THE GILDED HIDEAWAY

Robert West wants a change in stake it all for a chance to mak hundred thousand in cash from wife and friends behind, and he about a lawyer down there, Santos, who can guarantee him safety. All he has to do is pay Santos enough, and West is free to live the good life. That's when he meets Mercedes. She is everything he wants in a woman—innocently captivating, willing to share her life with him. But in a land where anything can be bought for money, does Mercedes have her price as well? And once West meets that price, will he be able to live with himself in his new-found paradise?

IN AT THE KILL

When auctioneer Jonathan Knox finds out that a construction company has ripped up the pavement in front of city hall, then fixed the hole expecting the city to pay for it, he sees a golden opportunity. He knows that bails of paper were buried when the original sidewalk was laid back in 1906. And that within that paper might lurk some very rare stamps. So he buys the bundles, sight unseen, from the construction company. The only problem is, the bundles are missing. And when Knox starts searching for them, he uncovers a much larger plot, this one involving some old photos and a deadly game of blackmail.

HEAT LIGHTNING

Holly Reed has been raised rough in the Kentucky hills and knows a lot more about men than her young years would indicate. She certainly knows that Brandy Elliot, the local bootlegger, is interested in her. He makes that plain enough. But she doesn't know love. Until the stranger comes to town, looking for a cabin. There's something about him that attracts Holly. She gladly agrees to help clean for him just to be near him. But the city-bred Larry Carter is not all he seems. There is someone else in town that shares a past with him. And soon Brandy gets an eyeful when he keeps watch on Larry's cabin. The hills already know lust, but before long, they will know violence as well.

"Ace published historicals, war novels, juvenile delinquent books, and borderline sleaze. They added a line of "singles" and the Ace Star series for larger and more expensive books, but they remained best known for their genre-oriented Ace Double Books."
—Richard A. Lupoff, *The Great American Paperback*

"In my teens I read every Ace I could find."
—Ed Gorman

THREE ACES

THE GILDED HIDEAWAY
Peter Twist

IN AT THE KILL
Emmett McDowell

HEAT LIGHTNING
Wilene Shaw

INTRODUCTION BY RICHARD KRAUSS

Stark House Press • Eureka California

THE GILDED HIDEAWAY / IN AT THE KILL / HEAT LIGHTNING

Published by Stark House Press
1315 H Street
Eureka, CA 95501
griffinskye3@sbcglobal.net
www.starkhousepress.com

THE GILDED HIDEAWAY
Originally published by Ace Books, New York, and
copyright © 1955 by C. P. Hewitt.

IN AT THE KILL
Originally published by Ace Books, New York, and
copyright © 1960 by Ace Books, Inc.

HEAT LIGHTNING
Originally published by Ace Books, New York, and
copyright © 1954 by Ace Books, Inc.

ISBN: 979-8-88601-027-5

Book text design by Mark Shepard, shepgraphics.com
Cover design by Jeff Vorzimmer, ¡caliente! design, Austin, Texas
Proofreading by Bill Kelly

First Stark House Press Edition: May 2023

ACES HIGH

By Richard Krauss

The year 1952 brought the best picture Oscar to *An American in Paris*, in a ceremony hosted by Danny Kaye; the first woman to hit number one on country charts, Kitty Wells' *It Wasn't God Who Made Honky Tonk Angels*; Charlie Chaplin's *Limelight* opened in London and the famed funny man was barred from re-entering the U.S.; Quality Comic published the first issue of *Web of Evil*; *I Saw Mommy Kissing Santa Claus* sung by 13-year-old Jimmy Boyd was released; and most importantly to paperback readers and collectors, Ace Books debuted with Ace Doubles.

Modern-day pulpster James Reasoner described his first Ace Single: "In the summer of 1964, my sister's boyfriend told me about this science-fiction author he'd been reading named Edgar Rice Burroughs. The name was familiar to me, probably from the Tarzan movies I'd seen, but I'd never read anything by him. I asked John to loan me one of the books, and one Friday evening when he came over, he brought me a copy of *A Fighting Man of Mars*, the sixth book in Burroughs' Martian series, in what was then a fairly new Ace Books edition with a cover by Roy G. Krenkel. At the time, of course, Ace didn't mean anything to me. But within the next year, in addition to more Burroughs novels I was reading Ace Double Westerns (I remember the cover of the first one I read, but I haven't been able to track down the author or title) and I picked up the first *Man From U.N.C.L.E.* novel by Michael Avallone, buying it off the paperback rack in one of the local grocery stores. That was plenty to convince me that Ace was a reliable publisher of books I liked, and I bought many more of them over the years."

Lifelong collector George Kelley began with science fiction. "I saw my first Ace Double in 1957. I was reading a *Batman* comic book when my uncle, who read a lot of paperback books, handed me D-53 Murray Leinster *Gateway to Elsewhere*/A.E. van Vogt *The Weapon Shops of Isher* (1954). It was the first time I had seen a book with *tête-bêche* format with two covers oriented upside-down with respect to each other. I loved the artwork on both sides of the book. But, in 1957, I was eight years old and van Vogt and Leinster didn't make sense to me no matter how hard I tried to read them. Little did I know Ace Books would publish 221 Ace Doubles in this format between 1952 and 1973!

"As I became an older and better reader, I started buying Ace Doubles displayed on a spinner rack (remember them?) at a drug store on my way to school. I loved the double covers and I enjoyed the variety of authors.

"In the 1970s, I worked for a consulting company that sent me to 48 states. After work, I visited every used bookstore I could, buying Ace Doubles when I could find them. But two Ace Doubles eluded me. I spent years trying to find D-36 Robert E. Howard *Conan the Conqueror*/Leigh Brackett *The Sword of Rhiannon* (1953) and finally found a copy in St. Catherines, Canada. It was on the shelf of a tiny used bookstore … for a dollar in Canadian currency (about 70 cents, US).

"The other Ace Double—rare and collectable—took me 10 years to find, but I stumbled on a copy in a bookstore in Madison, Wisconsin shelved in the Mystery section. D-15 William Burroughs (as William Lee) *Junkie*/Maurice Helbrant *Narcotic Agent* (1953) might be the most famous Ace Double of them all! And it only cost me a couple of bucks!

"I donated dozens of Ace Doubles (along with 30,000 other paperbacks) to the Special Collections Library at the State University of New York at Buffalo. You can visit them as I do at:
library.buffalo.edu/specialcollections/rarebooks/kelley/"

Author, publisher, and editor of *Paperback Parade*, Gary Lovisi recalled, "I first encountered Ace Books in the early 1960s in school. I was about 12. I was not a reader, in fact I hated books—because the books they forced us to read in school were dull and boring. I mean, who cared! But there was this kid in my class that first day of school who took out a dozen or more of the Edgar Rice Burroughs Ace F-series science fiction books and looked through them. I wondered where he got such wonderful books. All the cover art by Roy Krenkel and Frank Frazetta totally amazed me. I was hooked and had to get those books and read them. I soon read them all.

"I later discovered the Ace crime and SF doubles and the great S-series of hard crime and noir novels. These had incredible violent and hard-boiled cover art, some with great sexy gals. I loved them. They were a revelation and I still have them today—some a bit worse for wear from reading more than once! They were great reads—and still are!"

■ ■ ■

Aaron Abraham Weinstein (1898–1967), son of Jewish Russians, immigrated to the U.S. in 1891. He shortened his name to Aaron A. Wyn when he enrolled at City College of New York in the fall of 1916. After a few years he left and began his career as a proofreader at a printing company, progressing swiftly. A year later in 1930, he was hired to edit pulp magazines for Harold Hersey at Magazine Publishers. When Hersey left the company, Wyn began running the place, replacing its swastika logo (an ancient Native American good luck symbol) with an ace of spades.

Under Wyn the company was known as Ace Magazines, branching out into Ace Comics from 1940 to 1956. Wyn's pulps included over 50 titles and dozens of characters, perhaps most notably *Detective-Dragnet / Ten Detective Aces, Western Trails, Secret Agent X*, and *Love Fiction Monthly*. Wyn's wife Rosa Wyn was also part of the company, serving as an editor of both pulps and comics.

Miffed at an editorial in the *New York Times* dismissing pulp magazines, Wyn wrote a lengthy rebuttal, printed in its entirety in September 4, 1935. Here's an excerpt:

"Your editorial about pulp magazines headed 'Fiction by Volume,' in *The Times*, was so typical of the attitude of the partially informed and the misinformed that I cannot resist the temptation to answer it. As publisher of approximately ten Western, Detective, Flying, Spy, Mystery magazines, I am particularly amused by your characterization of this publishing world as 'little known and officially unrecognized.' 'Little known,' by whom? 'Officially unrecognized,' by whom? Certainly the 10,000,000 people who go to their news stands each month to buy pulp magazines know and recognize this publishing world."

In 1952*, Wyn branched out again into mass market paperbacks with Ace Books, specializing in genre fiction. He began with westerns and mysteries, but soon added science fiction capitalizing on the SF boom of the '50s. Ace published every genre, including gothic, media tie-in novelizations, romance, and nonfiction. Donald A. Wollheim was looking for an editor's job and courting Ace as well as Pyramid. When Wyn got word from Rosa that Wollheim had applied for work at Pyramid, he promptly hired him to start his paperback line.

The first Ace paperback was the beginning of their famous "Ace Doubles" line, pairing *Too Hot for Hell* by Keith Vining with *The Grinning Gismo* by Samuel W. Taylor, both mysteries. The novels were

---

*Most online sources cite 1952 as the year Ace Books began, and it was the copyright date of the first Ace Double, D-01. However, the timeline on the Penguin Group website lists it as 1953.

bound *tête-bêche* (French for "head to toe") to enable two front covers, with readers flipping the book head-to-toe to read the second novel. Other publishers had used this format, but the Ace series was the best-known proponent. Ace Doubles lasted 21 years and today are highly regarded collectables.

Although cover blurbs purported each novel was "Complete and Unabridged," that wasn't always true. Printing economics required total page counts between 256–320, and that meant if a book didn't fit, it was abridged. Ace Doubles often paired a well-known author with a lesser-known one in hopes of gaining new readers for the latter. Nearly every leading genre author of the 1950s and 1960s who wrote crime, westerns, or science fiction were included in Ace Doubles or later in Ace Singles.

A copyright loophole gave Ace an opening to become the first American publisher of J.R.R. Tolkien's *The Lord of the Rings* trilogy. A legal dispute followed and Ace agreed to discontinue its editions. Thus, Ballantine became the first "authorized" US publisher. A similar move brought the works of Edgar Rice Burroughs back into print. In this case the legal agreement that followed gave Ace the rights to many of Burroughs' works, with Ballantine gaining his more famous Tarzan and Mars books. Another milestone for Ace was the first publication of *Dune* by Frank Herbert.

When Aaron Wyn died in 1967, Ace Books was sold to a consortium with no experience in publishing. Donald Wollheim made an effort to hang on, but bills were not being paid and authors' royalty checks were often late. Eventually, it became too much. Wollheim left Ace in 1971 to form a new imprint in association with New American Library: DAW Books, focused exclusively on science fiction. Ace was soon sold to Grosset & Dunlap, which in turn was acquired by G.P. Putnam's Sons in 1982, where it became the SF imprint of Berkley.

In 1996, Penguin acquired Putnam Berkley Group including Ace Books, now part of Penguin Random House. Today, Ace is the oldest continuously operating SF publisher in the United States.

Ace Doubles and Singles published dozens of the most revered authors of genre fiction throughout the decades, featuring cover artwork by a similarly revered roster of artists. The volume you're about to read brings back three novels from Ace's library.

First up is *The Gilded Getaway* by Peter Twist, originally Ace S-107 from 1955. The name Twist was a pseudonym of C.P. Hewitt, who only published this one novel.

In At the Kill by Emmett McDowell was originally half of Ace Double D-445, paired with his own *Bloodline to Murder* in 1960. Although

Robert Emmett McDowell (1914–1975) was born in Oklahoma, his family soon moved back to their roots in Louisville, Kentucky, where he spent the remainder of his life. He began writing while serving in the Merchant Marines during World War II. He sold short stories in a variety of genres to pulps like *Planet Stories*, *Jungle Stories*, and *Action Stories*. His first sale was under his full name, but he quickly became known in print as Emmett McDowell.

In a profile for *Planet Stories* (Spring 1948), he wrote: "I like to write. I haven't any axe to grind, unless it's about people who think a story should fulfill some purpose other than entertainment. 'Didn't you enjoy it?' That should be the final criterion. I'd like to be able to write stories that you couldn't put down and that you regretted coming to an end."

When pulp sales declined, McDowell turned to the burgeoning paperback market in the mid-1950s. His first novel, an Ace Double (D-51), *Switcheroo*, was paired with *Over the Edge* by Lawrence Treat. His second Ace Double (D-329) paired his novels *Three for the Gallows* and *Stamped for Death*. By the time of his final Ace Double (D-445), he became more and more interested in the history and culture of Kentucky and joined with others in what eventually became the Filson Historical Society.

Switching to his full name, he wrote *Tidewater Sprig* (Crown, 1961) a historical adventure novel. It was followed by the nonfiction *City of Conflict* (1962), and later by a return to the mystery genre with *The Hound's Tooth* (William Morrow/M.S. Mill, 1965) by Robert McDowell. A follow-up called *The Sour Mash* was planned, but never saw print.

The final novel in this volume, *Heat Lightning,* was first published as Ace Single S-74 in 1954. Written as by Wilene Shaw, pseudonym of Virginia M. Harrison, who wrote several lesbian/JD novels including *The Fear and the Guilt* (Ace S-080, 1954), *The Mating Call* (Ace D-050, paired with *The Bad 'Un* by Orzo Grant, 1954), *See How They Run* (Ace S-263, 1957), *Out for Kicks* (Ace S-378, 1959), *Tame the Wild Flesh* (Ace D-464, 1960), and *One Foot In Hell* (Ace D-520, 1961). A short story by Wilene Shaw appeared in *High* No. 3 (October 1957), a short-lived men's magazine in an unusual format.

—February 2023

References:

BullittCountyHistory.org
eBay.com
Galactic Central
Wikipedia.org
FaceBook's Paperback, Pulp, and Collectors Anonymous group

Richard Krauss is the editor and publisher of *The Digest Enthusiast*, a book/magazine that explores the world of genre digest magazines through interviews, articles, and reviews. It also includes original genre fiction. Krauss is also the designer for Alec Cizak's *Pulp Modern* and several standalone volumes such as Roman Scott's *Oddities and Other Grotesques*, Clark Dissmeyer's *Through a Basement Window* (both edited by Marc Myers), and Bruce Chrislip's *The Minicomix Revolution* 1969–1989. larquepress.com

THE GILDED HIDEAWAY

Peter Twist

I

You may remember reading a few years back about a guy who stole a hundred thousand dollars and skipped. The newspapers played him up big for a while and then said he had been caught and the money recovered. That was a lie. He was never caught. I was the guy.

The newspapers, while I was copy, made like amateur psychologists. They tried to pep up the story with speculations about what made me do it. They missed. They invented nonsense and never did know about the real running, murder and confusion.

I'm not writing this now because I'm carrying a cross or wearing a hair shirt. I'm doing it because this is the last anyone is going to hear from me and I want everyone involved to know the truth before I fade out. I've learned some things. Hell! It could happen to you.

Finding a beginning is difficult. I don't want to start at the time my mind was made up—that wouldn't show anything. I could go back to the day when the doctor gave me my first slap on my backside and I gave my first scream of protest. A psychologist would want to start there, maybe earlier. But I can't see any point in going back those thirty-two years. They were moderately peaceful and ordinary. I started taking my life apart and reassembling it in an offbeat pattern right after the Long Island bank robbery. They didn't catch that guy either. I wonder how he made out?

According to the story, the guy who pulled the job (medium height, dark blue double-breasted suit, scar on chin) parked his car in front of the bank manager's house that morning. Since the manager lived only a couple of blocks from the bank, he used to walk. That day he didn't. The thief showed him a gun and the manager was convinced. He got into the car.

They drove to the bank and parked outside. The building wasn't open for business yet but employees were there. The vault had been opened to get the cash ready for the day's business, which was going to be heavy. When the employees saw the gun in their manager's ribs they were cooperative. They filled a suitcase the thief brought in with every dime in the place. The gunman left with the money and the manager. No one pushed the alarm. When they were asked about that, they said that they were afraid the robber would shoot if he heard it.

The manager was dropped off a half hour later on a lonesome road. The car was found that afternoon parked in front of a Queens' subway station. The whole thing had taken less than an hour.

I thought it was beautiful. I went into the kitchen and asked my wife whether she had read the account. She was busy with the dinner and wasn't interested.

I suppose there was nothing unusual in my excitement. It's an international tradition to exalt outlaws. Look where Robin Hood, the James boys and Pretty Boy Floyd stand in our folklore. And do you remember the talk after the Brinks robbery? You get excited by the bravado and the cooperation a neat job implies. It doesn't mean that you intend to do the same thing yourself. There may be more juvenile delinquency these days but you can't blame it all on the comic books. They are just another symptom of the same thing that makes kids go in for gang wars. They aren't a cause.

I was no ex-bad boy and I'd never been in any unusual jams. The worst thing that ever happened to me was when I knocked up a girl and had to pay for an abortion—a messy underworld sort of deal; I'm still not sure I was the guy. Besides that, and some drunken mischief, I had never thumbed my nose at the law.

I got through high school without being top or bottom of my class and went on to college. I lost my mother and father that year and moved in with my uncle, Malcolm West. Pearl Harbor came and I went into the Air Corps as soon as they would have me. Three and a half years later I was out, without a scratch. For me it wasn't a bad war.

I went back to college, finished up, and made my first bid for freedom. Uncle Malcolm invited me to go into business with him. He had no children of his own and he promised me the world. I still had two years left of my GI Bill and wanted to go to Mexico on it. He didn't approve. I went to Mexico anyhow.

Then my GI Bill ran out, but Malcolm came through. The job was still waiting for me, and I came back to New York.

The next year and a half were fine. Malcolm paid me more money than I was worth and I lived the life of a happy bachelor. (That was when I got the girl in trouble.) That winter Malcolm gave me a month's vacation. West Construction Company, like most building outfits, practically shut down during the snow months so it wasn't such a surprising gift. Naturally I went back to Mexico, but this time I had money in my pocket. I made the tourist run from Mexico City to Acapulco and I met Doris.

I thought I loved her. I didn't want to lose her but marriage was a big step. Uncle Malcolm clinched it. He thought it was time I settled down and he liked Doris. We got married and Malcolm gave us the down payment for a house on Fairwater Road as a wedding present.

We had resolved to save. I wanted to go back to Mexico and Doris said she did too. It was the place to build a life. All we needed was enough money to keep us for a few months while we looked around and a little capital to invest. Mexico today is like the States were after the Spanish-American War. Anyone that's willing to take some of our tried and time-tested know-how down there can make a fortune. But when the chips were down Doris didn't want to go. She never said so in words but her actions showed she was plenty content in smug, uneventful Fairwater Road.

On paper it hadn't looked as if it was going to be hard to save the money for the Mexican venture. I was making plenty and with two or three years of careful saving we could have had enough to take off. It didn't work that way. We did have the most modern sink, refrigerator, washing machine, ironer and mangler, TV set and phonograph, vacuum cleaner, storm windows and the biggest and best ice cube maker on the block. We were loaded down with time payments for the rest of our lives. The desk drawer was filled with those little books from the bank—and we didn't have a dime. I didn't like it. It bored me. I couldn't see any way out.

Uncle Malcolm was a rich man. He could have retired years before, but he stayed in business because he liked business and was good at it. He didn't need the dough. Sooner or later though he was going to have to quit and then the business was promised to me. I think Doris counted on that to bail us out when she rolled up her debts. When I had the business I could get rich. But I didn't want to wait till I was sixty to have economic freedom and I didn't like the business. What else was there to do? The guy who knocked over the Long Island bank knew what to do.

II

The morning after the bank robbery it rained. That meant there wouldn't be much to do at the office. Doris gave me breakfast but we didn't talk. I drove to work.

The Malcolm West Construction Company was the biggest home improvement outfit on Long Island. We did all the stuff that the builders didn't do. We resided, insulated, roofed and waterproofed houses. We built garages, expanded attics and finished cellars. You name it; we did it. We were the homeowner's friend. Nothing down. Three years to pay.

I came and went pretty much as I pleased, though sometimes when I said I was going to visit some village building department I was really going to a movie. I made good money. I was thoroughly unhappy.

A couple of our carpenters were in the office sweating out the weather when I got there. The rain meant that the schedule I had made out the day before could be carried over another day. All I had to do was pick up the phone to answer complaints. The phone was ringing when I came in. It didn't stop.

When the rain didn't let up, the carpenters left, either for the Long Rail, a bar across the street, or for their homes, depending on their marriages.

John Finlay, our foreman, came in to report. Only the men on inside jobs were working.

"This rain stinks. We need a drink to warm us up," he said. "Let's go over to the Long Rail."

It seemed like a hell of a good idea. The bar was empty. The carpenters had left. We took two stools.

I liked Finlay. He knew his trade. He was a big guy stretching up to six foot six and he was hard as nails. Nothing bothered him. He had come to us as a carpenter and moved up to foreman. I often wondered why he didn't move out and start an outfit in competition with us. There was plenty of room in the business and he had the brains and the background. The only answer was he was lazy. He took things as they came.

The bar girl was reading about the bank robbery. She didn't look up when we came in. Finlay reached across the bar and took the paper out of her hands.

"What a job," he said.

The bar girl must have had a hard night. She looked unhappy.

"He'll be caught before the week's out." She was tired of it all.

Finlay sneered. "Nuts! They don't even know what the guy looks like. All he has to do is slip south of the border and he's safe."

"What do you mean safe? The Mex government are good neighbors, aren't they? They aren't going to let a robber stay there. They'll send him back and collect the reward."

Finlay turned to me. "Tell her."

I was supposed to be the expert on Mexico. I had told Finlay a lot about it—or at least the things I thought he would like to hear. I repeated to her the Mexican attitude about crime and law. There was no kind of immunity that couldn't be bought there for a price. I told her a story I had told Finlay about Mattias Santos. No one has heard of him in the States but in Mexico he is considered shrewder than Fallon, Rogers, Geisler and Leibowitz rolled into one. I was introduced to him at a party once.

An American living in Mexico shot his wife between the eyes. Santos was hired to clear him. Santos claimed that the American was a magnificent pistol shot and that he often amused guests at his home by putting a cocktail glass on his wife's head and playing William Tell. The night she died they were playing this game. He shot as well as usual but she jumped. Suicide.

The witnesses were bought. The jury and the judge were bought. There were no problems. The American is still living in Mexico.

The bar girl didn't think much of the story. We ordered two rye and sodas. Her shirt was open at the neck and when she bent down to scoop ice I could see the top of her bra and the curve of her breast. She would have been pretty except for the pockmarks on her face and her sullen expression. I smiled at her when she stood up. She didn't return it.

Finlay wouldn't let me pay. I think it made him feel big buying Malcolm West's nephew a drink.

"How's it going?" he asked.

I shrugged.

"How's the old man treating you?"

I shrugged again, noncommittally. The drink tasted good and swept away some of the previous night's cobwebs. I wanted to enjoy it. I didn't want to discuss Malcolm. I had no special loyalty to him as a boss and the subject didn't interest me.

Finlay drank his drink as if it was a glass of water and ordered another. I wasn't ready.

"You know," he said. "Reading about the big haul at the Long Island Bank gave me an idea. You're in a position to make a killing. I've been thinking about it."

"Yeah?"

"Those FHA loans. You turn in about a dozen of them a week. The bank never knows what the hell they are doing. All you would have to do would be to set up some phony loans and keep the money yourself."

"Great!" I said. "Then what?"

"I don't know. I'm no brain. There has to be some way out. Go to Mexico."

I finished my drink and got off the stool. Finlay insisted I have another one. I climbed back up.

The girl put the drink in front of me. "He West's son?" she asked Finlay. I answered.

"No. I'm just a poor relative."

"I've never seen you around here before. You too good for this place?" A real pleasant sort she was.

"Lay off," Finlay said, showing her the back of his hand. "He's married."

She stepped back and snorted. "So are you."

She shrugged and walked back to her newspaper at the end of the bar. Finlay talked louder than he had to. They seemed to be old friends.

"A character. She looks like a dull tool but believe me she's a jackrabbit. Four-drink Greta. That's all it takes and then she's on her back ready to take on the whole carpenters' union."

She lifted her eyes from the paper and looked at Finlay as if he was a freak.

"Do you want four drinks?" I asked.

She actually thought it over. I could see the wheels turning.

"I get off at nine."

Finlay roared. "Stay away from her! You'll catch something."

I'd had enough. The love play of the higher vertebrates wasn't amusing me. I said so long and left.

It was a game then. I was solving a problem. I drove home slowly, not because the roads were slippery but because I was thinking. Finlay was right, more right than he knew. It would be easy for me to con the bank. I was sitting on top of the system.

I went to the bank everyday with a handful of FHA loans. We placed a half a million dollars' worth of business with them a year. The loans worked like this: Jones wants to build a garage. He comes to West Construction and we set up a contract pending approval from the bank. I make out a loan application for him listing his occupation, his income and his obligations. I take the application to the bank and if they approve it they give us a completion certificate and send him a payment book. When we have completed his job we have him sign the completion certificate saying he's happy. We take that back to the bank and they give us our money. Jones goes on paying for it, at four and a half percent, for three years.

The FHA and the government don't patrol the loans. That's up to the discretion of the bank. All the FHA does is act as an insurer. It makes the bank feel secure. They never showed any hesitation in paying out.

All I had to do was make out some false applications. I would have them OK'd, sign the completion certificates myself and keep the money. There were two problems.

What happens when the payment books get mailed out to the non-existent people and what happens if they check the applications and find out that there are no such people?

Problem two was easy to solve. About five percent of our customers paid cash. They were that strange breed that had money. They worried all the time and didn't trust banks. They were never the rich ones. I could be sure that their credit rating was good. They existed. I could use their names.

The problem of the mailed-out books was a stinker. I didn't know what to do about that.

But then it was all an exercise of my imagination. I wasn't making plans.

When I got home Doris was still in the kitchen.

"You're home early."

I kissed her on her offered cheek. "There's nothing doing today with the rain. Malcolm came in and said I could leave."

She smelled my breath and looked at me with disgust. "You've been drinking."

She didn't mind hitting the bottle. She was pretty good at it herself. What she meant was that I had been in a bar and she didn't approve of that. It wasted money that could be used on important things like new shoes for her, or a new hat.

I shouldn't have argued. I should have smiled and kissed her again. I could have pacified her. I didn't want to. I didn't give a damn.

"Sure. I went across the street with Finlay the foreman and had two drinks. It's been a long time since I've been in a bar. It was very pleasant. So what?"

She had a way of tightening her mouth and looking displeased. It was a schoolteacher mannerism.

"We can't afford to go to bars."

I took off my raincoat and threw it on the couch. She jumped after it and hung it in the closet. I could imagine what the rest of the afternoon was going to be like. I shouldn't have come home. I should have gone to a movie.

She stood in front of me with her hands on her hips. "Jane called. She asked us to come out to Jersey for the weekend." Jane was her sister. I didn't like her. Doris didn't like her either, but when she was annoyed with me she acted as if Jane was half of her heart and I was keeping them apart.

Jane was a dull, content suburban cow. Her husband Joe was no better.

"Tell them to come here," I said from behind a book. It seemed like a good gambit.

"They can't. Joe is working Saturday morning."

I could have smoothed it over then. She was calming down. I was showing her willingness to talk about it and whenever I did that I wound up giving in—in the past. This time she had a surprise coming.

"Good for Joe," I said. I didn't look up.

"I want to go," she said slowly.

"Easy," I said, putting the book down after carefully marking my place. I looked her in the eye. "Go."

It was good having her on unfamiliar ground. She looked disturbed.

"What's the matter with you today? Did something happen at the office?"

"No. Nothing happened. Nothing is the matter."

She had to hit back somehow. "Two-drink Robert West! What a man! I'm going!"

I asked her if I could help her pack.

She stomped out of the room. I enjoyed her anger. I enjoyed winning an argument with her, no matter how trivial. I didn't want to go to Jersey with her, that was for sure, but I was also slapping back about her bitching, her buying on time payments, my job, my relationship with Malcolm, suburban living—the whole complex of things that made my life hell. It felt good.

Then I thought what the hell! She was the way she was. I was the one that had changed. I didn't like the life I was living but it wasn't much different from the lives of my neighbors and they were happy.

I went into the bedroom after her and put my arms around her and told her I was sorry.

She pushed me away. She was ready for me to apologize but she wanted to hear it. She had to win.

"Are you coming with me?"

"No."

"Well, I am going alone then." She tried to make it logical. "Listen to me, Rob. I think that it's a good idea for me to go away for a few days. I want to have a sisterly talk with Jane. And besides I think that sometimes, even when people are in love, they need a rest from each other in order to think."

I tried to kiss her again but she pulled away.

"I mean it," she said. "I love you but I think it would do us both good to have a rest from one another."

"Is life with me that hard?" I asked her. That caught her up short. She wavered but she didn't fall.

"It's not that. You know it isn't that."

I knew it wasn't that. It was just that she had to win every time. I knew that with another word I could change her mind. We could hug and kiss and fall onto the bed to make love, but this time she was the one that had to make the overtures.

"I think it's good for married people to have a rest from each other," she repeated in a less certain voice. It wasn't what she wanted to say but she was stuck. "And it has been a long time since I've seen Jane. I know you are bored when you go out there."

I suppose she thought she was punishing me by leaving me home alone.

"Right!" I said.

I helped her pack and when I shut her suitcase I ended something.

III

I drove her to catch the six o'clock theatre train. Once she got to New York she would have to take a bus. I sat in the car and watched the serpentine of window lights pull out of the station. I decided to go back to the Long Rail and Finlay. I was going to get stinking.

The place was crowded. Finlay was still there. He didn't seem tight. I was glad to see him. The bar girl was working hard.

I squeezed in next to Finlay and ordered a drink.

"You back?" he said.

The bar girl brought me a drink. She was in a better mood. "Have an argument with the wife?" she asked.

Like most bars the Long Rail had a neighborhood crowd. Everyone seemed at home. Finlay was the only person I knew. He got off his stool and took me around introducing, not that I gave a damn who I was drinking with. I didn't remember any names. We played shuffleboard and we drank. Finlay wouldn't let me buy.

The bar girl must have had no home. When nine o'clock came she got out from behind the counter and became a customer. No one bought her a drink. She latched onto me.

By eleven Finlay's money was gone and I had started on my six dollars and change. That was gone by midnight.

I was tight. Bars are make-believe places. You create them in your mind. In one mood they are homey and an island in the sea. In another they are the modern centers for all inspiration and dialectic. In the mood I was in it was just a big smoky, smelly, crowded room filled with nonentities.

I went back to the john and Finlay followed me.

"We've thrown away enough money," he said. "Let's blow this place. We'll get a couple of bottles and a couple of girls and have a ball."

I was ready to go. We went back to the bar. I cornered the bar girl. By this time I remembered her name was Greta and I'd bought her a couple of drinks. Finlay was pounding the ear of a personality blonde at the end of the bar. Greta was all for a party. Finlay was successful.

The four of us weaved our way out and got into my car. Greta squeezed up next to me. Finlay and his girl got in back. The problem was where to go. My house was empty but I didn't suggest it. I didn't want to see it. Finlay's girl had an apartment. We drove there.

We killed a fifth talking about nothing. The sentences fell apart and so did the party. It was fairly obvious after an hour that Finlay would be glad to see me leave with Greta. He was wrapped around his girl on the couch whispering in her ear.

I didn't have much to say to Greta. I was having trouble seeing. I tried to concentrate on a graceful exit.

"Take me home," Greta said thickly and solved my problem. She staggered when she stood up. I gave her my arm and we went downstairs after saying good-by and getting no acknowledgment.

I wanted to get rid of her. I kept my foot down on the accelerator and crashed lights and went down one-way streets. We didn't hit anything. She pointed out her house and I swung up in front of it. She leaned over and cut the motor.

You could have heard her whisper in Canarsie.

"We got to say good night down here. My old man won't let me bring anyone in."

She was eager. I wasn't, but I felt compulsive. I leaned over and kissed her. That did it. My hands weren't fast enough for her. She guided them. The street light shone into the car and I felt as if I was in an exhibition case. She kept shushing me. She didn't need to. I wasn't saying anything. It was all mechanical. When it was over there was still nothing to say.

She sat up and smoothed herself out. "Thank you for a nice evening," she mumbled, remembering her manners. I told her it had been a pleasure.

She got out of the car and staggered up to her front door. I watched her open it and then took off.

I sobered up a little on the ride back. My head throbbed and I wanted a shower. I'd busted over the barrier and joined the club. In my daydreams I had thought that when the day came and I was unfaithful to Doris it would be different. I was depressed. I had revolted and gone out for spite and all I had to show for it was a headache. Life stunk! I wondered whether it might not have been better if I had been killed during the war—crazy thought.

I got home, showered and hit the sack. I couldn't get to sleep. I got up, went to the kitchen and opened a can of beer. I knew it would make my head worse in the morning but I didn't care. It was cool and fresh tasting.

I got to sleep at last and was out, dreamless, until the alarm slammed me into the next day. I stumbled into my clothes, had a beer for breakfast, which helped, and crept to the office. I worked hard, on the way down, piecing together the night. I hated the world.

There was a note waiting for me on my desk. It was from Malcolm. He wanted me to go to the bank and check on two slow clearing loan applications. Going down to the bank, talking to people, was the last thing I wanted to do. It was a morning to sit in a dark bar and nurse your head.

Leaving the note was the kind of thing Malcolm always did. He could have picked up the phone and asked about the applications but since he was paying me to follow them up I had to do it. Malcolm liked to keep his subordinates busy.

I debated whether or not I should use the phone myself. I couldn't hide. I decided to sweat it out. I wanted to talk to Charlie Diamond who had charge of the home improvement department.

I drove down to the bank. Charlie was at his desk. He looked glad to see me. He should. West Construction places a half a million bucks worth of loans with the bank each year.

I asked him about the two slow clearing applications. He checked, looking efficient. One of them had simply been mis-shuffled. He apologized profusely. The other one had been held up because the borrower had a record for being a slow payer on his other loans. I straightened that out. The bank wasn't fussy. When the deadbeat brought his other payments up to date they would clear him.

I made myself sound as nonchalant as possible. "What's the procedure on checking loan applications, Charlie?"

He gave me the word. There was a central listing of all bad payers. When an applicant came in, the bank checked the name with the listing. If the applicant wasn't there they then checked his name against a record with the names of all people that had judgments outstanding against them. If the name wasn't on either of the lists, the applicant was cleared. It was a negative process.

"It sounds risky," I said. My head had begun to pound again.

Diamond didn't think so. "On a regular loan we investigate pretty carefully, and we demand collateral and co-signers, but this FHA stuff is insured by the government. We haven't gotten into trouble yet."

"Government insured. Four and a half percent. It's a dream, isn't it?" I said to make conversation.

"That's the word. All you need is capital."

"Oh. And another thing," I said, trying to make it sound like an afterthought. "What gives with completion certificates?" They were the papers that the borrower signed, after his job was completed, stating that he was satisfied with the work. The contractor turned them into the bank and collected his money.

"What do you mean?"

"What happens to a contractor that gets the customer to sign the completion certificate before the job is finished and collects his dough before he's supposed to?" I knew that it was a fairly common practice. We didn't do it. Malcolm would give his customers a hard time after he got his money and he was rough on his employees but he played very cozy with the law.

"Technically it's fraud but between you and me and the clock on the vault it's the way it's usually done. The small contractor has trouble waiting for the money. As long as there are no complaints, what's the difference? It says on the FHA form that it's the borrower's, not the bank's, responsibility to pick and watch the contractor. We don't care."

Things were falling into line on my little theoretical problem. I knew what I wanted to know. I said thanks and started to leave. Diamond held out a paper to me.

"Have you seen this? It might interest you and your uncle."

I looked at it. A new deal from an aggressive bank. I read.

Summer was a coming in. Special offer! The Fieldstone Bank of Long Island—the homeowner's friend—was prepared to grant home improvement loans now on which the first payment wouldn't be due until fall. Does your house need painting? Do you need a new lawn? The time was now.

It sounded good. It gave the borrower three months before he had to lay out a dime.

"Great," I said. "What's the catch?"

Diamond is an honest man. "It does look fine, doesn't it? The brochure doesn't mention the fact that the borrower is going to have to pay four and a half percent on the total loan for an extra three months. That gives us an extra one percent the first year. Naturally all the borrower's subsequent payments will be higher. It's a good deal for someone who's short of cash right now but it's no gift."

My head was all right now but my heart was pounding. I was surprised he couldn't hear it. All the problems of my academic embezzlement were solved. I took a rate card from him with shaky fingers. We shook and said thanks back and forth and I left.

With three months before the first payment was due a man that turned in a phony application would have twelve weeks before the bank would find the application was no good. You could take a lot of money in twelve weeks.

I went back to the office. Malcolm had been in and out again. He left a list on my desk of things to do. I pushed it aside. I pulled out the file of completed jobs and flipping through at random tabulated the amounts that the people who paid cash for their jobs spent. I toted up the first twenty numbers on the adding machine: $42,609.00. An average of $2,130.45 per job.

I ripped the paper from the machine and crunched it into a ball. I tossed it into the wastepaper basket. It bounced out. I picked it up and put it in an ashtray. I lit a cigarette and touched the match to the paper. I watched the numbers go up in smoke. I crushed out the ashes. My hand smudged. It was hard to wipe clean.

I was in no mood to work. I wrote a note to Malcolm saying that I had to make a tour of the local village building departments to check on permits. It was Friday, payday. I still had some cash from the check I had had Finlay cash for me at the Long Rail. It would carry me until Monday. I said I would return to the office by five-thirty but I had no intention of doing that. I picked up the 'A' to 'G' book of old contracts and went home.

Of course the bed wasn't made. I had just tumbled out in the morning. The house was a mess. I forced myself to the icebox and opened it. I made two elaborate peanut butter sandwiches and took the top off a can of beer. I carried the lunch into the bedroom. The top of the desk was cluttered with Doris' junk. I swept it all into the top drawer. I straightened out the bed. I made myself eat. The first bite had trouble going down but I finished the sandwiches and washed the last bite down with the beer. I felt better.

I went to work. At the end of the hour I had thirty carefully culled names. They were all people who had paid cash for their jobs. That meant that the odds were against them being listed as bad payers, and they were all people that had had their jobs done within the last eighteen months. Our experience had been that people waited at least that between big obligations. There was almost no chance that anyone on my list would have initiated a loan on their own since we had done a job for them.

I added up the amounts. Just under fifty thousand dollars. At a nice secure six percent that was almost sixty bucks a week—a hell of a lot of money in Mexico, but it wasn't enough. If you are going to be a thief, you might as well be a big thief. The sentence isn't much heavier. I dropped my pencil and did some skull work.

To buy immunity and security in Mexico, figuring high, would take about twenty-five-thousand dollars. Besides that you wanted money for yourself. Seventy-five thousand made the total a hundred thousand, a nice round figure.

If I did this thing I would have twelve weeks until September. I had to allow at least three weeks to get away, lose myself, and arrange protection before the bank knew that something was wrong. That left nine weeks in which to operate. To raise a hundred thousand in nine weeks meant raising eleven thousand per week. At two thousand per application that would mean roughly five applications a week. With fifty applications or even a few less, the world could be mine.

Even if it didn't work and I was caught, assuming that I could bank the money and they couldn't find it, the most I would have to serve would be about seven years. That meant I would be earning about fourteen thousand a year. That would be more than I was making on the outside. I'd get out at forty a rich man. And if I wasn't caught! It was so easy. I wondered why someone hadn't thought of it before. The catch was the stigma. You'd have to give up all your friends, all your past. To me that would be a gift.

I left the desk and lay down on the bed. I closed my eyes and watched the beautiful figures swim through my consciousness. The numbers were too big to handle. They ceased to be quantitative.

I didn't want castles in Spain or fast cars and beautiful women. I wasn't longing to be a playboy. I just wanted to leave the swamp in which I was living and build a healthy good life. You needed dough to do it. You couldn't homestead any more.

It was a dream like the infantile kidnapping fantasy. It was a long step between the dream and the reality. Knowing how to do it and doing it were at opposite poles. I wasn't consigned—yet.

I thought about it for four beers—until I knew that I'd be drunk if I had another. I didn't want that. I felt very alone and lost. I was making my bed but I had to see Doris again before I could be sure. I wanted her near me. I almost ran to the kitchen to call Jersey.

I asked her to come home. She almost cried on the phone. "Oh darling. I want to come home! I waited and waited for you to call."

I told her that I'd pick her up at the station.

I straightened up the house, changed my clothes, and put the dirty stuff in the laundry bag after checking for lipstick stains. I set the alarm and slept on the couch until it was time for me to call for her at the station.

IV

The rest of the week went slowly. I had been glad to see her at the station. I liked her. She left me cold. I decided to start after the weekend.

On Monday morning I left the house and went to the nearest bank where I rented a safe deposit box. From there I went to the office. First I worked at bringing my things up to date. When my desk was clean, I took out a pad of FHA loan forms, checked my list, and started on number one.

We had built two rooms and a bath for Jacob Mulligan six months before. He had expanded his attic to make room for his new son-in-law and daughter. The job had cost three thousand four hundred dollars. He paid cash. I remembered him. He was a nasty garrulous old man. When we did the job, I thought with pity of the guy who had to move in with him. His life was going to be hard.

I filled out an application for a loan as if the job wasn't done. On our contracts we only put the details of the job and the method of payment. I had to invent information for the spaces on the FHA form that asked for occupation, income and obligations. I invented a signature and put the application with a batch of legitimate applications into my briefcase. I took them to the bank.

Diamond was cheery and friendly. He merely glanced at the forms when I handed them to him. He counted them. "Busy week, isn't it," he said happily.

"And getting busier," I said. "Will you let me know as soon as you can whether these will go through?"

He glanced through the forms again. "Righto. They look OK to me. Give me a ring in the morning."

I left the bank and as soon as I was back in the car I took a deep breath of air. I felt as if I had held my breath the whole time I was in the bank. I started the engine but didn't move off. I had taken the first step. I was consigned. The realization hit me hard. I had forged a signature on a bum application, defrauded the bank and the government. I was jail bait.

It wasn't too late. I could go back in and get the Mulligan application. I could say it was cancelled. No one would know, but if I did that I would be affirming my existence on Fairwater Road. The rest of my life would be foreordained. No go. I started the car and kept driving.

That evening at home was strained. Every time I looked at Doris I tried to see beyond her eyes to find out how she would react when I left her. I wished there was some way to prepare her but I couldn't say anything without tipping her off. She was sweeter than usual. It made it harder. I concentrated on the things she did that annoyed me—the rabbit way she moved her mouth when she ate, the stiff studied way she sat down on a chair, her demands.

She must have felt something, right from the beginning, but at that time she held back. She didn't make any overtures in bed and that made things easier.

The next day at the office I made out some more forms. I waited anxiously until I heard from Diamond. He called me shortly before lunch and said that all the applications had been approved. I took out a completion certificate, signed it with Mulligan's name and took it down to the bank. They paid in hundreds. I drove out and put it in my safe deposit box. I had closed the door.

The next two weeks were dreamworld. I sweated profusely, which I don't usually do, and acted as if I was in a semi-coma. I went through the process of living mechanically and felt incapable of desire, passion, anger or joy. I couldn't even see ahead to the point when I would have the money. It was all robot like. I was a zombie. I'd set off on this thing and I was following the path to the end, head down, barely conscious. I submitted ten more applications and completion certificates and had $28,000 and some hundreds in my book.

My attitude during those two weeks must have jolted Doris out of her suburban sloth. One night I came home and there was a pitcher of Martinis in the icebox, the way I liked them, cold, dry and unwatered by melting ice. There was a plate of canapes. She was the old Doris, the one I had married. It was very pleasant.

She got my slippers out while I washed. I drank the first Martini with the usual hesitation. The second was a dream. I needed it. Doris' solicitude pleased me.

"You haven't said anything." She was coy, waiting to be praised. She deserved it. The way I had acted the last two weeks, she had every right to spit in my eye. I had said hello and kissed her when I came in and told her it had been a beat day. That was all. If I was going to sweat out seven more weeks I had to relax and allay her suspicion. I drew her to me and gave her a big hug.

I said, "I love you baby," putting all the passion I could into it. I didn't feel a thing but the Martinis. I learned something about how guys that work and worry too hard lose the sex drive.

She nibbled at my ear. It usually sent me. "That's what I want to hear, darling. Are you very hungry?" When she got sexy her voice turned a little whispery and hoarse. It used to excite me.

"I'm not hungry at all," I lied.

She was eating my ear. "I am, but not for food."

It had had to come. I thought back. We hadn't argued since she had come back from Jersey but we hadn't loved either. In normal times we weren't rabbits. We made love a Kinsey average of times a week. She was hungry now. She had never needed to show her desire in the past. I was always ready and initiated most of the things we did. But now I didn't feel a thing.

I nibbled back at her ear and whispered another I love you. I wished some reflexive passion would come. I was limp. The world had no flesh or substance for me. I was in a mirage. Until I left, money in my hand, I was a bodyless thing.

She led me by the hand. Inside I was excited at this new show of need on her part. In my head it angered me. She had hidden it so long. She wasn't loving me. She just wanted sex and was working for it. Robert West, her husband, had nothing to do with it. I was just a piece of apparatus.

When we got to the bedroom I suddenly realized that this was a form of rape. It struck me funny. I had always wondered how women raped. If a man didn't desire he couldn't.

She had tears in her eyes. "Please," she said in pain. "Don't tease, Robby."

I felt like a heel. I closed her out. I thought of all the woman I had wanted and not had. It came back to me. I didn't open my eyes. If I saw her face it would go away.

It was over. I was back on Fairwater Road. She lay on my arm, panting and then she was still. My arm hurt. I wanted another Martini but I couldn't get up. I kissed her, and waited, and wondered whether she knew that she hadn't been with me. She knew. She turned her face away and got up, bent, like an old woman.

"I'll go make supper," she said in a tired voice.

The box I had taken at the bank began to fill up. I hadn't realized how much room money took. When I left I was going to be loaded down. In order to get through Mexican customs without arousing suspicion, I would have to have the money on me. It was something to think about.

It had seemed so easy. All I had had to do was hold myself in check until the time came to leave, then go to Mexico, covering my trail, but as the time to go came, new problems that I hadn't thought of came with it. I knew that the bank wouldn't know anything until September, but I'd forgotten that when I took off Doris and Malcolm would probably raise a hue and cry loud enough for the bank to hear. If they did and checked, then they would be after me too soon. I had to figure out a way to take off without rousing Doris' and Malcolm's suspicion. It seemed an insurmountable problem. One depressed day I almost gave the money back. If I did they would probably be so glad they would drop the whole thing. But as quick as the idea came it dissipated. I couldn't do it. I wasn't going to bear the stigma of a thief for the rest of my life without having something to show for it, and now it would be absolutely impossible to live with Doris. The very sound of the words Fairwater Road made me sick.

I began to have half-asleep nightmares during the day. In my dreams I was being chased. I ran, fled, hid. I was lost, alone, despised.

I knew Doris was worrying. Her life was a quiet sort of hell. I didn't argue or scream and I did whatever she asked me to, but I couldn't make myself care about her and she saw through my counterfeited manner. I couldn't break through my own restraint. She was a stranger.

Doris kept her feelings in as long as she could and then let loose. I knew she was really upset because she didn't scream.

"What's the matter?" she asked me one night.

"I don't know. Just a depressive swing, I suppose. I've been feeling lousy."

She played the little mother. She asked me what I had been eating for lunch. How my appetite was. About my bowels. She looked at my tongue and took my temperature. I put up with it.

"It's not that," I told her. "I'm a little depressed, that's all. It's spring fever. It'll pass."

Malcolm noticed nothing. If anything he was pleased with me because for the first time I was getting all my work done properly. In the past, in the office, we had never been intimate. He wasn't capable of open affection even in his home, but now we were beginning to have an easy, pleasant time in the office. He took me out to lunch about three times a week.

I had resolved that when the time came I would tell Doris that I just couldn't take it and needed a rest. I would tell her that I was taking off for two weeks. She would protest but I was just going to go. I was saved the argument that would have followed. The fates were good to me. I got a letter from Steve Larson who had gone overseas with me as co-pilot.

Steve was a hell of a guy. He only stayed with me ten missions and then got his own ship. I considered him my best friend. We didn't see much of one another because after the war he went back home to Kansas City and I went to Long Island. Neither of us were correspondents. We kept in touch and always managed to write a long letter when there was an address changed or something momentous was in the offing.

In his letter Steve told me about the birth of his second child. I answered it that night and sealed it before Doris could read it. In my letter I asked him to write me again in two weeks. He was supposed to say that a bunch of the guys from the old squadron were getting together and could I come for the reunion.

I lived in a kind of suspended animation for the next three weeks. I walked lightly and kept putting in applications and completion certificates. Larson's letter came back on time. I played it close. I didn't show it to Doris and ask whether I could go. I left it open on the desk. It took a day.

Malcolm called me aside when I got to the office.

"I hear that there is going to be a reunion of some of your old bombing squadron," he said.

It had worked perfectly. I had Malcolm figured. He still lived the best part of his life in his memories of the AEF and World War I. He saw his old buddies and was the organizer of the yearly party that his old battalion threw. He had always been surprised that the veterans of World War II didn't have the same spirit.

I restrained my pleasure at the success of my plan and masqueraded amazement at Malcolm's omniscience. "Yes. Some of the guys are getting together. How in the world did you know?"

Malcolm liked being in the position of a vaguely mysterious wise old owl.

"Never mind that. I want you to go down. That's an order. The friends you make in combat are the best friends you'll ever have. It's important that you young fellows keep in touch. You're the backbone of our country."

I showed bewilderment, and joy, the proper emotions. I think I did well. He was grinning, pleased with himself. I shook his hand enthusiastically.

"Now get on home and tell Doris. Get packed. You're on vacation."

"Suppose Doris says I can't go?"

He was the know-everything. He winked. "I am sure she will say go ahead." He pulled a roll out of his pocket and slipped me a hundred. "This is between you and me. Don't tell Doris." A bigger wink.

I grinned back and shot out the door. He wasn't a bad old cuss. It was a shame I had to fool him, but he would survive.

I raced home and when I got in the house I grabbed Doris and danced her around the room. Things couldn't have worked out better. She was pleased with my happiness, the first emotion I'd shown in two months.

Then she, good wife, told me, between blushes, how she had read my letter and she had called Malcolm and told him how depressed I had seemed. Malcolm was so pleased with the good work I had been doing that he agreed immediately.

I calmed down. The big act was going on. I tried to look as upset as possible. "It will be the first time we have ever been away from each other."

She laughed. "No. Don't you remember when I ran off to my sister."

I remembered.

"It will only be a week," I told her. "If I can stand being away from you that long."

"You need it. You deserve it," she said. "Come, we had better get your things together."

The next day I told Doris that I was going to the city to get my ticket and buy some shirts. I left the house and went to a luggage store. I bought a large dispatch case and went to the bank. I cleaned out my box. In the little room the bank gives you for privacy the money spilled off the table. I gathered it up, and stuffed it into the dispatch case. I wanted to count it dollar by dollar, but that had to wait.

I shot into the city and bought my ticket to Kansas City. I took it and checked my dispatch case through. It was a chance but I couldn't carry it with me. Doris would ask what was in it and where I got it. The man asked me if I wanted insurance. I said sure so he asked for an evaluation. I almost laughed in his face. I said it was worth a hundred bucks.

On the way home I stopped by the office. Finlay kept his personal papers in the safe. I opened it, saying I wanted something of my own, and took out Finlay's army discharge papers. I put them in my pocket.

I still had two completion certificates that I could collect on but I didn't want to go near the bank. I was on my way. I didn't want to pause. Malcolm came in as I was closing the safe. He insisted on taking me across the street to the Long Rail for a farewell drink.

Greta, the bar girl, ignored me. I guess she was hurt because I hadn't gone in again.

I packed that night and slept like a baby. Doris drove me to the station in the morning. Malcolm was there. When I first saw him I thought something had gone wrong but he was just being a good uncle to his brother's son. I tried to say good-by upstairs in the mausoleum of a waiting room but Malcolm insisted that they go downstairs with me to the track. He liked to watch the trains pull out. We went down and said good-by again. I kissed Doris so hard my mouth hurt. I sat down.

I hate looking through the window, waiting, at the people that are seeing you off. It makes me feel like a freak. As the train started Doris began to bawl. Malcolm tucked her head on his shoulder. Suddenly I wanted to cry too. I didn't want to hurt her. I didn't want to hurt anyone. I wasn't looking for revenge or retribution. I just wanted to be free.

The train cut through the tunnel and soon we were crossing the Jersey flats. I went to the bar car for a Scotch and soda. I was on my way. I closed my eyes and tried to plan. First things first.

V

I stayed in Kansas City just as long as it took to get a plane to New Orleans. From New Orleans I doubled back to Kansas City and then flew out to Brownsville. It would confuse things a little.

I got into Brownsville late. Texas is hot. Brownsville is hotter. I dropped my bags at a second-rate hotel and went out to eat. If I was successful, Robert West would have faded out in New Orleans.

The next morning I went down to the Mexican Tourist Bureau and used Finlay's discharge papers to get a tourist card. A U.S. citizen doesn't need a passport to go into Mexico—just proof of citizenship. The tourist card was good for six months.

I was through with public transportation. It was too easily traced. I needed a car. I spent the rest of the morning checking the used car lots. I could have bought a Jaguar and I was tempted, but it was conspicuous, and also it didn't represent the life my money was going to buy for me. I found a dark blue, unobtrusive, '47 Pontiac that didn't blow too much exhaust when I put the accelerator down to the floor boards. The salesman gave me a long spiel. I had already made up my mind but I listened. I didn't want to plunk down the cash right on the spot because that would have made an impression—even in Texas. I told the salesman I would think it over and be back.

I dawdled over lunch and two cups of coffee while reading the local papers and when time enough had gone by, I went into the toilet and took enough money out of the dispatch case to buy the car.

After I picked it up, I checked out of the hotel, stowed the dispatch case under the front seat, covered it with tools and dirty rags, and put the rest of my luggage on the back seat. I had never heard of Mexican customs being very thorough but I was a little worried. My shirt was sopping wet. I could have done justice to a cold beer but that could wait.

I bought a five-gallon, army surplus jerry can for emergency, had it filled, and headed for the International Bridge—a big one considering that all it does is cross the withered Rio Grande. In the middle there was a sign saying USA/MEXICO. I got butterflies when I passed it.

The customs men made me take my two bags out of the car. I didn't complain but I kept a five-dollar bill in my hand in case anyone looked as if they were going to search the car. There wasn't any trouble at all. They stamped my card and told me to go with God. I passed into Matamoros and had that beer.

The barrier of the border was between me and all the years, months, days. I was free as only the rich are free. I had the stuff with which to build any damned life I wanted. I had the power to be virtuous.

There was another customs inspection booth about twelve miles down the road. They didn't even stop me.

Afternoon is a hell of a time to travel in summer Mexico. I kept all of the windows open in spite of the dust. The road seemed to stretch out monotonously into forever, disappearing on the horizon without showing a curve.

I turned on the radio and listened to a Mexican station. The music was loud and robust, man music.... I was a bird. I was filled with exaltation. There was nothing left but details and they were easily solved with money. I had money. I hadn't hurt anyone. The bank was insured. Malcolm would be better off without me and so would Doris.

The rest was routine. I knew where to go. I wasn't going to run or hide. Once you started that you couldn't stop. I wanted to be in a position where I didn't care whether anyone found me or not. I could rely on Mexico. As long as I kept my nose clean, the government would be on my side. I wasn't an expert on extradition but I did know that American police had no authority south of the border. If they located me, they would have to go to the Mexican police to apprehend me and deliver me to the States, and Mexican police can be bought.

At the first town, about two hundred miles south of Matamoros, I pulled in to a pump and got a new tank of gas. Fuel consumption was good. I didn't need any oil. I sipped a coke as they wiped the bugs off the windshield. There was no hurry. I knew what I had to do. I had to see Mattias Santos. He had to be my lawyer. In other times he might have been an emancipator but now, in the days of stability, he was a lawyer's lawyer. Ethics or morality didn't figure in his scheme of things. Law was a game and he knew all the rules. He used them or broke them. He wasn't subtle before a jury like Darrow or Fallon or Rogers. With him going before a jury was like losing the first round. His office was a combination central intelligence and communications agency where bribe and threat were weighed against bribe and threat, or so I had heard. He was expensive. I could afford him. Nothing but the best.

My only problem would be how to keep him from owning me. I knew he would try to take all he could get. Hell. I couldn't blame him for that. So would I. So did I. But I felt that I would be able to trust him as thief to thief.

The dark came down slowly. I stepped on the gas and tore through the falling dusk. In the half-light my headlamps didn't do any good. The countryside was taking on a ghostly look. I half closed the air vent and listened to the wind whistling. I pulled into a town about nine at night and decided to stay until morning.

I got a room at the best joint in town, sent for a beer, showered, changed my clothes and felt a hundred percent better. I felt itchy, ready to test my new freedom.

I lifted the dispatch case off the dresser and put it on the bed. It was heavy. Too heavy. It was my albatross. Carrying a hundred thousand dollars in cash doesn't create confidence. I opened the case and the money spilled out.

I had crammed the dough into the safety deposit box and had crammed it into the case. The bills were bunched, creased and folded. I straightened and stacked the bills. I didn't have string so I tore up the tail of one of my shirts for something to tie up the ten-thousand-dollar bundles. I played with them. I tried stowing them all on my body. I bulged like a straw man.

I repacked the bills into the dispatch case and locked that in my valise. It could be safer somewhere else but I refused to worry about it. I had stolen to be free. I wasn't going to be enslaved to the dough. I wanted to relax.

I left the room, leaving the money behind, and with it all the bad parts of the last months. I had about three hundred bucks in my pocket and that was about as much money as I had ever had to spend on pleasure all at one time.

I had a lousy meal in the hotel dining room. It was a Mexican's conception of what an American would like. I made up my mind never to eat in a hotel again.

I wanted to spend some money. I went to the desk and changed some dollars into pesos.

There was music in the hot dusty night and most of the noise seemed to come from up the street. I walked towards it and hit a plaza. The bass guitars called guitarróns in Mexico were booming. There were violins, trumpets, tubas, more guitars. A uniformed band was playing on a stage in the middle of the plaza and wandering groups were playing on the periphery. No one seemed to mind anyone else. It was a lot of music.

The square was crowded. All the girls walked around in one direction and the men in the other. As they passed one another they smiled, bowed and handed one another flowers. There didn't seem to be much talking. I bought a dozen flowers from a vendor and started playing. I watched faces as I walked and gave flowers to the prettiest girls. It was like playing musical chairs with as many chairs as people. You gave. You got. I liked it. I'd come for this. You didn't need to talk. You weren't figuring the odds.

I had a couple of drinks and watched until the whole thing broke up. The one thing I didn't want just then was to go back to a lousy hotel room. I knew the whore houses stayed open all night and that in Mexico they were more than just assembly line sex. You could find a game of dominoes or a drink. I went over to the hack stand.

The cabbie drove me around and took me to a couple of joints where I looked in the doors and came right out. There was too much noise. I tried to tell him what I wanted. I spelled it out to him. I wanted some place quiet, some place where the better people go.

That was a stupid thing to say. I felt badly about it. I recovered. I stuck my neck out, thinking maybe he would get it. I told him I wanted a place that was too expensive for me. That he got. We drove through the night.

I hadn't made up my mind that I wanted a woman. I just wanted some place to go.

The cab stopped in front of a big well-kept house in what seemed to be a quiet, better, residential district. The driver told me to wait in the cab while he inquired. There was a conference at the door and then I was told that I could go in. I didn't pay the cab. I wanted to be sure he would be waiting when I came out.

There didn't seem to be much business. I followed a maid out to a tiled patio and bar. There was a couple sitting there—engrossed in one another—and the bartender and that was all. I sat down and the bartender brought me a beer. I heard laughter in another part of the house. People wandered in and out. I wondered whether this was a brothel. I saw no conclusive proof that it was. I wondered where the cabby had brought me and then two girls came out onto the patio.

They were lovely and well dressed. I knew they were inmates. Outside they could have been taken for the daughters of the upper class. Their approach was subtle. They sat down at the table next to mine. They waited and lit cigarettes and then one of them turned to me.

"We've been arguing," she said. "Maybe you can help us."

I asked whether I could buy them a drink. I could. I moved to their table. The one that had spoken to me smiled. She liked to talk. The other one was prettier but was silent and hid behind languid, great brown eyes.

"We've been arguing and it is bad for good friends to argue. Tell us. Which of us is prettier."

It was a hell of an approach. Picking a whore is usually a sordid affair. She was making it into a game. I wasn't going to play Paris. Look what happened to him.

"No man can choose," I said. "Everyman has his own taste."

The quiet one leaned across the table. I could see down her dress to her navel. "Please choose," she said.

"Yes," the other one said. "It is your opinion we want. Which of us is—you know."

Paris had had three to choose between. If I was going to invoke his help, I needed the right setup.

"This had been done before," I said. "But before there were three to choose between."

I didn't expect them to get it. The quiet one seemed a little shocked.

"Three?" she said.

I patted her hand. It was small palmed and long fingered—perfectly shaped. Her nails weren't too long but you could see she never worked.

"It's a classical allusion and out of place. Don't make me choose. It's a job for a master. You are both visions."

The gentle one was most earnest. She leaned toward me again. I didn't bother not to look. Her nipples were high and hard.

"But you must. We have to know."

I wondered who had taught them this line. It was well taken. It did everything it was supposed to. There was a promise in each word. I hadn't given the Mexican profession credit for its suaveness.

The more talkative of the two whispered to her friend. They stood up and walked across the room, watching me over their shoulders. The one that had whispered had a slink. Her rump had a special motion. It was cultivated and something to watch. The other one just walked. She didn't need to do any more. There was more cat grace in her than there was in a whole set of *Vogue* models with their dissipated faces, binding underpants and padded bras.

I felt everything they wanted me to feel but I wanted out. I realized that this too was what I could spend all my money on. It was a kind of life that wasn't for me. It was a little nightmarish. I'd had enough to drink to make it all seem unreal. I felt like Ulysses with Circe. I stood up and they came back to me, but quick.

"You can't go!" they both said at once, in their own way.

"You have to answer the question," the talkative one said.

"You are both make-believe. You don't exist. I don't want to start a war." I was talking too loud. The couple at the next table looked up. I remembered all the nights crossing Piccadilly, choosing. I didn't want whores. "You are both goddesses. I must go."

"You are being irreverent," the talkative one said looking shocked. She wore a big gold cross. It hung, catching your eye, in the deep valley between her bosoms.

A hurried whisper behind my back and each one of them took one of my hands. I didn't wait to be pulled. I walked with them out of the patio. The girl still sitting in the patio laughed softly. We went through the house and in a door.

It was a king's bedchamber. I sank in a chair and looked across the room at the subtly lighted, canopied bed. I felt tired. I wanted to sleep. I felt as if I was asleep, but my eyes were open. They were giggling and helping each other undress.

Without clothes it didn't make any difference. The clothes had added nothing and took away nothing. I was a sultan watching his harem. They came to me. Nothing bounced. They were full, ripe, all ripples. They stood in front of me.

"Choose!" the talking one said. There was no choice. The quiet one sat at my feet and looked up at me. Her breasts were on my knees.

"Do you really want a third girl?" she asked.

"No," I said. "It was a joke." I could smell the perfume of them. My tongue was thick. I could hear myself talking, far away.

"Has the night been busy?" I asked. I didn't care. She understood.

"We have been with no one. We were waiting for you."

"We are clean," the other one said.

I stood up. I pulled them with me to the bed. Whatever I had lost I found. They were helping me. They took off my shoes and tie. I shut my eyes. It was wondrous. I kept my eyes shut. It was a lottery. I used my hands and found one and when she was with me opened my eyes. It was the quiet one but she wasn't quiet anymore. The other watched.

It was the Arabian nights. It was all of the Decameron. Time went. It had been so long. I was smothered between them.

The light was out. I had been asleep. It was still dark out. Someone was whispering in my ear. My hands had learned to know them.

It was the quiet one. She wanted more. There was no more. I was awake. She wouldn't take my answer. She kissed me on the mouth. I pushed her away and sat up. It had to have been a dream. I reached out and they were there. I turned on the light. The talkative one was asleep. I looked at my watch. It was almost five. I began to dress. The quiet one looked at me hungrily. She turned to the sleeping girl and cuddled next to her. She held her breast.

I dropped two hundred pesos on the bed and went out. The lights were still on in the patio but it was deserted. I gave a hiss and the bartender came out rubbing his eyes. My bill was as heavily padded as possible. There was a week's worth of drinks on it. The hell with it. I had money! I paid and left.

The cab was waiting. The driver was asleep on the front seat. I got him up and went back to my hotel. I wanted to get up early, sleep or no sleep. Tomorrow's destination was Mexico City.

VI

The next day I drove on to the capital. I felt lousy when I got up, but coffee, eggs and beer helped. I almost stayed in bed. It had been nine years since I had spent a day in bed without being or pretending to be sick. If there had been an icebox a few steps away I would have delayed the trip.

It was hard driving. Numbers rolled around the speedometer, but I kept my foot on the accelerator and made the city by late Mexican supper time.

I was far enough away from the States to relax a little so I checked into a small, good hotel. I was starved. It was too late to do anything but eat. I went to 1-2-3, the best joint in town, and had a good dinner. I sat alone and didn't talk to anyone. I saw the familiar faces of the Hollywood contingent whooping it up and I saw an ex-politician who was making his home in Mexico. I bought a good cigar and walked back to my hotel. I had hit the building part of my plan now. The tearing down was over. The past was dead.

In the morning I took five thousand dollars out of the dispatch case and put it into my inside pocket. I went to a bank, rented a safe deposit box and stowed the rest of the money. I felt better without it near me. A telephone book told me Mattias Santos address. I debated whether or not to call for an appointment and vetoed the idea. An unknown, I wouldn't have a chance of getting in.

I walked to his building. In the old days it had been the town house of some Spanish grandee and still bore some of the rock marks of its ancient grandeur—big iron gates, finely worked stone front. What had once been a stately courtyard was now an arcade lined with shops: a tobacco stand displaying lottery numbers, a photostat and passport place, a dusty bookshop selling books by Henry Miller and Frank Harris. The old days were gone.

There was a board near the elevator listing the office holders. Santos' name was unobtrusive. He was on the top floor.

The elevator made it, which was remarkable, as it was old- fashioned. I asked and the elevator man pointed. The door was unmarked. I rang. I heard the lock click. I pushed and went in.

The waiting room was small. It held a scarred desk with a middle-aged woman behind, a couple of modern restaurant chairs—not too clean—a standing ashtray filled with cigarettes, a water cooler, and a table piled with newspapers. There was a switchboard on the receptionist's desk.

I asked to see the lawyer. She asked and I told her I had no appointment. I wanted to see him on business. I said my name was Finlay. She asked me to sit down.

I sat. I waited. I read three or four newspapers. A couple of preoccupied people came in, whispered to the receptionist, and were let through the inner door. Too much time went by. I was getting anxious.

I went to the old dame and told her that I would come back in the afternoon. That made her move. She called inside and a minute later I was greeted.

It wasn't Santos. The man was more my age. I pegged him for a clerk. He looked intelligent but he was a message carrier.

"I am sorry Señor Finlay but the *Licensiado* isn't in today. Can I help you?" He said his name was Lopez.

"Sorry," I told him. "I can only speak to the *Licensiado*. When can I see him?"

His smile was apologetic. "It is difficult to say. He is very busy man and he is on vacation now." The woman at the desk snickered.

Lopez was perceptive. I was annoyed and showed it.

"Won't you come in?" he asked.

I could figure out the layout once I was inside. It was spread like a railroad flat. There was a room behind each room and you couldn't get to the end without passing through the others. In the third room back there was a desk. Lopez got behind it. There was a full leisure chair next to it and I took that. I sat too low. It was good psychology.

"Are you sure that I cannot help you, Mr. Finlay? I am Mr. Santos' assistant and I really cannot tell you when he will be back."

He was polite and deserved a smile. I had to see the big man. I was in a position where I didn't have to wait. I took out my wallet and separated ten hundreds. I laid them of the desk side by side.

Lopez began to grin. "We welcome you as a client," he said. "Who shall I kill?"

"It's easier than that. I want to see Mr. Santos. Take him this message and find out how soon you can arrange an appointment."

He didn't get it. "Yes? What is the message?"

I pushed the bills over to him. He picked them up and put them in an envelope. I told him where he could call me and I told him to work fast. He understood a thousand dollars' worth of urgency. He promised to call me that afternoon.

I shopped and bought some Tillett sport shirts. I window shopped. I watched the tourists buying wicker and silver. I followed four Huichol Indians in white pants, red tasseled hats and no shoes walking unawed from the main plaza to the market. I bought a silver cigarette holder because at last I could afford it and I found one without the calendar stone cut into it. Then I went back to the hotel. There was a message at the desk. Fast.

Mr. Lopez had called. There was a number to call back. I went to my room and rang it.

His voice sounded different over the phone. "Mr. Finlay?"

"Yes."

"The appointment has been arranged. When would it be most convenient for you?"

"Yesterday!" I said.

He didn't get that right away.

"May I come to your hotel to discuss this further with you?"

I told him I'd be waiting in my room. He must have called from around the corner because it didn't take him four minutes to get there.

"You see," he said after he was seated and I'd put a Cuba Libre in his hand, "It is not exactly a vacation the *Licensiado* is on. It is business and it is rather important that certain people do not know where he is." He acted as if it was a big joke. "So he has grasped opportunity and turned this necessary absence from the city into a vacation. Can you go see him?"

"Where is he? Let's go."

"Do you know Cuernavaca?"

I knew Cuernavaca—the sunny place for shady people.

"Well—he isn't there." The gag almost convulsed Lopez. "But he is near there. Can you come with me tonight?"

Cuernavaca was less than an hour away. I wanted to get this part of the business over with. I answered him by calling the desk to get out my car but Lopez interrupted by telling me that he had Santos' Oldsmobile in front of the hotel.

Lopez drove like a man with a devil. He kept his foot down on the floorboards and wasn't too careful about watching the road. He didn't bother to turn on his headlights and when I couldn't see the sides of the highway I reached across him and switched the lights on for him.

He didn't slow up on the turns and he passed cars without waiting to see if the road ahead was clear. He was in a hurry. Driving must have been a real bolster to his ego. In no time we could see the lights of Cuernavaca ahead but we turned off on a spur before we got there. The side road wasn't good. Once it had been maccaddamed, but now most of the tar was gone. It curved like a snake down into a valley. We passed jagged overhanging cliffs and skidded on the edge of deep drops before we hit the floor of the valley. The whole dark hadn't descended yet and the moon was high and full. By the half-light the valley looked like a place of thunder. It was completely ringed by cruel rock mountains that had the look of a semi-fused H-Bomb hit would.

We passed a few scattered houses and came to a town. It looked dead but the huge church and great cobbled plaza spoke of a time when it must have been the center of something.

Lopez streaked across the square at forty miles an hour. At one end it led onto a road that dipped down at a thirty-degree angle. Lopez didn't slow up. We dove into hell. At the bottom of the road was a plain. I could see cultivated fields stretching on either side of us to the feet of the mountains. There were scattered big houses. Lopez slowed down and we turned in a gate.

"We are there." I followed him out of the car wondering what Santos was doing this far off the beaten track. If he was hiding, which I now suspected, he was well hid.

Lopez took off his hat before he knocked on the door. His confident manner faded and he identified himself for what he was, a clerk.

An old Indian opened the door. His face was seamed and mummy-like. He might have been as old as the sacrificial pyramid on which the town church was built.

"Is there here a *Licensiado* Santos?" Lopez asked.

The old man stared at us and shut the door. It was apparently the way it was done because Lopez didn't seem disturbed. We waited. When the door opened again the old man stepped aside. I saw as we walked into the house that he had a pallet beside the door.

We came in out of the night, through the barrier of two-foot-thick adobe, in an Arabian Nights cave. There was an inside garden lit with the jewel points of flickering candles. We crossed it and went into the inner house which was built around another patio fringed with elephant ears. House windows opened onto the patio and we saw the first honest light since day.

The old man pointed and we went to a door. Lopez opened it for me and we entered a room out of some other country. The house was adobe and stone but this room was wood paneled and lined with books. The proportions were so heroic that I felt three inches shorter. Out of one French window heavily bracketed in long full red velvet drapes I saw a lighted swimming pool built in an involuted curve. I was impressed.

Lopez stood, nervously, and waited. I took a big chair and stretched out my legs. It was an act as I didn't feel that comfortable. There was no sound from the night.

A door at the end of the room opened and Santos came in. He was taller that I had thought when I had seen him before and he held himself erect with none of the bowed shoulders that some tall thin men adopt. His face was happy and satanic. He ignored Lopez and walked toward me.

I had trouble getting up out of the chair but I managed.

"I'm Santos," he said when I took his outstretched hand. "You are Finlay?"

I told him so. He sat down in the seat I had been using and signaled Lopez to push another under me. Santos gave me a once-over. I gave it back. He didn't know me.

He wore black. His hair was black and came down to a long widow's peak. Against his dark complexion his white teeth and white shirt shone. He didn't take his eyes from me but held out his hand to Lopez. He snapped his fingers and Lopez gave him an envelope. Santos dismissed him with a wave and handed me the envelope.

"Your message was eloquent," he said. "I return it to you so that we can talk. What do you want?"

There was something solid about him—not the solid of a Rock of Gibraltar, ponderous, unmovable, impregnable, but sure, ready to move with strong winds, hard to kill. I had an urge to pour out the whole story to him so that he could plot a course but that was emotion. I decided to stick to essentials.

"We've met. At a party a few years back. You wouldn't remember me but I remembered you. I've come because I think you are the man to help me." There was no reason for the preamble but I didn't know how to start in the middle of nowhere—without background and apology. In the car coming down I had rehearsed what I would say. I had decided to put it straight—without excuses. Now that the time had at last come when I had to put into words the thing I had done, I felt a little tongue-tied. I couldn't talk without telling about Doris and Malcolm and Fairwater Road and those things had nothing to do with this man.

He didn't acknowledge my praise. He waited. He offered me a cigarette and lit it. I groped for the right words.

"It is quite possible, but not certain," I told him, speaking slowly, weighing my words, listening to them to hear how they sounded to him, "that people are going to be looking for me. It will probably happen within the next month. I may be traced to Mexico. If I am found the people that are looking for me will try to have me returned, to the States . . ."

". . . and jail?" There was a trace of a smile on his face.

"Exactly. I do not want to be returned. Can you help me?"

He sat back and stretched his arms over his head.

It was my turn to wait. I could tell him the rest in answer to questions. I had parsed the problem and shown him the color of my money. He brought his arms down slowly and placed his fingers tip to tip.

"If those that look for you do not find you then you will have no problem?"

"I want to be in a position where even if I am found nothing can be done," I told him.

He spoke like a patient professor. "Let me try and sum up your problem, and please correct me if I am wrong. The first thing you must worry about is extradition. The second problem is that you must have a legal status in Mexico."

"No correction needed."

"We proceed. Point one. What are you wanted for?"

I wanted assurances from him before I laid my heart bare. Still I knew that there wasn't much he could tell me before I gave him the scoop.

"I've taken some money."

"How?"

I outlined it for him without going into elaborate details. His eyes half closed, as he listened.

"And over how long a period were you forging these applications?"

"Two months."

He looked up at the ceiling. "I see. From a bank. That means you will be wanted by the Federal Government." He was thinking. His lips were pursed. He straightened up. "This is the extradition setup. No member of your government has any status here. They can look for you but they cannot apprehend you. If they locate you, they request that our police deliver you to them at the border. As I see it there is no chance of your not being searched for, is there?"

"No."

"And sooner or later you are going to be traced to Mexico."

It was certain.

"So we are back at our original position. Either you must hide and not be found or you must in some way see that when you are found you will not be apprehended. In the second case you must buy the Mexican police."

He put it all in little boxes stacking them as either/or dichotomies. I imagined he was a good chess player. I put another card on the table.

"I debated a long time before I took the money. I did it because I thought it would buy me peace, security and a good life. I don't want champagne, women, or the fastest car on the road. The money isn't an end in itself. It's simply the tool with which I can build a decent and worthwhile life. I seek tranquility. I felt that by perpetrating one big fraud I could avoid spending a life that was built on hundreds of little frauds. I want to get set. I don't want to spend my life making deals and buying off police."

"You only have to do it for seven years," he said. "That is, I think, the statute of limitations."

"I don't even want to play cat and mouse for seven years. I have my pie. I want to eat it."

He stood up and started to pace. "Now I will put my cards on the table." His voice was sharp and precise. "I can help you if you have enough money. To do what you wish, you must first have legal status in this country. You must adopt a name and a personality. You must have papers. Then when anyone comes looking for Finlay—" he paused. "Of course, that isn't who they will look for, is it?"

"No. My name is Robert West."

"Yes. When they look for Robert West, they will find a man that looks very much like him. But that is all. It will not be Robert West."

He was beginning to make sense. I asked him how it could be worked.

"Once again we have some alternatives. You could pretend to be a Mexican citizen. Since that entails being born in this country we would have to get you a very legal-looking birth certificate and arrange to have the birth recorded. Maybe we will do that later, anyhow. At present it wouldn't be too easy. I suggest you become a legal resident of Mexico, with the privilege of owning property, working, or going to court, for the time being."

It was my turn to pace. I knew all this.

"A map of the alternatives is of no interest to you?" he asked.

"No. You are supposed to be a sharp guy. I've come to you to pick the alternatives for me, not to propose them. What should I do? This is your country."

He nodded. "You become a man who has lived in Mexico a long time. You have papers to prove that you haven't even been to the States in years—or at least you have papers that will satisfy the Mexican government on that score. You laugh at anyone who says you are Robert West. The Mexican police laugh with you. That is all."

"Fine. Great. How do we do it?"

"I can arrange that you have papers, very legal papers—in a Mexican sense. I see that you have a legitimate, checkable record in Mexico."

"And the price?"

He snapped back. "How much money did you steal?"

"Your price?" I repeated. I didn't want to give him the amount. I had too much Yankee blood for that. I wanted his figure. Either I would meet it or not.

He slipped back into his resting self. "A relationship such as ours," he said softly, almost to himself, "is similar to a marriage. We both commit crime to help each other. We cannot testify against one another. We become mutually responsible for one another's welfare. If you would prefer I will give you advice and charge you a legal fee for it but then you must perform the work. If I do it for you, dipping my not too clean fingers once again into the pot of corruption, risking my reputation, I must naturally be paid all I can get."

"Your price!"

I knew that he was picking it out of the air.

"A hundred thousand dollars!"

If I had had a hat, I would have tipped it. "Good-by," I said as pleasantly as I could. "It's been pleasant."

"Don't be a fool. Sit down!"

I stood up. He began to talk fast.

"You are in my country, Mr. Finlay-West, and I don't wish you to think evil of it or me. I have been honest with you, however, and you must be the same with me. I am a scoundrel who lives by subterfuge and deception and I do none of these things for the 'good life.' I do what I do for money and I am unscrupulous. You were willing to steal and risk jail for money. I am willing to kill for money. See? I put my whole hand face up on the table. I would not take more money from you than I deserved. It would not be difficult for me, even now, to take everything you have. You are the stranger here. I could have you murdered before morning and no one would know! Believe me, I would only do this if you had much more money than you can possibly have."

I waited for the conclusion. When he said murder his eyes narrowed to slits. He wasn't just making talk.

"I do not want to kill you. I have many enemies who would love to find me guilty of murder. I must be a careful man. So we have bared our souls. Now you tell me how much money you have and I will tell you how much of it I want to protect you from extradition and make you secure in Mexico. Isn't that fair?"

"I have about a hundred thousand."

"About?" he asked. "How close is about? One hundred and forty? One hundred and sixty?"

I snapped. "I haven't counted it recently." I mentally added and subtracted from the last count. "One hundred and one."

He heard me and sighed. "Things look very good for you and your good life. Fifty thousand dollars invested in first mortgages should bring you in an income of nine thousand dollars a year."

I was out of my seat. Fifty thousand! "You want half?" I asked incredulously.

"Sit down! Of course not. I want it all!" He laughed and it was like a hen cackle. "But I acknowledge that you are the victor and should get the spoils. I said fifty thousand in mortgages because I think you should keep twenty-five thousand in cash for emergencies. My price is twenty-five. It should be more but I am interested in seeing how you go about building your good life. It is going to cost me about two thousand dollars to arrange predated papers for you and another three or four for the expenses of building you a history. So I'll make around fifteen thousand. I must confess you impress me. I would have guessed you took about thirty thousand."

"And if I had?"

"My price would have been ten, but it would have been easier work as there is not as much pressure on a thief who steals thirty as on one who steals a hundred."

I started to speak.

"Don't bargain. The price is firm, and I advise you to take it. I am the man you need."

It was what I had estimated, but I hadn't thought I was going to spend it all in one place. I felt confident in him.

"How long will it take you to get the rest of the money from me?" I asked.

He grinned. "That depends on how long you stay out of trouble. I have been hired to protect you from your American law enforcers and I will. If you do something foolish and I have to—let us say for the sake of argument—defend you at a murder trial, I will naturally need some more of your money."

The business was more or less closed. "We must make up a name for you. What would you like?"

When I was a kid I made up lots of names. I had some favorites but it would be better if I kept the Robert. I wanted to answer if someone called. I thought of Ambrose. What happened to him?

"Robert Bierce." I hoped I would remember it.

"Good enough. We have much more to talk about but you must meet the other house guests." He stood up. He looked tired. I wanted to get back to the city. I told him so.

"But that is impossible. I am here and you must stay near me for now."

I told him I had nothing with me but the clothes I was wearing. He said he'd send Lopez in for my stuff in the morning. "I want you to stay off the tourist run until your papers are in order. This is a good place for you to be for the time being. Come. I will introduce you to your hostess—" he smiled, "—our hostess."

VII

Thick adobe is a wonderful insulator and soundproofer. It wasn't until I had followed Santos to the other end of the house that I heard the music and voices. My head was still filled with his talk when we entered a room full of people. It was a lighter room than we had been in. It was filled with white walls, lots of color, native furniture and people. I made a quick survey. There were two couples at the bamboo bar. Two couples on a window seat listened to the musicians who must have been outside on the lawn. Among the scattered groups, I counted sixteen people—all dressed informally in summer dresses or slacks. No one paid any attention to us when we came in. Santos stood in the doorway looking for someone. He found her and she came toward us.

She wore the one long, floor-touching dress in the room. Until she was next to us I thought she was taller than she proved. Actually, the illusion was due to the way she held her shoulders and her long slim neck. All she used was lipstick. She didn't need makeup. She had big eyes, full lips, a nymph's figure.

"We are glad to have you," she said. "My name is Mercedes Ruhl."

I didn't falter. "Robert Bierce."

"I am sure, Mr. Bierce, that Mattias gave you a drink, sat you down and talked business. Have you had a chance to wash?"

I didn't think I looked that dirty.

"You have described my actions perfectly, Mercedes," Santos said with a bow. "I am inconsiderate and ungracious, but now that Mr. Bierce is in your charming care I need not worry. If you will excuse me." He walked away and left us.

"I'll show you to your room, Mr. Bierce." I followed her out. I was glad she kept calling me by my new name. I might get used to it.

She was in front of me and the special rhythm her rump was making kept my throat dry. She glided along as if she were on wheels. I caught up to her and made conversation. "Your house is very beautiful."

"It is lovely, isn't it? Once it was the hacienda of the owners of the valley, but during the revolution it fell into disrepair. We had to put a great deal of work into it before it was inhabitable. It's almost complete now. Have you been in Mexico long?"

Santos hadn't briefed me on my cover story. I evaded.

"Quite a while, but in the south." No one knew the south.

"Oh?" She was discreet enough to drop that tack. We came to a broad flight of stairs and I followed her up. At the end of a castle-like hall she opened a door.

This room too was overlarge but it looked comfortable. The oversize double bed was set on a dais which made it look baronial. I felt a little uncomfortable looking at it with her at my side.

"I'll have one of the boys bring up your bags," she said.

"I'm afraid there has been a misunderstanding. I didn't know I was expected to stay when I came out to see the *Licensiado*. My things are in town."

"Oh? Then at least let me get you a robe and a clean shirt." She sized me up and her stare was thorough. "Gilbert was about your size." She turned and left before I could speak. I went to the bed, sat down, lit a cigarette and waited. I smoked two cigarettes. I wondered whether she had forgotten me. I needed a shower after the dusty drive. I figured that a houseboy would bring the things and stripped for the bathroom. The shower was modern, with five outlets. I turned them all on full blast and let the needle spray bite in.

I washed my hair four times, feeling and enjoying that compulsion that makes you wash when you are in a shower. I was Robert Bierce! Robert West was no more. While I had been lousing up the applications, I had dreamed of the moment when I crossed the border to Mexico. In that dream I had watched Robert West step across from the U.S. side and miraculously become someone else. Robert Bierce. It was a name. I remembered too much.

I heard a bang on the door over the sound of the shower. I rinsed the soap out of my hair, figuring it was the boy with the shirt and stuff. I wrapped a towel around me and went out to get it. I asked who it was through the bedroom door.

She didn't answer. She just came in. She didn't seem to notice that I wasn't dressed. If it didn't bother her and make her pretend coyly, it wasn't going to bother me. She had an armful of stuff. I watched her walk across the room. Her dress hung on her, flowing over the curves. She undulated as she walked. She dropped the clothes on the bed and turned.

"This is better than a towel," she said holding out a terry cloth robe to me. I took it and put it on. "Though I must say a towel does become you."

Her eyes were twinkling. She had a face from a romantic's too perfect drawing. She was at home in the world and the light of it filled her. She had been drawn in all the fashion magazines, but she'd never been photographed because she hadn't existed till now.

She wasn't in a hurry to go. She looked around the room as if she hadn't been in it before.

"Are you comfortable?"

"I will be when I'm dressed."

"I'm sorry I barged in on you. I hadn't known that you had started showering." Her laugh was filled with bell notes and sent a shiver through me.

"No. But I am sorry I barged in on you," I said back.

"My God! How long did you say you had been in Mexico? It's wonderful to see a new face! And any friend of Mattias—you know." She curtsied. "My house is your house."

She went to the door but stopped before she went out. "Only one rule in the Ruhl house. No guns below stairs."

"I'm clean," I said. She smiled. I felt rewarded.

"See you soon." And she glided out.

She had brought me a couple of sport shirts and cotton slacks. The creases were in the wrong place as if they had been packed away. I dressed. I needed a shave but that could wait. I was getting hungry and it was getting late. I went downstairs and followed the music to the room. No one seemed to have moved. My hostess saw me come in, picked a Martini up off a passed tray and brought it to me.

"I won't tell you names," she said handing me the drink. "You wouldn't remember them anyway."

The Martini was dry enough. I was sure she didn't need to buy more than one bottle of vermouth a year.

"Are you a Miss or Mrs. Ruhl?" I asked.

"Mrs. But there is no Mister."

"Sorry."

"I'm not. Let's not discuss it, shall we?" Good enough. I didn't want to step on toes. She left me with a pardon and began to circulate. She was a good hostess. I looked for the tray passer and changed my empty for a full glass. I saw Santos in a corner surrounded by people and stayed away. I edged up to the bar and listened. Someone was talking about pre-Columbian artifacts found in the valley. I was interested. Supper came in as if it had been waiting for me. I was ready to feed.

It was served buffet-style: a big mole, the thing they make out of turkey, chilies, peanuts and chocolate; a big paella with every known kind of seafood. I was too hungry to be polite. I was the first around the table. I found a corner and began eating. It went fast. I tried another round. I finished that fast too, and then I felt fat, sluggish and ready to sleep. Unless I had another drink, I was going to sleep right there. I went to the bar and had the man make me a dry Collins. I wanted something long and cold.

I watched Santos get up and detach himself from his crowd. He left the room. I wondered whether he had had enough but he came back ten minutes later. His walk was jauntier. He looked around. His eyes seemed different.

A few couples were dancing. Santos went up to the best-looking girl and tapped her partner on the shoulder. The second man took one look at the lawyer and left.

Dancing was one way to hold Mrs. Ruhl. I looked around for her, but found that she had a partner.

Santos stopped dancing. The dance wasn't over. He simply dropped his arms and walked away leaving the girl on the floor. Whatever he had taken when he had gone out before had made him mean. He went to the musicians and told them to stop. They stopped. He wanted them to sing. They sang.

The acoustics in the room were good. The musicians were loud, the way Mexican musicians should be. Santos began to sing with them but he didn't look as if he was enjoying himself. There was a desperate quality to him. He was rolling, as if he was drunk, his tan face was a sickly beige; he was terribly intent. He was possessed.

The songs he called for were heavy with rhythm, unsentimental and filled with yodels and shouts of exultation. His voice wasn't good but it was loud. At the peak of one song, when he couldn't make the falsetto shout, he pulled out a gun. He fired, hardly aiming, at one of the overhead lights. It was a good shot. The light went out.

The room rang with the slam of the gunfire. Plaster trickled down from the ceiling and looked like the powdered snow you put on Christmas trees. The musicians kept playing.

It wasn't my kind of party. It was like a moving picture projector grinding to a slow halt. The dancers stopped. Everyone was waiting and everyone was scared. Santos gave a belligerent glance around the room and then refocused on the musicians. I saw Mercedes Ruhl going toward him.

The music was soft now. He had asked them to play a malaguena. The musicians seemed unperturbed by the fuss. Their faces were impassive. They were there to play. I could hear Mercedes' voice above the music but she wasn't talking loud.

"Give me the gun, Mattias," she said, her voice was even without bitterness or anger. "Give me the gun. There will no *macho* in this house."

He stared at her, but obviously had trouble focusing. He acted as if he wasn't sure who she was. He turned from her like a defiant child and let another shot loose at the trickling dust. The bullet ricocheted with a high dying whine.

"That's enough!" Her voice was a little louder now, but firm and cold. He stared at her. His eyes were wet as if he had been crying. He seemed at bay.

"When a Mexican wishes to shoot a gun, he shoots a gun." His voice was hoarse and tight. "This is our way. We do not first consult with our women." He made a mockery of a bow and turned back to the musicians.

"I do not give a damn what you wish, Mattias. This is my house. In it I am mistress. Put away your gun and stop acting like a child!"

His face turned green. "You will not talk to Mattias Santos that way as if he was a peon! Shout at me! Yell at me! Scream like a hag, but do not talk to me in your superior, well-modulated tones. I know you for what you are. This is your house by our grace. This is Mexico, a republic, and we have killed the *gauchopines*. We have driven off the overseers and castrated the *patrons*. It is with our blood and guns we bought our freedom. It—it—" He was spitting and having trouble finding words. He groped for something to finish with and found it. He slapped her. "Go to your kitchen, woman!"

I had had enough. I wasn't amused. Everyone else was playing the game of looking the other way as if that would make all this unreal. In the beginning I could just watch. He was drunk. We all get drunk, but it had gone too far. I didn't like the gun in his hand but he was acting too wacky to be much aware of what was happening. I got up, watching him, and edged around the room until I was in back of him. She saw me but she was calm. She didn't bat an eye or tip him off.

I stepped up behind him and grabbed his gun arm. I pulled it up fast and snapped it back down. The gun dropped. I kicked it away and gave him a push. He stumbled and went down. I picked up the pistol and put it in my pocket.

The shock knocked him out of it. He picked himself up and turned. I hoped he wasn't stupid. I hoped he wouldn't come for me. I had the gun. I didn't want to lose a lawyer.

He was smiling.

"So, Mr. Bierce? You aren't afraid of guns?"

"Sure I am. That's why I took it away from you."

"And you are not afraid of Mattias Santos?"

"We are born but to die. A man ain't nothin' but a man. I was having a good time. You were breaking up the party."

I sounded tough. It surprised me. I wasn't feeling tough.

He had trouble focusing his dilated eyes. "I have some bad habits. I shouldn't drink and—" He didn't finish. He rocked back and forth, purposefully, and got control. He looked for Mercedes. She was standing back watching with one eyebrow raised and a Mona Lisa smile. He went to her and lifted her hand to kiss.

"I apologize, Mercedes dear. Can you forgive me? It was unforgivable."

"Yes, it was," she answered gently. She seemed amused. They weren't talking about the slap or the gun. They were alone in the room full of people. They were sharing a joke.

"It is your guests. They bore me."

"But Mattias, darling, they are your guests."

The gun was heavy in my pocket. I watched them exchange courtesy for courtesy. Their manner was an insult to everyone in the room but no one seemed to notice. I felt that they enjoyed being insulted by Mercedes Ruhl and Mattias Santos.

"Will you forgive me, dear?"

"Of course, darling," she leaned towards him. He lowered his head and she kissed his cheek. She turned towards me and her smile made me feel like Galahad.

"Thank you very much, Robert." I liked her calling me by my first name. "And I think that Mattias thanks you too. May I have the gun?"

I gave it to her. Her honeyed behavior might be a sham, and she might even now shoot Santos for the slap. There was that about her; she didn't. She gave the gun to the bar boy and told him to take it to the lawyer's room.

She turned back to me. "You were very brave."

I couldn't say, "Shucks ma'am, it was nothing," so I merely nodded.

Santos had swept the room with his glance. He came over to us and put his arm around my shoulder. He didn't seem high anymore.

"Come, my friend, and drink with me. You have made me proud of the association we have formed. Away from the bar!" he shouted at the room. "We men do not drink with rabbits!"

A young man with pink hair and flowered shirt grumbled but everyone deserted the bar. The three of us went over, arm in arm.

He had recovered quickly. He was the Santos I'd met in the other room and laid my life in front of. We had brandy. He raised his glass in a traditional toast to health, money and love. I could drink to that.

There wasn't much party after the gunfire but as far as I was concerned there wasn't much to it before. The robot guests had been shocked from their complacency but I think they liked that. No one made a move to leave. We were watched. I didn't like being watched.

Mrs. Ruhl began making her rounds and patched some strained gaiety into the dying room. Everyone was well schooled. When they had been dismissed from the situation, they went through the motions of enjoying themselves. The fragile unity of a good party had never been wrought. Things went on. Santos had our glasses refilled.

"She isn't afraid of guns either," he said. He spoke to me but he was watching her. "A remarkable woman."

"You don't seem to think much of her guests."

He turned back. "They are dreadful people—the kind you and I must put up with. They depress me. I like people but I can't trust them so I must surround myself with clients I don't have to bother trusting."

I got it. I was one of them now. *Not me!* I swore.

"Are they then the happiness you've found?"

He leaned back on the bar. "God, no!" He looked tired again. "I had to leave the city for a while—a silly accident. I thought it was best to come here, but I hate the country. I wanted to laugh and relax so I asked Mercedes to invite this crew out. They make me laugh and they are harmless."

When he had said "hate the country," his voice had grown loud.

"I was born in the country. From the time I could walk I worked all day, every day, on a little group of fields built against the side of a hill. The hills were so steep that I had to attach a rope to a tree and hang on to it with one hand when I planted the beans and corn. And do you know what I got for this backbreaking work? Beans and corn! I slaved, like my father and my village, to grow food in order that I could eat and remain alive to slave to grow food in order that—. You see?"

I saw.

"So. The revolution came and I went with the other men in my village. I was taught to read and write. I fought, pillaged and stole like the other men, but with what I accumulated I didn't buy tequila or a silver saddle. I hoarded and saved and when it was all over I went to school. I became a lawyer filled with ideals. I would devote my life to defending the poor. I would be a politician and make great new laws. I would know what to do, as poor Zapata whose heart was so big had never known what to do.

"To do good one must have the will and the power. I had the will. I needed power. Money was power. I decided to get some. When I had money I would turn to virtue. I was successful in getting wealth.

"In the back of my mind I suppose my idea of peace was still married to land—land such as I had never had—land that was as rich and fertile as money and work could make it. Then I thought: if I bought land I would be the *patron*—the lord of the manor—and other men would work my land for I could never bring myself to tilling or planting another field. But if I was the lord of the manor then I would be one of those that I had fought so hard to overthrow. It was impossible."

He ordered another drink and stared into it.

"I had lots of ideas. First came the money. I was good at getting it. I protected my clients with any weapon at my disposal, and in time every weapon I used was turned back against me. I had to spend my time protecting myself and my money. Life became a constant battle. I did things to make me forget the life I was leading." He looked up from his glass. "Perhaps that is why I am interested in you—besides your money. You say you are looking for peace. Tell me, how do you find it?"

I didn't know. I was looking too, but I did know that I would never fall into his trap. He had made money but it had never been enough. I had enough. I didn't answer his question. I countered.

"If you had all the money you needed, what would you do?"

He was quick to answer. He stood tall. "I would do what I am doing I suppose. I don't know what else to do. Maybe I was happiest when I was planting corn and beans on the side of the hill. There was honesty in what I was doing. From where I sit I think there is no other honesty but the sweat on a man's face. Look at this apathetic group."

"And Mrs. Ruhl? Is she a client?"

He smiled tolerantly. "Of course, but of her I am fond."

"And—"

"She shot her husband. Terrible man. He was a client of mine too. Liked to be beaten with whips—wore a crown of thorns around the house. Naturally it was called suicide." He was watching my reaction.

"I've always liked people that are capable of positive action."

He stretched. "I'm tired. I am going to sleep. Do you wake early?"

"In strange houses."

"Good. That will give us time to talk at breakfast before these other slobs are up."

VIII

He left without a good-by to anyone but the bartender. I stayed on a few minutes hoping to talk to Mercedes Ruhl alone, but there wasn't a chance. I did catch her for a minute and said good night. I thanked her for letting me stay at her house.

"But I owe my thanks to you, Robert," she rolled my name. I wondered whether Santos had given her a rundown on me too.

I bowed out.

As soon as I got to my room I regretted not having taken a bottle with me. I was through with the party but I wanted a nightcap. I found a servant's buzzer and rang. I stripped and got into the robe she had brought me.

In spite of the stories about '*manana*', people move fast in Mexico. I had hardly stretched out on the bed when the knock on the door came. I yelled, "Come in."

It was Mercedes Ruhl. "Hello. Are you comfortable?"

I scrambled up. "Completely."

"But you just rang."

"Oh that. I wanted a nightcap and wasn't about to go back down into your lion's den."

"Of course." She went out before I could say never mind. I wondered what happened to the servants. She left the door open and was back a minute later with a tray. She put it on a table. There were two glasses.

"May I join you?"

"Is the party over?"

"Dear no. Now that Santos is gone they are starting. They'll go on until everyone has either passed out or picked a bed partner. I started it going. I'm through."

"How long has it been going on?"

"It seems like a week. Let me see. Santos got here three days ago. The worms crawled in two days ago."

She sat on the bed with a glass in her hand. She put it to her lips now and then but I could see that she wasn't drinking.

"I couldn't take it," I said.

"Good for you."

I wondered what she wanted. She didn't ask questions. She had nothing to tell me and my company wasn't that good. I wondered if it was the prelude to sex. I wanted that but I couldn't see a sign.

"What did Santos tell you about me?" I asked.

"He told me that you came here with a tremendous amount of money and that he wanted to keep you out of sight for a while."

"Did he tell you how I got the money?"

"Yes."

"Does he always tell you everything?"

She stood up. "This is my house and if he is going to ask me to harbor you—or isn't that the word?—then I want to know something about you. I do draw some lines."

I thought of the mob downstairs. "Where?"

She didn't bother with the pretense of drinking. She set her glass down. "Flagellants—they keep my guests awake. Satyrs because they are too aggressive. Lesbians because of prejudice. Homicidal maniacs because they make me nervous."

That got me. I must have shown it.

"Then Mattias told you about me too?"

"A little."

"He usually doesn't put things well. He isn't a courtroom lawyer, you know. I didn't shoot Gilbert. I gave him the gun. He shot himself."

So that was who Gilbert was. Her logic escaped me. "And he did? He was an obedient type husband."

"No. He realized that there was nothing to live for. He liked thrills. Suicide was a new experience."

"Being bored with life is a dangerous disease." It was hard to see her, beautiful, finely made, talking so calmly about her husband's murder.

"A disease that is harder on the family than the patient, as they say. Gilbert had become dull and unhappy. There was nothing for him to live for. He tried to invent sensations but he lacked imagination. It got him into difficulties. It upset him. He threatened suicide and I gave him permission."

"—and a gun."

"Yes. It was sticky."

"I can imagine. Was there a trial?"

"Of course not. It was suicide." She was serious.

"Do you have to pull the trigger to be a murderess?" I asked.

"Can you follow that point? If I ask you for your money and you give it to me, am I a thief? I asked for his life."

My glass was empty. She took it from me and made me another brandy and soda. "Shall we talk about something else?"

"Why can't Mattias Santos stay in the city?" I asked. I wondered how far her loyalty went. No one seemed to believe in secrets.

She told me. Everything she said should have told me something, but with her face before me I denied my reason.

"It was stupid! He was just about the way he got tonight. He was driving and stopped at a light. The car behind didn't stop in time and rammed him. Mattias' car was new. He claims that he fired the shot at the tire but it ricocheted and hit the boy. In any case the young man driving the other car was hit in the buttock, taken to the hospital; he died of tetanus. It's silly, isn't it?"

A shot in the ass? It seemed far-fetched.

"Mattias insisted it was an accident. Since the boy died of tetanus, he claims the doctor is the murderer."

"And the puller of the trigger?"

She shrugged. "It is accepted that people do not bump into the great Santos car. I am sure there will be no problem. And now good night, Mr. Bierce."

She was halfway to the door when I caught up with her. She turned the knob and started out. I took her hand from the knob and closed the door. She didn't move. We stood touching. This wasn't the kind, I thought, that you swept into your arms and all was right. She was cerebral. Words had to do it.

"Stay with me." My voice wasn't as even as I wanted it to be.

Her face was as expressionless as a death mask. "I am afraid that is impossible."

I could see her going to Santos' room. "Do you have another date?" I asked.

"That was nasty." She spaced the words. "May I go?"

I leaned down and found her lips. She didn't move. It was like kissing a statue. I stopped.

"I must go, with your permission," she said. "And I sleep alone."

She stood waiting. I opened the door. When she was gone, I poured myself a tumbler full of whiskey and took it to bed. I never finished it. I slept hard and had her in my sleep.

The house was a morgue when I woke. I dressed and went downstairs wishing I had a razor. I found Santos eating breakfast beside the pool. He shoved out a chair with his foot and swallowed.

"I spent most of the night thinking," he said. "I have big things in store for you."

It would have been impossible to tell that he had had a big night. He was dressed in another suit but it was still black. I ordered breakfast.

"I am going back to town today. I want you to stay here until you hear from me. Lopez should be here any minute with your things. Our problem is establishing you somewhere that will give you a cover story that can't be questioned. I think I have it solved."

"Have you seen Mrs. Ruhl?"

"Mercedes? Yes."

"Is it all right with her if I stay here?"

"Of course. She seemed pleased when I told her you would."

"And the other part. What are you going to do."

"I will send you to a little visited part of Mexico. It will be very pleasant."

"And how long will I have to be in hiding?"

"Hiding? No. You will be gone about a month but it will be an interesting trip. In the meantime there is a slight problem of money."

Yes, money. "First you do," I said, "and then I pay."

"In other words, trust you. Why should I?"

"Why not? You've said you could have me killed. I am in your hands and your price is high."

"But I haven't even any assurance that you have the money."

I answered that with a smile. I had to put myself in his hands but I needed an ace in the hole.

He shrugged. "Very well." That made me feel better. He had finished breakfast. I started to eat and talk in between.

"You are going back to the city? Is everything all right?"

"Ah? Mercedes told you about the ridiculous accident."

"Doesn't everyone tell everyone else everything here?"

"But no. Not everyone though it makes little difference. As for the stupid boy, I have avenged him. I have had the murderous doctor sent to jail and I have paid money to the boy's family."

That was one solution. He took a paper from his pocket.

"This is an *amparo*. I had Lopez bring it last night just in case. With it no one can put you in jail. It is good for a month. In a sense it is prepaid bail. Keep it with you at all times. I keep mine in my shoe." He wiped his mouth and stood up. We shook hands and he left.

The morning was quiet. I wandered the place and admired the fields which were irrigated with modern troughs and productive. There was a stable with riding horses off from the house and I wondered if the whole layout came with the hacienda. I saw no one. If I had had a knife, I would have whittled.

I sat at the pool and wished I had a bathing suit. A car pulled up and it took me a minute before I realized that it was the Pontiac I had bought in Brownsville. Lopez got out. He had checked me out of the hotel and had all of my gear in the car. I had my bags taken up to my room and gave myself a much-needed shave. It was a hot day and the clothes I had packed for Kansas City didn't do me much good.

I did change as best I could and went back down to the pool and sat looking up at the mountains. My watch said ten-thirty. The time for waiting had come. I'd sweated out the robbery and made the long run. Now, how long? and then what?

"Good morning," she tinkled. I looked over my shoulder. Her face was the same but she was a different person. She had on a full Mexican cotton skirt and a peasant blouse that emphasized her bosom which was so full for someone her size. She looked younger, and like a regular guy—the kind you could hold hands with, or skip. During the night she had been queen of a less wholesome world—somnambulant and lost. Now she was a respected citizen of healthland. She sat down beside me and stretched out her sandalled feet, her toes pointing to the sun.

"Isn't the heat glorious?" She closed her eyes and turned her face up to the sky, like a worshipper. It was hard to believe anyone so small could be mistress of a place so large.

"Have you had breakfast?" she asked without opening her eyes. I felt as if we had known each other forever. The woman I had wanted to sleep with me was as remote as last night's insane assembly of people.

"Hours ago. I saw Mattias off."

She looked at me with one eye. "Oh! Did he go?"

"Back to the city. About nine o'clock."

She jumped up. "Wonderful! Now I can clear the house of his parasites."

"What are you going to say?" I asked. "'Go now! Mattias is gone.'"

"Of course not. I will let them know that Mattias has gone and I have to leave too. They will have no choice. Wait."

She ran off across the lawn kicking her heels like a coed. Her skirts jumped. She was a lot of woman—the dream dame, the pal. I wondered which one of her was the real Mercedes. She played all the parts well. I tried to fit her into my shimmering mind-built house.

She came running back. "The servants will tell them I left with Mattias. Let's get away until they've gone. Do you ride?"

"A little."

We walked to the stable. She snapped orders. Two horses were brought out. She swung up onto hers tucking in her skirts but showing her bare, suntanned legs. I mounted and we walked our horses away from the stable.

We rode easily across the valley, and I was happy. "It's beautiful," I said, and meant it.

"I am happy here. I'd like to feel that it's my valley, but the local inhabitants won't let me. Without being discourteous, they let you know that they once owned the land and will again, when you, the outsider, are gone. I don't like being an outsider."

"But we always are," I said. She turned and looked at me.

"… and you don't feel that there is someplace where you can find peace and a sense of belonging?"

"I'm looking," I said.

Our trail wound up into the hills. From the bed of the valley it was hard to imagine a way but the path began easily enough. The horses accepted the climb but went slowly and cautiously. She told me about the hacienda and what she had done with it. The place was self-sustaining. She was proud of it. I would have been too.

We reined in and looked back and down at what we had left. From up here I could see her entire place, a group of houses separated by patios, connected with covered corridors, and all surrounded with a wall. It looked like a toy—a model railroad layout. There was nothing to say.

The trees began to cut off our view of the valley and the path got steeper. The horses began to work. We came to a trickle stream and let the horses drink.

"This water is good," she said and got on her stomach putting her face in the stream. I scooped water with my hands. It was cool.

"The people of the valley call the stream Uncle Sunday—Tio Domingo," she said. "In the rainy season it turns into quite a rush. This is as far as I've been. The horses can't go any farther. How do you feel about walking?"

We walked higher and higher between the sides of the interwoven hills. My leg muscles began to stretch and I had trouble keeping up with her. But I hung on, half ashamed of showing how tired I was. It didn't seem to bother her. We didn't talk. We needed all our breath for climbing. My second wind came and with it the labor went and I was able to see where we were going instead of just concentrating on the impossible path. We were gone from the world. This was wilderness. It was a personal paradise where one could mold a place out of scrub and rock. It needed an Adam.

The trickle of Tio Domingo broadened and became a proper stream. After almost an hour we came to a waterfall. We circled it. The stream above was lazy, slipping easily over worn rocks. We kept climbing and hit a level. We found a cactus that grew prickly pears and she showed me how to swipe at them with a handful of grass in order to get rid of the spines, and then how to wipe my hand in my hair to get the spines that hadn't been gotten rid of out of my skin. The fruit was crisp and cool. I was ready to lie on my back and stare at the isolated clouds. She moved on.

We stopped to watch dung beetles rolling their loot of burro droppings to a collection point. And we climbed. The undergrowth became thicker and there were more trees. The path was hard to find. Woodchoppers and gatherers didn't come this far, I thought, and then we passed a cornfield on the side of the hill. Ten minutes farther up the path leveled again and we came into a glade surrounded on three sides by massive cliffs—the sort of a cul-de-sac that regiments of contraband horseman used during the revolution. From high off one of the crags water dropped. The source of Tio Domingo was up there. We couldn't go any farther without pitons and climbing ropes. The water fell into the glade and the stream it made run quickly over shiny, worn, clean rocks. She sat down.

"We must have taken the wrong path. I know there is a way to get up there. I want to get to the source."

"I do too," I said and sat down next to her.

"We always want to go to the source, don't we?" She looked a little tired from the climb, but happy and relaxed. "Someday we will go to the source of Tio Domingo. That's the source you were talking about, wasn't it?"

She knew it wasn't. "When I said it I thought it was. Maybe it isn't."

I was pooped. I knew that she was too, but she jumped up as if sitting would lead to talking and talking to questions and she didn't want questions.

"Let's build a dam!"

I lifted my weary bones. We carried rocks to the stream and played at engineering. We raised the water in one section knee deep. We sweated with the work. When it was done, I surveyed it.

"It isn't as fancy as your pool but I prefer it."

"Oh, I do too!" she said with an enthusiasm I wouldn't have expected in the woman I had met the night before. "This is a real pool. We made it ourselves. That's the important thing."

I wanted her then, with my mind; my body was fatigued and ready for rest. All the conventions of courtship and compulsive sex were gone. We were alone in the woods and the world had vanished and I wanted her. If she said no, it would make everything dirty. I couldn't reach for her but I hoped she would come to me feeling as I did. I wanted her to come to me not so that I could say I had conquered, or cemented another block in the edifice of my ego but because I wanted her to want me.

"Shall we swim in our pool?" she asked, and my heart began to pound. I didn't answer because I would have stuttered. I nodded and watched her unzip her skirt before I looked away. I resented the fact that a woman shows no physical sign of passion. I stripped without looking at her. I heard her splash in and ran after.

The rock pool wasn't deep. You couldn't swim. If you lay on your back it covered you—and it was cold. All the showers I had taken to wash away my sins or past—and my past was my sin—had had no effect. But now in an instant the water cleaned me and I was rebaptized. I looked over at her and felt the passion more strongly and wasn't afraid for her to see me.

She was trim and fine. Her breasts were firm and hard with the cold of the water, and her nipples rose up virgin pink. The clean lines of her were like a miraculous statue—stone with softness, heat and light. There wasn't any fat on her. Her stomach was flat and strong, her rump tight—but she was woman, soft curved and elegant. Her symmetry was a completeness. I had never seen anyone so perfect.

She splashed me and I splashed back. We were like kids at the summer lake. I could splash farther and she kept coming closer. I moved away. I didn't want to be near her. My hand touched her and her skin was velvet smooth. She stopped splashing, looked at me and knew. I couldn't wait. I grabbed her.

She went limp and we lay in the water pressing together from cheek to toe. I kissed her cold lips and heard her small voice.

She said, "Please," and it meant, "Please, no." If she had been imperious or panicked, I would have carried her struggling to the grass. But her voice was the voice of an untouched child who is afraid of something she doesn't know. I released her and sat in the moving water looking away from her, trying to control my pounding heart, trying to still my breathing, trying to get the blood from my eyes. I heard her leave the pool. She called, as if nothing had happened.

"Let's sit in the sun and get warm. The water is cold." Like a stupid adoring slave I followed her up onto the soft grass. I didn't want to look at her in her nakedness. She was sitting, her bosom cradled in her arms. I lay back, half turned from her, my arm across my eyes and let the sun eat into me. I counted my heart. After a dozen beats she called me.

"Robert?"

I didn't answer. I was angry. I hated her for not wanting me, for making it no good, and I hated myself for wanting. "Look at me. Please, Robert?"

I looked at her, concentrating on her eyes, not wanting to see her breasts—her body—and think that she refused me.

"I'm not a prude and I'm not playing a game. I don't want you to touch me because I don't want to desire now, and if you touch me I will desire. I don't want to talk about it because talking about it will excite me and I don't want to be excited. I want to sit besides the pool in innocence.

"But don't be angry with me. Can you kiss me? Like a playmate?"

I sat up and kissed her waiting lips. We didn't put our arms around each other. We leaned forward like parent-encouraged babies and touched lips. Her face was still wet. We didn't close our eyes. She held her mouth to mine and kissed back until I pulled away and then she fell back on the grass with her arms behind her head, unashamed of her nakedness. I sat and looked at every inch of her. I watched her sky-pointing breasts rise and fall with each breath.

As I looked at her, I didn't feel brute desire anymore. I had love for her as I have never had for anyone including myself.

She rolled over on her stomach and put a blade of grass between her teeth. I sat, warm, knowing the heat. She looked up at me.

"You'll get burnt. You're not used to the sun. I think you should cover." She didn't make a move. Other suns had burnt her golden tan. I wasn't going to dress beside her nakedness.

She sat up and grinned. I didn't follow the joke but I grinned back. Maybe we were labeling the whole afternoon from the library of our worldliness.

"Besides," she said, "I'm famished. Shall we go back?"

I was tired of the glade. It was too strong for me. We hopped up and dressed. I had to help her with her bra snaps. I wondered who helped when I wasn't around.

We rode back to the stable without talking. A boy ran out to take the horses but she sent him to the house to see if the guests had gone and we unsaddled the horses ourselves. The kid came back and said that everyone had gone home.

We didn't bother to change. We were hungry and wolfed our food like starved adolescents. It was the first day in a long time that I was without a drink. I didn't want one.

"And now, with your permission," she said as she finished her coffee, "I am going to take a nap. I recommend that you do the same."

She didn't say good-by. She went through the door that led to the adjoining room. She didn't close the door behind her. I didn't know. Maybe I was supposed to follow her. She didn't have to close the door to let me know that it was a door. I walked out. If it happened, it was going to happen when she opened all the doors to me. Then she would never be able to close me out.

I didn't want to think about it. I went up to my room.

IX

I didn't think I could nap but the Tio Domingo had beaten me. I slept until Mercedes' voice called me from sleep. I woke with a start, wondering where I was. It was dark. I came back to the present. She was outside my window. I went to it.

She stood on the grass calling up. She was dressed in polka dots and moonbeams and looked like a prom date.

"I'll be right down," I yelled, feeling like a mixture of Juliet and Andy Hardy. I washed the sleep from my face, changed my shirt, and took the stairs three at a time. She was standing by the pool.

"You missed the sunset," she said. "I almost woke you."

"I wish you had. Seeing a sunset with someone is very important."

She gave me a long look that was all inside herself and wasn't meant to tell me anything. I must have hit some special memory.

"You hungry?" she asked.

The lunch had been fine but I was hungry.

"First I want a cocktail."

"Of course. May I have your arm?" I gave it to her. We went back inside to the room where I had met Santos the first night. First night? Last night! Only last night!

She rang for cocktails.

"This, Robert, is the room my husband used. At that desk. There was a lot of blood."

The Martinis were cold and the glasses were frosted. Sometimes I have trouble getting the first one down. This time it went easy. We had two and then someone came to tell us that dinner was ready.

We sat at opposite ends of the table and I didn't like being so far from her. It was a negation of the intimacy of the afternoon. I wondered why she wanted it this way.

Dinner was very stiff. The cook was excellent and the food was French. I wondered where she got the ingredients. I was careful and used my silver properly. I felt as if we had created a divorce. I missed her—and I could see her.

There was Armagnac brandy with coffee.

"Would you like a cigar?" she asked. I would have liked a cigar. I knew it would be a good Havana, but I said no.

"A cigar means that the ladies go to the other room. I want you to stay so that I can look at you."

"Then let us both go to the other room," she said, putting down her napkin as if signaling a table of diplomats that the dinner was over. In the absence of talk, I had eaten and I felt stuffed. I wanted air. I wanted to walk it off. I suggested it.

We strolled into the night, side by side, and then her hand reached for mine. I felt as if I had passed the test.

Her hand was cool and when I took it, it pressed mine.

We walked in silence. I felt she had something to say and waited. It came.

"Robert. I know you are going to try to make love to me. Don't. Promise not to."

I don't like women who think they are irresistible and all men rutting beasts. I held back my immediate tendency to blow steam and stalk off.

"No. I won't. I'd break it." I wanted to tell her true. For minute I thought she would leave me. Her hand went limp in mine and then grew strong and gripped.

There was a bench of wrought iron. It looked uncomfortable and as if it would dirty her dress but we sat down. She released my hand and looked up at the stars, not avoiding me, but not watching me.

"I'll tell you about Mercedes," she said after a while. She had thought it out and I wondered how deep into herself she had gone to find the words she was going to say. "I like fences," she said. "I want barriers—especially around my passion, my sex, my emotional life. I want my bedroom barred with a lock and key door. You see, I can't feel that physical love is a simple biological function without import or consequence. I can't make it part of a living routine. It's something special. I want physical love to be all things—communication, ecstasy, fulfillment. I want it to have reason—even one as naive as that the man I love and I want to bring flesh of our union into the world." She waited. I didn't say anything. She turned to me. "Don't ask me to make love to you."

"Are you speaking for tonight or all time—as concerns me?" I asked, trying not to sound too concerned.

"Who can speak for all time? No. It's the way I feel now. I don't know how I will feel."

"I want you," I told her straight and open. My voice sounded loud in the still night. "... and I understand you."

I don't know why the words hit her but she jumped up and walked away into the shadows. I didn't follow her. I knew she was leaving me and I knew that if I followed her, I wouldn't be able to bear not having her. Rape is ugly. I had to wait until she came to me and we could learn each other hand in hand. Most of all, I knew that sooner or later she would come. I couldn't feel the way I felt about her without her feeling something of it for me—and she came back—a cigarette later.

"Hello." She stood in front of me.

"Hello," I said.

"Do you still want to make love to this confused girl?" Her voice was as icy calm as it had been when she went to take the gun from Santos. It scared me a little.

"It will be an experiment this time," she said, in the same flat voice, "and if it fails, then you must promise me that you won't ask me to try again."

I should have spit in her eye. I should have laughed and said that I gave up experimenting when I found out that the girls I knew wanted sex and were as curious about sex as I was, but I didn't say anything.

She sat down beside me.

"I don't think that a woman can love with the same attitude a man can," she said. "I think it's because the climax is so much more definite in a man. I believe that a man can be what is technically called unfaithful without actually being unfaithful in his heart, but that a woman must love, no matter what she says and does—at least for the moment. I know women that make love often, with many men, and have one-night stands. I know that they wear no badge of shame on their breasts, but I don't think that it's sex alone that motivates their affairs. Sex is the manifestation of their disease, not the germ itself. I am sure that if you could probe deep you'd find fear, anxiety, anger and loneliness driving them."

"There are desires, urges to be answered. There's hunger," I said.

"... and there's control. I know. I don't condemn, Robert. Life is hard. We should grab at pleasure. It's just that, for me, I can't abandon myself to unquestioned pleasure. It has to be part of something bigger for me."

Her hand crept along the bench toward mine. She waited for me to take it. I didn't. She put it in mine. We sat a minute and then she stood up. We didn't have to say any more. I let her lead. We walked back to the house, across the patios, through the hall and upstairs to her room.

It was eerie. She walked away from me as soon as she had closed her door, and, as if she was alone, went to her dressing alcove.

I couldn't see her in the dark. I waited for her. She came out like a ghost. She was dressed in a diaphanous nightgown that billowed and flowed in the still air as she walked back to me. She stopped a few steps from me and then as if from a spring she flung herself at me and kissed me. Her lips were like eyes. Her tongue darted like a hummingbird's. She clung to me, pressing against me and suddenly began to shiver. It wasn't cold. I held her, tried to warm her with my arms. The world slipped away—even the dream of the mountain glade was too real to live in this room. I was in a waking sleep.

As suddenly as she had come to me she pulled away. For a frantic minute I thought that the real world had returned, that she remembered, that she regretted. I was furious. I hesitated a minute before going to her to take her—screaming, fighting, fussing, if that was the way she wanted it.

She hadn't stepped away to run or refuse. Her hands rose and held the material of her nightgown. They pulled and cloth came away in shreds. Like a madwoman, she tore off the dress, having made up her mind that there was no waiting.

I stepped toward her and she stepped back from me. The moonlight crossing her breasts made them seem even larger in the white and shadow. She stopped. The light caught her eyes and I saw that they were like an animal's and shining with cold brilliance. Her face, for all her frenzy, was calm. She called me softly.

It was slow and inexorable. Every move she made was calculated to be felt. My senses had never been so acute. She made love to me. There was no exhaustion. I didn't want to pause or sleep. We held each other close—and we moved apart until we might have been no oneness, however joined. I wanted light. I wanted to see her face which was in shadow.

Out of nothing she let out a moan. It was filled with hope and despair. It was the voice crying on the shores of the Mediterranean that Pan was dead. Her arms tightened around me and I was surprised at her strength. Then with a violent twist she moved from me and lay with her face buried in a pillow.

I closed my eyes to shut it out and I fell deeper and deeper into a pit. There was no sensation of falling. The bottom was coming up to meet me—like after the first jolt of an opening parachute. Then nothingness. A black deeper than black covered everything.

I felt her lips on my lips.

"Are you asleep?" she whispered. I kissed her and held her for an answer.

"Are you tired?" she whispered. Her voice was small, asking and ashamed to ask. I wasn't tired.

When we woke it was light—a soft morning—and we, half awake, still together, slowly, gently, delightfully joined the day. We laughed and clipped and kissed and toyed and did all the things the bawds love best. It was the same and new. Dimensions grew. The night had been a somber and terrifying initiation and now we enjoyed the joys of membership. It was the proof. It was the end. It was the way to move the earth. She held her breath and then there was a scream of exaltation. We lay embracing. We didn't go back to sleep. She uncurled my arm and bounced out of bed, laughing, happy. She leaned over and kissed me like a Christmas morning child. I still wasn't all awake.

"I love," she said. "I love you," she said gaily. I tried to pull her back to bed but she ran away. "I'm going to bring you breakfast in bed."

She ran out of the room, her robe flying behind her. I lay back and made the pillows right. She came back with coffee and juice. We drank, I in bed, she sitting cross-legged at the foot. I put away the coffee and reached for her again but she ducked away giggling.

We had breakfast by the side of the pool. The sun was high. My watch was upstairs. It was late. She ate like a healthy horse. I had two more cups of coffee and then was ready to smoke.

"God is good!" she said leaning back in her chair and stretching contently.

"I love you," I said and meant it.

Her face became serious. "I hope so. After last night I suppose my words should be 'I have never done that before' or 'I wonder what you think of me' or 'I'm not really that kind of woman' but you know that I have had lovers and that I've looked for thrills and tried to fill my loneliness. Still, everything I told you last night was true. My life has changed. In the other life nothing worked. I was tired of it. I swore I wouldn't do it again until I was sure."

I didn't want a morning confession. I was too happy. I kissed her.

"Then the experiment was a success?"

Her eyes were wide. "It is the first time it has ever been. You can't know that but it is true."

I looked at the ash on my cigarette.

She kissed my cheek and moved her chair nearer mine. "How does love come, Robert?"

"I don't know. You can't look for it. You don't build it. You wait. When it comes you know it."

"But the life span of a love. Can you know that?"

I thought of Doris. I would have said once that I loved her, and I thought of the others. Love? It was passion turned to disgust. Affection turned to boredom. "No. You don't know how long it lasts. You have to be happy when it is with you."

She leaned to me. Her robe draped open showing me her miraculous bosom. She pointed her cigarette at me parodying a schoolmarm. "But you see, Robert, my love, you are wrong. If love goes or disappears, then it never was love. Love is forever. You don't simply know love. You live it."

I wanted her again. Hers was the face in my dream. The talk was unreal and fantastical. I wanted to go back to bed or shut my eyes and be, without having to climb back in Tio Domingo's glade.

We didn't need words. She nodded. It was a question I understood. I stood up and took her hand for an answer and we raced back to her bedroom. We tumbled onto the bed, legs high, laughing when someone knocked on the door.

It was a maid. Lopez, she said, was downstairs waiting to talk to me. I told the girl to send him off. Mercedes insisted I go down. I went.

"Good morning, Señor. I hope I am not disturbing you?" I preferred him the way he had been when I first met him. When he hadn't known who I was, he had acted as if he was a man. Now, knowing that I was one of Santos' clients, he treated me with undue deference.

I waved my hand noncommittally. "Yes?"

"Señor Santos has sent me to ask whether you are ready to go."

Mercedes had come down. She stood beside me. "Go? Go where?"

"There is a private plane waiting for you at the airport. Arrangements have been made," he said.

"Tell your boss I'm not going anywhere," I said. "I like it here."

"But Señor," he whined. "You cannot. Arrangements have been made."

"Where is the Señor to go?" she asked.

"I am sorry, Señora, I cannot say."

"Tell her!" I commanded.

He shrugged.

"Yucatán. He is to live on the chicle land until his papers are ready."

"You tell Santos that I am fine here!" I wasn't about to go down to Yucatán. I'd found her and I wasn't going to leave her.

I felt her hand on my arm. "No," she said. Her eyes were sparkling. "Go. It will be fabulous."

I looked at her in surprise. I couldn't understand how she could want me to go after the things she had said.

"And take me with you. Please!" she added.

I told Lopez. I felt wonderful. "She comes with me!"

That didn't bother him. "As you wish," he said.

She almost jumped for joy. "Robert! Robert! It is a kingdom," she cried. "It's fairyland. You don't know how lucky we are."

To me a ranch is a ranch is a ranch and one in Yucatán was going to be hot. She wanted to go so we would go. That's all.

X

I knew she was beautiful. I hadn't realized how beautiful until I saw the stares she got at the entrance to the Mexico City airport. The tourists returning home forgot their bickering about overweight, stopped shepherding their wicker baskets full of pottery and silver, and crudely gawked.

A porter came to help us with her half dozen pieces of matched leather luggage. I had packed in five minutes and gone to her room to see how she was getting along. She was having trouble choosing what to take. I laughed at her.

"We are going to Yucatán, jungle country—to a chicle plantation. It isn't going to be like Metro Goldwyn Mayer's conception of Africa, replete with formal dinners."

She was too busy to argue. She pecked me on the cheek. "Robert. Oh, wait, Robert. You have such a surprise coming."

I had to sit on her bags to close them.

We had called Santos as soon as we hit a phone. He was waiting for us in the bar. He took us to a waiting Beechcraft at the other end of the field and gave us a rundown as we walked out.

"I want you to stay south until you hear from me. When you come back, I will have all your papers arranged and you will know enough about chicle to say that you have lived down there for the past five years. Being in chicle will account for your money."

"A hundred thousand?" I asked.

"I'll tell him," she said, bubbling. "How did you do it, Mattias?"

"My arms stretch far. Now be good children. Have a good time."

The pilot wasn't talkative. He made gestures and we got in. Mattias watched until we began to move across the field to the runway. I tried to speak to the pilot. I could swear his answer was in Russian.

I'd taken advanced training in a Beechcraft. It felt strange to be riding again. I held my breath on the takeoff. I know planes can't fly, but the miracle took place.

We ducked out of the pattern and I relaxed.

"All right, baby, now tell me true. Are you coming with me because you want to go to Yucatán or because you want to be with me?" I asked her.

"Silly! Because of you. But Yucatán? You mean you don't know where we are going?"

"Sure. Yucatán. A chicle plantation."

She shook her head in amazement and filled in the details. In the great uncultivated south of Mexico the world's supply of chicle grows and the whole domain is controlled by only a few men. They have built a kingdom—a domain—and on their land they hold the power of life and death. Their land is patrolled by their own armies and for all practical purposes it is independent of its mother Mexico. No one can enter the area without permission from its owners and those that do live there have unassailable refuge. The money made in chicle has been invested and the proprietors are among the nameless few that control the destiny of the world.

To me, until I saw it, it was still just jungle. Mercedes and I held hands and watched.

Six hours later we began to let down. I had to stare to find the strip hacked out of the tropical forest. It didn't look like a place to be excited about.

It wasn't the end of the trip. A command car met us. Under the shelter of the trees I saw long warehouses and other evidence of business, but we didn't stay there. We loaded into the car, which had a four-wheel drive and was equipped with a power winch in front, and started into the jungle along a well-worn road. Parrots screamed at us. We were in lost country. It was always a shock to pass other cars. There was no hail or salutation. I noticed that everyone carried a gun. I asked the driver why.

"To shoot snakes," he grunted. His Spanish was poor.

We came to a river. We stopped. The driver didn't want to talk. He got out and squatted on the bank smoking a cigar. The water ran fast but looked clean.

Our driver seemed disgusted. I asked him what we were waiting for and he grunted. It was no answer.

A boat glided up to the bank. It was built for this place, trim neat with a hull like a sled. Our driver put our bags on the boat. He spat in the water.

"Don't spit in my river," the boatman said. It was the only thing he said on the whole trip upriver.

We went against the flow for an hour. Once we thought we saw a house. I couldn't believe it. It was the light filtering through the trees. We came to a clearing on the bank. It looked like pictures I have seen of the African plains. I wondered what kept the jungle out.

We came to a fork and took the smaller branch. A half hour later we came to a lake. A waterfall plummeted into it from a cliff and on the cliff was a house. It was a shocker.

It might have been built by Frank Lloyd Wright. I wondered how it had got down here. The boat pulled into a wharf and we were handed out. A jeep took us up a curved path to the front entrance.

The man waiting for us looked like a Hollywood-built jungle-living Englishman with cork hat, knee-length shorts, bush jacket pipe and all. When he spoke he proved that the English part of the evaluation at least had been right.

"Good to have you," he said, without taking the pipe from between his teeth. "Expected you earlier. Been waiting."

"Boat was late," the jeep driver said.

"Damned thing is always late. Hope your trip wasn't too uncomfortable."

"It was wonderful," Mercedes said.

He took his pipe out of his mouth. "Amazing country, isn't it? You can't see it from the air. You'll like it I think, but I suppose you are tired and could use a little rest. It is a hard trip if you aren't used to it."

He motioned to the driver to take our things. We followed him into the house.

"But I'm not tired at all," Mercedes said. "I want to see everything." She was as excited as a rabbit in a cabbage patch.

"Everything is quite a bit," he said. "Come along. I'm sure you can use a drink."

The house was cool—not too cold—just enough to take the edge off the day.

"My name is Candle," he said to me when we were in a big comfortable room.

"Bierce," I said. "Robert Bierce, and this is ..."

I hesitated, wondering whether I should use her real name. I didn't want us to have separate rooms. He caught my pause and covered it.

"I am pleased to meet you Mrs. Bierce."

"Mercedes," she said and flashed him her charm. It rolled right off him.

"You seem to have everything here," I said.

"Naturally. It wouldn't be very pleasant if we didn't." He showed us around. There was a music room: organ, piano, as complete a collection of music and records as I have ever seen, fine reproducing equipment; a magnificent workshop; a tennis court; a billiard table—everything.

"No swimming pool," he said. "The lake is good enough."

We went back to the living room and he made us two icy long Collins. I was thirsty. I drank mine and when I saw Mercedes wasn't drinking hers, I took that too.

"How long have you been here, Mr. Candle?" she asked.

"Candle, Mercedes—just Candle. A long time."

He didn't want to discuss it. He stood up. "If you need anything, let me know."

"Is this your house?" she asked.

"Yes. This is my house. Now if you will excuse me." He left us with a jerky bow. A man came in and showed us to our rooms.

We had two rooms, adjoining, with a bathroom and a small pool of a bath between. I filled it and splashed in. She followed me. We lay, soaking up the cool. When we made love there were ripples.

We didn't see much of Candle. He ate with us and then left us and when we asked him questions he ignored them. The minute a meal was through he made his apologies. It was obvious that, for all his politeness, he would be glad when we left.

I had never in my life spent as much concentrated time with one person as I did with Mercedes. In the years of marriage with Doris our simple connubial proximity hadn't made us so close. There was something positive about Mercedes' presence, and we were alone in this lost world. We were forging a new identity, that special being that is two people joined by love. She loosened up about sex and though it became less frantic it was more solid and had larger dimensions. Her shyness disappeared. We would be walking down a path just out of sight of the house and she would stop.

"Shall we?" she'd ask.

And we would—on the springy, spongy floor of the jungle, not really caring whether anyone came by or not. We accepted sex matter-of-factly and the excitement increased because of it.

We learned about each other. I told her most of the history of my life. She told me hers. She had been orphaned young and had inherited a small fortune. She had dissipated it. She knew only the well-heeled life. She married Gilbert Ruhl. They spent their money. She decided to build instead of spend. She moved from the city to the hacienda. She built it into a paying enterprise. She learned that life could be good. Gilbert didn't like it. He spent. He tormented. He turned into a psychotic. He killed himself.

One night at dinner as Candle, our host, was getting up with his usual apologies, she spoke up and asked him to stay. I was surprised when he said yes.

We sat outside on the veranda, looking over the lake, watching the imported fish jump. He told us of the catalog he was making listing all the vegetation. He told us of the jungle which he knew intimately. He made the quest of a particular moth sound as exciting as a hunt for treasure.

From the time he had shown that he wanted to be left alone I had accepted him on his own terms. His business was his business and mine was mine, but now that we sat together pleasantly discussing the jungle there were other things I wanted to ask him. I toyed in my mind with words, trying to couch what I had to ask in terms that could be ignored. I couldn't figure out a means that was anything else but what it was—nosey and inquisitive. If he didn't want to answer, I figured, he could keep on talking about the varieties of moths, but he answered.

"I have been here fourteen years."

Mercedes leaned forward in her chair. Candle fascinated her. "And will you ever leave?" she asked.

I waited for him to go on about the moths but he answered.

"I don't think so. You see, I came here fourteen years ago, rather under a cloud—like you. Oh don't be shocked. Everyone here is hiding for or from something or other. I don't know what you've done. All I know is that you are waiting. So it was with me. I wanted the world to forget me.

You see, I killed a man."

I watched Mercedes. She paled and her lips parted. I looked at Candle. He was watching her as if she was an interesting insect—nothing else.

"When you kill a man," he continued, "you do not kill your memory of him, do you? If anything, when you kill, you emancipate the special ghost. Do you understand?"

She nodded her head slowly. He lit his pipe and we waited.

"You see, I killed my father."

Her voice came from the sepulcher. "Then you stay here to atone?"

He laughed. "No, my dear lady. I stay because I don't think that I could be happier anywhere else."

"But people," she said. "You see no people."

"Of course I do. I have simply been sketching a tale, not drawing it complete. I do leave the jungle for a few weeks a year, on the business of the owner of this world. And I find the few weeks more than enough. I am always glad to return."

"But women?" she asked quietly.

"Ah that! Yes. But remember, Mercedes. This is not the end of the world. People can and do enter—with permission. You came and it only took a day, and I am not the only person living here. Why do you ask? Are you lonely?"

"No. Of course not!" She was too emphatic.

"Would you like me to have a party in your honor? To show you the people?"

She seemed afraid. "No. Please no. I don't want to go to a party."

"I would like a party," I said. I wanted to see how it was done. A party in the jungle seemed impossible.

He stood up. "Righto. We shall entertain two days from tonight. Good evening then." He walked away. I felt a chill. He might have been dead.

The next day she was busy planning what she was going to wear. She must have tried a dozen costumes on for me. I thought she looked magnificent in all of them. Her enthusiasm came back.

"Darling, darling, darling," she cried the night of the fiesta. "This is what I've been waiting for. I can't wait. Button me."

She had picked her dress, but she was still nervous and making an awful fuss. Her cheeks were almost feverish red. I got a bottle. I had always believed that the most important drink at a party was the one you took before going.

"Drink it," I said. "It'll calm you down."

She pushed the glass away. "No, I can't drink."

I forced it on her. "Drink it," I said, as if I was giving a child medicine.

She took the glass. "You made me," she said. "I haven't had much success drinking."

"That was before," I said. "Life is different now."

The drinks didn't seem to affect her. She didn't lose her flush but simply became more attractive. She had calmed down.

I dressed and shaved twice. Now that there was going to be the party and people had been coming in through the jungle all day, I regretted having pushed Candle. Other people would break into our paradise. I wanted Mercedes to myself.

After much fixing, Mercedes said she was ready. I had never seen her so lovely. She was a queen. My queen. We went downstairs, she clutching my arm as if she was afraid. I hadn't thought I would ever see her so nervous.

A table had been set in the dining room and spread with a universe of food. Planes must have crossed half the world to bring things like Maine lobsters. The house was as crowded as a graduation ball—and still, through it all, I felt a heavy air of desperation as if most of the people didn't really want to be there and had been forced to come in order to prove something.

Mercedes and I went to the bar. I drank through nervousness and she drank with me, glass for glass. I couldn't feel the liquor and kept drinking to bring me up to party level. I thought she was getting a little tight. I'd never seen her high and encouraged it. Her eyes lost some of their brilliance but she was as beautiful as ever.

"No one is talking to me!" she said with a gasp. It was the liquor. It was true we had been left alone, but that pleased me. The groups were almost static. In spite of the crowd there was little mixing. I realized that wherever Mercedes had gone she had been the center of attraction—until that night. She didn't like it.

A wraith detached herself from a group and strode toward us. She was at least six foot four and as slim as a reed. She walked with determination as if she was going on orders into a lion's den. As she approached I tried to tell her age. It was impossible. She might have been a well-preserved contemporary of my dead grandmother. She wasn't of the human race. Her face was caked with spatula-applied makeup. She ignored Mercedes.

"Will you dance with me?" she asked in a reedy voice. I looked at Mercedes. She waved me away. I stood up, at last feeling the whiskey in my legs and took the zombie's arm. We danced. I felt the fool. She was two inches taller than I was, and she didn't dance. She walked around the floor, pulling me with her. When the dance was over, she thanked me and bowed. I almost ran from her. I went back to the bar. Mercedes was gone.

I felt a lost moment and then saw her on the other side of the room, looking happy, surrounded by men, being made a fuss over. I felt jealous and alone. I took my time and then pushed my way to her. I waited for a lull in the babble and whispered to her.

"Let's go to the terrace. It's hot in here."

She pulled her arm away. "Not now," she whispered. She staggered. She was tight. Really tight.

I get drunk. I don't act too well. All right. She was drunk. It happens. She turned away from me as if I didn't exist. That happens too when you drink. I walked away.

I waited the right amount of minutes and then thought it was silly to play her game. I went back to the main room to look for her.

The dance floor was deserted and all the people were crowded around something in one corner. For a panicky minute I thought that something had happened to Mercedes and rushed to the crowd, pushing my way through until I heard her laugh. It was a parody of a laugh, high pitched and touched with madness, but it was hers. It made shivers run down my back. I squeezed through the packed bodies and saw what they were watching. Mercedes was in the front row.

It was the tall thing I had danced with. She was on a couch. She was too big for it. Her skirts were up and there was a dwarf with her. She told him what to do. She commented on how it felt and how well he followed instruction—with asides to the audience.

Mercedes' face was flushed. I took her arm and dragged her unwillingly through the crowd and out to the empty veranda.

She had trouble focusing. "Are you having a good time Robert?" she asked thickly.

"It stinks," I said. "You are going to bed."

She pulled her arm from my hand and stepped back. He face contorted into hate.

"Don't tell me what to do! No one tells me what to do!"

"Listen baby," I said as gently as I could. "You're tight. You aren't at your best. Let's go to bed."

"Of course, I'm tight," she said. "And I'm glad. I've been bored. Inexorably bored and at last I'm enjoying myself. You are a dull lout. Your only virtue is your money. I'm willing to put up with you for it, but not tonight. See. Now go away. And don't try and tell me what to do!"

I slapped her. She laughed and I slapped her again. Hard. I had to hold her to keep her from falling. She squirmed out my arms. She leaned toward me like a fury.

"You've done it," she said.

"Are you coming with me?"

She stared. She didn't speak. I stepped towards her and she stepped back. To hell with her! I didn't want any more. I walked out and left her on the veranda.

Candle was waiting for me with a drink. He handed it to me. He must have seen it all.

"This is a party, Mr. Bierce," he said.

I took the drink. "To end them all!"

"But of course. Shouldn't we plan every party as if it is going to be the last?"

"I don't like your parties," I said.

"Everyone is doing what they want to do. I do my best see that they can. Isn't that a successful party?"

"I'm not doing what I want to do," I said.

"Aren't you? I have failed as a host. A party should be all things to all people, as they say. Won't you come with me?"

I followed him through the house. In other rooms they were not so drunk. He left me in the music room where a group of respectable looking people were sitting soberly, calmly listening to an old man at the piano. He was playing Satie, delicately with sounds that hung and could be tasted.

I couldn't take my mind from Mercedes. I walked out. Candle was waiting for me at the door.

"You see," he said. "You have been with the—let us say—wilder group. Their manners are contagious. They live what most people only dare to dream. You must be patient with Mercedes."

I agreed and he seemed to find that satisfactory. Everyone gets tight. No one makes sense when he does. The *in vino veritas* line is crap. I went back to find her.

I couldn't find her. I figured—and thanked heaven for it—that she had gotten some sense, realized she was tight, and had gone to bed. I went upstairs with joy. She wasn't in the room.

I wasn't going to make an ass of myself by acting the jealous husband and searching for her. I didn't want any more downstairs. I assumed she would come back up when she was ready. I lay down and waited.

I waited a half a pack of cigarettes and then I worried. She was so tight anything could have happened. She could have fallen in the lake. I got up and went back down. The party was taking shape.

Two women had stripped and were dancing together naked. No one seemed to notice. I searched the room for Mercedes. I couldn't find her in the house. I found Candle and asked him whether he had seen her. He said that he'd seen her going toward the lake. My first fears were increased and I raced out after her.

She was on the path, as we had been on the path, and she wasn't alone.

If I had had a gun, I would have shot them both. I didn't have a gun. My anger turned to disgust. I spat at them and went back to my room.

XI

I didn't sleep. I didn't undress. I lay on the bed and smoked until my tongue burned. I hated myself more than I hated her. In stealing the money I had risked my name and my life in order to find a good world. It was so easy to fall into sloth. I had thrown away all my ideals in order to be with her and she was flesh—only the flesh.

The sun was still below the horizon but it was throwing up the first rays of morning and cutting through the night when I heard the door.

She stood framed in the doorway looking lost.

"I'm sorry," she said in a little girl voice.

I couldn't answer her.

She began to weep. "He forced me. He made me. There was nothing I could do."

"Was it good?" I asked.

"No! No!" she screamed. "I was drunk. I didn't know what I was doing."

I got up and led her to the bed. "Get some sleep."

I didn't want to talk. She undressed. Her dress was stained from grass. She climbed onto the bed. We lay there without touching. I was tired and had to fight off sleep. My mind zoomed in crazy circles like a piece of paper in the wind. I held tight to myself, afraid that if I did relax and closed my eyes I would never wake sane.

But I slept—as if I had been drugged, straight through the day. I woke to see the sun sinking down behind the jungle. I was still dressed. I got up and showered and then got into other clothes. I didn't wake her.

Downstairs there was no sign that there had been a party. I found Candle on the veranda.

"Where are they?" I asked.

"They've gone."

I watched the water falling from the hill into the lake. I knew that he knew everything that had happened last night.

"Well," I said. "Say it."

"Don't be hard on her. None of us are beyond sin and what she did isn't really important."

"Throw a nickel on the drum," I said.

"Wake her up, man," he said. "And don't talk to her in the house. Take a walk, but don't do anything until you've talked to her. Don't make up your mind."

I asked him how long he had studied Freud and whether he had his certificate. He shrugged and walked off.

I wasn't going to go to her. I waited though, and when she came down she looked like the clean scrubbed girl of the Tio Domingo again. But I knew something now about the thing behind her eyes, about Gilbert Ruhl and the way she had tried to get Santos to give her his gun—and I knew about last night. I waited for her to speak. When she did she was in full control of herself.

"I am sorry, Robert. I drank too much. I was angry at the world and I wanted to hurt you."

"That's nice," I said. "I'm glad you weren't as angry at me as you were at Gilbert."

She winced. "I have a terrible hangover," she said. "Can you forgive me?"

"No." My mind made the words. "I don't think I can." She looked so good. I felt like crying. The night had been stupid, filthy beyond pardon, but I couldn't look at her. The woman of last night wasn't the one in front of me.

"Then there is nothing to say, is there?"

I remembered the rock pool we had built and how when we swam in it she had asked me not to touch her.

"Was it good?" I asked trying to hurt more. It didn't make me feel better to say it.

"No," she said with a weary sigh. "It wasn't good. It has never been good except with you."

"Candle said I should walk with you." I stood up. She stood up.

We walked past the house and into the trees.

"How much money do you have?" she asked after a while. I told her.

"I thought it was more."

"I'm sorry. I thought it was enough."

"If I stay with you," she said, and she sounded like a business woman, "and make all the promises you want me to make, and confess my guilt and shame, and plead for forgiveness, would you be pleased?"

I didn't know what to answer. I wanted her. I hated her.

"I would leave you when the money was gone," she said, matter-of-factly.

"When the money is gone?"

"Yes. Life is short. All the things that please me can be bought. Your money won't last."

If she had spoken in anger, I might have acted differently. She spoke so calmly that the image of her during the night, her refusal of me in Tio Domingo's glade, the words she had spoken before, the knowledge of what had happened to her last husband welled up in me. I meant to slap her, to stop her talking like this but my hand turned into a fist and she flew like an unstringed puppet across the path. She stumbled as she tried to stand. Her eyes were glazed at first, but when she gained her feet they blazed at me with the same unholy light I had seen in the night.

"You will pay me for that," she spit. "You are going to be hurt because of that. I will never forget."

"Good." I was shivering. I was cold. I was either going to hit her again or kiss her and beg forgiveness.

"You didn't try to understand. What I did was bad. Yes. But you had no compassion. I wasn't fresh and virgin clean when I met you. I had lived and loved and suffered and I carried scars from what I had done and seen. I had learned to fight back. Last night I was fighting. I was trying to hurt you. It was stupid. It was, I suppose, a kind of masochism. I couldn't believe in your love or that I was lucky enough, at last, to have real love and I tried to deny it. But it wasn't sin unto death. I was drunk. You didn't try to understand. You didn't try to help me."

Her hands began to clench and unclench at her sides and her face turned white. She shifted her feet like an untrustworthy animal. I didn't want her. I turned from her, left her on the path, and went back to the house.

She slept in the other room that night and in the morning when I woke she was gone. I had too much pride to ask Candle when and how she had left. He didn't say anything. It was as if she had never been there.

With Mercedes gone Candle spent more time with me. I found him ageless and filled with a mass of seemingly impossible-to-correlate information. Three weeks passed. I went with him into the jungle searching for specimens for his collections. We explored the lost cities. I worked all day and slept exhausted at night.

At the end of the month I heard from Santos. I was to return. I almost thought that Candle would ask me to stay. If he had, I would have and gladly forgotten the money that was in the safe deposit box. But Candle didn't speak.

Santos didn't mention Mercedes in his note. I wondered whether he had talked to her.

I left by boat and car and plane.

We landed in Mexico City before sundown. I got a cab and went directly to Santos' office. They were expecting me. "The story has broken," he said as he waved me to a chair.

He shoved a newspaper across to me.

I was called the usual names. There was an inaccurate biography. There were the usual comments: good neighbor, good husband, can't understand it, the war. Fairwater Road was shocked, Doris was shocked. Why? Why? Why?

Why! To have a hundred thousand dollars! I was tempted then to write them a letter.

West Construction Company was closed down. At first it had been thought that Malcolm West was in on it. He had cleared himself but the blow had killed his business.

The FHA announced that they were going to overhaul all loan procedures.

The big search was on. "Have you seen this man?"

"You have covered your trail pretty well," Santos said taking the paper back. "They don't seem to know, yet, that you are in Mexico, but of course it is only a matter of time before they do find out."

"Thanks," I said. "Now what?" I felt jumpy. There was no reason for it. I had known that sooner or later they were going to start looking for me. The time had come.

"Things go well," he said. "You do not know this Robert West man. Your name, of course, is Robert Bierce. Yes. You do look a lot like Robert West. Strange coincidence. You have spent your last five years working for the chicle raisers in the south. No one will ask you what you did. People do not inquire closely into the doings of men connected with chicle. Of course that will also explain your money. What is more you have invested your earnings wisely. You have paid taxes. I have receipts for you dating back five years. You have only one problem: you are quite possibly going to be seen by someone that knows you well, as you know them well. In that case everything is up to you. I advise ignoring them. No one can do anything to you without the support of the Mexican government and the Mexican government accepts the identity of Robert Bierce the chicle worker. Your fingerprints have been on file with them for five years."

He gave me a new *amparo*. He advised me to send anyone that spoke to me to him.

"Now. Where do you have your money?"

I told him.

"Get it out. As far as the government of Mexico is concerned you are safe, but banks are more international in their allegiances. If there is any doubt about your identity, they are within the law in sealing your box. It might be embarrassing. So … pay me and then put the money in a safe place. Put it in sound investments. I will help you if you'd like."

His calm calmed me. I felt better. He smiled.

"See? Everything is fine. Did you enjoy your trip?"

"It was quite a trip."

"I told you it would be exciting." I waited for him to ask about what happened to Mercedes. He didn't. I got up to go. He let me get to the door before he called me back and handed me the note with a silly smirk on his face.

I knew who it was from before I opened it:

> Dear Robert,
> I have made Mattias promise to let me know as soon as you come back. Will you have a drink with me at the Pasa Doble? I will be waiting.

I wanted to have cocktails with her. Flying home I had reviewed the insanities I had committed while I had been drinking. I had had no right to blow my top at her. We weren't married. I had tried, on the plane, to figure out a way to see her, court her, and apologize to her. I hadn't had much hope. I realized that she had been right about what the past can do to someone. I wanted to see her and try to make a new life for her that would compensate for the bad times she had had. But I hadn't hoped.

"What gives?" I asked.

"She gave that note to me three weeks ago, a week after she got back. She made me promise to call her as soon as you were to arrive. I called her as soon as you walked in the office. She's been staying in Mexico City waiting."

I ran out of the office.

"The bank!" he called after me. I skidded to a stop. The banks were closed but he had influence. He woke an official and we went down together. I took the money out of the box and put it in a briefcase I had borrowed from him and I rushed off to the Pasa Doble.

She was the loveliest woman in the room and I glided in on the beam of her smile. She gave me her hand, as if nothing had happened.

"I am so glad to see you back, Robert. Was the trip pleasant?" She was formal, like an old friend with whom you have never made love but her eyes were warm again.

"Fine," I said. "And your trip?"

"Awful. Bumpy and dizzy-making."

A dead pause. I ordered for us. I wondered how long she had been sitting, waiting for me.

"I made Mattias promise to let me know as soon as you came back."

"I know. I'm glad," and then it all started to rush out of me. "Look—about the whole thing. I've been thinking and berating myself and ..."

She cut me off. "I swore I would never talk to you again. I swore revenge. I never hated as I hated you."

"And?"

"No more. I feel shame and anguish. I must tell you—first—you must hear me out."

I gritted my teeth and hung on.

"I was drunk, so drunk. I don't know what happened. It was as if Gilbert was with me and the party was his disgusting party. I forced myself to become part of it to hurt him—and then you asked me to leave. When Gilbert thought I had enough to drink he would ask me to leave and then he would take me upstairs and start his filthy experiments. I felt you were going to be like him. I did what I did to spite you. It was awful."

"Don't," I said.

"It's the drinking. I can't drink. I know it. Do you believe me?"

"When you were trying to hurt me, you talked of my money. I have all of it in this briefcase. Here. Will you keep it for me? I believe you."

I was drunk on her words. The money seemed to say everything.

"I don't want to stay here," she said. "I want to go home." We left together.

We hid from the world. We wandered the hills. We built dreams for the future and might have gone on that way forever if Santos hadn't sent Lopez out.

I was supposed to come to Mexico City immediately. I told him to go to hell. Mercedes said I'd better go. I went.

When I got into his private office he jumped up and handed me a New York paper.

Big news! It said that the money I had stolen had been found. The story went on to say that I must have gotten scared and run away without the money. It was hidden in my attic with a note that I was sorry.

I couldn't figure it out. It threw me. I asked Santos. He shrugged.

"Insane," he said. "Insane. I'll find out what it is but it will take a few days."

"Whatever it is," I said, "it's wonderful. It means they will call the dogs off."

"Yes. Yes," he said impatiently. "But that isn't the reason I called you in. Do you know a man named Finlay?"

My heart rode a rollercoaster. I couldn't talk. My mouth was too dry. I nodded.

"Is he from the police?" Santos asked.

"Not unless he switched jobs," I managed to say. I told Santos who he was and how I had talked too much about Mexico and Santos to him. My head was reeling. Finlay here? In Mexico?

"Do you know why he is here?" Santos asked.

There could only be one reason. He wanted a cut. The thing that worried me was that if he got here so quickly then everyone would be right behind him.

"I don't want you to see him," Santos said. "He came to the office and asked for you. He acted wise and tough. I said I didn't know you. He wasn't satisfied. If you see him, you are going to have trouble. He looks like a desperate man on his last big do-or-die chance. I'll take care of him."

"You will? What will you do?"

I had to see Finlay. The papers only said so much. I had to know how Malcolm and Doris felt. I had to know what had really happened.

"I think the best thing to do is have Mr. Finlay disappear." It was a polite way of saying it.

"Never mind," I said. "I'll talk to him."

Santos jumped up. "Don't be a fool! He is probably being watched. If you are seen talking to him, or show that you know him, you will be sticking your neck out from here to there. Leave him alone. I'll take care of him. He asked for it."

"What are you worried about?" I asked. "The paper says they have their money. They don't want me anymore."

"Don't be an ass. Do they have their money? Where did it come from? It's a fraud. It's a sucker trick to make you feel secure."

"No," I said. "No killing."

"Don't be an ass!" he shouted. "I can have him put away for fifty dollars. No one knows him. No one will ask questions. It's the only way. You have to do it."

"There isn't anything dangerous about Finlay," I said. "I know him well."

I stood up. I was scared. "I'm going to see him first, in any case," I said. "Where is he?"

Santos gave me his address. He was staying at the biggest, best advertised hotel. When I got there I found myself in the midst of a convention. The lobby was strewn with banners announcing welcome to the great American chiropractor. I walked to the house phones and rang Finlay's room. There was no answer. I decided to wait a little while. I found a chair where I could watch the front doors and sat down, half hid behind a newspaper.

Finlay spotted me, five minutes later, before I saw him. He shouted across the lobby in the midst of the hustle bustle without causing any surprise. I almost jumped out of my seat.

"Bob-o!"

His arms were loaded with packages. He grinned like an old mate. I saw none of the desperation that Santos had mentioned.

"You old bastard," he said, pulling me up out of my chair. "It's good to see you. Let's have a drink."

Any one listening would have thought it was a chance reunion. He was a good actor.

I had never seen Finlay except in work clothes. He had sprouted new feathers—white Stetson, cowboy boots, tight pants. If he was trying to look Texas, he was doing pretty well.

I wanted the drink. On the trip with Mercedes I hadn't touched anything but beer. Finlay ordered a tequila and made a flashy show of licking salt and sucking lime. When he had proved that he was an old south of the border hand, he ordered something he liked. Bourbon. I had considered and stuck to beer.

"What a place," he gushed. "I didn't believe you back on Long Island when you told me how terrific it was but you were shooting square. I love it!"

"How long have you been down?"

"Two days. Three." He leaned towards me conspiratorially. "You're big news, Bob-o."

He took a mouthful of peanuts and talked through the paste.

"What happened?" I asked and hoped he was a good enough reporter to give it to me straight.

"Old Man West took it pretty hard when you wrote back from Kansas City and said you were going to be away another week. He pissed and he moaned. Then the week passed and no little Bob-o. And then the bank started calling. I don't know everything just like it happened mind you, I was only the foreman, but the cops came over. The old man handled things pretty well. He was pretty broken up because it meant the end of the business and the first day he cursed you. But then something happened and he calmed down. The coppers called me in too. I didn't know from nothing. When the business folded, I had to look for another job. I remembered what you had always told me about going into business for myself but that seemed like too much work. Everyone thinks you are somewhere in South America. While I was thinking how smart you were, I suddenly realized where you really were. I decided to take a vacation."

"And Doris?"

"Oh her. They smeared her across the papers. Say! She's a good-looking chick! She moved in with the old man." I had anticipated that. It made me feel better.

"It's time Malcolm retired," I said. "He has enough money."

"And how! You know I didn't know how well he was fixed—him working so hard and all that—until he put up the hundred grand."

This was it. I asked Finlay. He seemed surprised.

"Sure. Didn't you read about it. They found the money you took—or that's the story. What happened was that the old man worked a deal with the bank. I guess he wanted to protect you and your wife. You're in the clear."

Finlay sat back fat and comfortable. I should have been happy. I should have felt emancipated but I felt as if someone had hit me on the head with a sledge hammer.

I must have looked a little sick because Finlay nudged me in the ribs, laughed too loud and put his arm back around my shoulder.

"What the hell are you looking green about? You're the luckiest bastard in the world."

I was in a half trance. "No. I have to give the money back now."

Finlay took his arm off my shoulders and grabbed my lapels. People in the bar stared. His face was livid.

"The hell you say! You are staying here, in God's country, and little John Finlay is going to take care of you. We are going to live, man, live!"

I pulled his hands off.

"What's this we business?"

He looked mean, then, like an angry bull. He leaned his face close to mine. "Why the hell do you think I came down here? It took my last red cent. I had to walk out on my wife and kids. I came down because I want in. See? I've been waiting for this all my life."

It was pointless. I had to get away and think. I stood up and said good-by.

He grabbed my coat sleeve and pulled me back. I didn't want to fight in the bar.

"Listen, Bob-o," he said between his teeth. "You always were a nice guy. Stay that way. You always told me I should go into business for myself. I am. You're going to be my angel. There's a lot of room down here for a smart building operator. We'll clean up."

"Shakedown?"

He was smiling again. "Of course not. Listen, Bob-o, you have enough for ten people. You are going to give me some because you like me—for old times—or maybe because you're sorry you lost me a cushy job. You see I used to cut ten percent on all the bills I submitted to the old man. I was doing all right."

"Good for you," I said. "Thanks but no thanks."

"Listen," he snorted. He was taut as a drum. "Now that West has paid off the dough it don't belong to no one. It's for the taking and I'm the guy that can take it, in spite of your fancy double-talking Mexican lawyer."

"But it does belong to someone," I said, keeping my voice down. "It belongs to Malcolm West."

He looked at me in amazement.

"Listen yourself, Finlay. Have a good trip. There's lots a guy like you can do in Mexico. Build yourself a future. But don't threaten to play rough. This is Mexico. You're off your home grounds."

He laughed and turned his hand palm up on the table. It was a ham, hard and calloused. "See that? That's a working man's hand. While you were sitting on your ass behind school desks I was working. You can't hurt a man with hands like that. A man with a hand like that is like a mule. I come from a long line of people that have been pushed around. I was born to take punishment. Maybe a smart guy like you slaps me around ten times to the once I get my hands on you, but I can take your ten lumps better than you can take my one. See? I ain't a mule anymore. I'm about to start a new line of Finlays." He liked his speech. He sat back and laughed. "Maybe I'll do it with a little Mex *mamacita*. Get it?"

"I get it." I stood up but didn't move fast. The talk had slowed him down. He'd blown his wad. He stood up with me, without grabbing.

"Where are you going?"

"To think," I said. "You wouldn't understand that."

"I've done plenty of thinking, especially the last couple of weeks."

"Good," I said. "Stay here at the hotel and think some more. I'll call you."

I stepped back and walked away fast. He was still behind the table and couldn't make it. I lost myself in the crowd of the lobby and left the hotel before he could follow me.

XII

"Have him killed," Mercedes said. Her face was placid. She might have been talking about the weather. I'd repeated the conversation to her. She had listened all the way through without prompting or commenting. "Look at it this way. If you don't give him money, he is going to hound you. If you do give him money, it will be the beginning of a long sequence of dunnings."

"It's one thing to do a logical analysis of a situation that ends with getting rid of the object of contention. It's another thing to kill."

She didn't see it that way. I should have known. For the moment I'd forgotten Gilbert. "Everyone dies. All you are doing is hurrying up the process."

I couldn't be so cold-blooded about it. I knew I wouldn't let him be killed. I knew that he would ride me until I gave him some money and that he would be a monkey on my back for the rest of my life if I did but I had almost made up my mind. I told her.

"You can't!" she said shocked. "You have the world in your pocket and you're throwing it away. You've had the most fabulous luck in the world being bought out of trouble by this uncle. Be happy. Be grateful. You can't return the money!"

I didn't want her love if it had to be bought with a hundred thousand dollars. I couldn't afford that kind of love.

"I have to," I said. "We'll start over again, clean and heads high."

She threw her spoon on the floor. "No!" she shouted. "You mustn't."

I shouted back. "I'm going to! I don't like it. I risked everything for the money but if its price is Finlay's death I don't want it."

"You're a fool!" she snapped. "Think of me. Think of yourself."

"I am thinking of myself," I said as calmly as I could. "I want something decent out of life. You can't create that out of dirt."

"Man was created out of dirt!"

"Would you want me if I was always running? Would you want the money if it was sopping blood?"

She was exasperated. "You won't be running. Murder is nothing in Mexico. Finlay was in the war, wasn't he? He might have died and if he had he would have been a hero dying for a cause. Consider him a casualty if he is murdered—dying for a cause—his own cause."

"And my hand would be stained with blood every time I touched a dollar. I'm not thinking of Finlay. I'm thinking of myself."

"Money is money. It is all sopping in blood. What difference does it make where it comes from? It is the acts you have to distinguish between. You were willing to risk jail for the money. Finlay is obviously willing to risk death. You've won. He loses."

I looked away. She got control of herself and tried to soften it.

"Murder is nothing, Robert. Not here. Life is cheap. You live and you die and you have to do all the living you can during the few years you have to live. I don't want to lose you. I want you. I love you. I want you with me. I'd die if you went away."

Gilbert came in again. "I don't want to lose you. I'd kill to keep you."

"Keep me or the money?"

She looked me in the eye and shot it from the shoulder. I liked the honesty. I detested the words.

"Both."

She got up and came to me her voice butter soft. "Don't leave me. Don't think about it. I'll take care of it. Santos will take care of it."

"You need a drink," she said. She brought it to me. I swallowed without tasting. Things slowed down. She gave me another.

We spent the day drinking, or rather I spent the day drinking, she feeding me. Things seemed easier. She fussed around me, flirting, being sweet, coddling me like a sick child. Somewhere in the evening I grabbed her and carried her, staggering under the weight, upstairs to bed.

I woke with a hangover the next day. My head was pounding and I wanted out. I forced myself to shower and dressed with trouble. Buttons wouldn't go through buttonholes. When I went downstairs I couldn't find her. I didn't want to get drunk again but the only cure I knew for the daddy of all hangovers that I carried was another drink. I started on whiskey sours and weaned off on beer. It helped. I tried to put the pieces together again but nothing fit.

She showed up in the afternoon after lunch, which I had had to force myself to eat.

She was solicitous of my hangover and vaguely amused. She spent the day trying to please me but I was close to incapable of being pleased. I hated myself for getting drunk the previous night. I made smiles and sucked beer. I wasn't drunk again but I was riding high.

"You forget about it," she said, sitting beside me in the sun, holding my hand. "Everything is going to turn out all right." She was mothering me. I needed mothering. "Do you remember that once you told me that the life you would build with the money would prove your acts, not the life you had led before? You have to continue believing that no matter what happens."

"But the past won't stay dead. It's following me."

"No, darling," she patted my hand. "It doesn't exist." She stood up. "Come with me, darling. I know how to make you better."

I was still in my reverie and the words came out before I thought them through. "Where? On a jungle path?"

She stepped back as if I'd slapped her. "You'll never forget that, will you? Is that what's bothering you—or Finlay?"

She was beautiful—like a witch is beautiful. I couldn't see too well. I had to close one eye to focus. She watched me, her hands on her hips.

She sneered.

"You're another weak one—like Gilbert was weak."

"Give me a gun," I said. "See who I shoot with it."

"No. With you there are other ways. I've taken care of things."

I jumped up and grabbed her. She squirmed away. She walked off. I didn't want to stay at her place but there was nowhere else to go. Doris would have cradled me then and accepted my unthinking cracks for what they were. I didn't miss Doris but missed the response and sympathy she sometimes gave to my confusions. I had to get away and think.

Mercedes and I had dinner together. It sobered me up. I stopped drinking. She was aloof, polite, formal. Shortly after dinner a taxi drove up with a telegram for me. It was from Santos. I was to meet him the next day at eleven sharp, repeat, eleven sharp, at Finlay's room. I was to go up without checking the desk.

I was relieved to get the wire. It meant Finlay was all right. I'd hoped that Santos could figure out some way to make a settlement. I wished Mercedes had a phone. I wanted to speak to Santos and find out what was what.

She coasted through the rest of the evening on good manners. I learned how Gilbert had felt living in the same house with her and still being a stranger. She could shut you out without saying a nasty thing. I knew why Santos had blown his top the night of her party.

We slept together, because that was the way we had been sleeping, but she kept to her own side of the bed.

In the morning I felt better. I took a bromo to be on the safe side and then drove into town. I was stone sober but had a hint of the shakes. I turned the window panels out and let the air flash on my face. It made me alive. I purposely kept my mind away from Finlay. I wondered how to make up with Mercedes.

I'd tried her as severely as she'd tried me. I talked so damn much about forgetting the past and the minute I was upset I threw her past in her face. I wanted her. I had to control myself. I couldn't blame her. Everyone gets into an invisible plastic armor when they get pushed. I had done plenty of pushing.

I swore that I wasn't going to let anyone do anything to Finlay. If necessary I'd give him some dough with the understanding that if he asked for more *then* I'd push and push hard. That way he would be making the decisions, not Robert West, Mattias Santos or Mercedes Ruhl. All the problems seemed to be answered with that solution. Then I would go back to Mercedes and make everything all right.

I parked around the corner from the hotel and used the steps to get up to Finlay's floor. I checked numbers and found his door at the end of the hall. I knocked.

I had never seen the face of the guy who opened the door before. He was Mexican and had the lean hungry look. He seemed glad to see me and stepped aside to let me in.

Santos wasn't there. Finlay was sitting down looking a little green. He kept his eyes on the man who had let me in. I followed his stare and saw the gun. It didn't bother me. Everyone in Mexico carries a gun.

The Mexican smiled and pointed with the gun to an empty chair. He was polite. He asked me to sit down. I sat. I figured he was from Santos and had been sent up to throw a scare into Finlay. He was the boy to do it. His face was pinched and his smile as artificial as one painted on a puppet.

"I'm glad you've come," he said in Spanish. "This other one doesn't speak the language and I have no English."

"What's he saying?" Finlay asked.

"Hi, Finlay," I said. "What's new?"

"What's he saying!" Finlay sounded scared.

"He's saying hello," I told him. It was three minutes after eleven. Santos had said and emphasized eleven sharp. I wondered where he was.

"And now," the gunman said. "Tell your friend to look out the window."

I translated for Finlay. He looked back at me blankly. "What gives? This guy came in a half hour ago and has been covering me, telling me to wait. I let him in because I got a telegram from you last night saying you were coming at 10:30. I thought it was you at the door. Tell him to put up that gun! I don't like guns!"

"Talk in Spanish!" the gunsel shouted. He wasn't smiling anymore.

"He doesn't talk Spanish," I told him. "My friend wants to know who you are. Did Santos send you?"

He didn't answer. "Tell your friend to go to the window!" It was an emphatic order.

I wondered what Finlay was supposed to see out of the window. I got up and looked out. I couldn't see anything. I went back and sat down.

"You'd better go," I told Finlay.

I could see he was frightened. I didn't like the situation either.

"Not me," Finlay said, sinking deeper into his seat. "I'm sitting here. Who is this guy?"

It was a linguistic stalemate. The gun carrier didn't like talk in English. He was holding the gun tighter.

"When I count three," Finlay said evenly, "let's jump him." Though his voice was level it was tight and came out of his throat.

“Relax,” I said. “I have a friend that will be here any minute.”

But I wasn’t relaxing. Santos’ people had more finesse.

“This man has no money,” I said to the hood. “I have no money. What do you want?”

It was a ridiculous thing to say. We were in a hotel that charged six bucks a day for a single room. A Mexican master mechanica makes just about a buck a day. In parts of Mexico a pair of not too worn shoes would be a good haul for a robbery, but things like that didn’t happen anymore, especially in Mexico City in a top flight hotel.

“Go to the window!” The gunman screamed. “Both of you!” I stood up to go. There was no sense in playing games. Finlay took it for the signal to jump. I had started toward the window when the gun crashed. I spun around. Finlay went down like a big tree. The hole in his forehead was small and showed only a ring of red. When he hit the floor he half rolled and I saw that there was no back to his head. Just white brain tied in a snood of blood red threads. I looked up for the gun. If I was next, the son of a bitch was going to come with me. It had only taken a split second. The gun was on the floor and the door was closing.

I ran out and saw him heading down the stairs. I wasn’t going to stick around. People came out of doors into the hall. I ducked back into the room and got the key. I went back out and locked the door behind me in order to keep people out and get that much more time. There was nothing to do for Finlay. The hall was filling up. I put the key in my pocket and forced a smile. I nodded hello and walked down the hall as if nothing had happened.

The muscles in my cheeks hurt from holding the smile. I heard the increasing bubble of detached voices behind me. Someone was knocking on Finlay’s door. I got to the steps and as soon as I was out of sight raced down them three at a time.

The commotion hadn’t spread to the lobby. I couldn’t see the killer. I scooted across the lobby and cut out onto the street.

I never dreamed that dream about being naked on Times Square but I learned to appreciate it. No one stared at me but I felt that everyone knew what had happened. I wanted to run but I held myself to an inconspicuous walk. I put distance between me and the hotel. I couldn’t figure it. I needed Santos. When I was five or six blocks from the hotel, I hopped a cab and headed for his office.

The receptionist fixed me with an unknowing stare and asked my name. I’d been in and out enough so that she knew me but her sudden lack of recognition didn’t dawn on me right away. She told me to sit and wait. It was like the first time I had been up but I knew the routine now. She wasn't as blank as she acted. Instead of calling back, she took a key from her desk and unlocked the door to the inner offices. She took my name back in person. I didn't like being alone in the room. She came back in a matter of seconds.

"The *Licensiado* cannot see you this morning," she said. "He is very busy. Can you come back this afternoon?"

I was in no mood for games. I grabbed the key out of her hand and opened the door as she started pushing buzzers on her switch board.

Lopez was waiting on the other side of the door. "He is busy, Mr. Bierce," he said. "Can I help you?"

I felt like a trained rat in an unfamiliar maze. I should have poked Lopez and gone through.

"I've got to see him. It's urgent. Life or death."

"So? Just a minute."

He went to his own desk and sat down. He didn't call like I thought he was going to. He seemed to be looking for something in his drawer. He talked all the time.

"Are you sure it can't wait until this afternoon?"

That was it. I leaned over the desk, grabbed his tie and stretched his neck. It was beginning to dawn on me.

"You know damned well it can't wait. Now tell him I'm waiting."

He gasped and his eyes were panicky. That only lasted a split second. He brought a gun out of the drawer and slashed the sight across my arm. It cut through the cloth and I dropped him. I wished I'd taken the gun that killed Finlay. I stepped back. The fright went out of his eyes. Behind the gun he was a big man. The barrel didn't waver.

"Sit down. Careful. I am not fooling." I sat down. "Now friend, listen." He wasn't a lackey anymore. "I have a suggestion for you and I will charge you no legal fee for giving it. I think you should run, and run fast. You should try and hide. I say this because you are a nice man who was once almost a client of ours—if not for that I would hold you here and call the police. You have embarrassed this firm terribly. It is a most dreadful thing to shoot a friend—especially in a midtown hotel."

He was crazy. "I? Kill my friend?" It had to be a joke. It was insane. I was in a labyrinth of despair. There was no way out. Black was white.

"Santos! I want to see Santos!"

"He will not see you. Now go or I shall call the police."

I started for him and the gun came up. He felt at home with it. I couldn't have gotten within three feet of him. I took off.

XIII

I ran. I didn't care who saw me. I didn't know where I was going. I was fleeing hell. But there was nowhere to go. I felt like a baited bull. I needed help.

I cut back towards my car. I skidded short and stopped. There were cops and a crowd around the Pontiac. I turned away and headed for crowded back streets. I knew things for what they were. I was in the midst of a big frame.

The pieces began to fall into place, what with Mercedes taking off the morning before and the phony telegrams. Santos was in on it. I knew that from the office. They knew about the murder before it happened. Santos couldn't have set it up unless Mercedes was willing to split with him. All she'd wanted from the beginning was the dough. It was lovely. She and Santos hadn't bothered to kill me for the money. That would have been too simple. With a murder rap pinned on me, I'm lost forever and Finlay's out of the way.

I was cooked, but they weren't going to get the lousy dough. They were going to get it like Finlay got it and the money was going back where it belonged. That would make everything all right. Life wasn't so good or valuable that I'd run to save mine. They'd pay.

First I had to lose myself. Anywhere else I could go to the police and they could make paraffin tests and see that I hadn't fired the gun. It wouldn't work here. They'd say I wore gloves. Santos was a heavyweight at the other end of the seesaw.

The quicker I turned and fought back the better. I couldn't hide or run forever. Sooner or later, whether I wanted to or not, I had to hit a cul-de-sac and fight my way out back to the wall. The time to turn was now.

I was in front of a cantina. I went in and found a shadowed table in the rear. I ordered a beer.

I could look for another lawyer—but there was no other lawyer, and I didn't have the money.

I needed a place to sleep.

I was alone. I needed someone on my side. Who was there? I wracked my brains and found it.

When I'd met Santos he was on the lam. He'd been in a stupid accident, as he called it. All right. He'd straightened things out, but vengeance goes a long way with a Mexican. They would have no love for Santos—the family whose kid he'd killed. I had to find the name of the boy.

I thought back and counted days. I'd been in Mexico roughly six weeks. It had happened just before then. It was close enough. I called the barman and handed him a ten-dollar bill. For him it was a lot of money. I wanted back issues of newspapers between eight and six weeks old. The newspapers in Mexico have a blood page and list all accidents and police blotters.

It took the barman over an hour. I nursed my beer and prayed. I don't know where he got the papers. They weren't out of a newspaper office. The copies were smudged and dirty but they'd serve.

I went through them line by line. I couldn't find a word about the accident. Santos had covered well. I started through again hoping I'd missed something. I found it on the sports page.

The kid had been a *novillero*—one step below a full-fledged bullfighter. He must have been pretty good. The reporter said his death was a loss. Maybe it wasn't the same guy but he had died of tetanus after an automobile accident. They made a joke of it. He risks the dirty horns of a bull and lives. He drives a car and dies. The paragraph gave his name and address.

I showed the piece I tore out of the paper to the bartender. The address was on the other side of town. I paid up and took off.

I had to ask directions a dozen times before I was even in the area. My feet hurt. It was an old quarter behind the thieves' market. An old man pointed the way. I went down a nice sunny street that was lined with coffin-filled windows. The place stunk of formaldehyde. I couldn't find the address. I hit a dead end and asked. I was shuttled back. Finding the address was the most important thing in the world to me. I went into an embalmer's store. They are the same all over the world. He bent his head and rubbed his hands. He looked properly bereaved. I asked for the address. He pointed across the street. It was an alley.

If you were a hell of a driver and had worked twenty years on the big trucks, maybe you could have gotten a car between the buildings. The alley stretched three hundred feet. It was dank, dark and smelly, but at the end it opened into a sun-filled courtyard as big as a city block ringed with old tenements. Clothes hung to dry out the windows. It was quiet as death and that isn't natural for Mexico. I walked slowly.

It was empty except for an old woman bent over a tin tub washing clothes. I went to her and asked her where the Rojas family lived. Either she was deaf, didn't speak Spanish or didn't like my face. She kept on washing.

"Yes, Señor?"

He was at my shoulder. In California he would have been a zoot suiter, his jacket came down to his knees and I couldn't see how he got his feet through the bottoms of his pants. I didn't like his pencil mustache.

I asked him if he knew the Rojas family. His shrug was eloquent. He might. He might not.

I showed him some money. He took it but he didn't start talking right away.

"And why—with your permission—do you want to see the Rojas family? Or is it some one member of the Rojas family that you wish to see?"

"I want to see if we hate the same people," I said. That had the right Mexican flavor.

"Hate, Señor?"

"Of hate, yes—and revenge."

"Do the Rojas hate? Do they wish revenge?"

Hell! I didn't even know, then, that they were the people I wanted. "For the love of God," I said. "Will you take me to them?"

He didn't bat an eye. "My name is Antonio Rojas."

I pulled the clipping back out of my pocket and shoved it to him. "Is this a lie?" I asked. "Was your brother shot by *Licensiado* Mattias Santos?"

I got one flash from his eye.

"Will you join me in a little drink?" He didn't wait for an answer. He started across the courtyard. I didn't want to lose him. I followed. A door on the opposite side led down three steps into a cave of a room. There were a couple of bare tables and chairs and a heavy smell of urine. He sat down and hissed. He didn't need to order. The choice was small. A big fat man put a bottle, two glasses and the junk on the table. Antonio Rojas smoothed out the clipping in front of him and read it again.

"It says here that Dionysio Rojas died of tetanus after an automobile accident. It says nothing of shooting."

"I know. Who was the accident with?"

"With a man named Mattias Santos. A famous lawyer I hear."

"I know he shot your brother."

"So?"

I poured it out. "He shot a friend of mine. He made it seem that I shot my friend. He has stolen from me. He is looking for me."

"And you didn't shoot your friend?"

"No."

"So you have come to us to hide?"

I was tired of it. He made me work too hard. I was past playing. "Yes."

"And why should we hide you? We do not know you. Have we not worries of our own?"

I drank the tequila and tried to find words that would get through.

"Antonio!" He jumped up. He looked less man than boy. I looked over my shoulder. She'd come in like a ghost. It was the old woman of the clothes washing. In the dingy light of the cantina her face looked like a prune but now that she wasn't bent over her tub she stood straight and had no bow to her shoulders.

"Yes, Mama."

"You speak badly to guests."

I wondered how long she had been standing behind my chair.

"Yes, Mama."

She turned and walked to the door. "Bring him with you," she said without bothering to turn.

"Come," Antonio said. We left, without paying, and followed her across the court. I went with him to a building and up three flights of steps.

The apartment was meticulously clean but was so crowded it looked as if it harbored the fruits of five reincarnations. The furniture was Grand Rapids and highly polished. The main room, the one we entered, had a table, a few chairs and a bed. It was a living room, a dining room, and bedroom. The old woman wasn't in it. I could hear her in another part of the house.

"Sit down, Señor," Antonio said and went out to his mother. I sat down on the bed and waited. Half of life, I thought, is waiting. Three quarters of mine had been waiting. In the old days I was good at it. I'd lost the skill. I wanted to do now. It didn't make much difference what I did—the doing in itself was enough. I wanted to make each of my acts positive in order to affirm my existence. I was through with the conjectural world of thought and plan.

I lit a cigarette.

The old woman came into the room with a large parcel tied in brown paper. She opened the wrappings carefully with her boney fingers and spread back the paper. Inside there was a carefully folded Suit of Lights, the costume of a torero. She passed the jacket to me. It was heavy with silver—too rich for the house.

"This was his jacket," she said. "This was his suit. He would have been a great matador—like Manolete."

Antonio was leaning in the doorway. "Manolete was killed at thirty in a lousy little bull ring in a lousy little town in Spain, Mama."

His mother paid no attention to him. "My boy was shot by a man who might have been his brother—by a man who has forgotten his own past and misused his gifts. The man is called Santos but he is the devil. Our house is your house."

"Sleep," she said. "First you need sleep."

I stood up and stumbled after Antonio to the next room. I wanted to speak but I wanted to sleep. I wanted to shut out the day for a little while.

It was a tiny bedroom. I guessed it was Antonio's room. I sat down on the bed. He watched me for a minute and then went out when I didn't speak. I lay back, loosened my tie, and closed my eyes.

It was the sleep that comes immediately and is empty of dreams or even the awareness of sleep.

I didn't know that sleep had come until I felt a hand shaking me.

It was the old woman. "You have slept long. Now you must eat, son. Come."

I sat up. She walked out. I rubbed the sleep from my eyes and followed her.

The table in the main room had been set for four. Antonio was sitting there and across from him was a girl. I had never seen anyone like her. She made Mercedes look anemic. She watched me, appraising, but with no seeming curiosity or emotion. Neither she nor Antonio spoke. I sat down between them. Her eyes never left me. I avoided looking at her as long as I could and when it was impossible to look at Antonio anymore our eyes met. It was like an electric shock. All the hate in the world was in her eyes and it wasn't for me. She was telling me she understood.

The old woman didn't sit. She brought us our food. I ate without tasting. When we were through the girl got up to clear the table. I couldn't keep my eyes off her. She eclipsed Mercedes. Doris didn't exist beside her. It was hard to believe.

When the table was cleared we sat around it in the stiff-backed chairs not speaking until we had formed a sentence in our minds and silently tried it out.

"We will do whatever you wish," the old woman said after a while, speaking for her family. "What would you have us do?"

"Let me stay here a while," I said. When I said it, it was all I knew. The first and only known step, but as I said it I knew what I had to do. I had to kill Santos. The unvoiced resolve filled me with elation as if at last I had found a certainty. I wondered why they hadn't done it. Why hadn't they avenged their brother?

"And then?" the girl asked, leaning toward me as if she knew what my mind held and was urging it out.

"And then I must kill Santos."

She sat back. I'd said what she wanted to hear, but she didn't accept it.

"No! It is not for you to do. It is for Tonio."

Antonio looked as if he heard this before and was tired of it.

"They are right," he said, in a bored tone, "I will kill Santos, not you. The time has come."

The girl sneered. "Yes. You will kill Santos," she mocked. "When? Why is he not dead?"

"Time isn't important," he said. "I have been waiting. I wanted him to be very happy with his life before I took it from him."

The old lady ignored her son. She spoke to me. "You will be our son now, the brother of our dead boy. You shall avenge him. You will do what you must do."

I was in a nest of furies and I felt at home. Home is where they take you in. A simple declaration of the woman had made it so.

Antonio brought out a bottle of tequila. He set it on the table.

"You drink too much," his sister said.

"Is there something better for the poor to do?" he answered grinning.

"We are not poor," the old woman said. "Our blood is rich."

Antonio poured out a shot. "Yes. Six hundred years ago we were princes—so strong and brave that a handful of Spanish criminals took our country from us."

"We have taken it back," the girl said.

He drank his drink. "You are long on memory."

"It is better that memories are long," his sister answered. "One loses what one has by forgetting. Once we had the land. We lost it. We must get it back and then we must work and defend it. There is no solace in tequila. You can only pour oblivion from a bottle."

"I bless oblivion. May I pour a drink for my new brother?" There wasn't a trace of mockery in his voice. It was an explanation.

"It is good that brothers drink together," the old woman said.

I didn't want the drink but I had one with him. As he held up his glass in salute, his grin turned to a smile and his smile warmed the room and drew us together. I had something I had never had. They knew nothing of me except that I had been hurt by their hurt and because of that they took me in.

The old lady didn't bother to say good night. She got up and left. Antonio waited until she was gone. "I am sorry, brother, but I too must go. I have work to do. It is to feed us." He smiled at me and left and with that the girl and I sat across from each other alone in the room. A chill wind crept to the windows and seeped through the cracks. I felt it touch my back and shivered. She pushed the bottle to me. I poured another shot. It scalded going down and tasted green but it gave me heat.

I reached into my pocket and took out my wallet. I put all my money on the table and pushed it towards her. I knew it was more money than she had ever seen.

"Take this. It is for the family."

She ignored it. "Tell me what happened," she asked. I told her, right from the beginning, everything, and it was the first time it had been told. She drew the words and the thoughts from me without speaking.

Most of it about Long Island must have been incomprehensible to her. She neither smiled nor frowned. She hid behind her face. I wondered if she was listening and didn't care. When I was through so was the bottle.

"It's hard for you to hate," she said. "For us it is easy. You must fan your anger to white heat to hate. You must be in pain. We can harbor our hate, live with it, and wait. Tonio spoke true. He was waiting. His calmness was no lack of resolve. He can keep waiting if needs be. You say you must kill Santos. Do you know that you will feel the same way tomorrow?"

I knew it. I had to have his life before I could live my own.

"I will feel this way tomorrow," I said.

"Then good night." She walked from the room. I was alone. I smoked another cigarette. I wasn't tired after the sleep I had had in the afternoon. I had found friends.

I crushed out the last butt and went to bed. I tossed and turned. I saw things. They weren't in my mind alone. They hung in the room in front of me. I heard real sounds. I smelled real smells. I watched Finlay's cracked skull bulge brain, coral-like, expanding like an inflated balloon until it exploded with a gun's roar. Pasty white pieces fell. The echoes of the gun caromed around the room. I smelled Mercedes clean and white beside the pool at Tio Domingo. The things of the night pushed me into sleep.

XIV

The knock on the door was like a clap of doom. I opened my eyes and was instantly awake. It was a strange awareness. I knew where I was and what I had said the night before. I remembered everything like you remember the resolute plans you make while drinking but the resolve wasn't there.

"Come in."

The door opened and the girl came in.

"I have a gun for you," she said. I could see it.

I took it. A standard U.S. Army forty-five—hero of the islands—it was heavier than I remembered. The clip was full. I pulled back the slide and the bullet in the chamber flew out and skittered across the floor. She picked it up and dropped it on the bed.

"Where did it come from?"

"It was bought."

"What did it cost?"

"It is a present."

"What time is it?" My watch had stopped during the night.

"Nine o'clock. The day is ahead of you. You must wait until night if you are going to do this thing. I'll bring you breakfast."

I lay back and lit a cigarette. Last night it had been vows, words, threats. Now in the daylight all the words carried weight. I heard the promises again and let them sink in—the text for the day.

She came back with a tray loaded with coffee and hot milk, rolls, ranch style eggs covered with hot sauce. I wanted to be alone. She stood and watched me eat.

"This isn't for you to do," she said after a moment.

I didn't answer. I kept eating. I was hungry. I poured coffee. My hand didn't shake.

"Have you ever killed a man?"

"Thousands."

"No, not in the war. That was from a distance and your heart had been filled with ideals. Did you ever kill a man when you could look through his eyes to his fluttering soul?"

I wanted her to go. I wanted to think. I wanted to backtrack and see where it started. "Ask me tonight," I said curtly.

She didn't speak again until I finished the breakfast and had wiped my plate clean with a piece of bread.

I wanted to dress. I told her to take the tray out. She didn't move.

"I want to dress."

"Then dress."

I got out of bed and put on my clothes. She didn't take her eyes from me. It made me nervous.

"Haven't you ever seen a man?" I snapped.

She didn't bother to answer that. "No two men are the same. We see people's faces and hands. It is not enough to know someone."

"Then I don't know you?"

"Not yet," she said and then walked out.

I washed my hands and face in a basin of cold water. I combed my hair. I needed to shave but didn't ask for a razor. This day wouldn't call for a shave. I picked up the gun from the bed. It fit into the inside pocket of my coat and when I was buttoned it didn't pull the jacket too far out of shape. I left the room. I could hear her in another room. I didn't want to talk to her anymore. I went downstairs, crossed the courtyard, and went into the cave of a cantina. I hissed for service and ordered a beer. I poured the last three months into a glass and drank it down. Four months? That was the time on the delivery table, from the first birth pang to the slap on the back. Before that, there had been thirty-two years of gestation. I didn't know what was going to come next.

I nursed the beer, stretching out the bottle for close to an hour. Antonio came in as I was ordering number two.

He looked as if he needed sleep. He slumped into a chair across from me and signaled for the tequila bottle. I must have had a death look in my eyes. He spotted it.

"Today?"

"Tonight, I think."

"We must make plans, then," he said. "You cannot do it alone."

"I need no one."

"Of course not! Not to kill, but to come back safe you need someone." He yawned. "I am tired. I need sleep."

"Were you up all night?"

"Yes. Anything for money. I take the gringos to the whore houses. That is how I make my living. It wastes my night. See? That is Antonio Rojas, descendant of princes, and now a pimp."

He finished his tequila without salt or lemon and stood up. "I only need a few hours. Don't leave the courtyard. Wait for me."

Leave the courtyard! There was no place to go.

As the sun moved across the morning the slice of light that had pierced the cantina for an hour or two disappeared. She came in with the returning shadow.

She looked at the beer bottles and the tequila bottle her brother had drunk from.

"I don't want you to do it," she said again.

"Then you have forgotten your murdered brother?"

"No. But you are not avenging him. Only Antonio or I can do that. You are revenging yourself and in so doing you are denying us vengeance. And if your heart spoke true you would admit that you are not doing what you said you would do because you still want Santos' life but only because you are loyal to the words you spoke in temper last night. No, it is better that we, with knowledge settled in our hearts, kill him."

She angered me. I wanted her to drop it. I wanted her to let me alone. I cut at her.

"Santos gave you money. When you accepted it, didn't you sell your right to revenge?"

"He threw a hundred pesos at us. Is that the price of a brother's life?" A hundred pesos is a little over ten dollars.

I tried to read her as I felt she could read me. I could see nothing in her face but startling beauty. Some day she might be an aged queen like her mother—but she would never lose the thing she had.

"I have other things to talk to you about." Her voice was so low I had to stretch for it. "You showed me money last night. It was enough to buy good land. Come with me. We will buy that land and I will show you the freedom you spoke of."

"Together?" I felt she was tempting me. Her voice was a hand stretching to me in the night. Her eyes were alive but unfathomable. "You would live with me? Forever?"

"There is no forever. Until death."

"But you have no love for me."

"Love? It has not been planted. The seeds are in all of us. You watch it grow in good soil. You are a man. I am a woman. That is enough. I will work for you and with you. If you can do the same for me there will be love. You have to abandon dreams. I need your blood. You need mine."

"I see your face and I see your hands but I do not know you."

"That will come. Will you go with me?"

I felt that I was on a stage and that there was an unseen audience listening to all my words. "Do you go with me for me or my money?"

"Your money will buy our freedom." Her face tightened. I thought I saw a shadow smile. "I will go wake Antonio."

I ordered another beer.

Antonio came in. He hadn't slept long but he looked rested. I wondered how he did it. He'd shaved off his pimp mustache and put away his city suit. I preferred him to the man I had seen first and was glad to see him. I hissed for his tequila but he wanted a beer.

"Drinking is for men that think but do not do. This is a time to do. We must wait until night comes. I will go get a car. Then we will wait for him outside his mother's house."

My car was still at the hotel, as far as I knew. I told him about it. He asked me what it was. I told him. He didn't want it.

"The police are probably still interested in your car and besides I think we need something more fitting to the occasion. I favor a Cadillac."

I asked him where he would get it. He told me, grinning, that my brother Gringos were careless. I dropped that. I asked him how he knew that Santos would be at his mother's.

"I have watched him. He goes there every night for dinner. How do you feel, friend?"

I felt lousy but I snorted. I wanted to work myself into a passion and stab myself with memories so that I could face his fluttering soul.

Antonio stood up. "I go to get our car. It may take time. We have time. Wait in the apartment. Don't listen to my sister. Don't think too much."

Though the cantina was dark then I could see the blazing courtyard through the door. It was fiery bright in the noonday sun. I was hungry. I paid the tab and went back to the apartment. I wondered where the old woman was.

The girl had had her say. She didn't talk and I was glad. It was an effort to keep the picture of Finlay in front of me. My mind wanted to reject, but I had to keep the picture alive if I was going to kill. I had to hate.

She made lunch—beans and tortillas. I watched her pat the pancakes from hand to hand as the Aztec women had done. She dropped them on the tin griddle that covered the charcoal brazier.

"Have you thought that you might be killed yourself tonight?" She had spent a long time finding the right way to say it.

"Yes."

"This, then, may be your last day on earth."

"Yes."

"The world should be yours today."

I wanted to shut my eyes and be back five months ago before I'd filled out the first crooked application. I wanted to start over again. My resolve would be the same, but I would follow it steeled against illusions that merely gave the appearance of what I wanted. I could look back and see things for what they were now—uncostumed and stark.

"Wouldn't you wish to be with a woman on your last day?" Her voice was low. I ate. I didn't look at her.

"I am more than hands and face."

I didn't look up. "Would you have a man that might never return from his trip?"

"It is to such a man I would give myself. His journey is being made for me. There would always be an emptiness in me if I didn't."

She left me and went into her bedroom. I finished eating and placed my utensils neatly on the plate and then I got up and followed her. I was the sacrifice. This was the day of glory before they cut my heart out.

She was waiting. She put her arms up and pulled my head down to her. She caught my lip in her teeth and bit.

I'd entered the room automatically, passionless and she infused me with anger. I grabbed her and pulled away. She stepped back and waited, arrogant, defiant, like a brave torero. It was a dance. I went to her slowly and she edged back, calmly, step by step until her back was pressed to the wall. She couldn't go farther. She stood, not in terror, waiting.

I reached out and took her dress in my hand. I tore her clothes from her. Her naked body was earth. She was the fountain of life, full and eternal. She was fallow ground. Every inch of her seemed alive. Her muscles writhed like live things.

"Come," she grunted between her teeth. "Come to me, man—avenger of my brother."

There was no wild soaring flight of blindness and fantasy. It was struggle. Muscle against muscle. Combat. It held us. And it was over.

"That is love," she panted. "That is woman. Now kill for me. I will wait."

Strength! There was no illusion of tenderness or tranquility. We try to hide the fight in us. She carried her fight on her face, on her lips. She met it and accepted it. She did not know how to hide. She could kill and look in your eyes without bothering with the camouflage of a smile, a kiss and a knife in the back. I had to learn to kill like that. She had been teaching me.

I looked for her. She'd gone into another room. The door was closed and locked. It was silent behind the door.

I sat for an hour and then got up and went to her door again. She wouldn't answer my knock. I wanted her. She had something I had to have before I left. I listened at her door. It wasn't weeping. It might have been an invocation. I banged and demanded admission. There was no response, just the buzz of words.

I took out the gun and field-stripped it. It was in good condition, well-oiled and cleaned. I wondered where it had come from. The day was taking an interminable time to turn to night but dusk came.

With the dark I heard a car fill the courtyard with sound and looked out of the window, gun in hand. I couldn't see in the dark.

There were footsteps on the stairs. It was Antonio. He looked happy, as if he was going to a party.

"Everything is ready. Come." He looked around the apartment and fixed me with a searching eye. "I will wait for you in the car," he said in a strange voice.

He went down. I was ready. Maybe I was supposed to light a candle first. I knocked on her door again. She didn't answer. I called. Nothing. I could hear her breathing.

I was going out to kill! For me—yes, but for her too. I wanted to see her. Maybe I wouldn't come back. Santos had a gun too. I knocked again and when there was no answer my blood flooded my brain and I kicked the door in. The lock plate tore out. I was like a mad man.

She was on the bed, still naked. Her eyes were wide and bright and she was smiling.

"Good," she whispered. "I have been waiting."

I looked back at the splintered door. I went to her. She pulled me down beside her. We said farewell, frantically, furiously, quickly. I had no thought of her and she thought only of me. There was nothing to say.

She pushed me away gently. "Now go," she said, stroking my face. "I will wait."

XV

I could see the blood glow of two cigarettes as I crossed the courtyard toward the car. As I got nearer I saw that Antonio had done well. He had stolen a new Cadillac.

The front door was opened and I got in. Someone sat in back.

"Who is this?" I asked.

"A friend," Antonio said. "He is very good at this sort of thing. He enjoys it." I shook hands with the friend and when he leaned forward I saw it was the big bartender from the cantina. It was very friendly.

We glided out the narrow alley. Antonio was a good driver. He didn't hesitate.

"You've said your good-bys?"

There was no doubt about what he meant. He was talking of his sister. I didn't answer.

"I am glad," he said. "I have said my good-bys. It is what warriors do."

I wanted to change the subject. "Where did you get the car?"

"On the street. It called me. Nice, no?"

I wanted to talk. He drove slowly and carefully, but not so cautiously as to attract attention. "Your mother. Where is she?"

"Waiting for us."

I could feel the weight of the gun in my pocket.

The city was lit with neon and floodlight. We crossed the center of town, shot past the hotel where Finlay had bought his, and went out towards the Lomas.

Chapultepec Park is where the Emperor Maximillian built his castle. The streets bordering it are the streets of wealth. The houses got bigger and fancier. Antonio pulled over to the curb. He pointed across the street.

"That is the house. The car in front is Santos'. He is in the house with his mother. It is a formality and he won't stay long. We will be waiting for him in his car when he comes out. Paco will wait in this car in case we need help."

It was a main street but it wasn't too brightly lit. Santos' car was in shadow. People walked the street but it wasn't crowded. Buses flashed by every twenty minutes. I didn't like it.

Antonio slid out from behind the wheel. Paco climbed into the front and waited for me to get out. When I was next to Antonio he drove off.

We kept to the shadow and crossed. The shutters on the house were closed. We couldn't see in and I hoped they couldn't see out. The doors of the car were locked. Antonio took a punch and made a hole the size of a pencil in the back door window. He had a wire made from a coat hanger. He opened the door. I looked nervously around. He hadn't bothered to see if anyone was on the street watching. I didn't see anyone.

We got in the car. Antonio was grinning.

"That is how I got the Cadillac. Neat, no?"

It was neat, yes. I wished he wouldn't talk. We crouched on the back floor. The closing door made a lot of noise. My watch ticked as loudly as an amplified heartbeat.

Soon. Soon. Soon.

Crouched down on the floor we couldn't see the house. A few minutes later he sensed something. He pressed my arm.

"Now."

I took out my gun and pulled back the slide to get one into the chamber. It made a racket. I slipped off the safety. I heard footsteps on the pavement. A key in the lock. The front door opened. It wasn't Santos.

Antonio's hand clamped on my arm. I stayed still. The horn honked. More footsteps. Santos got in.

My heart leaped when I saw him. I could have shot him there, in spite of all my early qualms. The door closed and Santos started the engine. Tonio released my arm. We put our guns up together. I jammed mine into Santos' neck.

"Drive slowly, very slowly, to the corner and then stop," Antonio said. His voice was like a snake's rattle.

They didn't speak. They drove—very slowly—to the corner. I looked back and saw the front door to the house close.

"Stop!"

Santos stopped.

"Flash your lights twice, please."

The lights flashed. The Cadillac had been waiting. It pulled out in front of us blocking the way.

"Now, friend of Santos, go to the other car."

The man made his move. I saw his shoulder go down. I swiped him on the head. His head wasn't hard. He slumped.

Paco was out of the Cadillac. I put the gun back in Santos' neck. Antonio and Paco carried Santos' friend to the other car. They put the man in back. I heard them talk.

"Will you be all right?" Antonio asked.

Paco grinned. He didn't bother to say anything back. He took a billy from his pocket and gave the still unconscious man another rap. Then he spoke.

"It will be all right."

Antonio came back. "You drive," he said to me. Santos moved over. Antonio got in back. I got behind the wheel.

"Where?"

"Towards Toluca."

I made a U-turn and started for the hill.

Santos hadn't spoken a word. He kept his hands in his lap and looked straight ahead. When we passed the police booth at the foot of Toluca road he spoke.

"You have good friends, Mr. Bierce. You make friends quickly."

"My name is Antonio Rojas," I heard from the back.

Santos didn't associate it right away. He played it cozy. He acted less than afraid. If he knew how his calm affected me, he would have gotten on his knees and wept. I had sworn he would take a long time dying.

"How do you do?" he said. "I don't think I know a Rojas. Have you worked for me?"

Antonio laughed. "No. I have not had the pleasure. I thought perhaps I would see you at my brother's funeral but you were away on business."

"Oh? Rojas! Yes. I remember." He lapsed back to quiet. I lit a cigarette.

"May I have one?" he asked. "I do not like to borrow when I have cigarettes of my own but I am afraid of moving to get them with this man behind me."

I gave him a cigarette. They do that on firing squads. He took a deep drag. "You were very clever, Robert. Going to Rojas was wise."

"I went to you first."

"Yes. That was unfortunate, wasn't it?"

"For you."

We passed through Toluca. Antonio began to check the roadside. He told me to go slow and when we came to what I would have called a cow path he directed me to turn onto it. It looked too rough for the low pan of Santos' car. I put one wheel on the middle hump and one up on the side of the road. We went slowly.

"Can you drive without lights?"

I flicked them off. The moon was high again. It was the same moon we had had the night I first knew Mercedes.

I drove carefully, babying the car over the rough spots. It tired me and I thought the hell with it. I didn't have to protect the car. It belonged to Santos and he wasn't going to be in a position to care. I dropped back onto the path and made time.

We crossed the fields and up a dirt road between the mountains. The car was taking a beating. I didn't give a damn. After half an hour the road widened and then met another. It was easier going. We drove until we came to a village stuck in the midst of nowhere.

"This is it. Stop."

"Mexico is romantic, isn't it, Mr. Bierce. Filled with thieves in the night and all that," Santos said.

"We have them in my country too."

I got out of the car and covered Santos. The air was clean hill air. The village looked deserted and showed no light. Antonio searched him. He had a gun.

We prodded him along. He didn't need much encouragement. He walked firmly and held his head high. He was taking it better than I would have. I looked around the decrepit village. It was a hell of a place to die, but then he had probably been born in a village like that.

Antonio used his pistol butt to knock on a door. It opened. We went in. The room was lit by kerosene lamp. There was a dirt floor and no furniture. Antonio's mother had opened the door for us. Santos saw her and tipped his hat.

"And now," he said, turning. "Do you kill me immediately or may I make confession before?"

"Where's the money?" I asked.

He laughed.

I shot him. The gun jumped in my hand. His eyes opened wide and he was flung back.

I'd shot from my side without aiming. I'd pulled the trigger to answer the laugh. His shoulder was streaming blood. He leaned against a wall with his arm dangling loosely. If there hadn't been a wall he would have been thrown on his back.

"You are very brave," he gasped, "when I do not have a gun."

"My brother had no gun," Antonio said. "This isn't a duel. This is the sentence after trial."

Santos eyes showed his fear. "I've done nothing to you, Robert," he said.

It was my turn to laugh.

He began to talk fast. "She did it. I didn't know anything about it until a minute before you came to the office."

I lifted the gun and let him see it. "Then why didn't you let me in?"

Santos slumped down onto the floor cradling his bad arm. The blood squeezed through his fingers. I knew how it hurt but he didn't look like he was going to bleed to death. His voice had lost its strength and bravo.

"She had the money. She told me. You had no money."

"That's fine," I said. "Just fine. That explains everything."

"You're a fool." He said it wearily. "I wouldn't have given you my oath the day we met if I wanted to take all your money. It would have been easy to take it from you. You were simple. I could have had you sign a power of attorney and taken that to the bank and cleaned out your box the day after I met you, but I'd given my word. How long do you think I could have remained in the filthy business I'm in if I didn't keep my word?"

"Then why wouldn't you see me?"

The shock was wearing off and the pain increasing. Santos was talking between clenched teeth. In a little while it would get numb and then it wouldn't hurt so much.

"I'd fulfilled my promise to you. I got your identity. It cost me money—and I hadn't seen a dime from you. How could you pay me if she had the money? I wanted what was due me."

I squatted down next to him. "You are a hot shot, aren't you? You told me so yourself. Now you've made your mistake. You bet on the wrong horse. I'm going to get that money back—see!"

He laughed again. "Will you? How? You don't know her. You believed her story about Gilbert. I told you the truth but you believed her because I look like a slimy lawyer and she looks like a lady. She stood in front of him, Robert, laughing and shot him between the eyes. She is as cold as a snake. Yes, she is charming and a magnificent actress—and she's a good psychologist. She had you fooled from the beginning. Oh how stupid you were. She told me about the night in Yucatán. She was afraid. That was the real Mercedes. And still you forgave her. Did she tell you that the night she refused you in her house she came to me? She laughed as she told me how she had teased you. And do you know why she left me? Because you had more money. She swore to me she would get it. And she has it. You gave it to her! And you think you can get it back from her? I must see. Please, let me live to see this. She had killed twice for money—less than she has now. She would die before she would give it up."

He began to laugh. Tears streamed down his face.

"A woman has your money?" Antonio asked.

Santos was still on his kick. "His money? It is anyone's money. Your money, Rojas, if you get it. This one stole it and now it has been stolen from him. To whom does it belong? Tell me?"

"She killed your friend?" Antonio asked.

"She had it done," I said.

"Then I think she is a very bad woman. I think we should get this money away from her." He spoke with a straight face, very seriously.

Santos was hysterical. "Yes. She killed for the money. Death is not pretty. She is very good at killing. It is her specialty. She doesn't care who she hurts. She is not like you. Of course you, Robert West, are blameless, aren't you? You hurt no one? You stole from nothing but a big soulless building, didn't you? You do not think of the men that have lost their jobs because of what you did. You took their money—and didn't you tell me that money is life? And who pays for the theft? The big men? No. The little men. They pay for the insurance. And Finlay? You killed him as much as Mercedes. Would he be dead if you had not done what you did? And this uncle of yours? How many years did he work to earn the money he is paying for you? And—"

I fired the gun. I didn't try to hit him and I didn't, but I had to shut him up. He was going to stop this or he was going to die. He stopped talking.

"Do you have anything else to say before you die?" Tonio asked him.

Santos made an effort and sat up straight, redeeming some of his dignity. "Oh? So then it was already decided before I came. I do have a request. Would you shoot quickly and well. The floor is hard and cold and my arm is in pain. End it. I don't wish to think about my sins."

Antonio looked at me. I looked at him. Neither of us shot.

"I think that first we should go get this money," he said. "It sounds like a lot of money. We can kill this one later. If I cannot have the pleasure of killing him when he is happy then at least I can let him live a little longer in pain. Of course I propose this pending your approval. If you wish to shoot him right now please do."

I put my gun back in my pocket. "I'm going," I said. "Wait for me."

"No. I am going with you."

I had to do this alone. I told him. He nodded. "I will go to the city and wait for you at the apartment. I will drive. This one we will leave here. He will be taken care of."

He called. Two men came out of the back room. They were old and wrapped like mummies in serapes against the night air. They squatted down opposite Santos.

"Fix his arm, mama," Antonio said. "We are going to take the gold back from the conquistadors."

He drove back like a madman. I sat and thought about her. I had wished, after I crossed the border into Mexico, that I could be a new man but I had been the same man. Now my wish had come true. I was a different man. I knew that she could plead or weep and it wouldn't seduce me. I found love for Finlay and Malcolm and Doris.

We crossed town and dipped down toward Cuernavaca. Antonio cut the lights and turned off the ignition, letting the car coast in the moonlight. He switched them on a minute later.

"I don't know why I do that. I do not need to save gasoline. I have a brother who is going to be rich."

He was in high spirits. I watched his face in profile and wondered what he was thinking. Santos had spoken true. The money would belong to whoever had it. It was enough to kill a brother for. I didn't know whether it was the light and shadow of the moon, or what, but there was a new cast to his face. He had said he was going back to the apartment. I hadn't been thinking. He was still with me.

"When one brother is rich all the brothers are rich," I said. It sounded like a saw.

"A thousand thanks—but first let us see the money. No?"

I told him where to turn off. In the moonlight we entered a valley of thunder. It looked like a Doré Hell. I remembered lightning though I had never seen any there. Her house was dark.

"Wait," I said outside the gate.

I walked down the road to the house as silently as I could and was glad for the sound-muffling hard baked clay beneath my feet. I went over things fast. She'd arranged the shooting to get me out of the way. She must know that I had gone to Santos' office and been refused admission. It was possible that I was a bigger fool than I really was—in her eyes. When she saw me she might think that I had come to her for refuge. She would act it out. I thanked Fate that she didn't have a phone. I went over all the servants I had seen in her house. None of them seemed formidable.

I tapped at the front door. I looked at my watch. It was five in the morning. The roosters, which crow all night in Mexico, were crowing louder. Dogs yapped.

The old man opened the door a crack. He looked like one of his ancestor's ancient red clay idols. I didn't want to hurt him. I knew that if I tried he would die without changing expression but he would be hard to kill. He looked as if he had been to death once and come back with no terror of it.

"Is the Señora there?"

Five o'clock! He started to close the door in my face. I grabbed his arm and pulled him outside.

"She sleeps," he said.

"I am expected."

"You are not expected." His statement was simple.

"What are you paid?" I asked.

He was ready for talk. "I am an old man. I am not able to work in the fields and they have taken my land. My sons are dead. I am paid nothing here. I am fed, like the dogs. They give me a peso a day."

Eighty cents a week and food. I pulled out my wallet. He saw the gun as I opened my coat.

"I shall be blamed if there is noise," he said.

"Do you like it here?"

"I prefer the village in which I was born. It is far away. I am too old to walk there and I have no money for the bus. It has been a long time since I have been back."

I handed him five hundred pesos. "Then return. Start now. Come back here no more."

He took the money, looked at it, and handed me back two of the hundred-peso bills. "This is sufficient." He picked up his serape and shuffled off. I went in.

It was dark. Tile floors don't squeak. I walked across the patio and went up the stairs. I couldn't hear myself. I held my breath. When I couldn't stand it anymore, I let it out with too loud a whoosh. I stopped and waited until I could breathe quietly.

Her door was closed. I put my ear to it but couldn't hear anything. I put out both hands. With one I took the knob and pulled. With the other I pushed. I held the tension and turned the knob. It opened without a noise.

I walked to the bed. She was in it. She was alone. I put out my hand, ready to stop her scream, and switched on the bed light.

She jumped up as the lamp flooded the room, trying to focus in the new light.

"Robert!"

She didn't scream. I sat down next to her. Her nightgown had fallen off one shoulder exposing her breast. It was a good, round, firm breast. I remembered it.

"What are you doing here, Robert?" she whispered.

I kept my voice low. "I came for my money."

"Oh God, Robert. It isn't here!" She made her explanation sound authentic—as if she didn't know what was going on.

"Where is it?"

"I gave it to Santos. He said that you needed it."

I knew it for the lie it was. Santos wouldn't have loused up the truth with a bullet in him.

"Where have you been?" she whispered excitedly. "I've been so worried!"

"Have you?"

"Of course, darling. Where were you?"

Let me see. Where had I been? Hell and back? How many years had I been fleeing?

"I was running, Mercedes," I said. "Running for my life."

She moved toward me. She didn't bother covering herself. I moved away. Her eyes were filling with tears. She was very good. "Oh, why did you do it?" she wept. "I've been frantic. They say you killed that Finlay man. Everyone has been looking for you."

"Who said?"

"Santos, everyone."

I slapped her.

"That's enough," I said. "I'm angry. I don't want to hurt you. I don't want to talk. Where is my money?"

"I gave it to Santos!" She was Bernhardt, Duse and the rest of them rolled into one. Her voice broke. She didn't understand. I was acting irrationally.

"Santos is dying. I shot him. He has no money. He could have bought his life with money if he had any. He told me everything. Is your life worth a hundred thousand dollars?"

Her lips tightened. She hesitated and wondered whether to go on with the game. She must have decided against it. "There is only ninety-six thousand. I counted it."

I slapped her again. Her head rolled with it but she didn't try to move away. Her eyes half closed. "Hit some more," she said. "You've paid well for the privilege."

I slapped her again—and harder.

"You would be surprised at how much I enjoy being hit. Especially for a hundred thousand dollars."

I pulled the covers off her. I grabbed her arm and dragged her from the bed. She fell on her knees. I pulled her up. As soon as she was on her feet, she moved toward me, her mouth half open. She undulated her hips.

"Oh, hit me, Robert! Beat me a hundred thousand dollars' worth."

I didn't mean my fist to be tight. I meant to slap her again. My arm came up from the floor. She went across the room and slammed into the wall. She slumped to the floor like a dropped rag doll. Her cheek was cut. My hand hurt.

I went to her. I wanted to say I was sorry and detested myself for it. It hurt her to laugh but she was trying.

"That's good," she muttered. "Now Robert is a man. He beats the ladies but the lady isn't going to tell him anything. The lady likes to be beaten. Do it some more, Robert, but hit me where the bruises won't show the way Gilbert used to. I love it. It excites me. Shall I show you his whips?"

I yanked her up from the floor. She tried to help with her legs but they crumbled under her. I lifted her and threw her on the bed. Her nightgown had ridden up across her stomach and her legs were apart. She looked like a stringless puppet but she could talk.

"Oh yes! Hurt me. And then make love to me, like Gilbert. I like that. I like to be bruised and sensitive so that I can feel you with all of me. Gilbert would help me. He didn't like it when I did it to him though."

I took out the gun.

"But, Robert, if you shoot me, then I can't tell you where all the money is, can I?"

I put the gun away. If I held it in my shaking hand, I was going to shoot it—twice—once through each pink, pointing nipple bullseye. Then no money. I had to have the money.

It took effort but she pulled herself up. She didn't bother arranging her nightgown.

"So now you know," she said.

"Did you ever want me for myself?"

"You were my most exciting lover—a little old fashioned and without much imagination—but the most exciting. It surprised me. In the beginning I had to work very hard at holding myself back from you. You spouted such middle-class concepts I was afraid that you would be shocked if I gave myself to you too quickly. I thought life would be all right with you once you knew what to do with your money."

"Go on."

"Money is power, Robert. Power to command and power to do. I could have taught you to use it. I thought it would be such a waste if you returned the money. I took it from you. I could use it. I know what to do with it."

She waited.

"Where is it?" I asked.

She laughed. "Oh no. Never. You have lost it Robert. And what can you do? Go to the police? You are wanted for murder. Kill me? Then you won't get the money, and besides I don't think you can. No, Robert, forget the money. Forget me. Go your way. Live your life. Leave me."

I could search her house but there was no profit in it. It would take too long. She would tell. Everyone talks. But not here. I was in her domain. She had to come to mine. There were things I could do. It would be hard. I wasn't built for it. I would have to steel myself, but she was going to talk.

I remembered a story from the war. A soldering iron was inserted and plugged in. People talked.

"Get up!" I said.

She leaned farther back. "But of course not. I will go nowhere with you."

I pulled her from the bed again and stood her up. I twisted her arm behind her and she walked; either that or she broke her own arm. At the stairs she screamed. It was the cry of a staked vampire. It wasn't pain or fury. It was a summons. I got out my gun with my free hand and kept her moving. When we got to the bottom of the stairs I saw her bar boy. He had a gun. I didn't bother talking. I fired, not at him, he had done nothing to die, but to show him what I meant. His face went white.

"Do you want to die for her?" I asked.

He looked at us and dropped his gun. His face assumed a pasty smile. He stepped back. I told him to walk ahead of us and open the front door. I kept my back to the wall. As we went past him through the open door, he made a little bow.

I pushed her ahead of me down the path to the car. All she had on was the flimsy night gown and she was cold. Tonio opened the door and I shoved her in.

"Let's go back!" I shouted.

The motor was running. He put the car in gear and we started. "She is pretty, that one," he said.

"Give me your jacket, Robert. I'm cold," she said. I gave it to her.

"You know, brother of mine, when we get to the city she is going to scream. It will be embarrassing." Tonio said.

"It's true," she said. She seemed to be enjoying herself.

I had the gun in my left hand. I brought it up and down and hit her. I held back. I didn't want to break her skull. She slumped. I was getting good. There was no blood. I pushed her down to my feet.

"You have the money," he asked.

"No. She wouldn't talk."

"She will," he said.

I knew she would.

XVI

The sky was preparing for day when we reached the city. The gray light of morning was more dismal than the blue of night. The morning star still shone like a gem on the horizon. As we crossed town the first red rays of the sun bloodied the snow on Popocatepetl. Vendors on the street were getting their booths ready. Except for them the streets were empty.

We reached the street of the coffins and as we drove slowly down it I saw that an Indian had made a purchase. It was a little coffin—the size of a big bread box—painted white with a red rose on top. He carried it on his head and from his gait I could see that it wasn't empty. He sang as he walked.

We turned into Antonio's courtyard. It too was deserted. I hadn't been thinking where we were going. I'd been lost in my own thoughts on the silent trip in. I was surprised when I saw where we were. I'd assumed we would take Mercedes back to the village where Santos was being kept.

"Should we have come here?" I asked.

"It is all right. No one will care about a woman's screams. It is the sign of a happy home."

I felt her pulse before we lifted her out. It was healthy and strong. Antonio ran ahead. I picked her up, like a bundle of laundry, and carried her up to the apartment. She was lighter than I'd remembered.

Maria was sitting at the table. I dropped Mercedes on the bed.

Maria walked over. "This is the one you spoke of?" I was panting. I nodded. Maria rolled Mercedes onto her back. Except for the bruised cheek she might have been asleep.

"She is very pretty except for her cheek. Did you beat her?"

"Yes."

"Did she give you the money?"

"No. She likes to be beaten."

"She is a woman," Antonio said. "Maria, make coffee."

Maria went out to the kitchen.

"And now what?" Antonio asked. Mercedes stirred. Her hand fluttered and came to rest cupping her breast. "She is something," he went on reflectively. "Why can't beautiful women be good?" He was watching her as a museum-goer watches a statue.

Maria came in with the coffee. It was sweet and thick.

"I will wake her," she said. She pulled Mercedes' head over to the side of the bed and put a basin on the floor beneath it. Then she poured the water.

Mercedes came out of it like a spaniel out of a pond. She rolled away struggling. Maria grabbed her and wiped her dry with a towel.

Mercedes sat up and looked around. She shook her head once more. It must have hurt like hell but she didn't make a face.

"This is a filthy hole," she said at last, after surveying the room. She had trouble talking. Her lips were dry.

"Our house is your house, Señora," Antonio said. He turned to me.

Mercedes swung her legs over the side of the bed and straightened her nightgown. "Where is the bathroom?"

Maria took her. While she was out of the room, I tried to plan how to start. I didn't know where to begin. I wasn't indoctrinated in torture.

Maria and Mercedes came back. Mercedes went to the bed and sat down.

"Well?"

Maria and Antonio looked to me.

"Where is my money?"

"That? Still?" she laughed. It wasn't a funny laugh. "How long do you think you can keep me in this hovel before someone finds me? You are being very foolish."

I knew I could kill her without hesitation but slow death wasn't my style. I had to do something.

She looked away from me. "Do you have water here that isn't typhus ridden? Get me a glass!" she ordered Maria. Maria didn't answer. She went for the water.

"We will search her house," Antonio said.

"No. It would take too long—and besides there are probably police there now."

Mercedes began to laugh. She couldn't stop. Tears ran out of her eyes. She was shaking like an epileptic. I slapped her. It didn't do any good. I had to stop the insane cackle. I slapped her again on her bruised cheek. She shivered once and the shaking stopped. She began to talk through giggles and tears.

"Kill me. I don't care. Life is money and I have money. Enjoy yourself. Perform your pagan rites on me. It will make your crops flourish but the money is mine. Robert gave it to me."

Maria looked at Antonio and then me. We didn't move. When she saw we were not going to do anything, she went to Mercedes.

"Give me the nightgown!" she said. Her voice was low but her command didn't need noise. Her back was to me and I couldn't see her face but it must have told something. Mercedes' face went white. She stopped laughing and stared. Maria reached down and grabbed a hand full of material. She pulled. The nightgown was off.

"Stand up!"

Mercedes didn't move. Maria pulled her from the bed. There was no doubt where the strength was. Maria stepped back and looked at her, her head cocked, like a horse trader appraising a horse.

"The bruise is not good," she said half to herself, "but that will go. We can use her. There are many people that will pay well for her, Antonio."

"Yes," he said.

Mercedes looked frightened for the first time.

"What do you mean?"

"These men do not know what to do with you. I do. First we shall give her as a gift, Antonio. I owe the beggar a favor. Watch her."

Maria turned and left. Mercedes stood in front of us like a new Venus. She knew she was naked. It had never bothered her before. She pulled a sheet from the bed and covered herself. She cowered back from us watching like an animal at bay.

Maria came back with a man. Or he was more man than anything else. His skin was as old and hard as an alligator's and his age told itself in the crusts of dirt in the wrinkles of his hands. He shuffled into the room after Maria. There was no life in the slits of his eyes. I'd seen him and his brothers carrying packs because they were cheaper than burros. I'd seen them picking at the garbage for a meal. Once he might have stood tall as a man but now he was stooped and dwarf-like.

Mercedes couldn't look at him. She turned to the wall.

"Why do you turn away?" Maria said. "He is a man. Could you survive what he has survived? He is strong. His seed is strong. He has hunger. Once he had land. Maybe it was in the valley where your house is."

"No!" It was a wail of anguish.

I didn't like looking at this parody of an upright, rational, god-touched thing. I started to get up to stop it. I remembered Finlay.

"Go to her," Maria said gently.

His eyes hadn't left Mercedes. He walked, shuffled, toward her. She shrunk back until her legs touched the bed and she crawled onto it. He turned to Maria again for permission. She nodded. He was oblivious to Antonio and me. He reached across the bed and touched Mercedes with wavering fingers. She began to scream. It tore the air. It filled the courtyard. It came from her stomach.

Maria went to her and tore the sheet from her clutching hands. The thing reached out again and touched her. His hand was so hard that it scratched her skin.

I had had her on green grass in clean air beneath honest skies. I remembered that and knew that the girl I had been with had given me good days. But I wasn't going to stop it. I prayed she would speak.

"I'll tell you," she screamed. "Take him away. I'll tell you."

Maria called the old man. He came back to her like an obedient dog. She told him to sit. He ignored the chairs and squatted on the floor. Mercedes babbled. There was a safe under one of the floor tiles in her bedroom. The combination was in letters.

"There may be police at the house," Antonio said when I started to go. "I had better be the one that looks." It was my problem. I didn't want him to.

"No," he said. "You will be known for what you are. Maybe they have your description. I can look around the valley and everyone will think I belong there. I can watch and not be seen."

"And in the house?"

"Those in her house will see my eyes. They will be able to read them. I will have no problem."

"Take him with you," Maria said.

Antonio took the old man's arm and guided him from the room. Mercedes lay on the bed, curled like a fetal glob, pressed against the wall, sobbing silently.

I sat down next to Maria. We waited. I poured coffee for myself and then couldn't stand it. I took it to Mercedes. She wouldn't roll over to take it. I covered her with the sheet.

We heard a shuffle on the steps and Maria's eyes grew wide. It was the first time I had seen anything akin to fear in them. The old man came back in.

He couldn't talk. He pointed to Mercedes.

"No!" Maria said but her voice quivered. He ignored her. He went to the bed and firmly, definitely, gently pulled her from the wall. She sat and watched him, her eyes dilated like a cat's. She was speechless, soundless in horror. He looked at her and then stepped back. There was a clothes press. It was seven foot high and five feet wide. It must have weighed over three hundred pounds.

His arms came up slowly. They were long like an ape's and showed the size he had once been. He clasped the clothes press and lifted. It came off the floor. He didn't grunt or breath hard. He held it and then set it back down without a thump. He looked at Mercedes, not for approval—simply watching her, and then shuffled back out of the room.

Maria began to cry.

I sat in the room feeling alien. Something had been built between the two women that excluded me. Maria was still sobbing. Mercedes' face was calm, lit with the light of some mysterious understanding. She sat like an Egyptian empress, immobile, her head on its long neck held high. When she spoke her voice was soft and sounded like an echo from a tomb.

"And on this you are going to build freedom? You are as corrupt as I am—and as enslaved. He was a man."

Maria looked up. There was a flash of understanding between them.

Mercedes sounded tired. "We might have had a lot," she said to me.

"You betrayed me. Not I you."

"There is a sonnet. 'Love is not love which alters when it alteration finds.' You didn't love me."

"No."

"Are you going to kill me?"

"No."

"You must. If you let me leave here alive I will not rest until I have seen you dead. You know that."

Maria wasn't crying anymore. Her voice was as still as Mercedes'. It was a dialogue of the dead.

"Would you give your life to see him dead? For if you kill him you will die. I swear it."

Mercedes didn't answer. We all sat silent for minutes.

"Robert?"

I looked at her. I felt sick.

"You have won. This girl has won." It seemed to be taking all her strength to say it. I could see the tightness of her muscles. A tear began to trickle down her still stained cheek.

"Don't let them kill me, Robert. Don't let them kill me."

"No one is going to kill you."

"I had Finlay killed. I killed Gilbert. I should die, but don't kill me."

"No one is going to kill you."

She was falling to pieces. She shivered and her voice was small, shaking, insistent, repentant.

"But they have to kill me," she whined. "I shot Gilbert. I had Finlay killed. I would have killed you. Really I would have killed you." Her words were touched with madness. "Stay with me, Robert. I will be good. Take care of me. Protect me from the thing inside me."

I found water and dipped my handkerchief in it to wipe her face.

"He stays with me," Maria said. "Go your way."

Mercedes was sick. She lay back and opened the sheet. I turned around and poured myself a drink.

"Don't look away, Robert. Look at me. I am still beautiful. Look at me!" I turned to her. She covered her bruised cheek with her hand. "Don't look at that. It will go away. Make love to me, Robert. Show her." She was pleading. I didn't answer.

"Before they kill me. Before I die. Once more. Give this to me."

I didn't want her. I pitied her. She was insane. I went to her with my wet handkerchief to wash her face, to cover her, to hold her hand, to try to quiet her. As soon as I was near the bed, she lifted her arms and stretched out her hands to me. She took my arms and as soon as she held me her face contorted into a hideous, distorted mask. She tried to spit at me.

"So! You come when you are called, still, Goat! You're still mine!"

I slapped her.

"Bring me the ragpicker. He is a man!" she shrilled.

I threw the tequila at her.

She rolled and moaned and at last quieted and went to sleep.

Maria sat by me. We waited.

And we waited. Night came. Mercedes slept. My mind played with awful things and I refused to accept the truth.

"I am worried about Antonio," I said.

Maria seemed listless. When she answered me her voice was almost inaudible.

"I don't think you have to worry about him, Robert. I think, now, you must worry about yourself."

Mercedes stirred. She sat up. She looked around the room in bewilderment a moment and then asked what time it was. I told her. She thought about it and then began to smile.

"Poor Robert!" She began to laugh, softly at first and then louder and less controlled. I slapped her. She stopped. And we sat in silence.

Near midnight there was a knock on the door. I jumped up, upsetting a chair in my rush to let Antonio in. It was Santos. Alone. His arm was in a sling. He looked drawn and tired.

"I've come for Mercedes," he said in a flat, level voice. I stood in his way, staring at him.

"May I come in?"

I felt will-less and lost. I stepped aside. He walked past me and went to Mercedes. She sat up and clung to him.

"You know what has happened, of course," he said. "Oh, but you are a fool!"

I still couldn't believe it.

"He came back," Santos went on. "He had the money. He was quite honorable. He paid your debt to me." He reached into his pocket with his good hand and drew out a sheaf of bills. "Twenty-five thousand." He turned to Maria. "He told me to tell you that he would send for you."

"And me?" I screamed.

Santos had trouble holding back a smile. "He told me to tell you 'thank you.'"

Maria turned her face to the wall.

I went crazy. I began to scream louder. I took out the gun. Santos' voice cut my yelling.

"Put it away," he said. "What do you gain by that?"

My head was whirling. I couldn't think. I went to Maria and turned her so that she was facing me. She couldn't look at me. I grabbed her chin and lifted her face. I shook her.

"Did you know?" I shouted.

She shook her head. She was crying. "No. I didn't know." I pushed her away and went to Santos. I felt like a rat in a maze.

"And what am I supposed to do?" I yelled.

"You have a gun," he said. "Look for him. Take it back from him, but I don't think you can. I think you had better leave Mexico."

"Where?" I screamed. "I can't go back!"

He shrugged. "Who can tell another man what to do? But out of friendship I will help you. I promise not to call the police, and if they should ask me about you I will pretend I know nothing."

"Police!"

"That unfortunate Finlay affair. Have you forgotten? Our police are very upset about it. Such things are bad for the tourist business."

My mouth was too dry to speak.

"You'll need money," he said. "Consider this a loan." He dropped a hundred lousy dollars on the table. He helped Mercedes up. They went toward the door. I watched Maria. She didn't hesitate. She went to them. I stood there. I couldn't move. I couldn't think. And then I was alone.

And now I am alone. And what am I to do?

THE END

IN AT THE KILL

Emmett McDowell

1

Jonathan Knox liked fall. He liked the crisp, sparkling days, apple cider, and apple-cheeked coeds, even football. Halloween he could take or leave alone.

Generally he left it alone.

Last night, however, he had been inveigled into squiring Elly Watson to a Halloween party, where he had drunk altogether too much hard cider spiked with applejack—a damned treacherous concoction. He had a sour stomach, a throbbing head, and the disposition of a wounded water buffalo this morning.

Knox was sole auctioneer and chief proprietor of the Green Barn, Incorporated, a Louisville auction house that flourished like the proverbial green bay tree. At the moment he was trying to concentrate on his morning mail, but Elly Watson's desk was right outside his office and he could see her attacking her typewriter as if trying to kill it.

He winced every time she slammed back the carriage.

Ordinarily he found his bookkeeper very pleasant to contemplate. She was a strikingly pretty brunette who radiated innocence and virginity—a rank deception since Elly was neither innocent nor a virgin. In fact, she had been married, divorced, and still tended to regard men with a jaundiced eye.

Jonathan, though, was in no mood to appreciate either the sight or the sound of her, especially the sound.

With a groan, he got up and shut the door.

His office was cluttered with the overflow from the auction floor—a box of tools, a breakfront-secretary, a trunk, a china cabinet full of dishes. He threaded his way through the conglomeration into the lavatory, where he ran a glass of tap water, took two aspirins, then stared at himself in the cracked mirror.

His bloodshot eyes stared balefully back at him out of a lean and hungry face. He was a tall, rangy man in his middle thirties, with a long prominent nose, a wide thin-lipped mouth that was about as amiable as a bear trap. Jonathan, though, felt that whatever his features lacked in beauty, they more than made up for in character, strength and intelligence.

"Damn fool," he muttered at his reflection, and returned to his office. He felt he was getting too old to indulge in such nonsense as he had the previous evening.

He scarcely had seated himself at his desk again when the door opened and Elly cautiously stuck her head inside.

"Lieutenant Helm is—" she began. Then her eyes suddenly widened and, giving a startled squeak, she skipped through the door, which banged against the wall with a crash that nearly took off the top of Jonathan's head.

"What the hell's the matter with you?" he demanded coldly.

"He pinched me," said Elly in a furious voice, glaring back over her shoulder.

Lieutenant Ben Hardin Helm followed her inside with a broad grin on his red, good-natured face. Helm was head of Louisville's Homicide Squad—a big beefy man whose hard blue eyes perpetually contradicted the amiability of his expression.

"Morning, Knox," he said.

Jonathan acknowledged the greeting without enthusiasm. He entertained a certain grudging respect for the detective, but not too much fondness.

"Sit down," he said. "You're not here on business, I hope."

"Nope. Pleasure." Helm flicked an admiring glance at Elly's shapely bottom.

Jonathan said, "Do you mean to tell me you came all the way over here just to pinch her fanny?"

"I think you're both pretty disgusting!" said Elly hotly.

"You oughtn't to take it that way, ma'am," said Helm with a chuckle. "It's a tribute." He turned to Jonathan saying, "I've got a couple of tickets—"

That was as far as he got.

Elly snatched up a pair of pliers from the box of tools and clamped them down hard on the detective's lean flank.

Helm let out an agonized bellow, and for a moment Jonathan thought that he was going to climb right over the desk into his lap.

Elly dropped the pliers, suddenly terrified at the enormity of her success. She backed up a couple of steps, then turned and fled from the office.

"Jesus Christ!" Helm picked up the pliers, shook them under Jonathan's nose. "Look! Look at that!"

"I see them," said Jonathan.

"She pinched me with them, by God. Pliers! I didn't know what had hold of me."

He rubbed the seat of his pants, limping painfully around the office.

Jonathan began to laugh. He couldn't help it. He laughed till his eyes streamed tears.

"I don't see anything so damned funny about it," Helm said in an aggrieved voice. "That girl's a mental case. I was going to ask her if she'd like to go to the Kentucky game Saturday, but God-a-mighty, I'd rather take a snapping turtle!"

"I heard that," Elly called through the door.

"Yeah," said Helm bitterly. "Well, you haven't heard the last of it, either."

"You shouldn't take it that way, Lieutenant. Consider it a tribute."

Helm ground his teeth together.

Jonathan took out his handkerchief and wiped his eyes. "Sit down, Lieutenant," he said soothingly. "Have a drink."

"I need one." Helm lowered himself gingerly into the brown leather armchair beside the desk. He winced, shifted his weight to the opposite hip.

Jonathan hauled forth a fifth of bourbon and a glass from the bottom drawer, poured a healthy slug. Helm drained it at a gulp. He was badly shaken. "Jesus!" he muttered again.

"Another?" said Jonathan.

"Yeah."

Helm drank the second one a little slower. By the time he had finished it, he seemed to have returned almost to normal.

"This hasn't been my day," he said sourly. "I got chewed out this morning over nothing at all. It wasn't even my job. Hell, I'm Homicide. But they're all in a sweat down at headquarters."

"What about?" said Jonathan.

Helm essayed a feeble grin. "Well, it was the damnedest thing you ever heard. Somebody repaired the sidewalk in front of the courthouse during the night."

"What's so strange about that?"

"You don't understand. About nine o'clock last night, a couple of truckloads of workmen from the Emco Construction Company pulled up at the curb in front of the courthouse. There was a big crack in the concrete sidewalk where it had settled a couple of inches."

Helm took out a handkerchief and dabbed at his forehead. "Damn that girl! She oughtn't to be allowed to run around loose."

"Go ahead," said Jonathan impatiently.

"Where was I? Oh, yes. They set out horses and red lanterns and flares, rigged up floodlights. You know the county police have their headquarters in the courthouse. By God, the construction gang even ran their cables into the chief's office to get their juice. Then they tore up the pavement with jack hammers and dug a hole in the middle of the sidewalk. Hell, it must've been ten feet deep."

Jonathan was staring at Helm with a fascinated expression.

"You mean this repair work hadn't been authorized by the city?"

Helm shook his head.

"Didn't anybody question them?"

"Question who?"

"The construction gang."

"No. The county road department was closed up for the night. So was City Hall. A great many jobs are let out on contract. Nobody thought anything about it."

"Not even the cops on the beat?"

The detective lieutenant shrugged. "The courthouse is county property, but the sidewalk is maintained by the city. The county police said they figured the city was doing it, and the city police say they thought it must be work connected with the courthouse. But if you want to know the truth, nobody gave it a second thought."

"Is the hole still there?"

"No. And that's the strangest part. The construction gang filled it back in, tamped it thoroughly, poured a new concrete sidewalk. Then this morning they presented their bill. Seven hundred and eighty-five bucks. The street repair department went nuts trying to find a work order on it. Finally they refused to accept the bill.

"The Emco man showed them a letter under the Commissioner of Public Works' official letterhead and signed by Commissioner Mills himself, authorizing the work. They got hold of the commissioner and he said it was a forgery. Hell, he had no right to authorize it. The law says that the city has to take bids on any job over five hundred dollars.

"The Emco man said they would sue the city. The street repair department told them to go ahead and sue, that they hadn't ordered the work done and that's all there was to it.

"It looks like somebody with a goddamn peculiar sense of humor played a Halloween prank on the Emco people. I'm glad I'm in Homicide. The Detective Bureau is going crazy trying to find out who pulled the stunt. They haven't got a lead."

Jonathan had forgotten all about his headache. He was blessed—or cursed, depending on the viewpoint, with a mind that soaked up facts like a blotter. He never forgot anything, besides which he had almost total recall, and there was something he had heard or read about the sidewalk in front of the courthouse. It would come to him in a moment.

"What about the letter from the commissioner?" he demanded.

"It was a forgery. No doubt about that. Whoever wrote it hadn't even attempted to imitate Mills' signature."

"But it was on the commissioner's official stationery?"

"Yes, sure, but it must've been stolen. It wouldn't be too hard to swipe a few sheets of stationery."

"His office is in City Hall, isn't it?"

"That's right."

"Did the Emco people take anything out of the hole?"

Lieutenant Helm's raw red features slowly hardened.

"What the hell are you getting at? Are you on to something, Knox?"

"No," said Jonathan. "I was wondering why they would dig a hole ten feet deep and then fill it back up just to repair a sunken place in the pavement. Why did they?"

Helm slowly shook his head. "I don't know," he said.

Jonathan shrugged. "Well, it isn't important. Sorry I have to run along now, but I've an appointment to look over some furniture. It's been a pleasure to see you. You ought to drop in oftener." He stood up, reached for his hat.

"Look here, Knox," Helm growled suspiciously. "You know something, by God! You look like a cat with its mug in a saucer of cream. If you're concealing evidence—"

"Evidence of what?"

"I don't know," said Helm in an unhappy voice, "but I know you, and that's enough."

"I don't see what you're getting so riled about," said Jonathan. "There hasn't been a crime committed. Well, fraud maybe. The Emco Construction Company has grounds for a civil suit against the perpetrators of the joke, but that's all."

Helm got to his feet and Jonathan accompanied him, opened the door. The auction floor stretched off beyond, packed with used merchandise, lit dimly by naked yellow bulbs. Walter Reed, the clerk, was working alone inside the railed-off enclosure.

"Where's Elly?" Jonathan asked his clerk.

Reed shook his head. He was a tall, elderly man, a retired rural letter carrier, who made a fine appearance and was as meticulous as a watchmaker. "She left," he said.

"Didn't she say where she was going?"

"No. Just something about taking it on the lam," said Reed in a disapproving voice.

As soon as Lieutenant Helm had departed, Jonathan looked up the address of the Emco Construction Company in the telephone directory. Then he put on his hat and left, telling Reed that he might be gone for the rest of the day.

The Green Barn had begun its career as a brick livery stable—a long, narrow building with big carriage doors opening directly onto the street. It was a disreputable section of Louisville and the blended odors of sewage, meatpacking plants and the nearby stockyards assailed Jonathan's nostrils as he came out on the sidewalk. It was about eleven o'clock in the morning and people crowded the pavement, a steady stream of traffic rumbled past in the street.

Jonathan turned into the vacant lot next door where his car was parked—a 1956 Buick station wagon. Getting in, he started the engine, pulled cautiously out into traffic.

"Where are you going?" said Elly's voice from the rear seat.

Jonathan nearly ran into the car ahead, which had stopped for a red light.

"Where did you come from?" he demanded in a shaken voice.

"I was hiding until Lieutenant Helm left."

"Well, for God's sake, don't ever startle me like that again while I'm driving. Do you want to get us both killed?"

"Is he gone?" said Elly.

"Yes."

She raised up from the floor boards, where she had been crouched, climbed over the back of the seat, revealing trim nylon-sheathed legs as high as her garters. Elly had good legs, long, straight and shapely, and wasn't hesitant about showing them. Settling herself in the front seat, she straightened her skirts. She was wearing a dark wool plaid dress and flat-heeled shoes. Her hair, which was dark and glossy as a seal's, was done in a ponytail, making her look ridiculously young.

She lit a cigarette, puffed at it nervously.

"What am I going to do?"

"Turn yourself in," said Jonathan helpfully.

She flung him a rather bitter glance.

"I mean seriously. He's furious, Jonathan. I'm afraid to go back to work. He may be laying for me."

"What ever possessed you to nip him with those pliers in the first place?"

"I hate to be pinched. I wondered how he'd like it is somebody pinched him."

"Yes, but steel pliers! My God, you could have taken out a chunk of meat!"

"Damn!" said Elly. "And I really would have liked to go to that football game Saturday."

"Call him up. Apologize over the phone."

She sighed and shook her head. "I'd be afraid to go with him now. He's like an elephant. He neither forgets nor forgives."

They rode a short distance in silence.

"Where are we going?" Elly asked finally.

"The Emco Construction Company."

"I never heard of it," she said, giving him a puzzled glance.

"It's just a small concern. Specializes in building private drives, I believe."

"Why are we going there?"

"I don't know why you are, but I want to ask them some questions."

"Questions?"

"Yes, Somebody played a Halloween prank on them last night." He went on to describe how the Emco Company had dug up and repaired the sidewalk in front of the courthouse under a phony order from the Commissioner of Public Works.

Elly almost forgot her troubles in her amazement.

"Why," she exclaimed when he had finished, "that's the most brazen thing I ever heard. Maybe somebody did it on a bet."

Jonathan shook his head. "No," he said flatly, "and it wasn't a prank either. Somebody had a pretty compelling reason for pulling a stunt like that."

Elly had learned better than to contradict him. The most aggravating thing about Jonathan was that he was invariably right.

"What do you expect to get out of it?" she demanded.

"Nothing, perhaps. That depends entirely on what the Emco people say."

"But what are you going to ask them?"

"I'm going to ask them," he said, "what they found in the hole."

"Don't you know?" she demanded tartly.

"Of course I know. Seven bales of wastepaper. If they dug in the right place. That's what I intend to find out."

"Wastepaper! What would wastepaper be doing under the sidewalk? And what would anybody want it for?"

Jonathan reached over and patted her knee.

"Honey, I wouldn't trust my own mother with that information, let alone you."

2

The office of the Emco Construction Company was housed in a small frame building inside the yard where their heavy equipment was stored. Jonathan drove through the gate, parked in front of the office and got out.

"Wait here," he told Elly.

"Nothing doing," she said, scrambling out on her side and coming around the car.

He shrugged, held the door open for her, then followed her inside.

A red-haired girl in a white blouse was banging away at a typewriter as they entered. She stopped, said, "Yes?" questioningly.

The room was dusty, girdled with filing cases, map cabinets. The smell of hot oil and asphalt permeated everything. There were several doors, one open, showing a corner of a drawing table.

Jonathan said, "Who's in charge?"

"What is it? A complaint?"

"No. Business."

"Which one do you want to see, Mr. Emberger or Mr. Conrad?"

"Either one."

She pressed a button on the intercom, said, "Mr. Emberger, there's a man and a woman out here to see you."

The box on her desk squawked back at her. She looked up at Jonathan. "What's your name?"

"Knox," he said.

"A Mr. Knox," she said into the intercom, which rattled back at her again.

"What's your business?" she asked.

"Just tell Mr. Emberger that it's about that sidewalk repair work last night."

The redhead's eyebrows shot up.

"The city job," she said breathlessly into the intercom. The box on the desk was ominously silent.

The redhead looked from Jonathan to Elly and then back again. Her eyes were wide and green as limes. Her skin was pallid even under her pancake make-up. Her forearms were bare, freckled, and white as buttermilk. She didn't have a bad figure from what Jonathan could see of it, though she was a little on the stocky side.

"Are you from the newspaper?" she said finally.

"No," said Jonathan. "Have they got hold of the story?"

"Yes," she said. "There's been two of them around to see Mr. Emberger, and a couple of detectives, and a man from one of the radio stations—"

She broke off as the second door from the left was opened violently by a man in his shirt sleeves.

"Knox?" he barked. He was an older man in his sixties, but erect and trim. He was wearing a tie and his face was very brown and distinguished looking. Only his gray hair, which was badly mussed, betrayed his agitation.

"That's right," said Jonathan.

"You know anything about that business last night?"

"Perhaps."

"Perhaps? What do you mean, 'perhaps'? Either you do or you don't."

Jonathan shrugged. "Yes," he said. "I know something about it."

"Bea!" Mr. Emberger snapped at the receptionist. "Get the police. Tell 'em that joker's here in the office now. Hurry!"

The red-haired girl picked up the phone and began to dial frantically.

Jonathan stepped over to the desk, put his hand on the cradle, breaking the connection. The girl looked at him as if she'd like to bite him.

"Put it down," he said and turned back to the agitated Emberger.

"I didn't say I was the perpetrator of the joke. I said I knew something about it. There's even a possibility that you might get your money out of the job. Now, why don't we go in your office and talk this over sensibly? Then if you still want to call in the police, you're welcome to do it."

Emberger ran his hand through his hair, mussing it even more violently than before. Finally he said, "Very well. Hold the call, Bea, and ask Mr. Conrad to step into my office."

The red-haired girl said, "Yes, sir."

"This way," said Emberger.

Jonathan and Elly proceeded him into a big airy room with venetian blinds at the windows, a bleached mahogany desk and comfortable upholstered furniture. A mauve twist carpet covered the floor. Hung on the walls were framed photographs of asphalt and concrete driveways, simulated tile patios and walks.

Emberger motioned for them to sit down on a couch, then went behind his desk. He had scarcely seated himself when the door opened and a big, heavy-set man about forty-five or fifty entered the room, shut the door behind himself.

"Ben," said Emberger nervously. "This is Mr. Knox. He claims that he knows something about that business last night. Mr. Knox, this is Mr. Conrad, my partner."

Conrad eyed Knox, making no move to acknowledge the introduction. He had been a powerful man at one time but was beginning to go to fat. He was wearing a tweed jacket, contrasting slacks, and a brick-red bowtie that matched his complexion. He was smoking a cigar.

Pointing the cigar at Elly, he said, "Who's she?"

"Miss Watson, my bookkeeper," Jonathan replied. "She's here merely as a witness."

Conrad grunted, let his massive frame sink into a deep upholstered chair beside Emberger's desk.

"Go ahead," he said.

Jonathan said, "I want to ask a question first. Why did you dig so deep when you were repairing the sidewalk?"

"Those were our orders."

"Did you find anything in the hole?"

Conrad shrugged. "Dirt. What the devil did you expect us to find?"

"Weren't you supposed to be on the lookout for anything that could have caused the ground to settle under the sidewalk?"

"Yes," Conrad admitted. "The city agent thought there might be some bales of wastepaper that had rotted. He said years ago there had been an excavation there for sewers or, something, and when they filled up the hole they threw in these bales instead of hauling them off to the dump."

"Did you find them?"

"I don't know," said Conrad. "The foreman can tell you that, I reckon."

"Could I talk to the foreman?"

"Why?"

"Mr. Conrad, this morning you and Mr. Emberger presented the city with a bill for seven hundred and eighty-five dollars, which they refused to accept. I think it's a little high. However, I might be able to get your money for you. Might, you understand. It depends on certain factors. Now may I talk to your foreman for just a few moments?"

Emberger and Conrad looked at each other.

"Alone?" said Emberger.

"No. I would prefer both of you gentlemen to be present."

Emberger said, "I can't see any harm in that. Can you, Ben?"

"No," Conrad agreed grudgingly.

Emberger said into the intercom, "Bea, is Marks in the yard?"

"Yes, sir."

"Send him in, please. Right away."

"Yes Mr. Emberger."

There was a silence.

"Look here," said Emberger to Jonathan. "Why are you so interested in those bales of waste?"

Jonathan offered Elly a cigarette, lit it for her, then lit one for himself. He inhaled, blew it out, saying, "Wait till I talk to your foreman. Then we'll go into that."

Conrad said belligerently, "I think he's just fishing. I don't think he knows a thing."

"What have you got to lose?" said Jonathan.

"That's right, Ben," said Emberger.

"Hell, he's just bluffing," said Conrad. "He can't get our money for us."

"I'll make my proposition after I've talked to the foreman," said Jonathan.

Conrad's cigar had gone out. He relit it, chewing on it savagely. But he made no further objection.

Presently there was a knock on the door. "Come in," Emberger called out.

The door opened and a short stocky man in faded khakis and a soiled, gray felt hat entered the office. He had brown eyes, a weathered face, and bad teeth. He took off his hat.

"Bea said that you wanted to see me, Mr. Emberger."

"That's right," said Emberger. "This gentleman"—he indicated Jonathan—"wants to ask you some questions about the job last night."

The foreman turned about and faced Jonathan. "Shoot, mister."

Jonathan said, "Did you find the bales of wastepaper in the hole?"

"Yep"

"How many?"

"Seven. About three hundred pounds each."

"What condition were they in?"

"Looked to me like they was in pretty fair shape. Water hadn't got to 'em if that's what you mean. That's all sand around there. High, dry, and well-drained. They was packed pretty tight. I reckon they could've stayed there another hundred years without rotting."

"What did you do with them?"

"Put 'em in the inspector's truck. He said they was to be hauled to the city incinerator."

"What inspector?"

The foreman scratched his head. "I don't know his name. He showed us his papers, but I didn't pay much attention to 'em. He was waiting for us when we got on the job. He didn't bother us except to have us put the bales in his truck. Then he drove off. We went on and filled in the hole again. Had to have a couple of extra truckloads of dirt because of the bales that had been taken out."

"Had you ever seen him before?"

The foreman shook his head.

"What did he look like? Can you describe him?"

"He was a blond fellow. About thirty, I reckon. He was wearing a brown suit. I don't remember much what he looked like. Kind of tall and skinny."

"Any identifying marks like a scar, a mole, tattooing?"

The foreman started to shake his head, then said, "Wait a minute. He took off his coat when he got in the truck, and he had a broken heart tattooed on his forearm with initials in it, but I don't remember what they was. I only seen it for a second."

Conrad grunted.

Jonathan looked at him appraisingly. "Do you recognize the description?"

"Sounds like the city agent who gave us the job, but I didn't see the tattoo. He kept his coat on in the office."

Jonathan looked at Emberger.

Emberger said, "I never met the agent. My partner talked to him; I didn't. Mr. Conrad made all the arrangements."

I see," said Jonathan and turned back to the foreman. "Can you think of anything else?"

"No."

"What about the truck?"

"It was a green stake-body job. Two and a half tons. A 1954 Chevy."

"Did you get the license?"

"No."

"Have you told the police about the bales of wastepaper?"

The foreman shook his head. "Nobody's asked me no questions."

Emberger said, "The detectives questioned Mr. Conrad and myself and even Miss Sullivan, but the matter of the wastepaper didn't come up. Frankly, it didn't seem important, and this is the first time we've heard about an inspector. Consequently, neither the workmen nor the foreman were examined."

"Who's Miss Sullivan?"

"The receptionist."

"The red-haired girl outside?"

"Yes. Do you need Marks any longer?"

"No," said Jonathan.

Emberger dismissed the foreman who left, pulling the door shut after himself. The two partners turned on Jonathan.

"Well?" Conrad said.

Jonathan frowned. "It's a pretty big gamble. I don't know whether I care to risk it or not."

"What do you mean?" Conrad barked impatiently.

"Just this. You can't possibly collect from the city. You've been the victim of a fraud. However, you do have a legal right to the bales of wastepaper, if they're ever found. You could probably claim them to indemnify yourself for the expenses incurred in repairing the sidewalk."

"What are you getting at, Knox?" Conrad demanded.

Jonathan said, "It's a pig in a poke. Seven hundred and eighty-five dollars is a lot of money to pay out for a salvage claim to something that might amount to nothing."

Emberger said, "Do I understand, Mr. Knox, that you want to buy our claim to those bales of wastepaper found underneath the sidewalk?"

Jonathan grinned sheepishly. "Yes, but seven hundred and eighty-five dollars is a bit steep."

"Jonathan!" said Elly, speaking up for the first time. "Are you stark raving mad? You don't even know where they are, or who took them, or why."

"I think I know why," he said dubiously. He looked at Conrad, then Emberger. "I'll level with you, gentlemen. There's a possibility that I might be able to double my money if I could find those bales."

Emberger said, "You think you could get fifteen hundred dollars out of them?"

"I think so. In fact, I'm pretty sure of it. If they're found in time."

"How? What's in those bales?"

"Believe me, nothing but wastepaper."

"But—" Conrad started to protest.

Jonathan shook his head. "I said I thought that I could get that much from them. I might not. I might not get anything. I might get more. As I said, it's a gamble, gentlemen."

Conrad said harshly, "I don't like this."

"Why? All I want is an assignment from you for your claim to the seven bales of wastepaper salvaged from beneath the sidewalk."

"For that you'll pay us in full for the job?"

"I don't suppose you'd take five hundred?" said Jonathan without much hope.

Emberger and Conrad looked at each other.

"I'm afraid we must insist on payment in full," Emberger said.

"You don't stand a chance of collecting that fee from the city," Jonathan pointed out almost timidly.

"Seven hundred and eighty-five dollars," Conrad said.

With a sigh, Jonathan got out his checkbook.

Elly managed to contain herself until they reached the car.

"Well, that's seven hundred and eighty-five dollars you can kiss good-by," she said in a tone of infinite sadness.

Jonathan gave her an irritated side glance, started the engine, turned around.

Elly said, "Seven hundred and eighty-five dollars for what? For nothing. Seven bales of wastepaper. No. Not even that. For a claim to seven bales of wastepaper."

"Do you think I'm a fool?" he demanded sourly, as he pulled out of the yard onto the highway.

"You looked like one back there."

"I wanted them to think so."

"Well, they do, and so do I." She shook her head ruefully. "When it comes to money you're about as bright as a seven-year-old-idiot."

"I haven't done so badly."

Elly gave him a scathing look.

"Don't pat yourself on the back. If I had half your brains—just half—I could've been a millionaire by this time. You know everything about everything except the value of money."

"I thought I knew everything except how to get along with people. That's what you told me before."

"You don't know that either."

"Maybe not, but at least I don't go around pinching detective lieutenants on the ass with pliers."

"Don't be vulgar," said Elly. "And don't try to change the subject. What in heaven's name is in those bales?"

"Sorry, but this is one deal you're not going to chisel in on."

"Don't worry. I don't want any part of it."

"Okay," said Jonathan. "Just remember that."

3

Jonathan took Elly to lunch and then back to the Green Barn, where he consulted the yellow pages of the telephone directory again. There were eleven truck-rental firms in Louisville. Jotting down their names and addresses, he left hurriedly, abandoning Elly to her fate.

It was nearly two o'clock in the afternoon. The companies renting trucks were located in widely scattered parts of the city; one of them was as far out as Valley Station, nearly fifteen miles from the downtown area. He managed to visit five of them that afternoon, and then it was closing time and he hadn't gotten so much as a smell of the green stake-body truck.

Jonathan, however, had great faith in himself, and he set out undaunted the next morning. The newspapers had the story, but they were treating it humorously as a Halloween prank. There was no mention of the seven bales of wastepaper, nor of the bogus inspector who had carted them off.

He visited two more truck-rental firms. In the second one, he hit paydirt.

It was the Berry U-Haul-It Company. The manager, a young man with horn-rimmed glasses, a crew haircut and an affable manner, said, "Yep, we have a truck answering that description."

"Is it in?" Jonathan asked.

The manager shook his head. "No. It was rented out this morning for an eight-hour period."

"Do you have a record of who rented it October 15th?"

"Sure," said the manager pleasantly, but he showed no disposition to look it up.

Jonathan said, "I'm an insurance investigator for the Metropolitan Insurance Company. A 1954 Chevrolet truck with a green stake-body was involved in a minor accident October fifteenth and we're trying to trace the driver."

"Could I see your credentials?"

"Of course," said Jonathan, and he took out his wallet and showed him a ten-dollar bill.

The manager raised his eyebrows, but he folded the bill neatly, tucked it in his pocket. Then he went to a filing cabinet, rooted around in it, and returned with the rental contract.

Jonathan glanced at it eagerly.

The truck had been rented at 10:00 A.M. Thursday to a Miss Bea Sullivan, whose age was given as twenty-three years and who lived at 4019 Catalpa.

"A woman!" said Jonathan.

"Yep. A nice-looking, red-headed chick. We don't rent many trucks to women. That's why I remember her."

"Did she drive it out herself?"

"Yep. She called two days ahead and made a reservation. When she came in she was wearing blue jeans and a sweater. Boy, was she stacked!" The manager's eyes glistened reminiscently behind his glasses. "She plunked down her twenty-dollar deposit, climbed up in the cab and tooled it out like a man."

"When did she bring it back?"

"The next morning at seven o'clock."

"You got her name and age off her driver's license, I suppose."

"Sure."

"Did she say what she wanted the truck for?"

"Her girlfriend was going to move in with her, she said, and there was some furniture and things. The janitor was going to help them load up the stuff."

"I see," said Jonathan. "I'd better check it through, but I'm afraid it's not the right party. It was a man driver who was involved in the accident."

"You couldn't mistake this chick for a man," the manager said. "Not in a sweater, brother! No siree, bob!"

"Well, thanks anyway," said Jonathan, concealing his excitement. He handed back the rental contract without taking time to copy down the information on it. He had a photographic memory and could have written it out word for word, including commas, anyway.

"Sorry I wasn't more help," said the manager.

"That's okay. We're not even sure it was a rented truck," said Jonathan, and departed.

Catalpa Street was in Parkland, an older residential section of the city. The clean pungent smell of burning leaves hung in the bright October air as Jonathan pulled up at the curb, and the trees lining the street made gaudy splashes of yellow and vermilion. Forty-nineteen was a three-story, red-brick Victorian house that had been converted into apartments.

He went up the brick walk and tried the front door. It was unlocked. Inside was a hall and a stairway. There were six mailboxes on the wall. Miss Bea Sullivan occupied Apartment 2B.

He rang the bell and waited.

The faintly musty odor that clings to old houses in spite of any renovation or modernization lingered in the hall. Mingling with it was the smell of cooking cabbage. A muted murmur of women's voices came from the ground floor rear. Some place a door slammed.

He rang the bell again.

There was no answer. He hadn't really expected one. The plump red-haired Miss Bea Sullivan should be at work at this hour, sitting behind her desk at the Emco Construction Company, typing and answering telephones.

He climbed the stairs quietly but not stealthily. There were only two apartments on the second floor. 2B was in the rear. He paused at the door of 2A, however, and put his ear against the panel. Though he waited for a long time, he could catch no sounds of life inside. The occupant must be out. He should have the second floor to himself.

Moving down the hall to 2B, he knocked, then tried the door. It was locked.

It was a spring lock, though, and the door was old. It had contracted through the years until there was a wide crack between it and the jamb. The door opened inward. He rattled it, feeling the play in it. It was frustrating to be so close, to be prevented by such a flimsy obstacle from satisfying his curiosity.

Suddenly a noon whistle began to blow not far off. It was joined by a second and a third. On impulse, he put his shoulder to the door, turned the knob and pushed.

There was a screech of screws pulling loose and a sharp crack, the sounds drowned by the hoarse moan of the noon whistles. The door swung open.

Jonathan stepped inside a trifle breathlessly and shut the door. The catch, he saw, had pulled loose from the doorframe just far enough to release the lock. If he could find a screw driver or even a kitchen knife in the apartment, he could tighten it back so that it would pass anything but the closest inspection.

The room which he had entered was big and high-ceilinged, with a white cotton-shag rug on the floor. Three walls had been prepared with a stark white embossed paper. The fourth wall had a black background on which was a spidery modern design in red and silver, repeating cancan girls, champagne glasses and the Eiffel Tower over and over again. Draw drapes that matched the black wall paper in design sealed off most of the daylight. The furniture was modern—a big, low couch in gold upholstery, a long, low coffee table, a hi-fi set replete with several speakers, a record cabinet, a couple of low chairs, end tables and lamps.

All in all it was a rather startling room.

His steps were muffled by the thick shag rug as he crossed the room to a hallway. Reason told him that Miss Sullivan didn't get off from work until five. It was most unlikely that she would get home before five-thirty. Nevertheless, he could feel his heart thudding and his mouth was dry.

The hall led back to a kitchen and dinette. There were two other doors opening off the passage, but Jonathan went straight to the kitchen, rummaged around in a cabinet until he found a screw driver.

He returned to the living room, tightened the catch which he had torn loose in entering. Feeling slightly better, but only slightly, he commenced a rapid search of the apartment. Every minor noise from the street made him freeze, while his heart would leap spasmodically.

He simply didn't have the temperament for this kind of work, he decided.

The living room took only a minute. There was nothing there of a personal nature, aside from a framed and tinted picture of a blond man about thirty with a thin face and high cheek bones. It could've been the bogus inspector, but there was no way of telling. It was a studio portrait and had been made at the Burton Studios.

From the living room he went into the corridor, opened one of the closed doors. He was confronted by a feminine and messy bedroom done predominately in pink and gray—gray cotton rug, pink ruffled bedspread, pink ruffled flounces on the vanity, pink and white curtains. A smell compounded of powder, perfume, toilet water and bath salts permeated the stale air.

A pair of white nylon panties lay on the floor, a white nylon slip was draped over the foot of the bed. A dark-green wool dress was folded across the back of a chair. Nylon stockings were wadded up on top of the vanity, a garter belt had been kicked half under the bed. Dark-green lizard shoes with high spike heels reposed in one corner.

Jonathan shook his head.

When Miss Sullivan got out of her clothes, she apparently let them lie where they dropped.

He began to go through the drawers of the vanity. He didn't know precisely what he was looking for. A lead, perhaps, to where the seven bales of waste had been taken, a clue to the identity of the man who had driven the truck Halloween night.

He found everything except that. Miss Sullivan's drawers were a shambles—the contents topsy-turvy. No one could be that messy. And suddenly a light broke. Someone had searched the place ahead of him.

He was reworking an exhausted vein.

He straightened, wiped his forehead with his handkerchief. For some reason, the realization that he was following in someone else's tracks gave him a creepy sensation.

He abandoned the drawers, glanced quickly into the closet, then the bathroom. A light was burning over the washbasin. It was a big, old-fashioned bath with a tile floor, an oversized tub full of water.

Jonathan suddenly caught his breath.

Miss Sullivan lay in the tub, staring up at him through the water!

The shock of it literally drained the strength from his legs and he leaned weakly against the doorframe.

The naked girl was completely submerged except for her knees. Her red hair sprayed out from her scalp in delicate waves. Her green eyes were open, staring. Her skin was as white as the enamel of the tub.

Drowned, he thought. Drowned in her bath!

How long had she been there? Since last night, probably. He gingerly tested the water with his fingertip. It was cold. The bathroom was cold. What had happened? There was no mark on her that he could see. Had she fainted? Had she slipped and hit the back of her head?

It was horrible. He backed out of the room, feeling the coldness seeping through his arms and legs. A skim of perspiration covered his forehead. He wiped his face with his handkerchief.

Then he went through the apartment carefully and wiped off every object that he had touched in his previous search. When he had finished, he glanced at his watch. It was almost two o'clock. He had been in the apartment nearly two hours.

He was seized by a sudden overpowering urgency to get out of there, but he forced himself to pause in the living room, to think back and make sure that he had left no trace of his presence in the apartment.

He was standing there beside the door, looking back over the room, when he heard the key being fitted into the lock.

This second shock, coming as it did on the heels of the first, had a completely opposite effect on him. He was galvanized into action as the adrenalin literally must have squirted into his bloodstream. Snatching up a modernistic alabaster sculpture of a horse's head, he leaped behind the door so that as it swung open it would conceal him.

The lock clicked. The knob turned, twisting as if by its own volition. The door opened inward.

He could hear someone clear his throat. Then the figure of a man walked into view. His back was to Jonathan.

"Bea!" he called. "Bea, where are you?"

Jonathan brought the alabaster statuette squarely down on top of the man's head. Without a sound the fellow crumpled to the carpet like a sack of wet cornmeal.

Jonathan glanced into the hall. It was empty, thank God. The fellow had been alone. He shut the door, dropped to his knees beside the unconscious figure.

He hoped fervently that he hadn't hit him too hard. The man's pulse seemed to be strong and regular. He had merely been knocked unconscious.

Jonathan rolled him over. It was the blond man in the photograph on the record cabinet. Going through his pockets hastily, Jonathan found his wallet. It contained thirty-two dollars in bills, a number of cards and a Kentucky driver's license.

The license identified him as Peterson, Jack Elwood, 6269 Winter Way, Louisville, Kentucky. According to his date of birth he was thirty-two years old. He was five feet eleven inches tall, male, white, with blond hair and blue eyes.

Jonathan returned the license to the wallet, the wallet to Peterson's pocket. Then he pushed up the man's left sleeve. A blue broken heart was tattooed on the forearm enclosing the letters J.P. and R.S.

He had found the bogus inspector who had carted off the bales of wastepaper.

Standing up, he wiped off the alabaster horse's head and laid it on the floor, dusted off his knees and let himself out of the apartment, pulling the door carefully shut after himself, making sure that it locked.

The corridor was still deserted.

He had to suppress a violent impulse to go tearing down the steps at full speed. Despite all his self-control, he kept going faster and faster. Fortunately he met no one. He opened the front door, feeling the crisp autumn air on his face like a cleansing bath.

He half trotted down the brick walk, jumped into his car, started it up. There wasn't much traffic on the street. He pulled away from the curb. Nobody shouted at him or called to him.

He didn't draw an easy breath, though, until he was a good ten blocks away.

After cruising for a while he spotted a small red and white telephone booth against the outer wall of a drugstore. He pulled up in front of it, jumped out of the car, crossed the sidewalk and entered the booth. Depositing a dime, he dialed police headquarters.

A woman's voice answered.

"Give me Emergency," he said, "I want to report an accident."

There was a slight delay, then a man's voice came on the line.

Jonathan said, "Listen carefully because I'm not going to repeat myself. A girl has drowned in her bathtub at 4019 Catalpa, Apartment 2B. Got it?"

"Who is this?" the man asked.

Jonathan hung up, got in his car and roared away as if pursued by devils. He couldn't get the image of the drowned girl out of his mind.

4

Murder was one thing that Jonathan hadn't bargained for.

However, he had a seven hundred- and eighty-five-dollar investment to protect. Besides, if the prize was valuable enough to commit murder over, it must be valuable indeed—more so even than he had suspected. So he began to drive slower and slower, and presently he turned around and started back.

As he approached the neighborhood again, he could hear the wail of a siren rising and falling eerily. And when he turned onto Catalpa, he saw that a patrol car was pulled up to the curb in front of the apartment house and a crowd had collected. Then an ambulance wheeled around the corner, red light blinking, siren moaning, and pulled in behind the police car.

Jonathan drove on past, parked half a block away. He didn't get out.

Presently a dark-blue, unmarked sedan arrived. From his vantage point he saw the Homicide bulls pile out and go into the house.

The crowd had reached sizable proportions by this time. A cluster of small boys darted across the street. Jonathan continued to sit patiently in his car.

Finally he saw two detectives emerge from the house. The blond man, whom Jonathan had knocked out with the alabaster statuette, was between them. His head was bandaged, his wrists handcuffed. The detectives put him in a squad car and drove away.

Jonathan started the engine, set out for 6269 Winter Way, Jack Elwood Peterson's address as listed on his driver's license. The bogus inspector would be kept far too busy at headquarters to interrupt him a second time.

The address was in Portland—one of the oldest sections in the northwest quadrant of the city. Originally Portland had been a separate village, a tough, flourishing little river town at the foot of the rapids. Louisville, though, eventually had reached out and engulfed it. Portland was still tough, but it was no longer flourishing.

Number 6269 Winter Way was a narrow, one-story, white frame cottage, set cheek to jowl with its neighbors. Jonathan drove past it, turned the corner and parked out of sight around the block.

It was ten past four in the afternoon. Bobby-soxers in woolen skirts and sweaters strolled along the pavement in noisy groups. Most of the signs of Halloween had been removed, but here and there a candle-streaked window remained.

Jonathan got out of the car, hesitated, then took a wrench from the tool compartment, slipped it into his pocket. Locking the station wagon, he returned around the corner to 6269 and rang the bell.

There was no answer.

A brick-paved walk led around the side of the house to the rear. He tried the bell again, then strolled around to the back, feeling furtive and conspicuous. Through the glass pane of the door he could see into a kitchen with dirty dishes piled in the sink. He knocked and waited, and at length rattled the knob. The door was locked.

An unpainted shed stretched across the end of the narrow lot, while high board fences enclosed either side, giving him a reassuring sense of privacy. The yard was weed-grown and littered with trash.

A window was set close to the kitchen door, and, emboldened by the continuing silence from within, he took the wrench from his pocket, broke the glass. It made a loud tinkling sound. He waited with his heart in his mouth, but when there still was no alarm, he reached through and unlocked the window, pushed it up and climbed inside.

He found himself in the kitchen along with a gas stove, an electric refrigerator, a cabinet, a table and several chairs. The air had a stale smell of cold grease, ancient cooking, dead cigarette butts. A cockroach scuttled across the worn linoleum.

Jonathan was conscious of a tight sensation, as if his nerves had been keyed up like banjo strings. He unlocked the back door in order to provide a means of quick withdrawal, shut the broken window, pulled down the green blind to conceal the fracture, and brushed the splintered fragments of glass under the refrigerator. Then, with the wrench clutched in one sweaty fist, he set out to explore the house.

The floor plan was simple—a shotgun cottage, as the style was known locally, because of the fact that the living room, dining room, and kitchen were all in a row, one behind the other. The only variation was a bedroom and bath built into an offset towards the rear of the building.

The place was a mess, dusty and uncared for. The cheap furniture was worn and rickety, except for a twenty-one-inch television set in the living room. The only reading matter in evidence was the newspaper. The smell of stale tobacco smoke penetrated everywhere.

Within the bedroom, a threadbare carpet covered the floor. Dirty curtains drooped limply at the grimy window. An empty whisky bottle reposed in a wastepaper basket. A brass bedstead covered with gray, rumpled sheets occupied one corner. There was a dresser, a chest of drawers, an old-fashioned walnut wardrobe, and a slipper chair. That was all.

Outside a horn beeped and the shrill voices of children rose momentarily in the crisp fall air. A heavy vehicle rumbled past on the street, causing the floor to tremble.

With surprise, Jonathan realized that he was sweating despite the clammy chill pervading the cottage. Slipping the wrench back in his pocket, he went to work.

In the top drawer of the dresser he found the stub of a paycheck, revealing that Peterson was employed by the legal firm of Burton and Burress, though in what capacity was not made clear.

He also found a half-dozen letters from a Mary Peterson, whom he was able to identify as Peterson's ex-wife. The letters all requested money and were rather abusive in tone. Peterson seemed to be consistently delinquent with his alimony payments. According to the return address on the envelope, Mary Peterson lived at the Clayborn Apartments on East Ormsby. He made a note of the address, returned the letters to their former place.

The remaining drawers yielded little of interest. Neither did the wardrobe. The bareness of Peterson's life, as revealed by his home, was appalling. Moreover, there wasn't the slightest hint as to what he might have done with the seven bales of wastepaper after he had driven off with them from the excavation.

An unfloored attic contained nothing but dust, and the house had no basement. Jonathan even went out and looked through the shed, but it was quite bare.

Having exhausted all the obvious places, he returned to the cottage. This time he began a rapid search of the more unlikely spots, such as the backs of pictures and the undersides of the furniture.

The October days were short; dusk was beginning to fall, but he didn't dare risk a light. He was about to give up when he hit paydirt.

He had pulled out the bottom drawer of the old-fashioned walnut wardrobe. Upending it, he saw a large Manila envelope taped flat to the underside.

His fingers clumsy with excitement, he pulled the envelope loose. It was sealed. He hesitated. By this time it had grown so dark inside the house that he couldn't even read the face of his watch.

Should he chance a light?

The decision suddenly was taken out of his hands by the sound of an automobile stopping out front. A car door slammed shut.

Jonathan had been conscious for some while that he was cutting his time mighty close. Springing to his feet, he thrust the flat envelope inside his shirt, readjusted his shirttail, rushed to the window.

The bedroom was at the side of the house, however, and he could have seen nothing even had it been light enough. He started back rather frantically, heading for the door to the dining room, and in the dark tripped over the drawer which he had left on the floor, fell sprawling with a nerve-shattering crash.

Suppressing a curse, he rebounded to his feet, suddenly froze at the faint sound of a key being fitted into the front door. Then in the silence he heard the lock click.

He was trapped in the bedroom, which was at one side of the house and opened directly into the dining room. Whoever was at the front door had only to enter and flip on the lights, exposing Jonathan should he try to cross the dining room and skip out the back way.

Panic galvanized him into action. He spun about, rushed for the window, and fell over the drawer again. The crash he made could have been heard two doors down the street.

"Damn!" he muttered, with a despairing conviction that the drawer was deliberately and malignantly pursuing him.

Springing to his feet, he dived for the window, tried to yank it up. It was stuck.

Jonathan knew exactly how a cornered rat must feel.

He had no idea what the man at the front door was doing. Silence certainly was no longer of importance. Unless the fellow was as deaf as a post, he was bound to have heard Jonathan floundering around inside the bedroom.

Snatching the wrench from his pocket again, he smashed all the glass out of the window. It made a ghastly sound as it rang down on the brick walk.

A hoarse voice shouted, "Where did that come from?"

"Around the side," another voice cried.

"Watch him! He might be armed!" the first voice shouted. And before Jonathan could scramble through the window, there was a sound of footsteps on the brick walk. The beam of a flashlight lanced down the passage between the two houses. He drew back behind the curtain.

At the same moment, the front door was flung open with a resounding bang!

Jonathan stood perfectly rigid just inside the broken window as the man with the flashlight pounded along the brick walk. The window was about four feet from the ground. He clenched his fist around the wrench. Desperation steeled his nerves. He didn't have but a fraction of a second to wait. Then the man with the flashlight came opposite the window.

Jonathan reached through the broken frame and whacked him solidly over the head with the wrench.

The man crumpled without a sound. The flashlight hit the bricks with a clatter, but didn't go out.

Just then the light came on in the living room. Jonathan, though, was already skinning through the broken window. He came down with both feet on the body of the man he had felled, and almost fell himself. It was then that he got the rudest shock of all.

The flashlight had fallen so that its beam partially illuminated the unconscious man's face. With a hair-prickling sensation, he recognized Lieutenant Ben Hardin Helm!

"Oh Lord!" said Jonathan under his breath, and took off like an arrow from a bow. He didn't want to be within five miles of the lieutenant when he regained consciousness!

Jonathan burst out of the narrow passage between the two houses, sprinted across the back yard, whipped through the shed and into the alley. Then he ran down the alley to the side street where he had parked his car.

His fingers were all thumbs as he fumbled out his keys and unlocked it. Diving behind the wheel, he started the engine with a roar, pulled away, tires screaming. He didn't slow down until he was on a main artery in the thick of the six o'clock traffic.

His nerves were shattered.

In all fairness, he told himself shakily, he had thought it was the murderer who'd had him trapped. He hadn't suspected that it might be Lieutenant Helm.

He doubted, though, that this particular excuse would have the slightest mollifying effect on Helm, should he ever learn who had slugged him.

In the distance the converging wails of several sirens raised their voices above the sounds of traffic.

He shuddered as he drove with ultraconservatism. No well-publicized public enemy ever felt more hunted than he did at that moment.

Jonathan lived alone in a big two-story frame house in the south end of town. It was close to the park and his street was tree-lined, so that as he walked across the yard from his drive to the front porch, his feet made a rustling sound in the fallen leaves.

The big Manila envelope tucked under his shirt made a faint rustling sound also.

He was acutely conscious of it, and now that he'd had time to recover, at least partially, from his fright, his curiosity was devouring him.

Hastening up the steps, he unlocked the door and entered, switched on the lights. Adjusting the thermostat in the hall, he hurried back to the kitchen, where he put on coffee, made a cold roast-beef sandwich, and cut a wedge of apple pie.

While he was waiting for the coffee to perk, he took the envelope out of his shirt, hefted it experimentally, then slit it open and dumped the contents onto the oilcloth-covered kitchen table.

Several glossy eight-by-ten photographs slid out.

Jonathan stared at them in dismay. It was the last thing he had been expecting, and his disappointment was acute. In the first place, they couldn't possibly have come from the bundles of waste which had been buried under the sidewalk at the turn of the century. From their pristine state it was only too clear that the photos had been freshly printed—perhaps within the past few days.

He picked up the top one, stared at it, his puzzlement practically exploding. The photograph appeared to be an enlargement made from a snapshot which had been taken at a picnic.

But what a picnic!

Three men and two girls were lounging around a white tablecloth spread on the ground. One of the girls was tipping a whisky flask up to her mouth. It was the kind of flask so prevalent during the Prohibition Era, and the girl was clad in the long-waisted, short-skirted style of the twenties.

The other girl wasn't clad in anything at all.

She was a remarkably beautiful girl, slim and blonde. Jonathan didn't think she could have been over twenty-two or twenty-three. She was reclining on one elbow across the cloth, and was staring into the camera with a half-sullen, half-sleepy expression. Her hair was bobbed. Her breasts were young and firm, her stomach flat.

The men in the picture were only a little older than the girls. They were wearing white flannel trousers and were in their shirt sleeves. One was bareheaded and smoking a cigarette. The other two wore straw hats.

From the style of the clothes, it seemed probably that the original picture had been taken around 1926 or '27.

In the background was a large body of water that might be the Ohio River. Willows fringed the water's edge and the cloth was spread beneath a grove of tall slender cottonwoods. The ground appeared sandy and bare.

The second picture showed the same group in the water. There was a narrow sandy point with the willows forming a background. The men were all wearing swimming suits as were the girls. From the setting of the second picture, Jonathan decided that they were picnicking on an island in the river.

The third picture proved it, showing the narrow channel between the island and the shore. In the foreground was a skiff and the blonde girl was sitting in the stern naked again.

The fourth picture was more decorous, for all the picnickers were dressed and were unloading the skiff. The blonde girl was absent from the group and another girl was shown—a dark, vivid brunette in the short-skirted, long-waisted dress of the twenties. Her hair was done in a mannish bob, and she was wearing ridiculously high heels for such an outing.

In the last picture, all three girls were standing like the three Graces, simpering into the camera, and there wasn't a stitch of clothing among the three of them!

As he picked up the last picture, Jonathan discovered a small envelope about four by five, which had been lying under it. It was beginning to yellow and the paper was spotted. He opened it. On the inside were five postcard-sized negatives.

He held them up to the light, recognizing them immediately as the negatives from which the prints had been made. The negatives were old, but they were sharp and clear, with excellent definition.

On the back of the small envelope was written in a crabbed hand:

Steiglitz vs Steiglitz
Exhibits 1, 2, 3, 4 & 5

The coffee was perking away merrily. Jonathan turned off the burner, poured a cupful, then sat down and began to eat.

The name "Steiglitz" didn't ring any bells. He recognized none of the people in the photographs. And anyway, the picnic had taken place more than thirty years ago.

Furthermore, the picnickers were so self-consciously behaving in the best tradition of "the lost generation" that it was like something out of the worst of F. Scott Fitzgerald. Bathtub gin and home brew, gangsters, the St. Valentine's Day Massacre, wild parties, the Charleston. Hold that tiger!

Jonathan could close his eyes and almost hear the frustrated wail of a saxophone.

When he thought what he had gone through to get this mess of garbage, he felt like giving a frustrated wail or two himself.

5

The day before an auction was always slightly frantic. Jonathan was in his office arguing over the phone with the caterers who supplied the sandwiches and coffee, when Elly burst in from the sales floor in a panic. Her eyes, normally a clear light amber, were yellow with distress.

"Lieutenant Helm's here," she whispered frantically, pausing in mid-flight. "He looks like he's been in an accident or something."

Jonathan winced. "Where are you going?"

"Out," said Elly, whose courage was of a very low order. Without further ado, she whipped through the back door.

Jonathan hung up the phone, settled back in his chair with a distinct uneasiness.

It was a couple of seconds before Helm limped inside and closed the door ominously behind himself.

"Good Lord!" Jonathan exclaimed with hypocritical astonishment. "What happened to you?"

The lieutenant regarded him with inhospitable blue eyes. His head was bandaged, and when he moved over to the desk he hobbled pitifully, wincing as he lowered himself into the chair.

"I was sapped," he said.

"Sapped?"

"Yeh. Some bastard hit me over the head with a pipe or something. Then damned if the sonofabitch didn't jump on me with both feet. At least there are two heel prints on my back. When I catch him, I'll make him rue the day he was born."

Helm spoke with such cold ferocity that Jonathan's blood turned to ice water.

"I hope you get him," he lied.

"Oh, I'll get him. I'll get him if it takes the next ten years."

Jonathan swallowed. "How did it happen?"

"The bastard ambushed me."

"Any idea who it was?"

Helm shook his head, winced again.

"Knox," he said, "I'm not in any mood to beat around the bush. I've got six stitches in my scalp, a stiff back, and a blood blister as big as a hickory nut where your sadistic secretary pinched me."

"Bookkeeper," Jonathan corrected nervously.

"What the hell difference does it make whether she's a bookkeeper or a secretary? If you're going to hire a girl like that, you ought to keep her chained up."

"I'm sorry—" Jonathan began.

"I didn't come over here looking for sympathy, but for facts. I want to know why you paid seven hundred and eighty-five dollars for a claim to some trash."

Jonathan offered Helm a cigarette and took one himself, lit them both, which gave him a chance to reach a decision.

"After I heard about that girl being killed—what was her name? Bea Sullivan, wasn't it? I was going to come over to headquarters, Lieutenant, and tell you what I had learned, but I haven't been able to get away. I'm glad you dropped in—"

Helm's expression was skeptical. "When did you hear about the murder?"

"It was in this morning's paper," said Jonathan truthfully.

Helm merely grunted.

Jonathan said, "About those bales of wastepaper, Lieutenant, I bought the claim purely on speculation. There's quite a story connected with them—"

"Make it short."

"I'll make it as short as I can. Do you know what Postmasters' Provisionals are?"

"No."

"Well," said Jonathan, who'd refreshed his memory recently, "before adhesive stamps came into use, envelopes or letter sheets were marked

'Paid' or 'Due,' sometimes with pen and ink, sometimes with a hand stamp. Usually the amount of the postage and the town postmark were put on also. They are known among collectors as 'stampless covers.'

"Then the act of Congress of March 3, 1845 established uniform rates of postage, and a few postmasters in different cities began issuing Provisional stamps.

"This didn't last long, though, because the U.S. Government issued its own stamps July 1, 1847, and these superseded the Provisional stamps. Consequently the Postmasters' Provisionals are extremely rare, the most valuable of all U.S. stamps, in fact."

Lieutenant Helm's cold blue eyes had begun to glitter hopefully at the mention of rare stamps.

"You figure there are some of these Provisional issues in that trash?"

"Well, yes," said Jonathan.

"Why?"

Jonathan regarded the detective lieutenant without pleasure. "When that trash is found, it belongs to me. I've bought the salvage claim openly and legally."

"Sure," said Helm. "Of course we might have to impound it for evidence."

Jonathan's eyes narrowed. Suddenly he no longer felt guilty about clobbering the lieutenant. "Okay," he said. "Five per cent if the police recover the bales of waste."

"Ten," said Helm flatly.

"This is an out-and-out shakedown," said Jonathan irately. "I ought to report you to the chief of police. By God, I would if—"

"If what?"

"Oh, what the hell," said Jonathan resignedly, thinking that a ten percent cut might go far towards pacifying Helm should he ever discover who had laid him out with that wrench. "It might be worth it to keep you out of my hair."

Helm grinned amiably. "Right. Now, what tipped you off about that trash?"

"Just this. One group of those old Provisional issues is known as the St. Louis Bears. The stamps took their name from the fact that they show the coat of arms of Missouri, which has two erect bears holding up a circular plaque or seal between them. They were issued in 1845 and '46 by John M. Wimer, who was the St. Louis postmaster at that time. Three denominations: five, ten, and twenty cent stamps in a number of minor varieties.

"But the joke is this: For a long time only a single copy of the Bears was known. In fact a great deal of doubt existed about the stamp's authenticity. Some of the experts thought it was a fantasy. Not a counterfeit, you understand, but a fake.

"Then in 1900, a general housecleaning took place here at the courthouse—"

"You mean right here in Louisville?" Helm interrupted.

"Yes. Right here in Louisville. The Jefferson County Courthouse. Old files were cleaned out and put in order. Evidence that the courts were not required to keep—correspondence, empty envelopes, that sort of thing—was all thrown away. Seven bales of trash altogether, according to report.

"While the trash was being baled, one of the Negro janitors found a lot of covers with stamps on them. Over a hundred. He showed them to a nearby saloonkeeper who gave him five dollars for the lot.

"Meanwhile the rest of the trash had been baled. At that time there was a big excavation in the street in front of the courthouse where the city was repairing a sewer. Instead of hauling the bales away, they dumped them in the excavation, which was then filled in with dirt and the sidewalk laid over it.

"The saloonkeeper didn't know anything about stamps and he took them to a man by the name of Hassler, a local collector. Hassler's eyes must have popped out of his head. There were over a hundred of the St. Louis Bears, and on cover too. Considering their source, there could be no question of fakery. In fact, it established the genuineness of this particular issue. I reckon it was one of the biggest finds in the history of philately.

"Anyway, Hassler bought the Bears from the saloonkeeper for three hundred dollars, turned around and sold them to C. H. Mekeel of St. Louis for thirty thousand. That was in 1900, mind you, when thirty thousand dollars was big money.

"News of the sale leaked out. It created a sensation. The newspapers were full of it. Thirty thousand for a bunch of old stamps! People all over Louisville ransacked their attics. As a result there are no more finds of rare stamps to be made here now. They were all rooted out in the early nineteen hundreds.

"What's more, ever since then a rumor has persisted that a fortune in St. Louis Bears lay under the sidewalk in front of the Jefferson County Courthouse. Hell, I've heard a number of collectors say that the way Louisville's streets are perpetually being torn up and repaired, a man could hire a crew to dig up the sidewalk and the authorities could never question the work."

The glitter had died slowly out of Lieutenant Helm's eyes as he listened to Jonathan's explanation.

"Are you pulling my leg, Knox?" he demanded sourly.

"No, of course not. When you told me about the sidewalk having been torn up in front of the courthouse, that rumor was the first thing that leaped into my mind. So I went out to the Emco Construction Company, and sure enough, seven bales of waste had been recovered."

"How do you know the Negro janitor didn't get all the Bears?"

"I don't. But he was supposed to have gone through only a small part of the trash."

"And you mean to tell me that you paid seven hundred and eighty-five dollars on the strength of a rumor like that?"

"Yes," said Jonathan stiffly.

"Well, I'll be damned," said Helm in amazement. "If it was anybody but you, I'd say he was a liar. How did you get on the track of Peterson?"

"Who?"

"Peterson. Jack Elwood Peterson. The man who pretended to be a city inspector and hauled the bales away."

"I didn't," said Jonathan, feigning excitement. "Have you found the bales? Where did this Peterson take them?"

"Not so fast."

"But they're mine!"

"I'm asking the questions," said Helm coldly. "Where were you yesterday morning?"

"Making the rounds of the different truck-rental firms to try to locate the truck that had been used to haul off the bales." He told Helm with disarming frankness about tracing the truck to Bea Sullivan, the red-haired receptionist at the Emco Construction Company, who had been murdered.

Helm, though, didn't appear to be especially disarmed.

"What did you do then? Go up to see Miss Sullivan?"

"No. That was early in the afternoon. She was at work; at least I thought she would be. I decided to wait until she got home before calling on her. But when I got there I found a big crowd in front of her apartment and the place swarming with cops."

Helm regarded him out of skeptical blue eyes.

"That's going to be your story, eh?"

"Yes," said Jonathan uneasily. "Do you mind telling me a little more about this Peterson? How did you get onto him? What has he done with the seven bales of waste?"

"We got onto him because he was lying on the floor of Miss Sullivan's apartment. Someone had knocked him out cold with a marble statuette."

Jonathan nearly said, "Alabaster," but caught himself. "Are you holding him?"

"No."

"Why not?"

"I doubt that he killed Miss Sullivan, knocked himself out in her apartment, then phoned headquarters and tipped off the police."

"Oh," said Jonathan. "Was that how you learned about the murder? An anonymous tip?"

Helm nodded.

"But the bales of wastepaper? What about them?"

"Peterson denied all knowledge of them."

"Didn't the Emco foreman identify him?"

"Yes."

"And you still let him go?"

"The Emco people refused to press charges. They weren't interested anymore. They had their money."

"Damn!" said Jonathan, and smote himself in the forehead with the heel of his hand.

"We couldn't even charge him with destruction of public property," Helm continued. "He had the sidewalk repaired, not destroyed."

Jonathan felt like groaning. "But you have got a tail on him?" he pleaded.

"Yes," Helm admitted, "for the time being."

"Good. What's this Peterson's address?"

"Don't you know?"

"No. Of course not."

"Where were you at six o'clock yesterday?"

"Eating supper."

"Where?"

"The Jim Porter Room."

"Can you prove it? Would the waiter remember you?"

"I doubt it. I don't eat there very often."

"I see," said Helm, getting painfully to his feet.

Jonathan said, "How long had the girl been dead before she was discovered?"

"Roughly, eight or ten hours."

"That means she was killed early the same morning."

"Yeah," said Helm. "She was probably taking a bath before dressing for work. The killer hit her over the head, knocked her unconscious, pushed her face under water and let her drown."

"Couldn't she have slipped in the tub, struck her head on the rim and then drowned?"

"Not from the position of the bruise. It was murder, Knox—cold-blooded murder."

"Do you have any leads?"

"Yes. Unquestionably it was the killer who knocked out Peterson and slugged me."

Jonathan swallowed uncomfortably. "Why do you say that?"

"The M.O. for one thing. He likes to slug people over the head. That's the thing about crooks. They pull off a stunt in a certain way. It's successful, so they keep repeating the same method. Eventually there's a pattern. We'll get him. We have men ringing doorbells all over both neighborhoods. Somebody will have noticed him." He smiled amiably, said, "See you around, Knox," and limped out, leaving Jonathan to gnaw his knuckles.

Elly reappeared a few minutes after Lieutenant Helm had departed. Jonathan looked at her without really seeing her, and groaned.

"What's the matter," said Elly, giving herself a quick, uneasy glance. She was wearing a dark-green wool skirt, a dark green angora sweater and a wide green leather belt with a gold buckle. "Is my slip showing?"

Jonathan shook his head.

"What happened to Lieutenant Helm?" she asked. "Was it an accident?"

He gave a guilty start. "No. Somebody slugged him with a piece of pipe, he says."

"Really? But that's terrible."

"Oh, I don't know," said Jonathan. "The fellow who did it probably had a good reason. Sit down a moment, Elly. I want to talk to you."

She crossed the office, seated herself in the chair which Lieutenant Helm had just vacated, crossed her knees. Jonathan offered her a cigarette and lit it for her.

"Elly," he said, "how would you like to pick up a little extra cash?"

"Doing what?"

"Just some routine checking. I want to locate those bales of waste as quickly as possible, and I'm not altogether satisfied that those people down at the Emco Construction Company are as innocent as they pretend to be. That receptionist was involved in the deal. Maybe some of the others were, too."

Elly shivered. "Jonathan Knox, that girl was murdered!"

"I don't want you to do anything dangerous."

"No?" she said skeptically. "Then why aren't you doing it, instead of trying to inveigle me into it?"

"Because I can't pursue half a dozen lines of investigation at once. I told you I'd make it worth your while."

"So you did. How much?"

"A dollar twenty-five an hour."

"Am I supposed to do this on my own time?"

"Of course."

"Then I won't even consider it for less than a base rate of two dollars an hour, plus a fifty-cent bonus because of the risk involved, and my expenses."

"There isn't any risk," Jonathan said sourly. "I'll pay you a flat two dollars plus your expenses. Not a cent more."

"Well," said Elly, her native avarice overcoming her better judgment, "what do you want me to do?"

"Check first on Emberger and Conrad. They're both pretty prominent socially, and well-to-do. You shouldn't have much trouble. Find out everything about them—their families, their vices and hobbies, the works. After that you can start on the hired help."

He glanced at his watch; it was ten o'clock. Rising, he put on his hat. "I might be gone for the rest of the day."

"But—but where do I start?" Elly protested.

"Use some initiative," he bade her, striding through the door.

Jonathan headed straight for the Jefferson County Courthouse, a big neoclassic building surrounded by lawn. He ran up the broad sweep of steps, crossed the rotunda. Too impatient to wait for the elevator, he took the back stairs and climbed to the fourth floor where the circuit court clerk's office was located.

The records were housed in a lofty room that looked big enough to accommodate a basketball court. Three iron galleries, one above the other, lined two walls, and there was a rectangular counter in the center of the floor.

Jonathan hunted up the indexes of actions for the period covering the 1920's. The name Steiglitz was unusual, and there was only one suit in which both the plaintiff and defendant had that name:

Arthur B. Steiglitz vs. Alma W. Steiglitz

It was a divorce action and had been tried in 1927.

He wrote the style and number of the suit on a slip of paper, gave it to one of the file clerks—a buxom, middle-aged woman with rimless glasses and a portly bosom. She came back in about fifteen minutes with an apologetic air.

"I don't understand it, sir," she said breathlessly, "but that file is missing."

"*Missing?*"

"Yes, sir."

"Could somebody else have taken it out?"

The file clerk shook her head. "No, sir. Nobody has signed for it. We never give them out unless they're signed for."

"Could it have been misfiled?"

The clerk glanced rather helplessly at the thousands upon thousands of green metal file drawers lining the walls from floor to ceiling. "I suppose so, but—but." She shrugged.

"Maybe it's just out of numerical order."

"No, sir. I looked completely through the drawer. It's not there."

"Are these suits ever taken out of the courthouse?"

"No, sir."

Jonathan's first unpleasant suspicion that the Steiglitz vs. Steiglitz file had been stolen became a certainty. But why? What possible connection could a divorce action have with the bales of waste buried under the sidewalk and the murder of the red-haired receptionist? Bea Sullivan had been a baby at the time the divorce suit had taken place.

As far as that was concerned, what did any of it have to do with the St. Louis Bears?

Nothing about this case made sense, he thought angrily.

"Come along," he told the woman, and headed for the office of the circuit court clerk. "We've got to report this. It's a serious offense to tamper with public records."

6

When Jonathan finally got away, the circuit clerk's office was in a quiet, frenzied turmoil, like a disturbed ant hill. The present circuit clerk was a stickler about his records and was instigating an immediate investigation into the missing file.

Jonathan's curiosity by this time was thoroughly piqued, and he delayed long enough to look up the record which showed that Arthur B. Steiglitz had been granted a divorce from his wife October 16, 1927. That hadn't been tampered with. It was the trial transcript, containing all the evidence, the exhibits, the details of the action, that was gone.

From the circuit clerk's office he hastened across the alley to the Marriage Bureau in the annex. It didn't take him but a minute to find the marriage.

Arthur B. Steiglitz had married Alma W. Wilcoxson, the daughter of Hiram Wilcoxson, June 24, 1926. The marriage had lasted slightly less than a year and a half.

He raised his eyebrows. Wilcoxson!

In view of the photographs which he had found secreted in Peterson's house, he was beginning to have a pretty good idea of what had happened to the papers of the suit. The Wilcoxsons were an influential Louisville family—powerful socially, politically, and financially. The divorce action obviously had been pretty sordid, and they must have brought all their influences to bear on hushing it up, even going so far as to destroy the file in the circuit clerk's office.

Jonathan's curiosity now was at white heat. Armed with the dates, both of the marriage and the divorce, he returned to his car, drove to the library. In the Kentucky Room on the second floor, he asked for the microfilm of the Louisville papers of June 1926 and October 1927.

The librarian put on the reel for October 1927 of the *Louisville Courier Journal*. It took him an hour to go through the film. There was no mention of the divorce.

Clearly, the Wilcoxsons had been able to keep it out of the papers.

The marriage was different. He had no trouble locating it. The society columns for June were full of it, and on June 25th there was a full page spread of photographs, showing the bride and groom, their parents, the best man, the bridesmaids, pictures of the wedding reception. It had been a big church wedding, a social highlight of the season.

Jonathan stared at the pictures of the bride with a growing sense of triumph.

Mrs. Arthur B. Steiglitz, the former Alma W. Wilcoxson, and the naked girl shown in the photographs of the picnic, were one and the same!

There could be no mistaking the half-sullen, half-sleepy look about the eyes, the short-bobbed hair, the regular, almost classic features. It was the picture of a beautiful, spoiled, selfish young woman.

Jonathan shut off the reader, sought out the librarian and arranged to have prints of the newspaper pictures and articles made from the microfilm.

The film had to be taken out to a local processing company, but a ten-dollar bill, which he slipped to the messenger, helped grease the wheels and he was assured that the prints would be delivered to him that same evening.

For the first time, he began to feel that he might be making headway. But for the life of him, he couldn't see any possible connection between the divorce and the St. Louis Bears.

If there was any truth to the rumor at all, the trash containing the Bears had been buried beneath the sidewalk in 1900. Certainly the Negro janitor had found them in 1900; that much was history, irrefutable, a matter of public knowledge throughout the philatelic world.

The only unprovable part of the story was the persistent rumor of the trash having been dumped in the excavations. But the fact that the seven bales of waste actually had been found *in situ* seemed to clinch that too.

Peterson had to be after the Bears. Jonathan couldn't think of any other reason why he would have gone to such trouble to recover the bales of trash. Certainly he couldn't have been after anything related to the divorce, which had not taken place until 1927—twenty-seven years after the bales of waste from the courthouse had been entombed.

Jonathan wondered if he wasn't trying to find a relation where no relation existed.

With a thoughtful frown, he put on his hat and left the library.

Having skipped his usual lunch hour, the pangs of hunger were making themselves felt with mounting insistence. Consequently, he paused long enough to wolf down a hasty lunch, revolving the frustrating aspects of the case as he ate. It was like trying to put together a jigsaw puzzle in which none of the pieces fitted.

Meanwhile, with Peterson loose, he was confronted with another worry much closer to his pocketbook. Had Peterson started to dispose of any of the Bears yet? Such a possibility filled him with unutterable dismay. The Bears cataloged from four to five thousand dollars apiece, and on cover they would fetch a great deal more.

Should Peterson manage to sell just one stamp, the loss to Jonathan would be considerable. The very thought of it was enough to ruin his day.

Gulping down the last of his coffee, he reluctantly left a dime tip for the waitress, headed for the offices of the Jefferson Stamp Company. If any of the Bears had been offered for sale, Colonel Heyman, who was Louisville's foremost stamp dealer, would be the most likely person to know about it.

The elevator disgorged Jonathan on the third floor of the Republic Building. Hurrying down the corridor, he pushed through a glass door into the main sales room of the Jefferson Stamp Company. It was a spacious, L-shaped chamber with a counter displaying hundreds of the more colorful stamps under a plate-glass top. There was a showcase on the right with several sumptuous albums reposing invitingly on its shelves. Two private offices with glass partitions opened off the sales floor on the left. The back was crowded with tall metal fireproof cabinets.

Colonel Heyman, the proprietor, was personally waiting on a customer—a small boy engrossed in a stock book of the cheaper U.S. issues. Otherwise, the shop was empty.

Heyman glanced at Jonathan, said, "Hello, Knox," with no particular warmth in his voice. "I'll be with you in a minute."

Jonathan took a seat at the counter and waited.

The colonel continued to attend his customer with a friendly, helpful interest, though the boy's purchases probably would not amount to more than a dollar. Jonathan marveled at his patience. Colonel Heyman, he knew, was a retired army officer, and retired army officers are not noted for their patience. The colonel was seated across the counter from the boy, and even sitting he gave the impression of being tall and big-boned. His enthusiasm for philately was boundless, and he probably knew more about the inner workings the stamp trade than anyone of Jonathan's acquaintance.

The boy finally finished his purchases, a momentous transaction amounting in all to a dollar and twenty-three cents, and departed.

Heyman swung around in his chair facing Jonathan. "Well, Knox, who have you skinned lately?" His tone was not encouraging.

Jonathan, who had lit a cigarette, took a deep puff. He knew that Colonel Heyman didn't always approve of his methods.

"I'm after a little information," he said.

"Hmm," said Heyman.

Jonathan essayed a friendly, open smile with no noticeable thawing effect on the stamp dealer.

"Colonel," he said, "have you heard of anyone having some copies of the St. Louis Bears for sale?"

The colonel leaned back in his chair, regarding Jonathan with a rather diabolical expression.

"The Bears, eh?" he said. "So it was you who dug up the sidewalk in front of the courthouse. By God, I should have guessed it. What went wrong? Did your confederates double-cross you?"

"I didn't have a damned thing to do with it," Jonathan protested in some indignation, but he saw that he wasn't going to get anything out of the stamp dealer unless he made his position clear. So he went on to explain how, purely on speculation, he had bought the Emco Salvage Company's claim to the seven bales of waste.

Colonel Heyman suddenly chuckled. "How much did you pay for that junk?"

"Seven hundred and eighty-five dollars."

"Seven hundred and eighty-five dollars!" Heyman repeated, and his chuckle erupted into laughter. Jonathan had never seen him enjoy anything so much.

"What's so funny?" he demanded suspiciously.

Heyman got out his handkerchief and wiped his eyes. "Man, have you been taken!"

"Taken?"

"Yes, taken! Listen, Knox, there's not an old-time collector in Louisville who hasn't heard that rumor about a fortune in St Louis Bears being buried under the sidewalk in front of the courthouse." And off he went again into gales of laughter. "Nobody takes that story seriously," he said, when he could speak.

"Why not?"

"Well, for one thing, what makes you think that Negro janitor would have left any of the Bears?"

Jonathan regarded Colonel Heyman in annoyance. "Then there hasn't been anybody around trying to peddle some of the Bears to you?"

"No."

"You haven't heard anything?"

"No," said Heyman, "I haven't. Not a whisper. And if anybody in this area had been offered one of the Bears, I would know it."

"I expect you would," said Jonathan. He didn't know whether to be relieved or disappointed. If one of the Bears had turned up, at least it would have reassured him that he hadn't bought a pig in a poke.

He left the stamp company in a rather subdued frame of mind.

Jonathan had one more call to make—the offices of Burton and Burress, where Peterson was employed. The law firm occupied a suite in the Kentucky Home Life Building across from the courthouse. In the reception room, a very pretty, dark-eyed girl asked Jonathan if she could help him.

"Yes," he said, taking off his hat. "I'd like to see Mr. Burton."

"Junior or senior?"

"Senior."

"Do you have an appointment?"

"No," he said. "Police business." He flashed his honorary deputy sheriff's badge.

The receptionist did not seem impressed. "He's busy right now. If you'd care to wait, I'll ask him if he can see you. Who shall I tell him it is?"

"Lieutenant Ben Hardin Helm, head of the Homicide Department."

"You're not Lieutenant Helm," the girl said in a shocked voice. "He was here yesterday."

"I know. But I thought it might get me in quicker. Does Burton know the police chief, too?"

"Yes," said the dark-eyed girl with an involuntary giggle. "Are you really a detective?"

Jonathan sighed.

"No. The name is Knox. Jonathan Knox. Tell him that—that it's a matter concerning one of his oldest clients."

"Which one?"

He took a shot in the dark. "The Wilcoxson account."

The girl's eyes widened. "Really," she said, pressing a button on the intercom.

A rather harsh, impatient voice issued from the box. "Yes, Miss Ferrara? What is it?"

"There's a Mr. Knox here to see you, sir."

"Knox? Knox? I don't know any Knox."

"It's about the Wilcoxson account, sir. He says it's urgent."

The box was silent. The pause lengthened uncomfortably, then Burton said:

"Tell Mr. Knox if he will wait, I can see him in ten minutes."

"Yes, sir." Miss Ferrara released the button, looked up from beneath curly black lashes at Jonathan. "You heard him. Won't you have a seat?"

Jonathan sat down and lit a cigarette. "Do you have a fellow working here by the name of Peterson?"

Miss Ferrara arched her eyebrows. She was quite attractive in a dark Italian fashion. Her teeth glistened like porcelain. Her lips were full but delicately modeled. Her nose was short and straight, and she was wearing a simple white blouse that hinted at a splendid chest development.

"Yes," she said after a slight hesitation, "Jack Peterson works here. Why?"

"What's his job?"

"I'm not sure that I should answer your questions, Mr. Knox."

"Why not? Is there something dishonest about Peterson's work?"

"Oh, no! Nothing like that. He's sort of an investigator."

Jonathan was familiar enough with law firms to know that an investigator for a legal office spent most of his time tracking down reluctant witnesses, delivering messages, and going for coffee. He was, in fact, little more than an errand boy.

"I see," he said. "Where is he now?"

"He didn't come to work this morning. He phoned in that he'd had an accident. A concussion, he said. Anyway, the doctor's ordered him to stay in bed for a couple of days. Do you know him?"

"No," said Jonathan. "What kind of fellow is he?"

Miss Ferrara looked a trifle confused, apparently misinterpreting his question. "Really, Mr. Knox, I don't know what you mean."

Her reaction prompted him to say, "Did you ever go out with him?"

"Why—why, yes. Once or twice. What is the matter, Mr. Knox? Is Jack in trouble?"

"He's in trouble, all right."

Miss Ferrara's eyes widened in dismay, but before she could frame her question, the intercom on her desk squawked into life.

"Send in Mr. Knox," said the metallic voice of Mr. Burton, Senior.

"Yes, sir."

Miss Ferrara rose, and indicating that Jonathan should follow her, led the way through a door into a long, hall-like room, one side of which had been partitioned off with frosted glass panels into private offices. The subdued clatter of a typewriter mingled with the baritone murmur of voices coming from one of the cubicles.

Miss Ferrara, though, guided him past all the glass-partitioned offices towards a door at the very end. Jonathan, who was a step or two behind her, watched her switch along with undisguised appreciation. She had good legs, a trim waist, and a shapely bottom over which she appeared to have very little control.

Opening the door, she ushered him inside, saying, "Mr. Burton, this is Mr. Knox."

Burton didn't rise from the desk. He was a stout man in his seventies with flamboyant white hair and a crinkly pink complexion. He was dressed conservatively in a dark suit with a dark-striped tie and a matching show handkerchief in his breast pocket.

Waving Jonathan to a seat, he dismissed the receptionist with a glance, cleared his throat.

"I understand you're here about some matter concerning the Wilcoxson estate."

Jonathan had been glancing about the office, which was big and solidly furnished in mahogany and leather with blue carpeting. It was a very expensively furnished office, clearly proclaiming that Mr. Burton, Sr. was also senior partner of Burton and Burress.

"Yes," he said. He hadn't missed the attorney's use of the word "estate". "I'd like to clear up one thing before we proceed any further. The estate was left in trust, was it not?"

Burton nodded. He obviously was trying to figure out Jonathan and was still at sea.

"I assume," said Jonathan, "the terms of the trust are a matter of public record?"

The attorney frowned, saying impatiently, "Yes. Henry Wilcoxson left his entire estate in trust for his grandchildren, but Mrs. Emberger has the income during her lifetime."

Jonathan very nearly betrayed his astonishment at the mention of Mrs. Emberger. Burton had to be referring to the wife of Gerald C. Emberger of the Emco Construction Company. Anything else would have been stretching coincidence beyond the realms of possibility!

He said, "Did your firm handle old Hiram Wilcoxson's account?"

"Yes," said Burton thinly.

"Did you," said Jonathan, "represent Mrs. Steiglitz in the divorce action which her husband instituted? You might not recall it offhand. It was in 1927, over thirty years ago. Steiglitz vs. Steiglitz. She was the former Alma W. Wilcoxson, Hiram Wilcoxson's daughter—"

"I know who she is," Burton said with an ominous note in his voice. His face was set. His faded blue eyes glittered with a sort of cold, controlled anger. "Who are you? What do you want?"

Jonathan was taken aback by Burton's reaction. When he didn't answer immediately, the lawyer raised up out of his chair.

"Why did you come here, Knox, if that is your name?" he shouted; but even when he shouted it was done with deliberation.

Jonathan got to his feet rather hastily.

"Well, to be frank," he said in a mollifying voice, "I was just fishing for information."

This was so bald that the attorney was rendered temporarily speechless.

"The slimiest thing on the face of the earth," he said scathingly, when he got his voice back, "is a blackmailer! If it weren't for Mrs. Emberger, I'd hand you over to the police, Knox!"

Jonathan gaped at him. "Me?" he said in a dumbfounded voice. It flashed across his mind that his fishing expedition had been altogether too successful.

"You have your nerve coming to me," Burton said contemptuously. "But now that you're here you might as well get it through your head once and for all. I have already refused to let Mrs. Emberger have a penny of the capital, and as long as I'm administering the trust she won't get a penny of it! Do you hear that? Not a cent!"

"Why you crazy old coot—" Jonathan began in righteous indignation.

"*Out!*" Burton roared, leaning across the desk and shaking his fist under Jonathan's nose. "Get out before I have you thrown out!"

The door suddenly burst open and three grim-faced men appeared in the entrance. One was middle-aged and going to fat, but the other two were young and hefty. In fact, one of them was about six feet two with a crew haircut and an Ivy League suit. He had Harvard Law School plastered all over him.

"Throw this scum out of the office!" Burton, who had worked himself up into a deliberate rage, shouted.

Before Jonathan could pull himself together, they closed in from both sides, seized his arms. Harvard grabbed him enthusiastically by the collar. Then they marched him out past the wide-eyed secretaries, past Miss Ferrara sitting petrified at her desk, and propelled him into the corridor beyond.

"And stay out!" Harvard bade him in his clipped, precise English.

Jonathan had never been quite so incensed in his life. There wasn't anything calculated about *his* rage. Straightening his coat with a jerk, he strode back inside. The three attorneys stared at him in astonishment. Marching up to the stalwart young man with the crew cut, Jonathan hit him squarely in the eye.

Harvard sat down on the carpet with a thump.

Jonathan turned on his heel and marched out, slamming the door behind himself. His last glimpse of the office showed the young man sitting on the floor of the reception room, one hand clapped to his eye, and a startled, pained expression on his face.

7

Jonathan was really unnerved at having been taken for a blackmailer. So much so that he didn't go back to the Green Barn, but headed straight for home, a hot tub and some solid thinking.

He and the messenger from the microfilm company arrived at his front door simultaneously. Taking the flat Manila envelope from the deliveryman, he fished out a quarter, gave it to him, then let himself into the house.

A glance at his watch showed him that it was 4:35. The windows were still bright with daylight, but the hint of impending darkness was gathering in the corners of the room.

He went into the study, turned on a reading lamp over an easy chair. Making himself comfortable, he began to examine the copies of the newspaper photographs.

Newsprint isn't the best medium for the reproduction of pictures, and copying them hadn't improved their quality, but they were clear enough for all practical purposes. He lit a cigarette, then he retrieved the photographs of the picnickers from their hiding place in the cold-air duct. Jonathan wasn't given to self-doubts; but if he had been, a side-by-side comparison of the wedding pictures with the picnic snapshots would have dispelled them instantly.

The girl who apparently had been first to shed her clothes while on the island was young Mrs. Steiglitz, the former Alma Wilcoxson.

Although the trial record and depositions were still missing, it was clear to Jonathan that Arthur Steiglitz had used the snapshots as evidence against his wife in order to obtain a divorce on his own terms. While from the lawyer's reaction this afternoon, it seemed equally clear that the same photographs now were being used again some thirty years later for blackmail purposes.

Jonathan figured that the blackmailer knew Mrs. Emberger was wealthy in her own right and had tried to sell her the negatives. The hitch came because the money was held in trust for her children, and Mrs. Emberger couldn't touch it without Burton's okay. The attorney obviously had refused to let her have it.

Only one point needed substantiating. Was Mrs. Emberger the former Mrs. Steiglitz, nee Wilcoxson? Jonathan didn't think there could be the least doubt of it, but he went out into the hall, looked up the telephone number of the Emberger residence and dialed. He could hear the phone ringing in the distant house. Presently it was lifted from its cradle, and a maid's voice said, "Emberger residence."

"Is Mrs. Emberger at home?"

"Who shall I say is calling?"

Jonathan hesitated. "The newspaper," he said.

"One moment, suh."

Jonathan had a short wait, then an amazingly youthful, cultivated voice said, "Hello?"

"Mrs. Emberger," said Jonathan, "this is Bill Hertzmann. I'm with the paper. We're planning a series of feature stories on Louisville industrialists. The lead article is to be about your father, Hiram Wilcoxson. Could you give me the date of his death, Mrs. Emberger?"

"Yes, I suppose so." She didn't sound very enthusiastic about the idea. "It was in November, 1942. November tenth. But really Mr.—ah—Mr.—"

"Hertzmann," he said. "Thank you very much, Mrs. Emberger. Oh—one other thing. How many children did your father have?"

"I was an only child."

"I see," said Jonathan. "Grandchildren?"

"I have a son and daughter."

"We're just after a few dates right now to help with the preliminary work. Later I hope we'll be able to arrange an interview. Could you tell me when you were married to Gerald C. Emberger of the Emco Construction Company?"

There was a slightly longer hesitation than before, then she said, "June 11, 1931."

Jonathan decided to push his luck. "This is your second marriage, isn't it, Mrs. Emberger?"

The silence lasted so long this time that he wondered if she was going to hang up.

Finally she said in a tight, frightened voice, "Who did you say you were?"

"Bill Hertzmann."

"Thank you, Mr. Hertzmann," she said and did hang up.

Jonathan put the phone back on the cradle, returned to the study. There was a faint grin on his face. Mrs. Emberger was probably ringing the newspaper this instant to check on the fictitious Bill Hertzmann.

Sitting down beneath the lamp, he returned to his perusal of the pictures. He was looking at one of the wedding photos, when his eyes suddenly narrowed.

The picture had been taken at the reception and showed a young man accepting a piece of the wedding cake from the bride.

The caption identified him as the best man, Benjamin R. Conrad. So Conrad, Emberger's partner in the Emco Construction Company, had known Mrs. Emberger from the roaring twenties, from her flapper days.

Now Jonathan had been concentrating on Mrs. Emberger. For the first time he examined the other figures closely. There was something about Conrad's likeness that caused him to pick up one of the snapshots of the picnicking group, and compare them. He whistled softly to himself.

Benjamin R. Conrad had been present that day on the river also. He was one of the two young men in white flannels and straw hats.

And suddenly Jonathan was struck by an idea so fantastic that it nearly took his breath away.

How many of the other picnickers would it be possible to identify? There had been six who had attended the outing on that far-off summer day. He selected one of the pictures in which the three men were present, began a minute comparison with the newspaper photos of the wedding. But Conrad was the only man he could definitely recognize.

Then he tried the blown-up snapshot of the three naked girls grouped brazenly in front of the camera. They all had their hair bobbed and possessed the slim, straight figures so admired during the 1920's.

The girl in the center was a trifle taller than the other two, a statuesque brunette Diana, wearing nothing but a somewhat bleary, impudent expression. It didn't require much deduction to perceive that all three girls were pretty well loaded. Drinking had been smart during prohibition and one didn't drink the rotgut moonshine for any reason except to get drunk.

The third girl was also a brunette, small and rather more curvy than the other two. By comparison she was also considerably overdressed in a necklace of pearls.

Mrs. Emberger was an authentic natural blonde.

Jonathan grinned as he studied the nude figures. Now this was art! The 1926 Graces. He wished he had the nerve to frame the photograph and hang it on the wall.

Upon comparing the enlarged snapshot with the wedding picture, though, his grin slowly faded. Really, he was a little shocked at the results. Both the other girls had been bridesmaids at the wedding of Alma Wilcoxson. The brunette Diana's name was Ethel Crawford Sands. The third girl, wearing the pearl necklace, was Judy Jane Jointer.

Jonathan realized that he had succeeded in identifying four of the six picnickers: Alma Wilcoxson, who was now Mrs. Gerald C. Emberger; Benjamin R. Conrad, Emberger's partner; Ethel Crawford Sands, and Judy Jane Jointer, both of whom were probably respectable matrons leading respectable married lives at this moment.

The fact that he had identified them so quickly was due in part to luck, in part to the fact that their families had been socially prominent. He had no doubt but that he could identify the remaining two men without much more difficulty. Nor would it be hard to trace any of them right down to the present, providing they hadn't died in the meantime.

The implications crowded in on him so thick and fast that he could hardly assimilate them.

What he had done, Jack Peterson could have done, or Bea Sullivan, for that matter. What a gold mine it must have seemed to them!

Six staid members of Louisville's fashionable set, people, no doubt, of substance, with a certain standing, with families and children, whose youthful wild oats suddenly had caught up with them. For there was no doubt about it, those snapshots could wreck the lives of any of the individuals involved.

It gave him a rather eerie sensation to look at the pictures of the six picnickers; and he was suddenly conscious that any one of them might have killed Bea Sullivan. In one of them the seed of murder could have been planted that day, a seed that had not germinated until thirty years later.

Jonathan didn't feel like fixing his own supper. Returning the photos to their envelope, he hid them in the cold-air duct, then went upstairs to bathe and change his clothes.

He had a problem—a decidedly sticky problem.

The pictures should be turned over to Lieutenant Helm with a full explanation. However, he couldn't possibly do that without betraying himself.

Mentally he listed his crimes. He had forced his way into Bea Sullivan's apartment, temporarily failed to report a murder, assaulted Jack Peterson, broken into Peterson's house, stolen the photographs, thereby destroying evidence. And finally, he had hit Lieutenant Helm himself over the head with a wrench!

It was the last item that disturbed Jonathan most.

He wrestled with it as he soaked in the tub. He continued to think about it as he dressed and went out to eat. It wasn't until dessert that he came up with what he hoped might prove to be the solution.

Going to a phone booth he looked up Jack Peterson's number, dropped a dime in the slot and dialed. The phone rang a half dozen times before it was answered and a masculine voice said, "Hello."

"Peterson?" said Jonathan.

"Yeah?"

Suddenly it occurred to Jonathan that Peterson's phone probably had been tapped. He almost hung up. The thought of how nearly he had come to being trapped brought a prickling of sweat to his forehead.

He was growing careless!

"Hello!" said Peterson. "Hello! Who is this?"

There had been a rash of telephone salesmen recently. Jonathan pulled himself together, said, "This is the Wearever Aluminum Siding and Awning Company. We understand you own your own home, Mr. Peterson—"

"I'm not in the market for any siding," Peterson interrupted in an irritated voice.

Before he could hang up, Jonathan said quickly, "I see. Could you tell me the name of the people who live next door?"

"Norton," Peterson growled and banged down the receiver.

Jonathan thumbed through the phone book, found a Robt. A. Norton listed at 6271 Winter Way. He dialed the number, and presently a woman's voice answered.

"Mrs. Norton?" said Jonathan.

"Yes?"

"Mrs. Norton, we have an extremely urgent message for your neighbor, Mr. Peterson. We've been trying to reach him but his phone seems to be out of order."

"Hmph!" said the woman. "He probably ain't paid his bill."

"I hate to impose on you," said Jonathan, "but could you call him to your phone?"

"Who is this?"

"This is Ralph Burton, Sr. of Burton and Burress. I can assure you I wouldn't think of asking you to do this if it wasn't absolutely imperative."

"Hang on," said the woman reluctantly.

Jonathan leaned against the wall of the telephone booth, lit a cigarette and waited. In the background he could hear the children's voices. A television set was blaring forth also. The seconds dragged out into minutes.

At length he heard someone pick up the receiver. Peterson's voice said, "This is Jack Peterson, Mr. Burton. I was just using my phone. There ain't nothing wrong with it."

"That's what you think," said Jonathan. "The police have it tapped."

There was a startled silence, then Peterson said, "Who are you? What's this all about?"

"Your phone's tapped and the police have a stakeout on your house. Can you talk where you are?"

Again there was a hesitation before Peterson replied. Finally he said, "Not too good."

"Okay," said Jonathan. "Just listen. I have a package that belongs to you. The one you had taped to the underside of your wardrobe drawer. Do you know what I mean?"

"Yeah," Peterson said, the single monosyllable suddenly harsh as if he had bitten it off and spat it out.

"Good," said Jonathan. "I want to make a deal."

"What kind of a deal?"

"I'll return the package with the contents intact if you will tell me where you have concealed the seven bales of trash that you recovered from beneath the sidewalk in front of the courthouse."

"Why? Who are you, anyway?"

"Never mind who I am. Is it a deal?"

"No dice," said Peterson cagily. "I've got to know more. Call me later. Around ten tonight."

"Same place?"

"No. Winkler's. It's a beer joint on Rowan." He hung up.

Jonathan left the booth, returned to his car and started home. He figured that it would be safe to call the Winkler address from his own phone.

He had learned enough to want no part of what was going on. The minute he got his hands on the seven bales of waste, he planned to check the photographs at the bus depot and mail the key to Peterson, then bow out of the picture.

It shouldn't be too difficult to find some innocent way of tipping off Lieutenant Helm to what was afoot. Let the Lieutenant find the pictures on Peterson and take it from there. Blackmail was a nasty business and Jonathan didn't care to be associated with it, not even indirectly.

Parking the station wagon in front of his garage, he got out, started up the steps. Just as he reached his door he could hear the telephone ringing inside the empty house.

It was only about 8:30. Jonathan fumbled with his key, finally got the door open. The phone continued to ring. Flicking on the lights, he hurried across the hall and snatched it from its cradle.

"Hello," he said.

"Jonathan?" It was Elly's voice. There was a thick, dazed quality to it.

"Yes," said Jonathan in alarm. "What is it?"

"I'm out at Mr. Conrad's house, and I'm scared!"

"You're *what?*"

"Conrad's. Please, Jonathan, come get me quick! I can't say anything!" She sounded as if she were on the point of tears or hysteria or both.

"What the hell are you doing there?"

"Oh, dear, he's coming back. Jonathan, I'm—" There was a click and the line went dead.

Jonathan's memory of Benjamin Conrad, from their brief encounter in the office of the Emco Construction Company, was far from reassuring. Conrad, he recalled, was a big powerful man of fifty or thereabouts, beginning to go fat, with a brick-red complexion and thinning yellow hair. His manner had been overbearing and rude to the point where Jonathan would have kicked him gladly if he'd had the opportunity.

With considerable agitation, he thumbed through the phone book for Conrad's address, while frantically trying to imagine what kind of mess Elly had gotten herself into. He finally found the listing. Conrad lived at Prospect, all the way to hell-and-gone at the northeastern edge of the county.

Jonathan swore under his breath. It would take him the better part of an hour to get out there. And then he would have to make inquiries in order to locate the right place, because the houses that far out were not numbered. God alone knew what might happen to Elly in an hour with a man like that.

In fact, it might be happening now!

Dashing upstairs he got his revolver from a dresser drawer, checked the loads. It was a snub-nosed Colt .38 Special and there were shells in four of the five cylinders. Dropping the gun in his pocket, he raced back downstairs, snatched his hat and a trench coat and tore out to the station wagon.

Jonathan burned up the road to Prospect. At one time the community had consisted of a post office, a general store, and perhaps three or four houses at the end of the interurban car line. Now both the interurban and the post office were no more, and Prospect was only a wide place in US 42. The countryside had been pre-empted by big aloof estates inhabited by wealthy, aloof people.

Jonathan stopped at a filling station and was directed to a side road about a block further along. It turned out to be a winding country lane that led in the general direction of the river. He drove down it about a mile and a half, seeing only occasional houses; then, on the right-hand side of the road, his headlights picked out a big mailbox with the name B. R. Conrad in black letters.

A narrow asphalt drive bored back through the night to a low, rambling house that seemed to be spread along the crest of a ridge. Several lighted windows cut yellow rectangles out of the black mass, which was set back a good quarter of a mile from the road.

Jonathan guided the station wagon into the drive. He had no idea what he was getting into. He didn't even know whether Conrad lived alone or was married. He crossed a stone bridge. The drive rose sharply on the other side, debouched into a paved parking area at one side of the house.

There were no cars in the open, but an Oldsmobile, an MG and a jeep were parked in a four-car garage. The house itself was a one-story ranch-style brick with two spreading wings. A flagstone walk led up to the front door. The lights were burning in one wing. The rest of the building was dark.

Jonathan figured that his headlights had forewarned anyone in the house anyway, so he walked up to the front door and rang the bell. He could hear chimes bonging away inside, but there was no immediate response.

Suddenly two lights flanking the entrance came on, and the door opened. Conrad stood just inside, partially in shadow. He was in his shirt sleeves, a big hulking bear of a man, past his prime but still dangerous.

"Oh, it's you," he said in an inhospitable voice and making no move to unlock the entrance. "What do you want?"

Jonathan was at a decided disadvantage being in the light, while Conrad remained within the darkened hall. He said, "I've come to pick up Miss Watson."

"Who?"

"Miss Watson. My bookkeeper."

Conrad snorted. "What the hell kind of gag is this, Knox? I don't know any Miss Watson. Whatever gave you the idea there was a woman by that name here?"

"She called from your house a few minutes ago."

"Are you drunk?" said Conrad.

Jonathan said stubbornly, "Then you won't object if I take a look for myself."

"Of course I object! I don't know you, Knox. I'm not going to let you snoop through my house on such a ridiculous, trumped-up excuse. Now get the hell out of here! If you're not off my property in about two minutes flat, I'm going to fill your hide with birdshot."

And Jonathan suddenly found himself looking down the bore of a twelve-gauge repeating shotgun! Conrad apparently had been holding it at his side so that he merely had to raise it. At four feet even birdshot was capable of boring a hole through him as big as a broomstick.

Jonathan fell back a step, said in a shocked voice, "For God's sake, Conrad, have you got the safety off?"

"Beat it!" Conrad snapped.

"I'm going," said Jonathan, and backed away cautiously.

"And don't come back!" said Conrad.

Jonathan didn't answer. He was walking with as much haste as dignity would permit towards his car. Suddenly floodlights came on, bathing the black-topped parking area with a dazzling radiance. Jonathan felt like a man walking through a great empty lighted square in the midst of a darkened city. It was the most uncomfortable and conspicuous sensation he'd ever experienced.

Getting in his car, he drove out the way he had come. When he reached the lane, he turned toward the highway.

He glanced at his wrist watch. By the luminous dial he saw that it now was 10:18. It had been an hour and forty-five minutes since Elly had called.

8

Jonathan was so incensed that he was shaking. His first impulse was to go for the police—an impulse which he instantly quelled.

He had no evidence of foul play. Nothing, in fact, but an unsupported phone call. He wasn't unduly cynical, but neither did he have any illusions about just how much the rich and powerful could get away with. They might not enjoy complete immunity from the law, but they certainly were handled with kid gloves unless the evidence against them was overwhelming.

Frankly, Jonathan doubted that he could get one of the county police even to listen, let alone persuade him to barge in on Conrad without a search warrant. And a search warrant under the circumstances would be next to impossible to obtain.

Meanwhile, Conrad could beat Elly senseless, assault her, kick her out, and take refuge behind a battery of shrewd, unscrupulous lawyers. By the time they finished defaming her character, she—and Jonathan, too, for that matter—would be lucky if they didn't find themselves in jail for trying to work a badger game on Conrad.

Farfetched as such a miscarriage of justice might sound, Jonathan knew that it was entirely possible.

Consequently, as soon as he had rounded the first curve and his headlights were no longer visible from Conrad's house, he switched them off, turned around and started back in complete darkness. Fortunately the moon was full, sliding in and out of small scudding clouds, and he met no traffic on the country lane.

When he reached Conrad's gate, he turned into the drive, shut off his engine immediately, coasted off the asphalt onto the grass shoulder just inside the entrance and stopped among some bushes. Getting out of the car, he shifted the revolver to his trench coat pocket, started for the house afoot.

He had heard no dogs when he had approached the house before, and from the fact that Conrad had answered the door himself, it didn't seem likely that his servants—if he employed any—slept on the place. He still didn't know whether Conrad lived alone or not, but everything pointed to his being a bachelor.

The floodlights were still blazing down mercilessly on the paved parking area. Jonathan circled the house under the shadow of the ridge, came up behind the wing where the lights showed in the windows.

There was a moonlit, brick-paved terrace in the rear, and a swimming pool which already had been covered for the winter with a plastic film. The air seemed colder out here in the country. He shivered despite the trench coat. Then, with his heart in his mouth, he slipped silently across the terrace towards one of the lighted windows.

At first glance, it appeared to be empty. It was a big room, a den by its furnishings. Mounted trophy heads were hanging on the walls: Rocky Mountain goat, big horned sheep, an ibex, African buffalo. The walls themselves were paneled in walnut, the furniture solid, comfortable and worn. At the opposite end of the room a long, low couch squatted in front of a great fireplace with a wood fire smoldering in it. Above the mantel was a gigantic mounted sailfish, tinted the prismatic colors of the rainbow.

Jonathan, who couldn't hit the side of a barn with a bass fiddle, felt his blood run slightly cold. He was up against a man whose hobby was big game hunting.

At that moment Conrad appeared from the left, walking towards the fireplace. He had a drink in his hand and he was frowning slightly to himself. When he reached the fireplace, he stopped, stood with his head bowed, looking at something at his feet.

The couch blocked Jonathan's line of vision. He couldn't tell what was occupying Conrad's attention, but he had only too good an idea.

Finally, Conrad set the glass with the drink on an end table, stooped. He straightened with an effort. Jonathan realized that he was holding Elly under her arms. The girl's head lolled back limply. Her dark, seal-brown hair was undone, hanging down her back.

Conrad lifted her, propped her in a sitting position on the couch. Her head wobbled drunkenly. Then Conrad began to slap her.

Elly showed the first signs of life, trying to raise her hands to shield her face. Conrad seized her by the hair, yanked her head back, poured the drink down her throat.

Jonathan ground his teeth together. He tried the window cautiously, but it was locked.

Tearing his eyes away from the scene within, he slipped along the building, tried the next window, but it was locked too. So was the next, and the next. He came to a door; it was securely bolted. Another window—locked!

The screens had been taken down for the winter, storm windows and doors put in their place. The house was as tight as a fortress. The pressure of frustration was building up inside him until he felt that he must soon burst.

The wings formed obtuse angles with the main body of the house, so that they were widely separated. Conrad had Elly in the east wing. Jonathan suddenly began to run around the back of the building to the west wing, throwing caution to the wind. The house sprawled over so much ground, there must be so many rooms between the den and the west wing, that it presented his best chance of breaking in undetected.

Lifting out the storm glass of the first window, he clubbed his revolver, smashed a pane out of the regular sash, reached through and opened it. Then he was scrambling over the sill.

He literally dived inside, landing in the warm darkness on one shoulder and rolling. Scrambling to his feet, he stood panting, momentarily confused.

At that precise moment, a scream so shrill and penetrating that it nearly took off the top of his head, went off like a twelve o'clock siren right in his ear.

It was a shattering experience. He leaped straight up in the air, spun around. His trench coat got between his legs, tripped him. He lunged forward with his arms outspread, fell across a squirming, scratching, squalling figure on a bed.

Jonathan grabbed in self-preservation. To his distress, he found himself clutching a woman. He must have knocked the breath out of her, because she couldn't seem to make any further sounds except for rather tortured gasps. She was clad in some kind of flimsy apparel and was flopping around like a salmon trying to leap up a waterfall. Then he felt her breast swell nearly to bursting as she got her breath back.

He managed to clap a hand over her mouth.

"Don't yell," he panted. "I'm not going to hurt you." This didn't have any reassuring effect whatever.

"Goddamn it," Jonathan muttered rather unreasonably. "I told you I wasn't going to hurt you. Hold still!"

The woman practically exploded into action.

"Madam," he grunted, essaying politeness in the extremity of his desperation. "Please! I apologize. This—uh—is most embarrassing. I'm not a burglar. Not a rapist, either." Her thrashing grew less violent—probably from exhaustion. "Please! If you won't scream, I'll turn you loose."

She managed to signify yes by rolling her head back and forth slightly under his hand, which was still clamped over her mouth.

Jonathan hesitated, his ears attuned to any noise that might indicate her shrieks had been heard.

There was nothing but silence and darkness. Obviously her outcries had gone unnoticed. It was a long way from this bedroom to the east wing.

"Remember, don't yell."

He released her, slid off the edge of the bed to his feet.

He heard her draw a long, shuddery breath. Suddenly there was a *click*. A bedside lamp sprang on, shedding a soft yellow glow.

Jonathan found himself looking into the wide green eyes of a red-haired girl about nineteen or twenty. She was crouched on her knees on the bed. She had on sheer pale-green pajamas. The jacket had been torn open so that her breasts were fully exposed. The pants were twisted and gaping at the side where a couple of buttons had been snapped off.

His initial shock was doubly compounded.

"Who are *you?*" he demanded accusingly.

"Who am *I?*" the girl gasped.

"Yes. What are you doing here?"

"I live here! I'm Jane Conrad!"

"Oh," said Jonathan. "But—but, I didn't think—I didn't know … Are you Conrad's daughter?"

"No," she said in a quavery voice. Her face was as white as buttermilk. "I'm his wife."

"His wife! You?"

She swallowed and nodded fearfully.

Suddenly Jonathan said, "Do you mean to tell me that you've been here all the while your husband … You went calmly to bed while that old goat was—was—"

Jonathan tugged the revolver out of his trench coat pocket, waved it at her. "We're going to the den."

"Like *this?*" she wailed. "But he has someone with him!"

"You're damn right he has. Now move. I'm not having you take a pot shot at me from the rear!"

Mrs. Conrad got shakily off the bed, clutching her jacket together. But when she stood up, her pants started to slide down. With a despairing gasp, she grabbed at them and her jacket gaped open again. She threw Jonathan an anguished glance. Her chin quivered. For a moment, she looked as if she might burst into tears.

"C—couldn't you let me get a s—s—safety pin?"

"No." Jonathan felt that as long as she had to hold up her pants, her movements would be greatly hampered. "Get going,"

Mrs. Conrad stumbled across to the door.

"Who else is in the house?" he demanded, suddenly wary of a trap.

"N—n—nobody but Ben and his guest."

"Guest?"

"Y—yes. It's business."

"Business!" said Jonathan expressively. "How old are you?"

"Twenty-two."

He said, "If you're a day over twenty, I'll eat my hat. Are you really his wife?"

"Of course."

Jonathan shook his head. "What's the matter with you? Have you got a father complex? Or was it his money?"

Mrs. Conrad just stared at him wildly out of large, frightened green eyes.

"Okay," said Jonathan, "let's go."

Clutching her pajama pants with one hand, she opened the door with the other, switched on the hall lights. A thick runner covered the floor. The house seemed abnormally quiet to Jonathan, who was used to the noise of the city.

"Please," Mrs. Conrad said tearfully over her shoulder as she led him along the hall. "Wh—what are you going to do?"

"That depends." Mrs. Conrad's pajamas were so sheer that he wondered why she bothered to hold them up. They must lend her psychological reassurance, he supposed. She was the long-stemmed American Beauty type, but Jonathan suspected it was her extreme youth that had appealed to Conrad.

"D—depends on what?" she asked.

"Don't ask so many questions."

The girl shuddered.

With Jonathan keeping one step behind her, they passed through another door into a spacious living room, on across a dining room, then into a second corridor. Finally they came to a third closed door. He was no longer surprised that her cries had not been heard.

"Hold it," he bade her. "Is this the door to the den?"

She nodded.

Stepping forward, he put his hand on the knob, flung the door wide, pushed the girl in ahead of him.

"Put up your hands!" he yelled.

Jonathan had leaped into the room like a giant grasshopper. He waved the gun around, but it was purely a reflex action.

Elly was sitting beside the fireplace, her face a little strained, but otherwise perfectly composed. Conrad was ensconced in a deep leather chair across from her. He had been puffing composedly at a cigar. But now both of them had turned their heads and were staring at Jonathan in amazement.

For a full second the tableau held, then Elly said in a bewildered voice: "Why, Jonathan, where in heavens name did you spring from?" Her tongue might have been a little thick, but that was all. There wasn't a mark on her. "We didn't hear your car drive up."

A horrible suspicion lodged in Jonathan's mind.

Conrad's eyes swiveled from him to his wife, and his neck began to swell, his face grew even redder. "Jane! What in God's name happened to you?" he demanded in a dumbfounded voice.

Jane sniffled. She was standing beside Jonathan, holding up her pants, with a pitiful air. "He—he—he—" she said, and burst into tears.

"He *what?*" Conrad bellowed, leaping to his feet.

"He—he—he—" Jane stuttered.

Jonathan was in agony. "For God's sake, tell him!" he shouted, suddenly finding his voice.

Jane gave a violent start. "He attacked me!"

"I did not!" Jonathan yelled.

"He broke into my room," she said, "and jumped on top of me."

"Oh, my God!" said Jonathan in despair.

Conrad made a choking sound. His face turned an even deeper, richer red. He lunged at Jonathan.

"Keep away, Conrad," Jonathan warned him, "or I'll put a slug in your belly. Your wife is hysterical."

Conrad pulled himself up short. "Why wouldn't she be?" he raged.

"Ben," said Jane in anguish, holding her arms out to him.

Her pants promptly fell down around her ankles.

Jonathan groaned.

Conrad stared at his wife, who was stooping and trying rather frantically to haul them back up. "Go get some clothes on!" he thundered.

Jane Conrad burst into mortified sobs and fled from the room.

Conrad swung on Jonathan. "I'll kill you for this," he said in a grating voice. A vein stood out in his temple from the violence of his passion.

"Oh, shut up," said Jonathan, who had reached the limit of his endurance. "Go sit down and cool off. I didn't assault your wife. I came here to find Miss Watson. If you hadn't run me off with a shotgun, none of this would have happened. You haven't anybody but yourself to blame."

Conrad made a supreme effort to get hold of himself. He ran his hand through his sparse blond hair, giving Jonathan a peculiar look.

Elly suddenly giggled.

Jonathan turned and regarded her thoughtfully. "Elly," he said, "are you drunk?"

"Who me?" said Elly, with another giggle.

"Yes, she's drunk," Conrad said with icy contempt. He went over and lowered himself into his chair. "Knox, that girl's a lush. Get her out of here, but I'm not through with either one of you. I'll get to the bottom of this, and when I do …" He let his words hang threateningly in the air.

Jonathan was not impressed. "Where did she get the liquor?"

"I gave it to her to loosen her tongue. I kept pouring it down her and nothing happened. Jesus! I thought she must have a hollow leg. Then all at once, she just keeled over. Passed out. I was trying to sober her up when you rang the bell."

"Elly's no lush," said Jonathan. "She just can't hold her liquor, that's all. What were you giving her?"

"Vodka and lime juice."

"Hell," said Jonathan, "she probably didn't even realize it was spiked."

"I did too," said Elly gravely, "but it wasn't very strong."

Jonathan winced. "What were you pouring down her when I looked through the window?"

"Alka-Seltzer. Now get her out of here."

"How did she get in here in the first place?"

"I brought her. She came into the office, gave a false name and tried to apply for the job left open by Miss Sullivan's death."

Elly winked at Jonathan—an exaggerated, conspiratorial wink.

"Of course I recognized her immediately," Conrad went on.

"You did?" said Elly accusingly.

Conrad ignored her. "We had a couple of drinks in the office, then I brought her out here to try to find out what she was up to." His voice hardened. "I'm not sure just where you fit into this mess, Knox, but if you're smart, you'll deal yourself out."

"What mess?" said Jonathan.

Conrad gave him a long, thoughtful glance, his blue eyes cool and unwinking. Finally he shrugged.

"It's your neck," he said indifferently.

Jonathan felt an icy shiver run up his spine. He had an uncomfortable conviction that Conrad would shoot a man with as little compunction as he had the beasts whose heads decorated the walls of his den.

Elly, it developed, could sit with more aplomb than she could walk. Jonathan helped her into her coat, half supported her out of the house, and led her down the darkened driveway to his car. Pouring her into the front seat, he got in behind the wheel, started the motor, backed out onto the country road.

"What time is it?" Elly said sleepily.

He glanced at his watch. "A quarter to twelve."

She fumbled in her handbag, got out her little black book, made a notation.

"What are you doing?" he demanded suspiciously.

"Keeping my time. It'll be twelve-thirty before you get me home. That's eight hours at two dollars an hour. Sixteen dollars." She put the notebook away.

"You aren't serious?"

"Why not?"

Jonathan muttered something under his breath.

"What did you say?" she asked.

He didn't think there would be much use arguing with Elly in her present condition, but he couldn't refrain from saying, "Did you get anything out of Conrad for my sixteen dollars besides a skinful of vodka?"

"Yep."

"What?"

"Well, not from Conrad exactly. From the foreman. Mishter Marks. We were discussing the Sullivan girl's death, and he said Mr. Emberger was taking it hard. He said Mr. Emberger had been sweet on her. Gave her presents, jewelry."

"Emberger?" said Jonathan, in an unbelieving voice.

"Yep. That's what the foreman said. Gerald C. Emberger himself. And him with a rish wife, a married daughter, and a boy in Dartmouth. *Men!*" Elly's voice registered her intense, if somewhat bleary, disrespect for the entire male sex.

Jonathan drove in silence for several miles, digesting this piece of information. He didn't know whether it had any bearing on Bea Sullivan's death or not, but he supposed he should pass it along to Lieutenant Helm.

And that made him think of Jack Peterson.

"Damn!" he muttered.

He had forgotten all about calling Peterson at Winkler's bar at ten o'clock.

"Do you realize," he said bitterly, "that this idiotic stunt you pulled tonight could have caused me to lose out on those bales of waste?"

Elly's only answer was a gentle snore.

9

Thursday's auction at the Green Barn was not scheduled to start until ten o'clock. Jonathan, who was in his office, glanced at his watch. It was only nine, but a low mutter of voices already was rising from the auction floor.

Through the open doorway he could see Elly behind her railing, checking the cash box. She had come to work this morning with a hangover, for which she blamed Jonathan, by some inexplicable feminine logic, and consequently was treating him with scrupulous politeness.

He shook his head ruefully. Looking up the number of Burton and Burress, he dialed the law firm, recognizing Miss Ferrara's voice when she answered.

"Is Mr. Peterson in?" he asked.

"No. He's not here."

"Could you tell me when you're expecting him?"

The receptionist hesitated, then said, "Mr. Peterson isn't with us anymore."

"He isn't?" said Jonathan in surprise. "Was he fired?"

Miss Ferrara evidently found the word "fired" distasteful. "Mr. Burton let him go this morning."

"Why?"

"Really, I'm not at liberty to give out that information."

"Why not?"

"It—it just isn't done. Who is this calling, please?"

"Sergeant Donovan. Homicide."

Suddenly Jonathan became aware of a figure filling the doorway of his office. He glanced up to discover Lieutenant Helm's hard blue eyes boring into him.

"Have you been demoted?" said Helm caustically. "Yesterday you were passing yourself off as a lieutenant."

Jonathan hung up the phone.

"Come in," he said with false heartiness. "Sit down, Lieutenant. I have some information for you."

Helm limped over to the chair beside Jonathan's desk, lowered himself into it. His gray felt hat was cocked at a rakish angle, due to the bandage on his head. His raw, red features were devoid of expression.

"What information?"

"Peterson's been fired."

"Yeah?" Helm didn't seem especially surprised. "Is that all?"

"No. I've got something else for you. Emberger was playing around with the murdered girl."

"Emberger? Why, he's sixty if he's a day."

"What's that got to do with it?"

Helm rubbed his nose thoughtfully. "Nothing, I reckon. There's no fool like an old fool. How did you find out?"

"From Elly. The foreman at the Emco Construction Company told her. He said that Emberger had been interested in Miss Sullivan, implied that they'd been having an affair. Of course it might not be anything but malicious gossip."

"There wasn't a hint of it in the girl's apartment," said Helm. "Nothing."

"I know—"

"Oh, do you?" snapped Helm, catching him up instantly. "How did you know?"

"You didn't let me finish," said Jonathan, feeling sweat prickle his forehead. "I was starting to say that I know you wouldn't have missed any evidence like that when you went over her place."

Helm raised his eyebrows.

"So," Jonathan continued, "I wondered if her rooms could have been searched before the police got there?"

"Well, you can quit wondering. They had been searched. Wiped clean of fingerprints, too. You wouldn't know anything about that, would you?"

Jonathan shook his head.

"I didn't think you would," said Helm. "This is the damnedest case I ever ran up against. The girl lived there quietly. Minded her own business. Didn't have many visitors."

"What about men? A pretty girl like Bea Sullivan must've had some dates."

Helm shrugged. "Peterson called on her pretty regularly. Then there was an older man who brought her home once or twice."

"Ah," said Jonathan significantly.

Helm frowned. "It could have been Emberger, I reckon. But I doubt that we can get an identification. If it was Emberger, he was plenty discreet. We haven't been able to locate anyone who got a good look at him."

"Is that all you've turned up?"

"All?"

"Yes, *all*," said Jonathan irritably. "Damn it, Miss Sullivan wasn't born full grown out of Jupiter's ear like Minerva."

"Minerva who?"

"I meant merely that she must have had parents, relatives, friends, acquaintances."

"Oh, sure," said Helm.

Jonathan said in exasperation, "It's like pulling teeth to pry information out of you. Why the hell are you being so cagy? Do you want me to locate those bales of waste, or don't you?"

"Well," said Lieutenant Helm reluctantly, "according to her birth certificate she was twenty-three. Her mother is a tramp, a drunk who lives in a rooming house over on Second. Her father abandoned them when the Sullivan girl was thirteen. At fifteen she was sent to Children's Center, and her mother to jail for contributing to the delinquency of a minor. Some mess involving an older man. She ran away from Children's Center, was caught and sent to Ormsby Village. When she was released from Ormsby Village, she was given a job in a tobacco plant. While there she went to a business school at night. That's where she got her secretarial training. The school got her the job with the Emco Construction Company.

"Her employment record was excellent, though she didn't hit it off too well with her fellow workers. No girlfriends. Not too many men. She'd been running around with Peterson about two years. Like I say, there were some other men, but we haven't been able to get a line on them.

Is that what you want to know?"

Jonathan sighed. "It's not much help, is it?"

"That's the trouble with this goddamned case," said Helm bitterly. "No motive, no suspects. No nothing!"

Jonathan's conscience gave a guilty twinge, because he was pretty sure that he could supply the motive and no end of suspects.

"Do you still have Peterson under surveillance?" he asked.

"Why?"

"I want to go out and talk to him."

"Who's stopping you?"

"I just don't want any reasons for visiting Peterson misunderstood," Jonathan replied stiffly.

"Knox, I've got a feeling that if I really understood your motives, I'd lock you up and throw away the key."

"I've always been honest with you, haven't I?"

"No!"

The lieutenant's tone didn't invite argument. Jonathan took out a cigarette, lit it. From the auction floor came the swelling buzz of voices as the prospective bidders assembled. In a few minutes he would have to start the auction.

Just then Elly stuck her head in the door, saw Lieutenant Helm and started to withdraw it with considerable haste.

"Oh, come on in," the lieutenant told her. "I don't bite."

Elly advanced dubiously. She was wearing a smart, brown wool suit, high heels, and her pony tail had been converted into a businesslike bun at the nape of her neck. She looked very young, very efficient, very feminine—and also very wary. Elly wasn't one to rush in where angels feared to tread.

"Then you aren't sore at me anymore?" she asked.

"No," Helm said amiably. "Of course not."

"I'm sorry—"

"Forget it," said Helm.

Elly gave a sigh of relief. "No hard feelings?"

"No hard feelings," said Helm.

She approached Jonathan's desk, making a rather wide circle around the lieutenant's chair in spite of his reassurances. Helm abruptly stood up. She jumped skittishly, and a small involuntary shriek escaped from her lips.

"You startled me," she said.

"Put out your hands," Helm said in a suddenly grim voice.

"Wh—what?"

"I said put out your hands." The lieutenant's raw, red face was as hard as jasper.

"Wh—wh—why?"

"I'm taking you downtown for questioning." And whipping out a pair of handcuffs, he snapped the bracelets on Elly's wrists.

"You're joking," Jonathan said in a stunned voice.

"Joking, hell!"

"But handcuffs," Elly wailed. The commotion in the office had drawn the curious gaze of a number of people who had been milling about the auction floor. They peered in through the open doorway, their expressions sober. She shrank from their gaze.

Jonathan said, "You can't do this! The auction starts in a couple of minutes. What will I do for a cashier?"

"That's your lookout," Helm said in a hard, implacable voice.

Jonathan went over and closed the door, shutting out their fascinated audience. "Listen, Lieutenant," he pleaded. "Be reasonable. Why can't you question her here?"

The lieutenant's expression became absolutely diabolic. "We want to talk to Miss Watson without interference. We've got a special room in the basement for just that purpose. She'll spill her guts after we've had her in there for a while." He reached for her arm.

With a terrified shriek, Elly whirled, flung herself into the lavatory and slammed the door. They heard the bolt *snick* into place.

The corners of Lieutenant Helm's mouth twitched faintly.

He turned to Jonathan, said in a low voice, "Let her sweat it out in there a few minutes before you tell her I'm gone."

Jonathan blinked. "Then you're not taking her in?"

"Hell, no! I'd just as soon haul in a sack full of wildcats."

"Well, you certainly had me fooled," said Jonathan.

Helm grinned, started for the door.

"Hey, wait! said Jonathan. "You're forgetting the key to those handcuffs."

"There isn't any key," Helm explained amiably. "It's an old pair that was lying around the office. The key's been lost for years."

And with a chuckle, he departed, leaving Jonathan staring after him in consternation.

Elly's sense of humor wasn't her strong point. Her relief at learning that Lieutenant Helm had only been ribbing her lasted less than thirty seconds, and when Jonathan had to confess that he couldn't unlock the handcuffs, her comments would have blistered a stone.

Moreover she refused point-blank to work in public with her hands manacled like a common criminal's. So there was nothing for it but to locate a locksmith and have him come over and saw them off.

Consequently they were late getting started with the auction, and even later getting away that evening.

Elly was still simmering when Jonathan locked up.

"Isn't there anything that can be done to a police officer who abuses his authority?" she asked bitterly. "Doesn't an ordinary citizen have any protection against such monsters? Are we living in a police state?"

"How about dinner?" said Jonathan soothingly.

It was against Elly's principles to turn down a free meal and she accepted without hesitation. Jonathan, who rarely did anything unless he had a good reason, had invited her partly to smooth her ruffled feathers, and partly because he had come to the conclusion that if she was to be of any real help to him, she would have to be briefed about the true facts of the case.

Thus, while they were eating, he broke the news to her about the snapshots and the probable blackmail angle.

"Blackmail!" she burst out.

"Shhh!" he said, glancing around at the other diners, but no one seemed to have noticed her startled exclamation.

"Is that why the Sullivan girl was murdered?" she asked nervously.

"Could be."

"Wh—who was she blackmailing?"

"I'm not sure. Mrs. Emberger, certainly. Perhaps Conrad, as well. Maybe she and Peterson were blackmailing all the picnickers."

"And so they killed her?" she said, her eyes wide, yellow, and fearful.

"For heaven's sake, quit scaring yourself to death."

Elly shuddered. "What are you going to do?"

"I haven't decided. But I don't see how the extortion racket can have any connection with those bales of waste that were dug up from beneath the sidewalk. They were buried in 1900, and the snapshots weren't taken until twenty-seven years later. Peterson is the link, though. I think I can pressure him into revealing where he's hidden that trash; but for my own protection I need to know who I'm up against. We have Mrs. Emberger and Conrad pegged, and I've identified the other two girls, but I still don't know who they might have married, or where they are now. I don't know anything about the men except for Conrad. What I want you to do—"

"Whoa!" said Elly, who had been listening with her head slightly cocked. "I'm going straight home and lock myself in my room. That's what I'm going to do!"

"Why?"

"Because I don't want to end up on a slab like Bea Sullivan."

"They keep them in refrigerated lockers and not on slabs, you miserable coward. And anyway, the only thing I'm asking you to do is spend a couple of hours at the library going through old newspapers. That idiotic stunt you pulled last night wasn't *my* idea."

"Are you sure that's all?"

"Of course."

"What am I supposed to look up?"

"You're to try to get a line on the other four young people who were at that picnic. The identities of the men. Who the two brunettes married. Whether any of them are still living in Louisville."

"But I don't even know what they look like."

"We'll fix that. We can stop by my place. You look the stuff over and take one of the least objectionable pictures along for comparison."

"Well," said Elly dubiously, betrayed by her curiosity. "Are they really so scandalous? The pictures, I mean."

He shook his head. "It's what they imply that makes them dynamite."

Jonathan dropped Elly off at the library, then drove to Portland. Parking boldly in front of the house, he looked up and down the lamp-lit street, but there were too many cars drawn up to the curbs on both sides for him to spot Lieutenant Helm's men.

Jack Peterson was an unknown quantity, but the knowledge that the house was under surveillance by the police lent Jonathan a reassuring sense of security. He got out, went up to the door, rang the bell.

A light was burning inside, but the blinds were drawn. Presently he heard footsteps approaching.

"Who is it?" a man's voice called through the door.

"Knox," Jonathan replied. "Open up, man. I can't shout my business from the street."

For a moment there was no answer, then he heard a bolt being shot back. The door opened inward.

"Come in," Peterson's voice bade him, but the man himself was careful to keep to one side, out of Jonathan's range of vision.

With a shrug, he stepped inside. Instantly the door was banged shut behind him. His shoulder was grabbed, and he was slammed around facing the wall.

"Hold it!" said Peterson in a tight, nervous voice. Jonathan knew it was Peterson, because in the brief glimpse he had been allowed, he had recognized the tall blond man whom he had knocked unconscious with the alabaster statuette.

Peterson now proceeded to jab him in the kidney with the muzzle of a gun, while frisking him quickly and expertly.

"Okay," Peterson said when he was satisfied that Jonathan was unarmed. "You can turn around."

Jonathan did so rather gingerly. The man he found himself facing was about thirty-two and had a shiny chromium-plated .45 caliber revolver clutched in his fist. Jonathan took a closer look at it and said, "I'll be damned."

It was a most realistic cap pistol!

Peterson laughed, tossed the toy revolver into a nearby armchair. He was wearing a bandage like a turban on his head, and his face was lumpy and in need of a shave. His sleeves were rolled up, and Jonathan could see the heart with the initials tattooed on his forearm.

"Who are you?" he demanded.

"Knox. Jonathan Knox. I've bought the salvage claim to those bales of waste that were found under your sidewalk."

Peterson's blue eyes narrowed. "You're the guy on the phone. You gotta nerve coming here. I oughta bust you one."

"Are you alone?"

Peterson jerked his head in the affirmative.

"Good," said Jonathan. "I came here to make a deal."

Peterson pursed his lips; then, as if reaching a decision, he walked over to a worn, lumpy, overstuffed chair and slumped into it.

Jonathan opened his topcoat, sat down on a battered couch, conscious of the odor of stale tobacco smoke permeating the room. A gas burner was glowing in one corner, adding its fumes to the over-all stuffiness.

"I'm not going to beat around the bush," he said dryly. "I have some negatives that you need and I don't."

"How'd you get 'em?"

"That's unimportant. I have them. If you want them back, you'll tell me what you did with those seven bales of waste."

"What's about that trash, fellow?"

Jonathan had been prepared to dislike Peterson and he wasn't disappointed. The blond man's eyes were set too close together, his lips too thick and red, so that he seemed to be perpetually pouting. He ignored Peterson's question and asked, "Why did you dig it up?"

"You oughta know, fellow."

"Who tipped you off about that trash?"

Peterson considered this before answering. Finally he said, "I don't mind telling you that. It was Mrs. Hazelip."

"Emma Hazelip. She used to be old man Burress' secretary. Of Burton and Burress?"

"Yeah. But it was Burress and Burton then. She was the queen bee around that office as long as old Burress was alive. After Burress died they reorganized and Mrs. Hazelip was let go."

"Why did they keep Burress' name?"

Peterson shrugged. "Burress' nephew is still with 'em, but he don't cut no ice. Burton's the senior partner now. Emmy had been there more than thirty years when they gave her the boot. She didn't like it."

"Is she in on this deal?"

"What deal are you talking about, fellow?"

"Blackmail, you lousy sonofabitch!" said Jonathan, who was at the end of his patience. "Don't you think I know what you and that Sullivan girl were up to?"

Peterson's face set in mean, lumpy lines. "You've got no call to talk to me like that. I oughta bust you one." But he made no move to do so.

Jonathan regarded him with disgust.

"For two bits, I'd walk out of here and throw you to the wolves, Peterson. It wouldn't take the cops long to squeeze the truth out of you what you've done with those bales. Is that what you want me to do?"

Peterson licked his lips. "Leave the cops out of it."

"Then where are those bales?"

"I ain't seen no negatives," he said doggedly.

Jonathan figured he had pushed Peterson just as far into a corner as it was safe to push the man.

"I didn't bring them with me," he said.

"That's okay," said Peterson. "I'll show you them bales when I get the negatives. But I gotta be sure you ain't gonna double-cross me. It ain't no simple exchange. When you know where the stuff is, what could I do if you was to hold out the negatives? Nothing, that's what."

"What do you suggest?" said Jonathan dryly.

Peterson hesitated. "I gotta protect myself," he said again. He got up and began to walk back and forth, back and forth, a scowl on his face. "You said over the phone that the cops are tailing me?"

"That's right."

"How do you know?"

"I have my own sources of information."

Peterson's frown deepened at this but he didn't challenge it. Finally he said, "What kind of car you driving?"

"A 1957 Buick station wagon. It's out front. Take a look at it."

The blond man went to the window, pulled the blind aside a crack and peered out. "What's the license number?" he asked, turning back into the room.

"K 41-517."

Peterson wrote this down on the back of an envelope. "Tomorrow night," he muttered, "about eight-thirty, I'll walk over to Winkler's for a couple of beers. I'll make a trip or two to the john during the evening. At a quarter of ten, I'll go to the john again. There's a back entrance. I'll duck out that way into the alley. You be waiting at the Twenty Sixth Street end of the alley with that station wagon. I'll jump in and you hightail it out of there. You get the picture?"

"Yes, I get it," said Jonathan.

"Remember! A quarter of ten. And have those negatives with you."

"I'll have them," said Jonathan.

"You better," said Peterson nastily. "Because if you foul up, I might just figger to leave you holding the bag. I ain't that hot on this deal, Knox. Not since Bea got it, I ain't."

10

The library closed at nine. Jonathan had found an empty meter on York and was parked in front of the entrance when Elly came out.

"Over here," he called, when he caught sight of her. He opened the door. The night was cloudy and a fall rain was beginning to sift down.

"What about a drink?"

"Ugh!" said Elly in revulsion. "I can still taste that stuff from last night."

"Some coffee then?"

"I wouldn't mind a cup of coffee."

He pulled away from the curb and at the corner turned south on Third. The streets were wet, black, and shiny. The oncoming headlights of traffic seemed to glitter like sparklers. Red, blue and green neon signs turned the city into Aladdin's jeweled cavern. The windshield wipers made a hypnotic swish-swish sound.

He fished a cigarette out of his breast pocket, lit it with the dash lighter. From the corner of his eye, he was aware of Elly sitting bolt upright, even her posture conveying an air of suppressed excitement.

"What did you find?"

"Well," she said eagerly. "I didn't think you were ever going to ask!" And then she laughed. "The little brunette, the one called Judy Jane Jointer, married one of the boys on that picnic. His name is Donald Henderson III, and they're in the phone book! They've got a place out on Upper River Road!"

Jonathan raised his eyebrows. "The hell you say! How do you know he hasn't been divorced? This could be the second Mrs. Donald Henderson III."

"I thought of that," she informed him triumphantly, "so I telephoned and asked for Judy, and when she answered I asked if she was the Judy Jane Jointer I used to know at Kentucky Home. And she said that I must be mistaken because she had gone to Collegiate. So I hung up before she could ask who I was."

"That was a neat piece of work," he said with respect.

"That's not all." Elly was so pleased with herself that she almost wiggled. "The other girl, Ethel Sands, married a boy from California—a Philip Evans—and went out there to live. So you can scratch her off."

"Maybe," Jonathan agreed; "but it's not impossible that they moved back. Did you try the phone book for them?"

"No, but you can eliminate the last boy for sure. His name was Mel Davis and he was killed in a perfectly ghastly automobile accident on the River Road."

"Well, that's it," said Jonathan with satisfaction. "The Davis boy is dead. For the time being, we can eliminate the Sands girl. That leaves Conrad, Mrs. Emberger, Mr. and Mrs. Donald Henderson III."

"Do you think one of them killed Bea Sullivan?"

"I don't know," he confessed. "I just don't know."

They drove a while in silence.

"I thought we were going to get some coffee," Elly spoke up presently.

"We're almost out to my place. We can make a pot there, and it won't cost ten cents a cup."

"Oh," she said, entirely satisfied by such a thrifty motive.

The rain was beginning to come down much heavier by the time they reached the house, and they had to dash across the front lawn. Inside, it was dark and a little chilly.

Jonathan turned up the thermostat, helped Elly off with her coat, sent her back to the kitchen to make the coffee. Then he kindled a fire in the open fireplace, put a stack of LPs on the record player, got a bottle of cognac from the pantry, dimmed the lights in the living room. When Elly finally emerged from the kitchen, bearing two cups of coffee, the strains of *Pretty Baby* were wafting softly, seductively on the air.

She took in his preparations with raised eyebrows.

"You haven't forgotten to stash the contraceptives some place handy, have you?" she asked with interest.

"What?" said Jonathan, in a shocked voice.

"I was just making sure you hadn't overlooked anything."

He winced.

"I suppose," she said, going to the fireplace and setting the cups on the hearth, "you want me over here on the rug." She took off her jacket, revealing a frothy white blouse, kicked off her shoes, and seated herself on the floor in front of the blaze.

"Cut it out," said Jonathan sourly.

She looked up at him from beneath her lashes. Her eyes were brimming with amusement.

"Sit down." She patted the rug.

Jonathan glowered at her suspiciously, then lowered himself to the floor beside her. Elly giggled. The dam broke and suddenly she began to laugh.

"It's not that funny," he said with a certain bitterness.

Her eyes softened. "I'm sorry. I just couldn't resist it." Unexpectedly she leaned forward, kissed him lightly on the mouth.

"There! Don't look so disappointed." She kissed him again.

Jonathan brightened hopefully. At that precise moment the doorbell rang. He and Elly exchanged astonished glances. Outside the wind had risen and they could hear the rain beating against the house in gusts.

"Damn!" he said. "Who would come calling on a night like this?" He glanced at his watch. "It's after ten."

The doorbell rang again.

"I'll get rid of whoever it is," he assured Elly, and scrambled to his feet. Going into the entrance hall, he switched on the porch light, opened the front door.

A woman in a wet plastic raincoat was standing on the porch. She was a well-preserved, beautifully groomed, expensively clad fifty-five. Her eyes were blue and worried. Her hair beneath the transparent hood of the raincoat was ash-gray and artistically tousled. A cream-colored Cadillac was parked in Jonathan's drive behind his station wagon.

"Mr. Knox?" she said questioningly.

"Yes."

"I hope I'm not disturbing you." Her accent bespoke a finishing-school background. "I am Mrs. Gerald Emberger. May I come in?"

Jonathan nodded shortly and stood aside. His surprise wasn't great enough to prevent his guessing instantly that Mrs. Emberger's visit boded no good. With rather poor grace he ushered her into the study, which was across the hall from the living room.

"May I take your coat?" he said.

"Thank you, but that won't be necessary." She opened the coat, sat down in a wing chair, put her handbag in her lap. "Mr. Knox, I slipped away from a party to come here." She bit her lip. "I—well, frankly, Mr. Knox, I thought that if I could only talk to you in person, I could make you understand."

"Understand what?"

"We have a boy in college, Mr. Knox. A junior at Dartmouth. Don't you see what this would do to him? And my daughter. She's married and is expecting a baby. It isn't fair to make them suffer for an indiscretion that I committed before they were born."

Jonathan was pretty annoyed at her assumption that he was the blackmailer.

"Why tell me this?" he asked coldly.

Mrs. Emberger drew an unsteady breath. For the first time he noticed that beneath her make-up her skin appeared bloodless. Her blue eyes were intent, almost glassy.

"Because of the money, Mr. Knox," she said in a low, hurried voice. "I can't possibly raise twenty-five thousand dollars. The money is in trust. Don't you see, I can't touch the principal. I—I've brought you this." She fumbled with her pocketbook, opened it, and drew forth a long white envelope which she held out to him. "Here is five thousand dollars, Mr. Knox. It's all I could raise. Please take it. Please, Mr. Knox, and give me those negatives."

He refused to touch the envelope, shaking his head.

Mrs. Emberger's shoulders slumped. Her hand holding the envelope began to tremble.

"How can you be so inhuman?"

Jonathan was furious.

"I think you'd better go," he said between his teeth. "What the hell do you take me for? Coming here and offering me a lousy five thousand dollars."

Mrs. Emberger gave him an agonized look. She returned the envelope to her bag. When her hand emerged, it was holding a little pearl-handled .32 automatic.

"I must have those negatives," she said in a high, brittle voice that trembled with incipient hysteria. "I don't intend to leave without them."

Jonathan felt his mouth go dry.

"Mrs. Emberger," he said, "I am not a blackmailer. I am not flattered at being taken for one—"

"You really don't expect me to believe that," she interrupted, her voice rising. "I'll shoot, Mr. Knox. Believe me, I don't intend to stand supinely by and see my children's lives ruined by a—a low creature like you!"

Jonathan glared back, but he could feel gooseflesh rippling up his spine. The little .32 automatic was trained on his stomach, and Mrs. Emberger held it as if she knew how to use it. The hopelessness of trying to argue with a hysterical woman whose mind had been made up beforehand, filled him with a sense of utter frustration.

He was conscious of the strains of *I'm in the Mood for Love* floating in from the record player. Mrs. Emberger's shrill, hysterical tones must have carried plainly back to Elly in the living room. Why the hell didn't she do something? Phone the police, create a diversion, anything!

He wet his lips. "Mrs. Emberger, I feel it's only fair to warn you. We aren't alone."

"I don't believe you," she said in a startled voice.

"My secretary is in the next room where she can hear every word. She's taking down our conversation right now."

"It's not true. You're trying to frighten me."

"Elly!" Jonathan called. The record player started in on *Cuddle Up a Little Closer*.

"*Elly!*" Jonathan shouted.

Mrs. Emberger waited. She looked badly rattled, but determined.

"It didn't work, Mr. Knox."

"She's there," said Jonathan doggedly. "She's afraid to answer because of the gun."

"I think I shall call your bluff on that," she said, tight-lipped. "You first, Mr. Knox. Keep your hands up in the air."

With his hands shoulder high, Jonathan preceded her across the hall into the living room. There was no sign of Elly.

Her shoes were gone, her jacket, too. Only one cup of coffee remained on the hearth. There wasn't even a lipstick-stained cigarette butt in any of the ashtrays.

"Well," said Mrs. Emberger from behind him. Then he heard her suck in her breath. He turned around.

Mrs. Emberger's eyes were fastened on the blown-up print of the snapshot which Elly had taken to the library. It was lying face-up on the end table, damning Jonathan forevermore. He knew that nothing he could say would convince her now that he wasn't the blackmailer.

She was only a few feet from him, her whole attention for the instant riveted on the snapshot of the picnic. He wasn't likely to get another such chance.

He leaped, slapped the automatic out of her hand. It hit the floor, went off sounding like a cannon inside the room. The bullet smashed into the record player, which squawked and stopped in the middle of a phrase.

Mrs. Emberger screamed.

Jonathan dived for the automatic, scooped it up, snapped on the safety. Dumping it in his pocket, he pulled out his handkerchief, wiped his perspiring face. Not until then did he become aware of the doorbell, which was ringing again.

Then whoever was out front began to kick the door and yell, "Open up! Open up!"

From the bottom of his heart, Jonathan wished that he'd never heard of the St. Louis Bears.

He glanced at Mrs. Emberger. Her nostrils were distended as if she couldn't get enough oxygen. Then she sank weakly into a chair.

Putting his hand on the little pearl-handled automatic in his jacket pocket, he returned to the hall. "Don't tear the door down," he shouted, unlocked it, and flung it open.

Emberger was standing on the stoop. There was a wild expression on his face. His fists were clenched.

"Where is my wife?" he shouted. "What have you done to her? If you've harmed a hair of her head—"

Jonathan was so exasperated that he reached through the door, grabbed Emberger by his coat lapels, and literally snatched him into the house.

"What are you trying to do?" he said savagely. "Rouse the whole neighborhood?"

"My wife," Emberger said rather breathlessly. "I heard a gunshot! Where is she?"

"In the living room." He gave Emberger a shove. The older man tottered into the next room.

"Alma!" he exclaimed.

"Gerald!" Mrs. Emberger said in a frightened voice. Wh—what are you doing here?"

"I followed you," he said.

"You didn't follow her closely enough," Jonathan said sourly.

Mrs. Emberger began to cry, dabbing at her eyes with a tiny handkerchief.

Emberger straightened his hat, a dark blue Homburg. He was wearing a dark blue topcoat as well, and was a lean, erect, hard-faced man despite his sixty years. Jonathan sensed the streak of ruthlessness in him. No man, he realized, could have spent his life handling gangs of tough construction workers without possessing a certain toughness of fiber himself.

Emberger turned away from his wife and looked at Jonathan with the beady-eyed fierceness of a stringy old fighting cock.

"Knox," he barked. "I want an explanation."

Between her sobs, Mrs. Emberger said, "He's—he's blackmailing me, Gerald."

"Nonsense!" Emberger snapped.

"But—but he is, Gerald. You don't understand. I've been afraid to tell you. He—he—"

"I know about those negatives," Emberger interrupted. "And I tell you this isn't the fellow. I had him investigated. He's an auctioneer—"

"You know!" Mrs. Emberger gasped. "But—but how?"

"I had a talk with Burton after the bank manager notified me you'd been trying to borrow twenty-five thousand against the trust."

"But he promised—"

Emberger said in his clipped voice, "Don't blame Burton. I didn't give him much choice." He regarded his wife dispassionately. "You should have come to me in the first place, Alma."

"I was ashamed to," she said in a stifled voice. "Those pictures …" Her voice trailed off.

He shrugged impatiently. "We all do idiotic things in our youth. Though I must say that business of hauling along a camera on a party like that just about tops the lot. Who brought it?"

"I don't remember. One of the boys." She drew a deep breath. "Gerald, you said Mr. Knox isn't the blackmailer, but he has one of the pictures. Look!" She held up the enlargement.

Emberger's eyes narrowed. It was the one where the picnickers were unloading the boat. Fortunately they were all dressed. He swung on Jonathan.

"How do you explain this, Knox?" he demanded, his voice sharply suspicious.

Jonathan sighed.

"I got it from the blackmailer."

"Then you know who he is?"

"Yes."

"Who?"

"A fellow by the name of Jack Peterson."

Emberger took the eight-by-ten glossy enlargement and studied it. Suddenly his eyebrows shot up.

"Jesus Christ!" he exploded. "That's Conrad! My partner. Was he on that party, Alma?"

She nodded unhappily. "That's why I didn't want you to know. I was afraid it might cause trouble between you."

Emberger laid the picture down on the end table with an expression of repugnance.

"Knox, you said you got this from Peterson. How?"

Jonathan shook his head. "I'm not ready to divulge that yet."

"Why not?"

"I'll explain that after I've learned where those bales of waste are hidden."

"You expect to find some rare stamps among those papers, don't you?"

"Yes. How did you know?"

"I told you I had you investigated. Colonel Heyman of the Jefferson Stamp Company explained your interest."

"I see," said Jonathan.

Emberger regarded him shrewdly for a moment before saying, "Do you think you could get the negatives from Peterson?"

Jonathan hesitated. "Take off your coat and hat," he said finally. "Let me get you a drink."

Emberger removed his hat, ran his fingers through his gray hair. Getting out of his coat he seated himself on a long, low chest which had been converted into a window seat. "Whisky, if you have it, and a little water."

"What about you, Mrs. Emberger?"

"Nothing, thanks."

Jonathan went through the dining room and the pantry into the kitchen, but there wasn't any sign of Elly. Looking out the window, he could see his car in the drive so she hadn't taken off in that. He was beginning to worry.

Fixing Emberger's drink, he returned to the living room.

The contractor swallowed at least half of it at a gulp. "Well?" he said.

"I don't know," said Jonathan dubiously. "Bea Sullivan and Peterson were in this together. If the girl was murdered because of those negatives, it would be suppressing evidence."

Mrs. Emberger said quickly, "Mr. Knox, I offered you five thousand dollars when I thought you were the blackmailer. I'll gladly let you have it if you can get them away from that horrible man."

She opened her pocketbook, took out the envelope and handed it to him.

This time Jonathan took it, glanced inside at the sheaf of green currency.

"Damn!" he said. "I don't know what to say. There's a chance that I can get the negatives away from Peterson." He explained tersely about his arrangement to see Peterson on the following night.

"How did you persuade him to show you where he's hidden the bales of waste?" Emberger asked when he had finished.

Jonathan shook his head. "That's not important. The thing is, after what's been going on, I don't know whether I should accept money for the negatives. It—well, it's too close to blackmail." He tossed the envelope back into Mrs. Emberger's lap.

"No, no!" said Emberger impatiently. "Take it, man! We're paying you to recover the negatives."

But Jonathan continued to shake his head.

"No," he said firmly. "Wait till I get them back for you; then if you still feel this way, you can pay me."

"It's a deal!" said Emberger, and thrust out his hand.

The Embergers departed a few minutes later. Jonathan saw them to the door, watched them drive off separately in their cars. The rain had settled into a steady drizzle by this time, and it was turning much colder.

Returning to the living room, he lit a cigarette.

A sepulchral voice said, "Have they gone?"

Jonathan froze, gave a suppressed exclamation of pain as the match burnt his fingers. He flung it into the fireplace, wheeled, staring about the room. There were no closets, neither was there any furniture that a person could hide under.

"J—J—Jonathan," said the muffled voice again.

It seemed to be coming from the chest under the window. He went to it, raised the lid.

Elly was squeezed in it like the Hindu boy in the basket trick.

"How the hell did you get in there?" he demanded in an astounded voice.

"I'm stuck," she wailed. "Never mind how I got in. How do I get out?"

11

Every time Jonathan thought about Elly hiding in the window seat instead of coming to his rescue, he grew more incensed. Consequently, by the next morning he was in a rather bitter frame of mind.

The day following an auction was generally slow and he decided not to go to the Green Barn at all. Instead he called Burton and Burress and, by pretending to be Mrs. Hazelip's nephew, obtained the address of the former secretary to the late Mr. Burress.

Mrs. Hazelip, it turned out, was a gimlet-eyed widow of some sixty-odd years, who made her home with a married daughter. The minute Jonathan started to ask questions about the Steiglitz vs. Steiglitz action, she refused to answer and ordered him out of the house.

Jonathan left, his disposition not exactly improved by the encounter.

Dropping in at police headquarters, he was informed that Lieutenant Helm was out, so he ate lunch by himself and finally went home. He spent the rest of the afternoon reading. At six o'clock he broiled a steak and fixed a salad for his supper. He sat around watching television until eight-thirty, when he got the negatives out of the cold-air duct. Then he went upstairs, shaved, dressed in dark clothes, put on a trench coat and a dark snap-brim hat, thrust the snub-nosed .38 revolver in his pocket and left the house. At a quarter of ten he was parked on Bank near the mouth of the alley leading behind Winkler's bar.

The night was clear and crisp, but there wasn't any moon. He sat there in the station wagon, feeling the coldness seep through his car. The seconds ticked by with agonizing slowness. He was just lighting his fourth cigarette when a figure slipped from the alley's mouth, hurried up to the station wagon, opened the back door and jumped in.

"Step on it!" came Peterson's urgent voice.

Jonathan started the motor, pulled away from the curb. "Which way?"

"Have you got the negatives?"

For answer Jonathan pulled the Manila envelope out of his pocket and tossed it into the rear seat. As they were driving past a garish neon sign, he noticed Peterson checking them against the light.

"O.K.," said the blond man at length, "head East."

With Peterson directing, they soon arrived at a neighborhood of dark warehouses lining both sides of Main Street. This was the oldest part of the city. Many of the buildings were vacant, big piles of stone or brick five and six floors high, their windows dusty and blank.

Peterson guided Jonathan into an alley, told him to park behind one of the empty warehouses about halfway down the block.

"Okay," he said, "douse your lights. This is it. The trash is inside."

They got out. The alley was narrow and black. No lights showed anywhere. Peterson pointed out big double doors in the rear of the warehouse. When he spoke, his voice was tight:

"This place is part of an estate administered by Burton and Burress. It's been vacant about six months. I borrowed the keys from the office. You can drive a truck right inside. I dumped the bales on the floor. This way."

He moved to a smaller door at one side. His foot struck a tin can which rattled loudly against the cobbles with which the alley was paved.

Jonathan's heart pounded wildly, and for a moment he felt as if he couldn't get enough air.

A tight, brilliant beam of light suddenly lanced from Peterson's hand as he tugged a flashlight out of his pocket and directed it at the door. He had a bunch of skeleton keys, and in a moment he pushed it open.

There was an empty, musty smell inside, and their footsteps resounded hollowly from the worn wooden floor. They edged past an open elevator shaft, then a boxed-in office, and came out finally into a vast echoing cavern of a room.

The beam of the flashlight traced a course back and forth, rested suddenly upon a mound of waste taller than a man's head. It was heaped on the floor just as it had been dumped.

"There it is," said Peterson.

"Why did you dig it up, anyway?" Jonathan asked, though by this time he was fairly certain that he knew. His only hope was that he was wrong, but that practically never happened.

Peterson's answer destroyed even that slim possibility.

"To get the negatives," he said.

"Were they there?"

"Yeah. In the first bundle we opened."

Jonathan felt like groaning. Why the hell couldn't he have been wrong this once? He reached the pile of trash, and the first thing he saw was a scrap of newspaper. It was dated June 11, 1927. Despite the persistent rumor, the trash couldn't have been buried in 1900. He had suspected for some time now that two separate incidents had become mixed up in the telling.

In 1900, the janitor had found the St. Louis Bears among some old trash. But it wasn't until 1927 that the courthouse had been cleaned out and the bales of waste dumped in an excavation.

There would be no rare stamps in this accumulation of waste. After the 1900 discovery, the courthouse had been ransacked by people in search of valuable stamps. With his toe he turned over the junk, seeing bound depositions, old magazines, printed circulars, an envelope with the stamp torn off.

"Well," said Peterson nervously, "what do we do now?"

Jonathan's shrug was invisible in the dark. "How did you know the negatives were in this trash?"

"I told you it was Mrs. Hazelip who tipped me off," Peterson said. "She was sore as a boil about being canned and got to talking about all she'd done for Burton and Burress. She told us about this Steiglitz divorce because she knew Mrs. Steiglitz was married now to Emberger, and that Bea worked in Emberger's office."

He lit a cigarette, the flare of the match causing his face to glow in the darkness.

Jonathan said, "How did Mrs. Hazelip know about the negatives?"

"Hell, Burress paid her to slip the transcript of the case and the exhibits out of the circuit clerk's office. Once she'd done it, though, she lost her nerve before she got out of the building with 'em. Instead, she sneaked them into a crate of waste. She said she'd hung around until the waste was baled and she'd seen the bales dumped in an excavation in front of the courthouse."

He drew a deep puff and the ember glowed brightly.

Jonathan said, "Then she knew what was in the snapshots?"

"Yeah, she knew all about them—who the people were—everything. Hell, it was enough to make your mouth water. Those negatives could be worth a fortune if they were used right. Of course it was a gamble. Moisture might have got into the bales and ruined them, but it was worth it. What I can't understand is what you wanted with this junk."

"Rare stamps," said Jonathan in disgust.

"Rare stamps?"

"Yes. And you've just queered that."

"How?"

"You've proved this junk was buried too late. There wasn't a valuable stamp left by 1927. Let's go."

"How do you know?" Peterson dropped his cigarette on the floor, ground it out, then began to poke about among the loose papers.

"Take my word for it," said Jonathan. "You won't find anything."

The blond man, however, began to circle the head-high pile, rooting in the bales, several, of which had burst open. Jonathan waited impatiently in the darkness. Peterson disappeared behind the heap, but the reflected glow of his flashlight was still visible. The rumble of traffic on the street in front of the building seemed muted and far away.

"Hey!" he heard Peterson suddenly exclaim. There was a solid, meaty crunch, followed by a thud. The flashlight clattered to the floor, its beam shooting off across the emptiness. There was the sound of two more blows in rapid succession.

"Peterson!" Jonathan called.

There was no answer.

The beam of light continued to blaze forth motionlessly.

Jonathan snatched the revolver from his pocket, started to edge around the mound of trash in the opposite direction from that which Peterson had taken. In spite of his best efforts, his steps made a betraying shuffle against the bare boards. About halfway around, he experienced a sudden thrill of horror.

A body seemed to be slumped on the floor.

The flashlight had rolled a dozen feet off and was pointed away from the mound of trash. Suddenly, from the light-sensitive corner of his eye, he thought he saw a movement among the shadowy bales.

Instinctively he pulled the trigger. By the flash from the gun's muzzle, he did see a figure charging at him.

Jonathan had time only to point the revolver as he would point a finger, and fire.

A .38 Special carries a tremendous punch. The figure seemed to be hurled backwards. Something metallic clanged to the floor.

Jonathan dashed for the flashlight, feeling as if he were moving in molasses. He scooped it up, directed it in the general direction of his shot. The beam centered on a man who was sitting on the floor and holding his thigh. Blood oozed from between his fingers. His leg, bent at an awkward angle, clearly was broken.

Jonathan let the light travel up to the man's face.

"Emberger!" he said.

The contractor's eyes were squeezed shut. He didn't say anything. Jonathan moved the light about, picked out a two-foot length of one-inch galvanized pipe lying on the floor. One end of the pipe was covered with blood and blond hair. Then the beam touched Peterson. He was sprawled face down. His skull was crushed like an eggshell.

Jonathan jerked the light away quickly, suppressing an almost overpowering urge to retch.

He directed the light at Emberger again. The older man was still numbed from the shock of the .38 slug and had not begun to experience any pain yet. When the light hit his eyes, he opened them.

"The negatives?" he said faintly.

"Peterson has them," Jonathan replied. "Why the hell did you want to kill me?"

"Get the negatives," Emberger muttered. "Don't let the police see them. No need to involve Alma and the kids in this mess."

Jonathan forced himself to go over and search Peterson's flaccid body. He found the envelope with the negatives and slid it into his pocket.

"I was beginning to suspect it was you," he told Emberger as he stood over him.

"Hindsight," the contractor muttered sarcastically.

"No," said' Jonathan. "Bea Sullivan had to be murdered by someone who was intimate with her. Who else could have caught her in her bath like that? I've suspected you from the time I learned that you were playing around with her. Why did you kill her? Jealousy? Blackmail?"

"They tried to work the old badger game on me," Emberger said bitterly. "That bastard broke in on us with a camera. They demanded fifty thousand dollars. I was furious. I walked the floor all night, and the longer I thought about it, the madder I got. Finally I drove to her apartment, let myself in with the key she'd given me. It was early in the morning. She was in the tub. She thought I was Peterson.

"I'll never forget her expression when I burst into the bathroom. She started to scream. I grabbed her by the hair, smashed her head against the faucet. She slid under the water. I let her drown. I hadn't meant to kill her, but God help me, I deliberately let her drown."

His face suddenly squeezed tight with pain as the shock began to wear off. "For God's sake, Knox, call the police before I bleed to death!"

"What's the hurry?" said Jonathan callously. "I'll only saving you for the chair."

He was still angry because Emberger had tried to kill him also, but he started for the front of the building at a lope anyway.

It was a few minutes after quitting time—Reed had already gone home, and Jonathan and Elly were just preparing to leave—when Lieutenant Helm entered the Green Barn. He started down the aisle for the office, and ran into Mrs. Emberger, who was on her way out.

The lieutenant tipped his hat, giving her a rather surprised look.

Mrs. Emberger was dressed in black and heavily veiled. It had been three days since the arrest of her husband, and she looked drawn and unhappy. She said, "Good afternoon, Lieutenant," brushed past him and hurried out, her heels making a tapping sound in the silence.

Helm frowned, then went on into the office.

Jonathan, who had seen the encounter through the open door, said, "Hello, Lieutenant, have a seat."

Helm said, "Hello, Knox. Hello, Elly."

Elly Watson was stirring the fire in a potbellied stove. She nodded rather stiffly. She hadn't forgiven the lieutenant for the trick he had played on her with the handcuffs.

Helm grinned, said, "Why don't we let bygones be bygones?"

She came over, propped one hip on Jonathan's desk. "That's what you said before."

"Well, I mean it this time," he replied affably. "Wasn't that Mrs. Emberger I met leaving your office?"

Both Elly and Jonathan stiffened imperceptibly.

"Yes," said Jonathan. "It's the first chance I've had to talk to her. She wanted to know the truth."

"Yeah?" said Helm. "And what is the truth, Knox?"

Jonathan shrugged. "I didn't feel it would be any kindness to her to lie. I told her that her husband admitted that he had been having an affair with the Sullivan girl, and that he had killed her when she and her lover had tried to work a badger game on him. He had to get rid of Peterson after that because Peterson could send him to the chair. The only thing I don't understand is how Emberger knew where Peterson had hidden the trash. Did he explain that point in his statement?"

Helm grinned, but his eyes remained rather bleak.

"Yeah. The Sullivan girl told him where the trash was before he murdered her. But why? That's what I'd like to know. Why was Emberger so goddamned worked up about that trash. There weren't any St. Louis Bears in it."

Jonathan said, "I guess he was pretty hot under the collar because they'd used his company to pull a fast one."

Elly said, "It was sort of adding insult to injury, wasn't it?"

"Then you think Peterson dug up that waste because he thought it was full of rare stamps?" Helm asked in a silky voice.

"Why else would he dig it up?"

"That's what I'm asking you," said Helm rather bitterly.

Jonathan and Elly both shook their heads.

"You seem to be taking it pretty calmly," Helm snorted.

"Taking what, Lieutenant?"

"The fact that there weren't any Bears in that trash. You're out seven hundred and eighty-five dollars."

Jonathan winced. "No use crying over spilled milk," he said.

"A couple of other things haven't been explained satisfactorily," Helm went on. "For instance, who cracked me over the head with that pipe?"

"But I thought that was Emberger."

"He says not."

Jonathan shrugged. "With both Peterson and Bea Sullivan dead, there are some things, I suppose, that never will be explained."

Helm didn't seem to find this answer very palatable. His frosty blue eyes shifted from Jonathan to Elly and back again. Then, with a disgusted grunt, he stood up and settled his hat gingerly on his head. He was still sporting a bandage, though it was much smaller. Bidding them a rather surly good night, he stalked out.

When he was gone, Elly leaned back and patted her chest breathlessly. "Do you know that the last of those photographs was still burning when he came in?" she said. "I thought I'd die. There's not any chance that Emberger might talk, is there?"

"About those snapshots of the picnic?" said Jonathan. "Why should he? He hasn't anything to gain by bringing more embarrassment down on the heads of his wife and children."

"Well, I hope not!" said Elly.

Jonathan took the envelope that Mrs. Emberger had pressed on him in spite of all his protests, and extracted a crisp thousand-dollar bill.

"Your share," he said, handing it to Elly.

"A thousand dollars!" she breathed. "Oh, you beauty!"

"I've often wondered," said Jonathan, "what you would do if I were to dangle a thousand-dollar bill in front of you."

"Why don't you hand over another one and find out?" she said sweetly.

But Jonathan had no intention of losing a thousand dollars just to prove what he already knew.

THE END

HEAT LIGHTNING
Wilene Shaw

CHAPTER ONE

Lightning flashed like hot blades of steel knifing into the semi-darkness of the countryside. Loud deafening cracks sounded as the blade crashed into timber, and split open the humid air. The wind pulled with vicious intent at the straight, unseamed sackcloth skirt of Holly Reed as she walked down the main highway that was a ribbon of black, shining and glass-surfaced under her searching feet. Slowly, the drops of rain stepped up their momentum until they beat down relentlessly on her bare black head. Washing untouched down her broad cheeks, they fell onto the shapeless shoulders in the shapeless brown dress.

Through the thick downpour that followed could be seen the yellow lights of the houses along the road and on the hillsides surrounding the village.

Here and there, Holly's toes came in contact with the bubbled, slick surface of a toad's back. They jumped in front of her like splashes of rain against the pavement, hopping ahead of her, gathering thicker and thicker as if falling with the rain.

On the front porch of the store where a yellow light burned dimly, a tall, skinny youth yelled out above the clamor of thunder, the splash of water over the eaves, and the cracks of lightning.

"Here comes Holly; here comes Holly," the lad yelled. "Bet she's a hotter number than she looks like. Bet she's got something under that ugly dress, Jeb. What you wanta bet, Jeb?"

The man called Jeb turned a threatening gaze on the youth and stepped menacingly toward him on the porch. He was a tall man with stooped shoulders. From beneath graying brows peered out the calm, searching eyes of a man who missed nothing.

"Ain't I told you many a time to call me Pa?" Jeb Buckley asked, walking toward the lad. "Ain't I waited three years, being patient with you? Ain't I?" he demanded. He closed in on the lad who rushed indoors, and clambered behind a sack of potatoes near the big pot-bellied stove.

"You ain't my pa; you ain't my pa," the lad said. "I don't have to call you Pa, when you ain't my pa. You ain't nothing but my stepdad, that's what you ain't!"

Jeb Buckley loosened his belt. It was wide leather with a bright brass buckle set big and vicious-looking on one end. Holding it in his hand, he walked around the sack of potatoes. But when he reached out, the lad leaped behind a chair in which sat a short, chubby woman. The woman's hair was pulled back from over her rounded forehead, and her hands were busily turning a needle in and out of the bright gray sock in her lap.

"Come on outa there," Jeb Buckley commanded, stumbling over a crate of eggs beside the chair, and bumping headlong into the card table near the stove. "Come on out and let me skin the brass outa you!"

"I'll quit school, that's what I'll do. You lick me and I'll quit school. Then I'll never be a lawyer, and you an' Ma will never get to move into town. I'll quit, that's what I'll do, Jeb," the lad sang out threateningly.

Jeb looked at the boy, Ronny, and then he looked at the woman who continued sewing. He looked back at Ronny.

"You ain't gonna talk back to me," Jeb said, but his voice was less convincing. He looked at the woman in the rocker again, and her gray eyes came up to meet his. A faraway, dreamlike quality shone in her eyes.

She said, "It would be nice to get into town, wouldn't it, Jeb?"

Jeb hesitated, looking at her. His own face became softer, melancholy as he watched her. "Yeah. I guess it would be nice to get into town." He looked at the lad as if to say he wasn't through, but that he would forget the argument for the moment.

Jeb started threading the belt back through his faded blue trousers. He was still looking at Milly with the sewing in her lap when the door of the store opened and slammed shut. Jeb came out from around the stove to look at Holly Reed.

Holly wiped a big awkward hand over her forehead and down across her lips, and flipped her hand so the water dropped off of it onto the floor.

For a moment she stood uncertainly inside the door while Jeb went around behind the counter. Busily he began refilling the bean bin. Then he wiped a dirty cloth along the top of the counter on which were a number of items: candies, cigar boxes and cigarettes, sun glasses, key chains and long black strands of licorice.

Holly walked over to the window. She remained there quietly. Soon the farmers and the village men would come in and gather around the store, and cluster around the card table. Monday was always a big night for Holly Reed, though she couldn't have explained exactly why. It never amounted to anything except to strengthen the pain she always felt when the big city bus pulled up front for a moment or passed by without stopping.

The bus came from the city on Mondays and Fridays, and it went on east and north to another big city. Sometimes it stopped to let off one of the village people who had gone to the city. Usually it was Jim Melchior's wife, Babs. Sometimes Babs went into the city to buy nice clothes, but she was almost the only one who ever went. No one except Babs could afford to go there shopping for clothes and things, and even she didn't often go. She hadn't gone today, but the bus would come by just the same. It came by twice a week.

On the day it was to pass, she would arrive at the store. She would look out through the dark window at the faces on the bus, seeing them briefly when the lights flicked on. Then she would dream. She would hurt all over with that strange hungry ache in her stomach. Her head feeling heavy and sick on her shoulders, she would press her face against the glass of the window.

Today somebody said, "Hi, Holly," like he was just being kind. When she turned away from the window, Karl Tincher was sitting across from her at the card table. He wasn't even watching her, just sitting there waiting for the others so that he could play rook for a while before bedtime.

The men never looked at her. If they did, they never saw her. It was never the way they looked at Babs Melchior, or even the way they looked at Holly's Ma, Alice. And they didn't look at any woman the way they looked at Nellie Byrd.

Except for Milly Buckley who owned the store with her husband Jeb, there wasn't any other woman in the place but Holly. And though usually the men would be looking at a woman in the place, they didn't look at Holly.

The ache rose up inside her so that she looked away. The lad, Ronny, was watching her, but he didn't look at her like the men looked at women. He was big for fourteen, but he didn't look at her the same way men looked at women. It was like he was just wondering, not knowing that there was really something more to her than the straight loose sack dress that covered her body.

"I bid eighty-five," Karl Tincher drawled. "How about you, Jeb?"

"Can't outbid you," Jeb said slowly. "Ain't got a thing to bid on."

Holly looked at Jeb. She could remember when Jeb Buckley had been a dreary bachelor who hated women. She could remember when he wouldn't have anything to do with anyone when he came in from the farm where he worked as a hired man. But now he was different. Three years ago he married Milly Buckley right after her husband was killed on a runaway wagon. Milly's first husband had left her a small farm which she and Jeb sold. They used the money to buy the store from old John Bently who had run it for years. Ever since that, Jeb had been just like anybody else. Although he was not as interested in other women as most men, at least he was interested in Milly. And he did everything just about as Milly wanted. But this was natural since it was her money which bought the store for him and set him up where he could learn all the gossip practically firsthand. Now he could give out advice just as quickly as Karl Tincher.

Karl usually got his information firsthand, and he passed some of it on to his wife, Dora, who was a first-rate broadcaster. Karl was the acting preacher when the regular preacher was at one of his other churches—which was often. Because of this he had gained the nickname of "Preacher," and it stuck.

Preacher got around more than most of the men because he was a trucker. He picked up cows and calves and delivered them to the stockyards for the farmers. In winter, he delivered their tobacco crops to the warehouse for the sales, and he hauled firewood and, sometimes, coal for the village people. When he wasn't busy working with loads for the country people, he sometimes hauled lumber for one of the lumberyards in the city.

Preacher was a big man, rough of figure and smooth of mouth. Holly knew firsthand how smooth he was because she had been passing the Nellie Byrd farm one afternoon when— She turned away to press her face against the window. It was cold and hard against her nose and hot, feverish cheeks.

The sound of airbrakes, like the sharp intake of a giant's breath, heralded the arrival of the bus from the city. The lights flicked on inside the big monster, and the pale white faces, weary with fatigue, looked out into the darkness and to wet streaming rain.

A pain shot up through Holly's stomach and she pressed her face harder against the glass window. Every time the bus stopped she imagined herself walking out of the store and climbing up the steps, then settling herself into a rear seat. She sat there and rode and rode into the night until the city lights popped up around her and lit up the whole world. That was when she would not be Holly Reed any longer but a woman searching for something—the something that was strange, foreign, and desirous to her though she couldn't say what it was.

It was just a hunger, an impatience inside her that twisted and turned and sent agonizing pains through her legs and arms every time that bus came by. She ran a tongue along her lips, and felt a hot, salty tear in the corner of her mouth.

After a moment, the lights went off in the bus and the engine moaned. Then the tires clicked down the road and away into the darkness.

The interior of the store had become suddenly deafeningly quiet. Holly turned about as the screen door of the store closed softly and the rustle of a man's bags hit the oak floor.

He was not a tall man but he was rounded, well-fed, and dark. He wore a hat—a city hat—and his hands were soft-looking and long-fingered, and his nails were neat. He wore a brown suit, rich-looking in the yellow light of the store, and his coat came down slowly over smooth hips and disappeared into the color of brown trousers that were tight and neat against his body.

His eyes met Holly's across the room, and a voice rose up inside her and died. He stared at her like the men always looked at their women, with his lips loose and his eyes shining, his shoulders sagging a little. Then he looked at the table where the men played rook, and the slender round-shouldered Jeb rose and walked around behind the counter.

"Stranger, ain't you?" Jeb said. And the man nodded. He held on to a big flat wooden square that was tucked up under his right arm.

Jeb said, "From the city, I reckon," and the man nodded again, looking about him furtively, as if half-expecting someone to leap on him and tear him apart to see what made him work.

"I'm looking for a place to stay," the man said. "Name's Larry Carter."

"Work around here?" Jeb asked.

"I paint pictures," Larry Carter informed Jeb softly. He smiled, and the white teeth showed even and bright in the yellow light. The corners of his mouth turned up, coaxingly, and he leaned a little forward. "I'd like to stay awhile. I understand it's a nice countryside you have around here. It would be pretty on canvas."

Jeb grunted, looked at Preacher, and said, "I reckon Dora could put him up, couldn't she, Preacher?"

Preacher nodded his big head; a shock of black hair fell over his forehead, and he pushed it back with one big hand. "I think she might," Preacher admitted.

Jeb looked at Holly. "You going home now, Holly? Couldn't you show the man where Dora lives?"

Holly nodded mutely. She came forward slowly, avoiding the dark eyes of the stranger. Walking past the man, she held the door open for him to follow her. Behind her, Jeb said softly, "Ain't no good going to come of it."

Holly walked off the porch into the rain, careful to keep ahead of the stranger. When they came to the big house that sat back off the road, she motioned toward it with a wet hand.

"Aren't you coming in to dry off?" Larry Carter inquired of her. "It's raining, you know," he added gently.

She shook her head, not looking at him. After a moment he went toward the house, and she knew that the pain inside her had risen higher and higher until it throbbed against her sides. She broke into a run down the small hill toward the culvert. She kept running until she passed it and reached the yellow house that sat back on the right.

In the shadows of the porch, she saw the big slumped figure of Brandy Elliot. She slowed to a walk as she came up the wooden steps and wiped the rain from her eyes.

"Why don't you stop drinkin' so much, Brandy? Why you wanta look so foolish?"

He was big and red-headed, with a long red beard. He raised the beard off his chest and looked at her through bleary eyes. Then he sank back in the swing with a grin that revealed his large yellow teeth.

"When you say you'll marry me, young un," he said quietly. "When you say it, I'll stop drinkin', I guess."

She sat down beside him. "You know I can't marry you, Brandy."

"Why not? You keep saying it, but why not? I ain't more than fifteen years older than you, and I'm younger than a lot of men my age. I'm big and strong, and I make a good living."

"Bootleggin'," Holly said without emotion.

"There are worse ways of making a living. Ways like Nellie Byrd, fer instance, or like your Dad. He ain't so good, either, you know. And I reckon your Ma could see a little of that religion Preacher keeps talking about prayer meeting nights."

"No use talking to you," Holly said. "Go on home and sober up. Watcha do if the sheriff catches you like that? He be sure to ask where you got all that cheap stuff."

Brandy laughed as if he thought it were a joke. He laughed and shook the swing and slapped his knee. "You're sure a good one, Holly. You sure are a good one!" Holly got up and went inside, and the door slammed noisily behind her.

She went through the almost bare living room and into the kitchen. From there she moved into a back room. She didn't even light a lamp. She just pulled back the sheets and lay down. She twisted on the mattress and then lay still until she heard the faint familiar noises from the other bedroom.

They came through the paper-thin walls as if they—the two of them—lay beside her on her own bed. The soft squeak of the springs, the muffled noises, and those other—

She turned over and pulled her legs up to her chin. She rolled over on them, hugging them against her until the pain was sharp in her breasts. Then her legs stretched out and convulsed back, pressing against her, her knuckles white and aching around her knees.

After a while the noises stopped and Holly ran a dry tongue along her cracked lips. Her legs went down softly, relaxing slowly against the mattress. Inside her, her heart seemed to stop beating. The pain stopped and she knew suddenly what it was that she had always wanted for so long now.

All summer long she had lain and listened to the sounds from the other room, knowing the pain in her stomach, and hating herself and everybody for it. But now she knew what it was that she had wanted all summer long—now that the stranger had come and looked at her like men always looked at their women, she knew. She understood why she ached, and why she cried, and why the noises sent her squirming into bed so that she couldn't sleep.

She rolled over on her stomach and thought about the stranger and what he had made her realize. Now she would know what to do about the aching inside her, because now she knew what caused it.

After a while, the rain stopped against the roof and Holly rolled back onto her side. She went to sleep with a hand curved upward around the cloth that covered her young breasts.

CHAPTER TWO

Holly Reed rolled over and propped her head on an elbow, keeping her hand just behind her right ear. The bedroom was dim and stuffy with an odd, stale odor about it like from damp cloth. She got up slowly, putting one foot on the cold floor and feeling about until the spot was warm. Then she lowered the other foot and stood up, unkinking her back and brushing down on the sack dress so that some of the wrinkles fell away to reveal dark ugly patches.

She went to the closet and pulled out a dress, not unlike the one she now wore, and slowly changed into it. Then she opened one of the two small windows and saw that the sky was light and clear. The sun was about to peep over the eastern slope on the other side of Brandy Elliot's private hill.

She heard the uneven footsteps of Alice Reed in the kitchen, and the murmur of pots and dishes as Alice undoubtedly prepared the usual breakfast of hot cakes and molasses.

"Ma," Holly thought aloud to herself. "My ma—crippled and hungry all the time just the same as me."

Picking up an old comb from the one chest of drawers in the darkest corner of the room, Holly combed her hair thoughtfully. She could feel of it where the dampness last night had curled the ends of it lightly upward. Her hair was long and silky; it was the only obviously pretty thing about Holly.

In the kitchen, she glanced once at Alice Reed and then went out one of the three doors. Outside the air was crisp and chilly with late summer frost. It was clear like the air always was after a good rain.

The brightness was the only reminder of the rain, until one looked at the hillsides and saw the gutters that had been washed down their sides. There was also the split hickory tree down by the culvert where she had walked by last night. And the ground was mushy yet … Autumn—the moment before the end of summer and the beginning of winter; the instant before the end of living and the beginning of death; the few short, depressive weeks in which to feel sorry that the summer was over and feel dread of the winter.

She walked by the woodshed that needed a coat of paint and would never get it. She saw the caving roof that the snows might crush, the loosely hanging door. From inside the shed came the faint, shuffling noises of activity, and she walked to the door and threw it back. Dick Reed looked up with surprise and quickly went on about his work.

He was busily taking the dried, cured tobacco leaves from the strands of wire stretched across the length of the building. These he worked into little twists of tobacco.

Holly walked away toward another smaller building in the back of the yard. When she returned, Dick Reed was closing the door of the shed; without speaking he walked ahead of her into the house.

Inside, he pumped water from the pump that sat on the edge of the sink. He washed his hands in the little pan of cold water and dumped it into the sink where it could drain through the pipe back of the house.

Dick was a short man, rather large with a big hairy belly that showed where the button on his faded blue shirt was torn off. His hair was mousy gray, dirty-looking and unkempt. He dried his big hands on the dishtowel Alice held hanging down from the pan of hot molasses, as she poured the syrup over the hot cakes on the three plates.

At last Alice broke the silence. "I wish it would never rain," she grumbled bitterly. "It always makes my back hurt worse than ever. Reckon I'm just gonna have to go to bed for the rest of the day," she whined. She looked at Holly. "Where was you last night, eh? Ain't been messin' around none, have you?"

Dick Reed looked up, swallowed a mouthful of food and muttered, "Wouldn't hurt her none if she did, would it? Brandy's been wantin' to marry her. He'd do it, too, I betcha. And he's give us a good livin', too." He looked at Holly from under long grayish brows. "Ain't so bad, now is he?"

Holly shook her head. "He drinks too much."

Dick laughed, coughed softly and looked at Alice. "Listen to her, will you? Ain't she the righteous one, eh? And knowing all the time that me and Brandy drink together!"

Alice glanced at Holly and then looked more seriously at Dick. "Don't you be drinkin' none till you get that work done fer Nellie Byrd. Don't you be spoilin' it, now."

Dick grinned, looked down at his plate and swelled up like a man with a big secret all his own. A woman wouldn't understand.

After a while, Dick stood up and tightened his pants by lifting them further up on his waist. "You workin' today?" he inquired, looking at Holly.

Holly shook her head. "Nobody asked me to work today."

"Well ..." he drawled slowly, turned to walk into the barren living room, and glanced back with that soft gleam in his eyes. "Don't you be waitin' fer me fer dinner. Might be long time."

When he had gone, Holly asked, "What's he doin' fer Nellie?"

Alice picked up the plates, rubbed her back with her right hand smoothing down her white fat hips. "She's havin' her bedroom done over, I reckon. Doin' it in pine. Dick says it'll be the prettiest bedroom hereabouts."

Holly looked at her plate. It was empty. So was the pan and the skillet which had held the hot cakes. She was still hungry. Reluctantly she got up and helped clean up the dishes that never had quite enough food on them to satisfy a growing girl's stomach.

She thought how good it would be to have meat and eggs and coffee and fried mush heaped up on a plate just for her to eat. She thought how wonderful it would be just to look at a plate of food with all those good things on it. She licked her lips as she thought about it.

Holly waited until she heard Alice go back to bed, the springs groaning under her weight. Then she started for the front door and stopped. Preacher was standing in front of her with one big hand raised to knock on the screen door. He looked down when he saw her as if he were embarrassed, and Holly wondered why that should be. It was nothing new to see him standing there five minutes after Dick Reed walked out of the house.

"How's your ma today, Holly?" he asked with interest, a professional look frozen on his broad face.

"She ain't feelin' very good today," Holly said. "She's in bed," she added, and walked on past him down the steps.

When she looked back, he had stepped inside and was hooking the latch on the screen door. She went on down the yard and into the road. Maybe Jeb and Milly would know of someone who needed her help. She could still taste all that food that wasn't there for her to eat. The only way she would ever get it was by earning her own money.

She walked faster as she thought about it. Ronny Buckley came out on the store porch on his way to school. He yelled at her:

"Hi there, Holly!"

"Hi yerself," she called back, grinning a little. She always felt like grinning at Ronny when he spoke to her. He tried so hard to sound like a big grown man, and to every appearance he was, except for the lack of a beard. Ronny had a thick coat of fuzz growing on his upper lip and along the outline of his face, but he was fourteen for all that. He wasn't what she wanted.

Across the road from the store, Jim Melchior was climbing into his old model A Ford truck. He started the motor and it sounded even and steady in the morning air. He called to her through the broken window of the truck.

"Hi ya, Holly," he yelled. "Can you help Babs do some papering today?"

"Sure I can, Jim," she said rushing across the road. She stopped by the truck, leaned against it and looked at him.

Jim Melchior was tall, sober of face and action, and with thin, narrow features and deep-set dark eyes. When he looked at her, Holly felt as if he saw clear through her to the straight tight strap that held her breasts against her chest, and the big pin in the back that fastened it.

Jim said, "She's doin' some fall house cleaning, and I guess she could use you. Told her you were the best worker around here. She thought I'd stay home today and help her hang the paper, but I guess you can do it better, can't you, Holly?"

Holly smiled faintly. "Not as good as you, I reckon, but I always thought it was a woman's job to paper."

Jim nodded, grinned appreciatively. "Guess you're right, too. Can't stand that goo on my hands anyhow." He grinned broader, and put the truck into reverse. It shot backward on the road. Then the gears grated and the truck shot forward, a swirl of black smoke coming from the pipe under the truck bed.

Holly knocked on the Melchior's door, and after a minute, Babs came to let her in. "I was just doing the dishes, Holly," Babs explained.

Holly saw that she still wore one of those pretty bright robes like you sometimes saw in the Sears and Roebuck catalogue. Babs wore clothes like the women in the book, too—always neat and tight. And no matter what she had on, one got the impression that she had a lot of curves that ran up from her thighs all the way to her big, full breasts.

Holly stood in the bedroom and watched her change. She didn't have on anything under the robe, and Holly knew suddenly why the men always looked at Babs Melchior with those misty dark eyes.

Babs pulled on a thin pair of pink things that hid nothing. Over them she put a pair of blue shorts that concealed very little. She put on a pink thin thing that pulled her breasts upward. They weren't as round and hard as they might have been, but they looked firm enough when she fastened the garment in the back. And then she slipped on a sweater that came up around her neck. She pushed the long sleeves up so that her slender arms, smooth and dark pinkish, peeped out just enough to suggest that there was more to them.

Holly stopped watching Babs Melchior and looked about the bedroom. The bed hadn't been made, and there was a cigarette ash tray on a stand by the bed. A big chest of drawers stood along the wall at the foot of the bed, and there was a large vanity along the far wall with a mirror that could show a woman's feet as easily as her face. Holly saw herself in it, and she shuddered at the straight unimpressive appearance she made.

On the chest was a folder of pictures: Babs facing Jim. But Jim held a funny-faced, dark-looking child no more than a year old, and Holly wondered about it.

Folks said that while Jim was in the Army, he had met lots of girls and maybe got a few of them into trouble when he was in Japan. Maybe the child was from one of the girls. The kid had funny dark slanted eyes, and bore no resemblance to Jim's lean almost homely face.

It was said that Jim had met Babs while he was in the Army, just after returning from overseas. She had come from somewhere in California, and the men said that she was one of the whores who hung around soldiers. But no one mentioned this so Jim would hear. And no one ever acted like she was a whore, not the way they acted about Holly's ma, Alice, or Nellie Byrd. The men treated Babs like she was beautiful and untouchable and smart. Maybe they did it because they actually felt that way about Babs, but Holly doubted it. Holly knew they treated her that way, with a certain distant approach, because they knew instinctively that Jim Melchior would have slit their throats as easily as he gutted a pig's belly. They couldn't act otherwise to his pretty strange wife.

Everybody had seen Jim's temper. He was quiet and reserved, but he was like a stick of dynamite that was harmless until you touched it off with mistreatment or carelessness. He had that undercurrent of danger in him, and everybody in the country had seen it explode at least once while Jim was growing up. And he hadn't changed now that he was grown, unless it was to become more potent, more dangerous. Men respected him, almost feared him.

Babs said, "It isn't his child, Holly," as if it mattered whether it was Jim's child or not. It wouldn't have changed her opinion of Jim.

"He had it taken while he was in Japan. It's one of the kids at the orphanage his company helped support while he was overseas."

Holly nodded mutely. "Reckon we better move this stuff back from the walls," she suggested self-consciously.

By evening, they had the room almost finished and Holly was wiping off the baseboards with a damp cloth to get the paste off. The room smelled new: the smell of wet paper and fresh ink. And it looked … oh, it looked wonderful, with black paper and a scarlet rose design running the length of each paper. Then Holly thought, *it looks just like Babs*. It was feminine, sexy, and—one could almost see Jim Melchior carrying that big blond-haired woman into the room and throwing her onto the bed, moving with that soft, deep laugh of his.

Babs looked at the room and smiled with satisfaction. "It's a pretty room. I like pretty things," she said softly. "Sometimes I miss them. I used to have so many pretty things and go to so many pretty places and dance and dance and dance. And there were always handsome young men to tell you how pretty you looked in a new dress and …" she paused and looked at Holly. "Do you know what it's like to miss seeing handsome young men? Here they treat me like I was poison, and there …" She stopped talking, a wistful look on her face. Holly suddenly felt sorry for a woman who had so much and wanted more. She felt real sorry because she knew what it was to want.

"Maybe it won't be like that always," Holly suggested hopefully. "There's a stranger in the village, now. He come in last night on the bus. Went over to Dora and Preacher's to stay awhile."

Bab's expression became one of intense interest. "A stranger? What did he look like, Holly? Handsome? Gosh, I hope he's handsome. I get tired of looking at dirty men with filthy, crumbling cigarettes in their thin lips, and …"

"He's real good looking," Holly assured her, remembering the way the man looked standing in the store—the way he looked so wise, and worldly, and handsome.

"Well, that's something," Babs said. "What do I owe you, Holly? Will two dollars be enough?" she asked, holding out the long, green bills.

Holly took them and nodded happily. She murmured her thanks and rushed out of the house and headed across the road.

Two dollars was practically a fortune! She stepped up on the porch of the store and burst in through the screen door. For a long time she stood looking at the shelves of food, the loaves of bread, the onions and potatoes in the bins. The money would buy a real good meal!

But as always Holly realized with a letdown that the two dollars would have to make more than one meal for them. So she began, carefully, to add up the prices of the things that would go furthest. And they were just plain foods, and there would never be enough—when you ate them, you would still be hungry.

The door of the store opened, closed softly, and she turned to stare wide-eyed at the handsome stranger who called himself Larry Carter. For a moment she forgot about the food and knew an intense hunger that had nothing whatever to do with two dollars or a can of beans.

She waited, heart bounding, for the sound of that deep sensitive voice to wash over her aching muscles, to send something cooling into her blood stream.

"Hello," Larry smiled, raising his brows. He no longer wore the brown suit in which he had made his appearance the previous night. Instead, he wore casual slacks of a gray denim material and a blue cardigan sweater which was open.

His right hand had moved inside his pocket, and his right shoulder was thrust slightly forward. His free hand hung loosely at his side. Holly's glance fell to the thick-soled cloth shoes which he wore on rather large feet.

She looked away, glancing down at her own small bare feet. She saw the drab brown sackcloth dress she wore. For the second time in her entire life, she was embarrassed by her own shabbiness.

Jeb Buckley looked from the man to the woman with suspicion in his small eyes. He cleared his throat noisily and spoke much too loudly. "What did you want, Holly?"

Holly glanced at him without seeing him. She fumbled for the things she had intended to purchase. "Beans," she said without looking again at the stranger. "Beans and potatoes and a pound of side meat."

When she looked at the man again, he was smiling amusedly. The smile disappeared when Ronny came running in from the front porch. From outside rose the soft purr of Jim Melchior's truck returning for the night to the yard across the road.

"You're gonna miss it, you're gonna miss it," Ronny yelled into the dim interior of the store. His words brought life into Jeb Buckley who hurried out onto the porch. And the stranger seemed puzzled by the sudden commotion. He looked at Holly who moved forward with Milly Buckley so that they could see across the road. The strange young man moved ahead also. He seemed to think he might be left out of something, and moved onto the porch where the other men were.

Preacher's truck had backed up to the front of the store and Preacher had stopped unloading the few sacks of potatoes onto Jeb's porch. Martin Manley, a young man of delicate appearance even in dirty jeans, stood on the bed of the truck with his father, Herb.

"What is it?" Larry Carter inquired of the man nearest him, but no one paid any attention to his question. The men stood on the porch with heads turned, looking toward the Melchior yard while Jim got out of his truck and hurried inside his house.

After a moment there was the high, joyful laughter of a woman's voice, and the deeper commanding voice of a man. And suddenly the screen door of the Melchior home burst open, emitting the big and beautiful Babs Melchior. She wore a pair of blue shorts and a tight knit sweater. She was barefooted. She ran across the yard aimlessly, laughing happily.

A second later, Jim Melchior burst through the screen door and was halfway across the yard before it slammed noisily in the still September air. He seemed to leap and bound across the yard, smiling with wide, generous lips. His hands reached out suddenly as he fell on the grass. And even as he did so, his fingers twined around the ankles of Babs Melchior, and the next minute Jim and Babs were lying on the grass laughing.

In that instant, Babs faced the men across the street. For an instant the smile left her face as her eyes came to rest on Larry Carter. Then the instant passed, almost as if it had not happened, and Jim Melchior was carrying her, laughing, back into the house.

Preacher sighed loudly, ran his hand back across his heavy head of hair, and bent over the sacks of potatoes. Martin and Herb Manley followed his procedure of picking up the sacks and moving them onto the porch.

Jeb Buckley tucked a thumb inside his belt and lifted his trousers further up on his flat belly. He glanced at Larry Carter as if he were seeing him for the first time.

"Some doin', eh?" Jeb laughed insinuatingly. Larry stopped rubbing the side of his cheek with one long forefinger, and looked at Jeb questioningly.

"Yep," Jeb obliged. "Every night he comes home from work, she takes off like that and he has to catch her. Ain't it something? Just like wild beasts, eh?"

Larry Carter didn't look very happy. "Like wild beasts," he repeated with disgust.

"Well," Jeb said, coming back into the store, "ain't a man among us, I reckon, who wouldn't be delighted to do the same thing. Somethin' about the way he chases and catches her …"

"It's childish," Larry Carter announced decisively. "Why chase her when she's his wife? It's primitive."

"Reckon it kind of adds to the excitement of the capture," Jeb answered wisely. "Reckon he just likes it that way. He's that kind of man."

"She likes it that way too," Holly said defensively. Then, realizing she had spoken too boldly, she turned suddenly red and went to the counter where Jeb had laid out her groceries.

"Did you want somethin' special?" Jeb asked Larry. Holly moved back as if to leave, hesitating to hear the answer.

Larry Carter leaned against the counter, one forearm resting along its top, and his right leg stretched outward so that he looked enormously long and thin. "I think I'll stay awhile," he answered thoughtfully. He looked at Jeb a long moment.

He said, "Is there any place where I could live alone? Perhaps a small farm house, not in the village? I've work to do, and I'd rather be alone to do it. You understand, the less interruptions, the better my work can be."

Jeb scratched his chin where a day's growth of whiskers attempted to show. "Don't know of any place like that. People hereabouts live on their farms, and—No," he said, jerking his head up to look at Larry, "I reckon there might be a place at that. Seems to me there ain't anybody livin' in the old Hinkle place." He looked at Holly. "Know the place, Holly?"

Holly nodded. "It's empty all right," she said. "But there ain't much in it to live. Got an old cook stove, and a built-in bunk, and maybe a table and a chair or two. It belongs to Brandy, Jeb. It's his tenant house."

"Yeah, it does," Jeb admitted. He looked at Larry Carter. "You ain't got no furniture, have you?"

Larry smiled. "I think I could get by with a stove and a bunk. Could I move into it right away, do you think?"

Holly said, "If it was all right with Brandy, you could. Why don't you talk to Brandy?"

Larry stood up. "Where do I find this Brandy?"

"Show him, Holly," Jeb suggested.

She put her groceries on the counter again and started out of the store. "It's a long walk. You wanta go see him?"

He followed her onto the porch and they started walking down the road, Holly a little way in front of the tall handsome Larry. She pointed toward the hills and the valley that ran between them to the south.

"He lives up there on the East Hill, west side of it. The empty house is on the east side of the West Hill with the valley in the middle. 'Bout a mile and a half up there."

"Long walk, isn't it?" Larry said thoughtfully, and added, "But I think I'd like that." So they walked down the road and across the culvert and started up the sled-width path that went through the valley.

A wide creek ran beside the path for a half mile, and then Holly picked her way slowly up the side of the West Hill. She walked around beneath the oak trees, and the hickory and the walnut, her feet mashing into the leaves that had fallen and were still wet and mushy from the heavy rain.

Down below them, on their left, the creek ran on through the valley as if it were following them. After a while they came to the big thicket of pine trees, and Holly walked more slowly, avoiding the sharp-pointed needles.

"She was right," Larry Carter said softly.

Holly turned to look at him, and he added, surprised, "I was thinking out loud. Someone told me it was beautiful in these hills. They were right," he finished. She turned and walked on without looking back.

They came to what appeared to be the end of the thick undergrowth and forest and looked out onto a flat piece of land on the side of the hill. There was a group of buildings and several trees among them. The biggest building was the big black barn; and the next biggest, close to the rim of the hill, was the house. Its porch faced the valley and seemed to sit on the very brink of the ledge that formed the cliff. On the porch sat the big bearded figure of Brandy Elliot and a big black hound dog lay stretched beside his chair. Another such dog walked about the porch, stretching, and bowing its back, and emitting odd noises that sounded like a big man's waking sighs. The third dog sat in the yard under a big oak tree, watching the porch. A fourth hound dog was smelling at some bushes.

It was this dog that suddenly faced Holly and Larry. A second later as they came into the clearing, the dog began to bark fiercely.

Larry Carter halted and looked from the dog to Holly. Brandy Elliot faced them and his deep voice spoke and the animal turned silent. Holly smiled.

"They know me," she said, "but they don't know you. Brandy likes dogs," she added.

"I can see that," Larry said.

"And he keeps them for another reason, too." She was thinking of the bootlegging Brandy did—accounting for his name—but she didn't tell Larry that down at the head of the valley, just below that ledge on the East Hill, were the barrels and shed that make up Brandy's bootlegging equipment.

"Hi, ya, Holly," Brandy called, and looked disapprovingly at the tall stranger who walked so boldly beside her.

CHAPTER THREE

Brandy Elliot did not bother to rise, but he motioned to a chair toward the other end of the porch. Holly sat in it and watched the two men as they looked at each other with obvious aversion.

"Stranger around here, eh?" Brandy asked. He pulled a sack of tobacco from the pocket at the front of his blue shirt and poured a little into the white paper. Rolling it up, he licked it with the long pointed tip of his tongue and put it in the corner of his thick lips. "You musta wanted to see me," he suggested, and ran a stick match along the top of the chair. The light flared up orange, and he puffed on the limp cigarette and threw the match over the edge of the mountain with a careless gesture.

"He paints pictures," Holly said from her chair. "He wants to live in your shack on the East Hill.

"Does, eh?" Brandy looked at him suspiciously. "It ain't a very good house for a city man. Ain't anything much in it, and it's damned lonesome up there fer a man alone, I expect."

Larry leaned a shoulder against one of the worn posts that supported the roof of the porch, and picked under his fingernails with the end of a sharp stick. "I won't get lonesome," he said, without looking at Brandy. "I need privacy. To me the place sounds like it'd have that."

"You plan to stay long?" Brandy asked, "Not that I care. If you pay me twenty a month for the shack, I don't care if you die there. But it gets snowed in sometimes up there unless you got a horse and a sled to get you down off the hill."

"I hadn't thought of that. I understood it never snowed that much around here—at least until late in the winter."

Brandy raised a brow and looked at him, his eyes narrowed. "Know a lot about it, don't you? As a matter a fact, it don't usually snow till the middle of December, and maybe two or three good snows a year. Anyone of them could snow you in, though."

"I'll take the chance," Larry Carter said. "I can keep enough groceries in the place to take me through the heavy snows."

Brandy raised himself as if it were an effort he didn't want to make. He drew on the cigarette and then tossed it over the edge of the porch and down the side of the mountain. "The shack is over there," he said, pointing with his forefinger to the trees on the opposite hillside. "In a clearing up there. You can see the path along the cliff, there," he added, pointing upward and across the gaping valley between the two hills.

"You wanta see it?" Brandy asked. One of the dogs came up and sniffed at Brandy's heels, and he touched its head with a big hand, and said, "Go 'way, boy. Ain't goin' no place where I need you."

"Isn't it rather late to walk back down this hill and come up again over there? Could we make it before dark?"

Brandy nodded. "Got a swingin' bridge that goes across the valley," he said. "Down there in the bushes. Only a half mile from here up to the shack, I reckon."

They walked into the woods and came out by a swinging bridge that was wide enough to hold a single file of men. They walked across it, Brandy leading the way and Holly following behind Larry. It was maybe three hundred feet down to the valley floor. If anyone happened to fall off that bridge, there wouldn't be anything recognizable left of them.

Holly held tight to the big cable that ran along one side, high enough for a person to grab onto. Larry walked carefully ahead of her, not looking down at all, and taking short careful steps. They walked on short narrow boards that were attached to the cables, and the bridge swung back and forth from their weight and motion.

The shack was small. Brandy opened the main door that hung loosely on its hinges and squeaked as it went back against the outside of the shack. Inside, there were cobwebs, dirt on the floor, and a big gaping hole in the wall on the north end.

It was desolate looking, but Brandy said, "You could have Dick Reed fix it up a little if you wanted to. He's a carpenter, you know. Might stay sober long enough to do it."

Larry said nothing, and they walked into a lean-to that was built on the south end. It held a slab bed with a torn, dirty mattress. And to the west was the long narrow kitchen which held a wood-burning stove and a wobbly table with two chairs.

Holly looked at Larry, who had an expression of disappointment on his dark, smooth face. His lips had puckered up thoughtfully, and she spoke hurriedly.

"I could clean it up fer you," she said. "I could clean it up while Pa fixed the leaks and things. I could maybe put up some new paper and ..."

Larry was looking at her hopefully. "You could do that? You could come up here and do that and it would be all right with your folks?"

She looked startled. "Sure, it would be all right," she said quickly. She glanced at Brandy and he looked away from her.

"I suppose I could have some furniture shipped in," Larry said thoughtfully, running a forefinger along his sharp chin. "I could get some paper for you to put up, too, and some curtains ..." he paused, smiled pleasantly, and added, "I think it will be all right." He pulled out a roll of bills from his hip pocket and handed two of them to Brandy. "Twenty dollars a month," he said, and put the rest back into his pocket.

Later, Larry stood and looked back into the place. He smiled that same mysterious satisfied way as if he expected something special to come of that shack. Brandy nudged Holly, and they walked away ahead of Larry.

When he caught up with them, they had reached the shack in which Brandy lived. They all went inside and sat down by the big fireplace, which Brandy lit because the sky was getting dark and a chill had come into the autumn air.

Over the fireplace, supported by two curved pegs, was the big, ten-gauge shotgun, shining blue in the waning light. Holly looked at it and then she turned to Larry. He also had been staring at it.

She said, "He always keeps the shotgun there. He likes guns about him."

Brandy looked at her. He frowned, and then said, "I reckon you wouldn't like somethin' to warm your insides?"

Larry glanced up inquiringly. He smiled. "Yes, I would. I've heard they make good liquor in these hills."

Brandy smiled appreciatively. He went out, and, after a moment he returned with a big gallon jar. He poured a half glass of the reddish liquid from the jar and handed it to Larry, then he poured himself a full one.

Larry sipped, smiled, nodded his head up and down. "It's good," he said, and quickly drank the rest of it.

Brandy smiled. "Yep," he said, gulping his own drink. "I make it good and tasty. Ain't no fun in drinkin' the stuff if it ain't got a good, mellow taste to it."

Brandy poured again, and the two men drank while Holly watched. It was difficult for her to keep her eyes off the younger man. Somehow, something about his spread legs—his long outstretched, spread legs—kept pulling her eyes back to him. She watched the lean waist and the way his trousers were pulled up so that a little of his bright, plaid socks showed above the edge of his slippers.

Brandy saw her looking, and Holly looked straight at him for a long moment. She didn't care if he saw her look at the younger man. She didn't care who saw her look. What she saw there was something special and different, and she wanted it desperately.

An impatience took hold of her, and she stood up. "It's dark already," she said thickly. "We better go back."

Obediently, Larry stood up. His face was flushed under his dark olive complexion, and his eyes glowed with a dark fire. "Yes," he agreed.

"I better go along," Brandy suggested, picking up a heavy plaid jacket and putting his arms into it.

"No," Holly said sharply. "Ain't no use you goin'." She looked at him with a hard gleam in her blue eyes. "You don't have to worry none with Larry along. He can take care of me."

Brandy hesitated, seemed about to ignore her, and slowly removed the jacket. He sank down in the rocker before the fireplace, and looked for an instant at the shotgun as they went out into the darkness.

She walked ahead of Larry down the path. Once she turned to look back at him and wait until he caught up with her. She said, "It's nice when it's dark. You can smell the niceness."

He stopped and looked at her. For an instant there was a friendly, almost hungry look about his lips in the darkness. She almost felt his breath on her cheeks and she leaned a little toward him so that she could see him better, and so that she could feel the warmth on her face from the sweet smell of his breath.

"How old are you?" he asked suddenly.

She looked down at her flat chest and her flatter belly. "Almost nineteen," she said slowly, as if the young age were a disgrace.

"You don't look that old," he said, thoughtfully. "I would have said you were sixteen at the most."

She kept looking at the ugly front of her dress that showed no signs of development, and she felt the nearness of him pulling at her until she leaned further toward him in the darkness. She felt it until the ache came into her stomach and her legs, and she felt the hard pointed beads of her breasts rising with need. She felt them pushing against the hard unrelenting band which she wore pinned about them, and she could have torn it off with the madness and the desire that was in her.

She faced at him, and he no longer had that look. His face was still flushed with the moonshine, and his teeth gleamed white as she smiled in the darkness. She turned abruptly, humiliated, and ran on down the hillside toward the village.

He came running after her and at last he caught her hand by the edge of the woods that opened on to the road. He pulled her about.

"What's wrong with you?" he demanded. "What are you running away from?"

His hands bit into her wrist, and she twisted it away from him and stared at him angrily. She wouldn't tell him that she was not a child, and he was a man. She wouldn't tell him that beneath that ugly dress was the body of a woman and the blushing, youthful breasts of a girl who wanted her man. She walked ahead of him to the road, and there she said good night, and walked hurriedly on up the opposite way toward her own house.

Going up the step to the porch, she remembered the food she had left at the store and reluctantly turned and went back to get it. As she passed the Tincher house, she saw a light go on in the guest room, and she knew that it was *his* light.

Preacher came out of the house and stepped onto the road. He spoke to her as if she were a child and walked a little way beside her down the bank to the culvert. There, he turned off toward the north, taking the valley path up the creek through the woods, and Holly swore softly. Preacher was going to the woman who lived on the small farm up there in the north woods. He was going there, and the woman would lay with him and be happy with herself.

Holly cursed the woman who was able to get men; she cursed her because she could have them while Holly went hungry, and ached with a wild passion inside her that cried wildly to get out.

Finally returning from the store, Holly went inside and put the groceries on the kitchen table. After a moment, Alice came in and put them away. Holly moved off into her own room, throwing back a glance at Alice Reed.

Inside, she closed the door and locked it. She stood in front of the one small mirror, and her hands were claws that snatched at the throat of her dress and ripped it away down the middle. They grabbed maliciously at the white band about her chest, and the band came off revealing her full rounded breasts, pushing out and upward and hurting. She looked down at the naked white belly and the lean, throbbing thighs. Then she threw herself angrily on the filthy bed and cried into the dirty mattress until she went to sleep, and the aches stopped …

CHAPTER FOUR

Nellie Byrd stood on the porch of her small white and green farm house. Dick Reed had finished with his work and gone down the valley whistling to himself in the cool evening air, and carrying the quart of moonshine Nellie had given him for making her bedroom beautiful.

The bedroom was her business, and she had to make the best of it to keep that business coming and satisfied and happy. Dick Reed had wanted to try it out, but he went away without meeting her in there. He wasn't the man that could break in that bedroom. No man who ever came there was the man for that job, but at least one of them came nearer to it than the others. So she could stand on the porch in her thin black veil with the slight breeze blowing it against her long legs, and out behind her like a wedding gown. She could stand there and wait because he never failed her, and he would come soon after the sun took the darkness away.

She had done considerable waiting in her thirty-three years in this deserted, hungry country. It hadn't always been for this one particular man. There had been much waiting before she realized what it was that she wanted: years that had been listless, unimaginative, hopeless. It was the way all people lived in the hills—from one moment to the next without thinking of the future and the reason people lived at all when there was nothing to live for. They needed nothing, no more than the day's work in the fields or in the timber. They needed no more than the year's crop of tobacco which would bring them enough money to keep them alive on beans and potatoes. That would last until the spring when the gardens were grown with fresh vegetables, and crops began again. The endless circle of nothingness, going nowhere and never ending.

And she had been alone in her waiting.... But once—she could just remember once when she had not been alone. That had been when she didn't know what it was she wanted. That had been when she was younger ...

A little girl in pigtails running through the woods, chirping like the sparrow, mooing like the cows, and crawling through the tall grass by the creek to sneak up on the Indians. They had been gone for years, but they came back to drink from the creek for a little girl in pigtails.

And there had been a heavy, large woman with her print dress wrinkling over her fat hips, and sweat oozing over her hairy upper lip. The woman always called to her just when the Indians were all gathered and bathing in the creek, and she had to go away before they were finished.

Rose Byrd had been a righteous woman who was ashamed of human nature, and she never let Nellie forget that shame. When Nellie had been just a child barely weaned away from the big fat breasts of Rose Byrd, the man had run away with another woman. Rose Byrd never let Nellie forget it.

Men were ugly and beastly and sinful. They were something that came to you in a hot summer's bed and demanded to mash your breasts with big fat hands, and drive at your soft pink flesh with hard unrelenting passion, madness and beast-like hunger. Rose made it quite clear how men were with women.

One day Nellie ran down the slope of the bank at the creek while trying to get a better look at her invisible Indians bathing in the creek. She ran into the water and thrashed at them, trying to find them, trying to touch the hard unrelenting flesh that Rose spoke about. But in the end she had to crawl out of the creek with disappointment. She lay in the tall grass with her face buried and her soft young body pressing insistently against the earth.

She lay there until she found the Indian. Then she rolled over on her back and bowed it, and lifted her knees toward the bright morning sun and felt the hurt from his big hard body pressing against her. It was a delicious, realistic and hungry dream.

And then she opened her eyes, slowly, reluctantly and looked at the big fat face of Rose Byrd staring down at her with piercing angry eyes. The thing in Nellie died and the shame rose up in her like a devil that screamed out hysterically into the still morning air.

Her hand felt like a leaden weight and she lifted it slowly, painfully, until it was near her breasts. Her face grew hot, and she knew that the thing was in her arms and written across her twisted lips in big heavy black scrawls: *shame … shame!* The eyes kept staring down at her and the shame was also in them, staring, accusing … disgusted.

She rolled over on her belly and dug her hands into the grass and clawed at it, and the sobs broke loose. But she knew that the eyes still stared accusingly down at her.

After that day, Nellie never went alone to the creek. Whenever she walked out of the house, Rose followed her watching her. She was never to forget that shameful moment by the creek.

Rose talked to her, lectured her, preached. And at last the shame grew heavy inside the girl, so heavy that the outside of her mind began to see that men were ugly and beastly, and the thing they did with their women was dirty, defiling and sinful.

For a long time, Nellie Byrd lived for just the days and the winters when she could go to school. Her one salvation was in her being clean, unreasonably pure for the rest of her life.

When she was fourteen, she began the long walk to the town high school, and afterward she went away to college. But she was enrolled only a year.

People said that Nellie Byrd was an old maid. They said that she was fine and good and wholesome, and no one talked about her the way people usually talked about girls in the hills. She kept herself plain but clean, and she learned from books. She was given charge of the village grade school, and she taught it carefully and with all her heart. The years had wiped away her shame, and she could hold her head high, and proud, and know that she was serving a purpose in life through her teaching.

Even after Rose Byrd died of a heart attack, Nellie Byrd went on with her teaching and her living alone in her own small, wholesome world.

It wasn't until she was twenty-nine that things began to change. Somehow, the children became irritable, and Nellie Byrd frequently lost patience. When she found the hole in the partition between the two toilets that stood in the back yard of the school, she swore softly for the first time in her life and tried to find the culprit who was responsible. When she found him, she whipped him with a vengeance that admitted her secret satisfaction from the incident.

And when she saw the bigger boys chasing the small girls, she would fly into a rage and bring out the board. She'd spank their lean buttocks with a pleasure she dared not admit.

In the afternoons when she had to say good-by to them and sit for hours going over their papers, she would stare at the narrow walls of the one-room school; she would stare with a blankness and an emptiness and a hunger that rose up inside her.

She was sitting this way one afternoon when the big boy with fuzz on his cheeks and the dumb illiterate look on his face came back to tell her he couldn't come to school on Friday.

"I gotta help Pa with the crop," he explained, standing there in the doorway with his legs spread apart and the front of his overalls tight against his thighs.

He was a big boy—so large and heavy and strong. He was the oldest boy in the school and not the least bit bright. But he was so big—even for sixteen, he was big, bigger than any man she had ever seen standing there. And she looked at him with a sudden overwhelming ache in her.

"I'm sorry about that, Ricky," she said slowly, watching him as he looked at her. He looked with the eyes of a man, and he looked with disgust and a sneer on his thick, fuzzy lips. He turned to leave and suddenly she couldn't let him go. She stood up uncertainly and called to him. When he turned, she froze like a chunk of hot ice and her legs wouldn't move.

"You sick or somethin'?" he asked suspiciously, watching her. She had sank back slowly into the chair and now she smiled, slowly.

"Come here, Ricky," she said carefully. "I want to talk to you. Close the door."

He closed the door and came forward, eyeing her with a strange uncertain look as he stopped beside her desk.

"You're the boy I whipped for carving that hole in the toilet wall. Why did you do that? You never told me why you did that."

The sneer was back on his thick lips, and he looked at her with secretive eyes. "So I could look," he said. "I looked lots a time, but you spanked me once and you ain't gonna spank me no more. Ain't nothing wrong with lookin'. Can't hurt 'em, any. 'Sides, I seen girls before, lots of times."

Nellie Byrd looked down at her hands, twisting the papers on the desk, mashing them, tearing them as she worked them into long curled stubs. "Just girls?" she choked. "You've only seen girls?"

"Well," he moved his big feet uncomfortably. He had never talked to a woman about such things. Women didn't talk about it. "I seen Pa take the cows out to Jason's to see the bull."

Nellie shivered, pulled her legs tight against each other, and sat forward, suddenly brave and anxious and aching. "But never a woman?" She lifted a hand to her own breasts, and ripped the buttons that fastened the blouse neatly over them. Underneath, the lace of her slip spread and hinted, and the boy's eyes grew large and his face flushed.

"A boy as big as you are should have seen a woman by now," she said, and caught her fingers in the lace and tore it. She held one firm hard breast in her fingers and looked at him. "Go on. Touch it. I'll bet a boy as big as you are could do something to a woman ..." Her voice trailed off, quivered as the boy's hand touched her bare flesh. Her own hand slid over his, grabbed it, pushed it into her flesh with an insistence that startled the lad so that he pulled back.

She stood up, crying out to him not to leave. She forgot all the purity and wholesomeness and decency which she had worked so diligently to build. Standing there before the startled boy, she tore off the skirt and the slip and the thin shimmering underclothes. She threw herself against the hard, unrelenting, probing flesh of the boy.

Suddenly, the boy broke loose from her arms, and the door of the school slammed, and Nellie Byrd stood a moment in frozen anger. Then she turned around and ripped the papers to shreds. Her fingers tore at them, threw them on the floor, and her legs carried her across the room to the blackboard. The erasers burst against the windows of the school, and her fists hammered the blackboard with merciless anger.

After a moment, she stood still. She was trembling and she knew quite at once and without any doubt, or shame, or humiliation that she had discovered the want inside her. She knew the purpose of her life, and she knew what she wanted from life. Very carefully she put her clothes back on. She pinned the blouse, and she walked with her head high up the valley to her own house in the woods.

She stopped by the creek where she had seen the Indians, and she saw them again, this time with a smile. There was no need for a dream now.

She entered her house and went to bed. The next day when she returned to school the lady was there. The lady told her she was unfit to be a school teacher, and Nellie Byrd smiled.

All her life she had hated the children and the teaching, the daily routine that made her come to school at eight o'clock and to look at dirty-faced children. She loathed the stringy hair of the girls with their long skinny legs, scratched knees and grinning yellow teeth. She hated the illiterate faces of the boys with the fuzz on their fat faces, the fuzz on the back of their necks, and their baggy, patched overalls, and the bruised, naked knees.

All the years of her teaching she had hated it. And now she was glad that it was over. The pretense had dropped away and she had come out of her shell like a young moth, fresh and alive, eager for life as she knew it and wanted it.

There was a new teacher, a younger one: a tiny wisp of a girl in a bright cotton dress who wouldn't have any secret desires like Nellie Byrd.

Nellie walked out of the schoolhouse, and headed down the narrow black-topped road into the village. She walked past the Reed house and her hips swayed as she walked. She moved on like a woman in a dream. She went on past the Tincher house, and she called out a hello to Dora Tincher, and smiled the way Nellie Byrd had never smiled, with wisdom, knowledge and happiness.

She saw that Preacher Tincher had his truck backed up to the store porch and was unloading sacks of potatoes. Nellie Byrd walked up to the porch and stopped near him. She looked straight into his eyes, and then she looked down the thick heavy body, and back again to his eyes. And there was a light in his eyes when she looked back.

Watching him, it was as if she said, "I know all about you, Preacher. I know about your women and your bastard kids. I know you real well, and pretty soon you will know me also." And then she flipped her hips about and walked into the store. There were a few things she didn't need but which she bought. When she came out again, Preacher's eyes were on her back. She knew that he would not fail her.

In the evening, she bathed in the creek and went back to the house where she put on a cotton dress that opened down the front. She wore nothing under the dress.

There were fresh sheets on her bed. They smelled of soap, clean air, and a bit of perfume which she had kept secreted for so long. She hadn't known why she bought that perfume so long ago, nor why she bought the other things; the rouge, the powder, the black eyebrow pencil. Now she knew why and she used them.

Just after dark, she lit one single lamp in the living room. She put a smaller one with a thick pink shade on it in the bedroom on the stand. She lit it also and a dim rosy glow filled the room, and she felt good … marvelous … lustful.

When the knock came on the door, she was lying back in the big chair by the library stand. She called, "Come in."

He came in slowly, almost uncertainly, and when he looked at her, the uncertainty fled and he smiled. "I heard you wasn't working at the school anymore."

Nellie Byrd watched him push the hair back from his forehead. He stood there like a large stallion, with his big hands tucked into the pockets of his trousers. She giggled without intending to, giggled because she knew so much about him.

When she got up, she felt his eyes on her and heard his big heavy feet following her into the bedroom. She smiled to herself. It was so easy … so very easy.

She unbuttoned the dress, slowly, leisurely, with the knowledge women are born with. As she neared the last button, she saw him stepping out of his own trousers. Then he grabbed her and threw her onto the bed.

For a while, she was clothed in a sodden fear that numbed her legs, clouded her brain. But then the fear … slowly … gently …

Afterward, she lay a long time while she watched him dress. The tranquility that was in her made her smile, and her flesh glowed, satisfied.

On his face was the look of accomplishment, of attainment, and she smiled because she knew why it was there. He had not expected a virgin, and somehow, to Preacher Tincher, it was an unexpected treasure.

He started to go out, and she said slowly, in a deep voice that was new and womanly and wise, "Two dollars … put it on the dresser, dear."

He looked surprised, smiled slowly, winked, and put the two dollars on the dresser. When he walked out, she got up and looked at the window. In the half-light of a quarter moon, she saw him striding down the hillside to the valley.

And how often, how very often she had stood waiting on the porch, knowing he would come. And how very much she had learned in these three years since quitting school. He had taught her many things, and she had taught him—the things a woman instinctively learns and knows about the life she wants, and has to live, and needs.

Now, as she leaned against the post in her new dress, with her perfect new bedroom a reality, she waited for him to come to her. When she glimpsed his large figure through the trees, she went inside to wait.

CHAPTER FIVE

Threading his way through the bushes along the creek that followed the North Valley, Karl "Preacher" Tincher reflected on the past which had brought him thus far to this unfavorable disgraceful crossroad of his life.

For many years now, he had been slowly degenerating into a listless, lustful and illiterate beast. He felt this more pronounced each time he visited Nellie Byrd, and yet the habit had become a part of his daily need, a vengeance against what he did not yet know.

He considered the years behind him: his mild, sheltered and religious youth; the careful coaching under his foster parents on the little farm outside Edsville where he had attended high school and studied so hard to become a local preacher.

In those years, there had been no time for the physical pleasures, and no desire for them. His entire world was in the small, impoverished attic room, where he kept his books and his Bible, and the schoolhouse where he learned how to use those same books and Bible.

He had lived an ascetic kind of life entirely suited to his desires, working toward one large, luminous goal: to preach. Preaching was in his body, in his brain, and it bubbled over his lips in rich, ripe words of encouragement and dark, frightening warnings of sin and lust and shame and women.

Everything a man could desire, he had found in his pulpit as acting minister of the small church near the village. He had obtained that lofty and revered position at the early age of twenty-two. And he had maintained it to the satisfaction of himself, and the congregation—at least he had done so until quite recently.

In the front pew was seated, always, a tall narrow-shouldered young woman with small hidden breasts and wide, generous hips. She sat there with her thin mouth open. In the evening, under the yellow lights, her teeth would gleam, and the tip of her tongue would flick outward and up as she murmured "Amen" to his ever-important denouncement of sin.

In time, he began to look forward to his sermons from a standpoint of whether she would be there ... whether *she* would like what he had to say. And it was inevitable that they should finally meet and marry.

Everyone said it was a perfect match: the quiet, reserved, tall young lady and the young preacher. They moved into a house in the village, and for a while his sermons were richer and fuller, and his voice was deep and hopeful. And then, somehow, it began to change, and he began to change. And now he had come to this—this visiting with Alice Reed, with Nellie Byrd and with the farmers' wives in the surrounding hills.

He knew definitely of three bastard kids he had fathered. There was the first one, nearly nine years old now, and not knowing that its father wasn't really killed in an automobile two weeks before it was born. The first one was a boy—and they saw each other often, this boy and the father.

He bent his head, shamed, remembering that incident. He had been called by one of the farmers at the store one evening. There had been a heavy storm, and the night was wet and muddy. The rain came down in ice cold sheets, signaling the coming of winter.

The farmer said there was an illness at the Barker farm, and would the Preacher please go to comfort the family and speak to the sick one.

Preacher took his truck, which he had only recently purchased to help supplement the small pay which the country church paid to him, and he drove up to the South Valley as far as the big double wheels of the truck would go through the mud. Then he walked and walked through the rain, with his hat brim pulled downward and his plaid jacket turned up about his hairy throat.

He had never been to the Barker farm before. They were a fairly new people, and he did not know how many were in that family. But it wasn't important to a man who served God. The important thing was for him to talk to the sick, and so he was angry when he arrived and there was no illness.

At first, he planned to say that the people in his territory were trustworthy, decent people. But a young girl looked at him with wide pleading eyes across an almost barren supper table, and he forgot to be angry.

There was the young girl, small but mature, the old grandmother and the old man with the cane. Soon it was apparent that they wanted to talk to him about the young girl. So he sat by the fire and dried his clothes and listened to them.

"We ain't been in these here parts long," the old man said, punching at the fireplace with the tip of his cane. "And I reckon it ain't very pleasant for a young one like Belle, there. She had a boyfriend over in Devil's Valley, but she ain't got none now, and a girl gettin' her age ..." He paused and grinned with big, jutting yellow teeth. "Me and Ma, here, we got 'nuf to worry us. We ain't so young anymore."

Preacher looked at the girl and turned back at once to the blazing fire. The steam was beginning to roll off his jacket, and the heat of it burned at his flesh. He wondered why he just continued to sit there staring at the fire instead of moving back.

"Reckon the preacher would know a young man for our Belle," the little old lady spoke up to her husband. She sat in a rocker, her fingers shaking as she threaded a needle.

Preacher looked at her, thought about moving back, and knew suddenly why he didn't. The girl, Belle, stood directly behind him, her arm on the top of his chair.

Afterward, they talked about the farm and the weather, and Preacher said he would look into the matter. "That's hardly in my line, you know," he explained, and was ready to leave when the rain came down again, hard and unrelenting.

"Reckon you'll have to stay the night," the old man said, closing the door.

Preacher was aware suddenly of the small house. It appeared to have three rooms: a kitchen, the big living room, and what might be a bedroom off to the right of the fireplace.

He shook his head. The old man said, "Sure. You can sleep on a pallet by the fire. The girl sleeps over by the kitchen doorway. Got a mattress she pulls outa the bedroom fer that."

He remembered that night very well indeed. For he had lain a long time before that fireplace, feeling the girl's eyes on him from the darkness across the room. He couldn't see her, but he knew that she saw him in the light of the fire. And that night something began to stir inside of him—something strange and different than anything he had ever known.

His wife, Dora, never stirred him like that. After they were married, he had been gentle and sweet with her. Love, he said to himself, came afterward. Respect was enough to begin with in a marriage—respect and virginity. But somehow there had never been the satisfaction he wanted from Dora.

He found her sharp-tempered, impatient and belittling. And when in desperation, he reverted to the animal in him and pulled her roughly to him and took her quickly, she said that he was a beast. He was a hairy dog, Dora said of him. And after that, when in anger and in hunger, he took his wife, he always felt the tinge of guilt, shame and filth upon him.

His relationship with Dora became less satisfactory and more infrequent. It happened only when, as he told, her, it was as God would wish it. He would tell her, "God said to marry and to replenish the earth." But she would say to him, "You're like a beast, Karl. You're dirty and like a beast."

He thought about his relationship with Dora as he lay there before the fire with the girl's eyes on him. And he knew that Dora had never been able to stir the feeling that was in him now.

It seemed hours that he twisted and turned, trying to drive out the unhappiness that made him susceptible to the admiring glance of a young girl. He told himself the important role he had to play in his religion. He reminded himself of all that God was to him.

Then he thought of the child he and Dora had never had, and he felt anger rise within him. And when he might have been strong enough to go to sleep, he felt her body close in against him there by the fireplace.

There had been no questions, no refusals—simply the giving and the taking—and when it was over, he said to himself that it was a good thing he had done. He had made a girl happy, and he had not hurt her; she was not a virgin.

But there had come the boy that he could not claim.

Yes. A stranger had given Karl Tincher a son. Not his wife, but a hungry, lustful woman who was a stranger in his bed.

Afterward, he felt himself pulled slowly into the whirlpool of sin, and he did not try to avoid it. There were other women, some of them many times over. Some of them, like Nellie Byrd, tasted life for the first time through his body—a body he had once dedicated to the service of God ... And the change grew until he knew that he was as Dora said, a beast.

Walking up the valley toward Nellie's house, he felt suddenly and irrevocably unclean. For so long he had lived this double life for the village people and the farmers: preaching on Thursday nights when the regular pastor was away; on Sunday night telling the people how to live the way he knew people should live—the way he didn't live any longer.

They listened to him, liked him. Some of them knew that he was not a fit preacher, but they never said it aloud. There was Holly Reed who had come upon him with Nellie one afternoon. Holly Reed knew that he was a beast.

And there was the young, girlish son of Herb Manley who followed Holly around with that dead-calf look on his face. He knew too because he had been with Holly that afternoon when they came up the valley to Nellie's place.

It was a funny thing about Holly Reed and the boy, Martin Manley. Preacher had seen them many times swimming in the creek or sitting under a tree with the boy, Martin, leafing through a stack of note paper, and talking ... always talking and looking at Holly as if he thought she were something completely new to him—so new that he dared not touch her.

Preacher had thought about Holly himself, once. But only once. Last night when the stranger arrived on the bus, and Holly had stood with that odd expression on her face—he knew that expression and had been nearly surprised enough to joke about it. Except that, in a way, she was so much like Jim Melchior that he didn't dare joke.

Holly would be like Jim Melchior if she loved a man: stubborn, insistent and possessive. And every man knew how Jim Melchior would be about his woman.

He wished he could feel the same possessiveness for Dora. If she had held her patience with him or if she had given him a child … He had nothing. He was completely void and empty. Life was a mountain which you kept trying to climb, but you always slid back as far as the step you had just taken. And then it seemed you went nowhere except downhill.

Finally he had reached the bottom of that hill, and the depression and anger was deep inside him. It was like a boulder, crushing his guts, pinching his chest.

Nellie Byrd opened the door to him, took one look at his stone-like expression, and led him into her new bedroom. He didn't wait for her to take her clothes off. The thin, lovely gown in which she had wanted to dedicate her new room was no handicap to Preacher Tincher.

He threw her back on the bed with a big, strong arm, and unleashed his anger upon her. And when it was over, he walked heavily into the living room and sat down by the lamp. He buried his head in his hands.

"It's rotten, Nellie!" he cried at last. "It's rotten! I come here for no other reason than to shame you. To vent my anger. I've been trying to explain to myself why I'm angry, and I don't know that I've discovered the reason even now. I feel like I've been tricked. Do you know what it feels like to be tricked, Nellie?" he asked, turning savagely on her.

She seemed not to hear him, but picked up an undergarment on which she had been sewing. Her fingers began to work nimbly through the cloth.

"I can remember when I was a decent man. I could hold my head up and be proud, and I could talk to God. Yes, literally, I could talk to him," he spat angrily. "But now! Why should I talk to him now? I spent all my life building something for God—denying myself the things most men want—pleasures: a woman to sleep with, moonshine to make a man feel brave, cigarettes to calm a man's nerves. I had none of them. I was a servant of God. I did everything He wanted me to do. I married a pure woman, and she turned into a gossip, a hypocrite. I wanted a child and I got a barren wife. I asked so little in return for my servitude and I got nothing!" He looked at her helplessly. "I've been tricked," he spat angrily.

Nellie Byrd got up slowly and walked into the kitchen while he watched her. She came back with a jug of moonshine, pink and pretty in the yellow light, and she uncorked it and handed it to him.

"Drink," she said, and raised it to his lips. He drank and leaned back slowly while she sat the jug on the stand beside him. When she went back to her chair, he looked at her again.

"I've been going downhill instead of uphill, Nellie. I've been getting more and more rotten all the time, living in filth. And it ain't because I want to live that way. If I wanted to live that way, I wouldn't feel ashamed and I wouldn't hate myself for it and I wouldn't be …" he was searching for the right way to say it, and went on … "I wouldn't be such a beast. I guess it's because I'm angry—angry with God." He paused, his eyes suddenly popping out with fright and the sweat coming through the pores of his forehead, a cold clammy sweat.

"Angry with God …" he murmured with sudden realization. "Angry because I gave him so much, asked so little, and got nothing. Angry because I married a selfish, suspicious woman, a woman who couldn't give me a child!"

She looked at him now and nodded slowly. "Yes. I could have told you that a long time ago. It's in the way … you take me. The way you take them all. With a vengeance and anger, and almost sadistic pleasure. Yes," she murmured slowly, "I could have told you that."

He slapped his palm downward on the tabletop, jarring the jug of moonshine which he seemed to see for the first time. He put it to his lips and drank deeply.

"What am I going to do, Nellie? How much further can I go? Maybe God will get impatient with my anger. Maybe he—" He stopped, startled, and said slowly, "I wish I knew what to do. Right now I almost feel there isn't a God. God isn't cruel, and yet what is this life of mine but cruelty? Nothing—anger and beastliness and nothing."

She said, "You'll find a way to believe again, Preacher. You'll find a way to stop the anger."

For a while he said nothing. He sat there while the moonshine set his body aflame, warmed his feet and calmed his mind. And then, finally, he stood up and went to the door and disappeared into the darkness.

Nellie Byrd sat a moment staring at the floor of her house. It seemed to her that all people wanted so little and got nothing. What she wanted was not far away: the man she had waited for ever since she could remember, but who would never come to her. She asked only for that one man, but she never got him. Instead she got a substitute, and how much longer would she have even that?

CHAPTER SIX

Jim Melchior helped close up the garage in which he worked in Edsville as a mechanic. He pulled the big steel doors to and locked them with the large Yale lock. Bob Farley, the owner, called good-by and went out the smaller single door. Bob was a wealthy, fat little man who looked soft and too well fed. He enjoyed making smart cracks about women, marriage and love.

Jim went into the washroom and began to bathe and change into clean clothes. He liked to be clean when he went home to Babs. Being clean was an important thing to him, a religious habit. Somehow, in being clean, a man could feel that he deserved all the soft, feminine beauty of a girl like Babs.

In the beginning, it had been difficult to believe that it could happen to him. A big, tall, almost skinny man with a homely, honest-looking face—it was ridiculous for him to wish for someone as lovely as his wife. But in the end, he had learned to believe. He could accept the fact that his dream had come true, really happened to him, the chosen man, the homely man.

It was strange how he had met Babs—purely an accident that a soldier might dream about and wish for, but which would never actually happen to him. He was visiting the NCO club in Los Angeles, California, just before he was to be shipped overseas from the port of Long Beach. And there she was: a tall, creamy blonde with long silky hair, and round full breasts.

She slipped into his awkward arms like a phantom, and he danced with her with his big thin mouth open in amazement, and his eyes bugging out like a schoolboy having his first look at a female in the suit she was born in.

He found out all about her that night too, but only because she kept talking while he was too stupefied to speak. She had once been a model. He could easily understand that. She seemed to like a quiet man with strong arms, a man who was taller than she and who had the look of strength about him.

He wrote to her from overseas. He told her all the things he had wanted to tell her in person: about the place where he had been raised, and the silly, friendly people he knew. He told her about his plans for the future and he told her that he had fallen in love with her, that he wanted to see her again.

Much to his surprise, he did see her again. He met her when he returned eighteen months later. He married her in Mexico and he then brought her back home.

There was a great deal he didn't know about Babs when he married her, much that he still didn't know. But it seemed enough that anyone as beautiful as she could love him. He needed no questions and no answers. As far as he was concerned everything was perfect.

He remembered that first night in a small motel by the ocean. It was a dirty little room with sunlight coming in the window and the ocean roaring outside and sounding like the bass fiddle in a band. He remembered her standing across the room from him, her eyes wide and her lips parted—those full, rich lips that he had barely touched, and which he could now taste to the satisfaction of his every wild, lustful desire.

They both laughed, looking at each other across the room. And then the spell was broken and he grinned as he started toward her. She took off in that silly, teasing way she still used. When he caught her, he picked her up and held her while he very carefully unbuttoned her clothes. He stripped her with the sunlight gleaming across her pink and cream body, and her large rich breasts close to him. He kissed her the way he had dreamed ... with passion and a prolonged anticipation. He kissed the tips of her small delicately shaped ears, the throbbing cup in the center of her throat, and the moist hollow pits of her arms with their fresh soap smell ... and the tips of those perky breasts with the odor of woman about them. Woman—lovely ... and his!

He kept kissing her even while he climbed out of his own clothes. Then when he stood against her, warm and naked, she laughed. It was a deep, sensual laugh. Then, after that, came that moment, that instant that seemed barely to exist—a second that was spun in the sunshine of invisible little threads that wrapped them together in space.

And this hadn't changed in the years of their marriage. Instead, it had grown better, richer and deeper. They learned to know each other, to love without passion and to fulfill this love with passion.

He learned about her love of fine clothes and he gave them to her gladly, knowing that he alone would be allowed to admire and then discard them, revealing the life underneath. He learned of her laughter—her deep, haunting, teasing laughter. And he learned the little things she did that made his heart lift, his blood pound in his veins and his body respond.

He went home to her and she did not speak to him. Instead she laughed and then he laughed. She ran into the yard and he ran after her and fell beside her, then to pick her up and carry her into the house.

He took her into the bedroom, and for a moment he looked at the beautiful room she had created for their love, and he loved her more.

And when it was over, he was reminded of something he had known for a long time. He was aware of what she meant to him. She was his life. Everything he had wanted, she was. And if anything ever happened to her …

He stood and watched her slip into a robe, her blonde hair falling over her shoulders, disarranged and wanton looking.

She saw him watching her and she smiled. She came over and pinched his chest. He slapped her hand playfully and she shoved her face forward against him. Feeling her teeth against him, he grabbed her.

"Lovely, lovely Babs," he murmured into her hair. "You always make me so happy, Babs!"

She pulled back and reached up and gave him a quick playful kiss. Then she twisted out of his arms and laughter was in her voice.

She was unusually quiet during supper, and he kept thinking about the years of their marriage, their love and their future. He mulled over something that had been on his mind for a long time.

"Babs," he said at last, "why don't we have a kid?"

He thought she looked startled and he said hurriedly, "I don't want to rush it, honey, but ain't we been married long enough for a kid?"

She hesitated. "I—yes, I suppose we have. Only …" she looked at him pleadingly.

"Only what, honey?" he prompted.

"Well," she said, fingering her fork uncomfortably, "couldn't we wait just a little longer? It—I don't know, but I keep thinking about—about what it does to a woman."

He laughed, and buttered a biscuit and bit into it. "Only for a while. It don't stay that way," he assured her.

"It's much more fun just to make love, Jim," she said quietly.

When he looked at her, she was staring down at her plate, and he thought she was going to cry. "Gosh, honey, it don't keep a man from making love!"

"But there would be the kid, and we wouldn't be as happy. We'd have to be more careful and sort of hide …" Her voice trailed off.

He got up and went around to the end of the table and put his hands on her shoulders. He bent over and kissed the top of her head.

"I thought you'd want one," he said. "A man ain't a man till he's had a kid, Babs," he announced, grinning, and walked toward the door.

"I'm goin' over to the store for a while. Maybe play some rook with the fellows." He smiled at her and winked. "Don't make up the bed," he finished, and went out knowing full well that when he returned the bed would be made up again, that she would be freshly bathed again, and that she would be waiting for him.

That was one thing he liked about Babs most: she loved him just as much as he loved her. She didn't try to hide it from him either, and she didn't pretend not to like his kisses.

"That's the kind of a woman a man needs," he thought happily. "Gives it to you 'cause she likes it." He smiled and walked across the road to the store.

CHAPTER SEVEN

Babs Melchior got up from the table and carefully washed and dried the dishes. When she had straightened the kitchen, she pulled down the shades and made herself a pan of hot water. Then she bathed luxuriously, and changed into fresh skimpy night clothes.

Afterward, she stood in the bedroom and brushed her long blonde hair into waves with ringlets at the bottom parting over her shoulders. She would look good for him when he came back from the store.

Strange, she thought, that she really did love Jim Melchior. It hadn't been sudden, the way it was with him. It had come to her after that first night in their marriage bed. Then it came to her steadily afterward—and in spite of the guilt she sometimes felt.

Oh, it wasn't about the loving that she felt guilty. It was the knowledge that their marriage wasn't really legal, and why it wasn't legal, and the fact that Jim didn't know about it.

She had been just another little stage-struck girl in a big city—a lonely young girl with a good body and no use for it. And in the end, she hadn't been a model at all, but a cheap little five-dollar-a-night whore.

It came about because she had to eat and not because it was in her to be cheap. It happened because she was lovely, desirable and hungry, and men saw this and offered to pay for it.

While she was in the madam's house, it had been more or less decent. She had gotten a commission there, and she had met some important men who pretended to be interested in her future. But they always forgot their promise after the act was finished.

She had met Larry Carter that way. He was one of the important men who had come to the house. The difference was that Larry Carter kept coming back, kept wanting her for his own. And without intending to, she had at last given in to him and married him.

For a while it was all right, their marriage. But as Larry worked less and less, and got poorer and poorer, he kept insisting that she go back to the House and bring home money. Months passed while she made money for Larry Carter to buy canvas, oils and brushes for his painting.

And then, she had gone with a friend to that N.C.O. dance, and there had been the tall, skinny young man with that fresh country look, and the admiration in his eyes. She hadn't taken it seriously, his infatuation. She hadn't taken it seriously until he came back. She was tired of whorehouses, and he offered her a way out—a way to disappear to a place Larry Carter could never find. And so, she had married Jim Melchior and come to live in his house in the hills of Kentucky.

But life had a way of catching up with you in the form of a conscience. So she wrote to Larry Carter and begged him to get a quiet divorce.

Correspondence followed: letters from Larry which always came in care of general delivery in the city, and which she picked up on her frequent shopping trips. And then, last night, she had seen him standing on the porch of the store with a surprised and then a disgusted look on his face.

Larry Carter with the full sensitive lips, irresponsible, selfish, egotistical. He thought she couldn't forget him—*him* with his loving that built up and up with passion, and then so often left you broken, empty and dissatisfied.

He promised so much, Larry Carter did. He made love so well, so thoroughly, and then did nothing about it. He fell flat on his soft belly when it came to doing something about it.

She threw herself onto the bed, remembering Larry's full searching lips against her own … remembering his rounder, softer body pressing against her, and his soft, almost feminine, hands on her shoulders and her bare, hot back.

So much—and then he would roll over exhausted. "Not now, baby," he'd say. "I've got too much on my mind, baby." And she could lie there and ache, dying with longing while he did nothing about it.

Sometimes he did, though. Sometimes … But when he asserted himself, it was always sudden, quick, and without any buildup. It was something sharp, painful, and screaming inside of her.

Why had he come here now? To torment her? To threaten her? To ask for money?

Her mind whirled with questions, unanswered, disturbing. It brought back the feeling of guilt—things she wanted to forget because she did love Jim Melchior.

The child he wanted was all right too, if he really wanted it. It was only that now she didn't want to face Larry Carter with a child in her body, not Larry Carter who would sneer at her and laugh and tell her she looked vulgar.

No … When she saw Larry, it would have to be at her best. She could do more with him if she looked her best. She could control him if she made him want her. It had taken a long time to learn how to control that body of hers in such a way that it could drive men the way she wanted them to go. Now she could command them like sheep: giving just a little, leading them a little, compromising a little. A man would do anything for a woman's body if she used it right.

Experience in a House had been to her advantage, because now she would use it to assure herself of happiness. It would be used to make the future secure for herself and Jim, and the child he wanted.

Distantly, she heard the door open and close softly. She heard big feet crossing the living room and entering the kitchen, the sound of water splashing and his soft, murmuring voice.

She heard him stepping barefooted across the floor toward the bedroom, and she faced the door and waited expectantly.

CHAPTER EIGHT

Dick Reed puckered his lips and sent a stream of brownish tobacco juice skittering down the top edge of the steps. It slid to a stop about a foot from the bottom step, a green fly buzzed over, came to a halt and bathed in it while Dick watched with open disgust.

When he glanced up toward the road, the farmers with their wives and families were beginning to come out of the valleys and the hills—graying old men with canes, and women with closely knotted gray hair pinned at the back of their necks.

He saw the Barker family with the girl, Belle, and the boy child whose father had been killed in an automobile accident; the Masons with their three ragged girls, and the squat big man with his unshaven face and drooping eyes like a cocker spaniel's.

Up the road a bit, Preacher Tincher came out of his house with his gossipy, sour-faced woman following him. Dick hated Dora Tincher with a passion. If she knew how to keep her mouth shut, folks would be a damned sight happier.

It was Dora Tincher's fault that the farmers came out of the hills on Thursday prayer meeting nights and walked by with their noses in the air. And the men walked beside their high-nosed women with their own noses digging into the pavement.

They had an idea that the village was a hotbed of sin, and nothing anybody could say now would change it. But the farmers had a way to get around this supposed condition. In the evenings, one could see them coming into the village for groceries. Sometimes they didn't come all the way. They stopped off at Nellie's house up the North Valley, or crossed and went up the South Valley to Brandy's house on the West Hill.

The farmers got their out-of-bounds sex and their moonshine, and went back to their farms and their illiterate womenfolk as pure as a newborn child on Christmas Eve. Then, like tonight, they came down with the whole family and sat in the church and pretended not to like the sin the village offered them, and which they took. They pretended they were courageous and big-hearted and pure.

Well, maybe they believed all that stuff and nonsense about church, but Dick Reed didn't believe it. He believed in three things: women, tobacco and moonshine. And he believed in them in that order.

Alice happened to be the only woman he wanted, but he didn't deny that he liked it. He didn't pretend about it. He could hear Alice bustling about in the back part of the house, putting away the few groceries he had bought with the money that new guy, Larry Carter, had given him for his first day's work on the old Elliot shack.

He could hear her and he almost forgot how much he had hated working on a hot autumn day for that stranger. Sometimes, when he was sober and had earned money, he felt good about it. Maybe the way Alice always looked at him when he brought home money had something to do with it. She had a way of making you feel like you were really something whether you were or not. She could make you feel it most acutely when she crawled into bed with you.

That was why he liked Alice, he supposed. He liked her because she didn't try to hide that normal desire either. She could up and make a man reach high whether he felt like it or not. She could put the idea in your head, make you stretch up and work for it.

If he was tired, he didn't care about women. He was even repulsed by her closeness and the strong body odor that went with it. But she had a way of putting the idea in your head anyhow, making you forget you were tired, making you ashamed if you were too tired to get up and move.

He liked his moonshine mostly because it made him feel good. When he had a little moonshine, he never felt ashamed of his inertia. He didn't mind that Holly brought home most of the money to buy the food. He was still the king of his house if he had a drink. He could lie down, feel lazy and contented, and not care about anything.

Sometimes, if he wasn't drinking, he would get so ashamed he felt awful. When it got like that, he would go get the stuff out from under the hay in Brandy's barn. He would sneak it out while in his stocking feet, and he would stop behind the barn and take a big swallow of the burning stuff. Then he would feel good and lazy and unashamed again—which was how a man ought to feel.

He leaned back on an elbow. He let the kink go out of his right leg as it slid down over the steps. If he had a drink now, he wouldn't care at all what Dora Tincher said to the farmers. If he had a drink, he wouldn't be tired and sore from climbing over that old shack's roof. He wouldn't be thinking so much, either, because he would be feeling just lazy and contented.

Mind you, he had worked all day for that no-good tramp who wanted to throw away money on stuff for that old shack. The smart-aleck kid with a big strut and a big seat in his pants!

He only had to see that smooth, leering face to know that the guy was rotten clear through. A man with lips like that, and big pretty eyes and soft hands— Only a lazy son of a gun had soft hands in this country. And that guy was the laziest.

Larry Carter commanded him about like he was a dog. He made him work on the roof in the hot sun. Then when it was cooler he had him come down and fix the hole in the wall of the house. It should have been just the opposite, but Larry Carter liked to command men. He liked the feeling of strutting with his legs spread apart while a man pulled his guts out trying to climb onto a roof.

Dick had seen that lazy slob lean up against a tree and watch Holly's legs as she bent to scrub the front porch. He'd seen the glint that came into the stranger's eyes. And he had seen Holly looking up at the punk kid, her face turning red. And then she had run inside like a frightened hen trying to escape thunder blasts. And Larry Carter had stood there, a hand poking into his pocket and a silent laugh on his lips.

Right then, Dick had wanted to throw the hammer at the black curly head. He had wanted to slam a big fat fist into the side of the smooth face. But if he had, the smart-aleck kid would have whined like a spoiled brat. And who wanted to hit a whining brat anyway. Dick Reed wished he had a drink so he could forget how mad he had gotten. He slid the kink out of his other leg and leaned back with his head resting against the top step.

Let them all go to church if that was what they needed. Let the smarty-pantsed kid look at Holly with that glint in his eyes. He didn't even care if Alice had plans about the night. Nothing bothered him, right then. He was one big aching bone, and he was tired. He wished desperately he had a drink.

Not that he wanted to get drunk—just a drink to loosen his tired muscles, just a drink to warm his guts so he wouldn't have to think about Holly growing up, and about her acting that way with Larry

Carter, and about her looking so haunted, so strange and different lately.

The screen door slammed, and he rolled over to look. Holly stood on the porch with her hair combed and her dress ironed. Her cheeks had that pink glow about them. He spat tobacco juice onto the steps below him.

"You goin' to church too?" He looked at her while she nodded, and he tried to grin a fatherly kind of grin that he didn't exactly know how to form.

"Well, don't let 'em put none of them silly ideas in your head. They don't know no better, that's all. Fussin' about religion and high livin' and stuff. Don't you pay no attention to 'em, Holly, me girl."

"You're drunk again, Pa," she said, and started down the steps.

He sat up, staring at her. "Why, I ain't had a drink all day!" he said, surprised. She went on up the road, and he sat up and pulled his legs up closer to him.

"Damnation," he muttered unhappily. "A man might's well be drunk if he ain't got no credit comin' fer staying sober!"

After a while, the farmers disappeared; they stopped coming through the village, stopped making him think so hard when he didn't like to be thinking. He got up and went inside.

Alice hadn't lighted a lamp. She was sitting over by the window with her head back and her eyes closed. She opened them when he came in, and he looked at her a long minute. He had a complaining woman, but one that was good at pleasing him.

"You goin' to bed, Dick?" she asked lazily. She stretched, and her big arms went over her head, and her breasts stood out like a pillow with two eyes pointing at him.

"Yeah," he said, hesitated, then shuffled into the bedroom. "I'm tired as hell," he added, stepping out of his pants and unbuttoning the dirty blue shirt.

She went past him, bent over and pulled her dress over her head, and he smelled the scent of her in the room, and then she threw the dress onto a chair and lay down heavily on the bed.

"I'm tired, too," she said, and he saw her pull one big fat leg up to her stomach and she was naked in the dim light. He muttered something without thinking and climbed into bed with her.

She had a way of making a man stretch up to get her, and after the first lazy reluctance, he rolled over to her.

CHAPTER NINE

Holly knew early in the afternoon that she would go to church when it came time to go. Usually, she felt bad about going because all the farmers and the village people would look at her in her awful brown dress with a sad, sympathetic look in their eyes that she didn't like.

She didn't need their sympathy and she didn't want it. She hated them, all of them. Well, nearly all of them, at any rate. The exceptions were all men. Jim Melchior. She liked Jim. He made a woman feel good when he looked at her. He was kind of friendly and unaffected and wise. She liked Preacher, too, a little. She liked him because he did just as he pleased. That made him a little like herself, or like she wanted to be. She wanted to be able to do as she pleased. She kind of admired Nellie Byrd for that same reason. Nellie did what she wished and got what she wanted, and she didn't give a hoot in hell who knew about it, either.

That was the way life ought to be. It ought to be open. It shouldn't ever be shackled and hidden, something you stole in little pieces, or never obtained at all because you didn't have the nerve to steal.

A girl ought to be able to see what she wanted and then go get it, either that or lie back and accept what she had. That was life. It was the human way. It was the way it ought to be but never was.

She came to church mostly just to see them all: to see Preacher standing up there in the pulpit with his big shoulders wide and warm looking, and his big fists banging on the Bible stand, and his lips moving and speaking such frightening things.

The minute she walked into the church, however, she wished she hadn't come. Subconsciously, she had expected Larry Carter to be there, and when she saw he wasn't she wished she hadn't come either. She could have stayed in the village, or maybe gone for a walk with him, or just watched the house where he was staying.

All day she had worked for him with a distinct pleasure, and yet a very positive unhappiness. She enjoyed scrubbing the floors and papering the walls; even with Pa there, it had been nice to fix things for Larry Carter, knowing all the time that his eyes were watching …

On the porch, he had looked at her with that look a man had for a woman. Just an instant—a second in which her legs had chilled, and her fanny had squeezed up like a pig's mouth, and the hair had raised up on the back of her neck. It had lasted a minute, and then she had felt her face coloring. And then she had that ridiculous urge to flee, and then she had heard his soft, taunting laughter while she worked indoors where he couldn't see her.

Yes, there was something about Larry Carter that she liked. Or maybe she didn't like it at all; maybe it was just something that she wanted—something she had to have, and soon!

Preacher was finishing the sermon, closing the Bible and motioning to Jean Brothers to begin the singing. Watching him, she saw Preacher look at her with that same peculiar, scrutinizing gaze she had seen him use earlier at the store, the night the stranger came in on the bus.

Dora Tincher's sharp, hard voice cut into the stillness, and the singing began. And behind Holly, the young people began to talk and giggle, and two young girls stood up and slipped outside holding hands. A second later, one of the farmer boys followed, and a face that had been pressing against the window disappeared.

Even the young girls got what they wanted. Holly sat and stared down at her hands in her lap, and when she looked up she saw that Martin Manley sat on the end of the seat from her. He sat looking at her, wide-eyed and unabashed. And she smiled, slowly, and then she winked at him. His face flushed, and she felt a sudden giggle rise inside her and she put her hand over her mouth to stop it.

Nobody knew Martin very well. She had played with him, had gone swimming with him in the creek and sat under a big maple tree and listened while he read his poetry to her. She knew him best of anyone, but she didn't know him well. He was a puzzle to her, and now as she watched him she wished she knew him better.

If anyone could have given her what she wanted, Martin Manley could have. He had opportunity many times. Now that she remembered, it puzzled her that he had not tried. He had looked at her like a man might, but he had never treated her with that intimate anticipation with which men usually treated their women. She began to wonder why.

Perhaps she had frightened him off. She hadn't known until the stranger arrived on the bus what it was that she wanted. She hadn't known when she sat with Martin Manley under the maple tree or when she went swimming with him.

His poetry had stirred an ache inside her, but she hadn't known why. Now that she knew, perhaps if she had put a hand on his arm, or given him a look or a wink …

Martin Manley moved across the seat, sat beside her and looked straight ahead. "Filthy girls," he muttered, and Holly smiled. He had noticed that the girls had gone out, followed by a young boy.

"It's just life," she said, smiling contentedly. "Don't you care about life, Martin?"

He glanced at her, made a face and said, "Can't you see we're in church? What they going to think if they see us talking in church?"

"Who cares what they think?" she said softly, but she stopped, and turned to watch the singers. Somebody had crept up to the altar. He knelt there and beat on the railing with his fists and cried like a kid with a torn finger. Preacher stood looking down at him. There was wonderment and a great sadness in his eyes. It was as if he didn't think any man could cry like this and beat on the railing like an idiot. Preacher stooped down and the singing stopped. A dozen men and women gathered around the miserable creature at the altar. The beseeching prayers rose, the crying caught, and the noise became horrible.

Holly frowned, touched Martin's hand on his knee and whispered into his ear, "Do we have to stay and watch this?"

He looked at her as if she had suddenly gone insane. She said, "Well, why? Ain't it enough to sit here and crawl all over like you had bugs without having to watch it too?"

She got up and went outside. Martin followed slowly after her. He came up to her and pulled her about. "You don't like church?" he demanded.

She stared at him angrily. "Maybe I do and maybe I don't." Her head came up defiantly. "I wouldn't know. All I know is that I don't like to sit and watch all that when I think it ain't real. They ain't pure the way they pretend. And they ain't righteous. They just know how to hide their sins better, that's all. They just sneak around and—" his hand had slipped over her mouth. When she stopped trying to talk, he took his hand away and started walking down the road.

"No use telling the world about it," he said finally. "You may be right. Sometimes I think that's the way it is, too. But I keep it to myself. It won't help any to tell them what you think. They just talk more about you being bad, that's all."

She walked beside him, quietly. He walked lightly, gracefully, almost like Babs Melchior walked—with that lift to his head, that spring in his step and a kind of sway in his hips.

"Maybe we're different," she said. "I guess we are," she added at last with certainty. "We're different," she repeated, liking the sound of it.

He stopped. "Don't keep saying that," he commanded. "We ain't any different than anyone else. Not that way. We just don't like all the sentimental gush, that's all. Ain't nothing wrong with that, is there? Me, I got other things to think about. I got better things like books and places and things to think about."

They started walking again. The moon had come out and the road shone yellow in the light. She thought, *this is a perfect night. This is autumn. This is life, waiting to be taken and lived.*

"What do you think about, Martin?" she asked. "What kind of things?"

He hesitated. "Maybe like you think about. Like people being so smart thinking they're always right and the other guy is wrong. Like maybe there is another kind of life somewhere. Like getting away and going somewhere to find that life."

"Well, *why* don't you go away and find it then? If I was a man, I'd go away. I wouldn't stay here if I wanted to go somewhere and find a new life."

He had come to the culvert and he leaned against it. She leaned beside him. "I couldn't. Pa would kill me. He would hunt me up and kill me. Besides, I couldn't do that."

"You're too scared. If you wasn't scared, you would go."

He frowned. "Suppose I went. Suppose I got to the city, and I found that what I'm looking for isn't there. Suppose there isn't anyone who feels like I do—then I'd die. I'd die just from hurting and being afraid and hating myself."

Holly gasped, leaned nearer to him in the moonlight. "You talk silly. If you want something, it's got to be out there somewhere. All you have to do is go get it."

"You gotta know for sure what it is you're looking for first. You gotta know for sure, and then, if it ain't what most people look for, maybe you won't find it at all. Maybe you'll find out you're just a damned freak, and—" He paused, looked at her with frightened, startled eyes. "You don't know what I'm talking about, do you?"

She shook her head and he said, "I don't know for sure either. Maybe it ain't like I think. Maybe I'll find out it ain't like that; then I can stay here and be happy just like the others. But I keep thinking I'm not like them. I keep thinking I couldn't be happy just smoking or drinking and going to bed with a filthy woman."

She stepped back and looked at him. "You mean you don't ever want that? Every man living wants that, Martin Manley. Every man lives on that. And I reckon you will too … in time. You ain't even tried it, I bet. I bet you don't even know what it's like. You just keep lookin' at a woman and you don't do nothin' about it."

He stared at her. "Gosh, Holly, you sound like you want me to do it!"

"Well, why not?" she demanded angrily. "What makes you think you're any different than everybody else?"

"But you …" he said, astonished. "You wouldn't let me …" His eyes got large and became frightened, and she turned red.

"I couldn't," he said flatly.

"Why couldn't you?" she demanded angrily. "Ain't nothing to it. You just lay down close and—" His hand again slipped over her mouth.

"Don't talk like that. I just couldn't, that's all. It's too dirty, too filthy. I just couldn't!" he pleaded, and his voice slid into a high, pleading note of desperation.

She turned to go away, and he said, "Don't hate me, Holly. Maybe—maybe if I think about it. Maybe if it was you ..."

But she had gone on up the road, alone, without listening. After a while, she stopped by the steps of the house, and she saw him move away from the culvert and head up the valley toward the hills where he lived.

She swore softly into the stillness. Someday she would make him do it. Someday she would. Why, she couldn't even get a young sissy to give her anything. He just said he couldn't.

God, something awful must be wrong with me—something awful and filthy and undesirable. Only one man ever looked at her as if she was to be desired, and that was Larry. But even he showed no signs of wanting her. He just looked and grinned.

She went into the house. In her own room, she lay down on the bed. She said to herself again and again that she would ... she would ... until she went to sleep, knowing that somehow she would get what she wanted.

She was awful tired of waiting, and wishing. She was getting angry about it. She was getting angry about lots of things. And a woman couldn't stand to be angry very long without going crazy. She just had to do something about it ... soon!

CHAPTER TEN

Martin Manley squatted under a tree and watched the shack where Larry Carter had been living for several days. Now that the tobacco crop had been ripened early by the slight frost and was cut and hung in the barn to cure, he had nothing to do in the afternoons until it was time for the evening chores.

For a number of days now, he had come to squat under the tree that was up on a knoll. This way he could look down on the shack. Ever since he had talked to Holly that night by the culvert, he had come to the knoll to watch. It was part of his plan to learn the truth about himself, part of the carefully contrived plan to build himself up to a point where he could, and must, learn about himself.

Several interesting things had happened as he watched the shack. On the day following the Thursday night meeting, Preacher had helped

Brandy and the young man, Larry, bring up a sled with odd pieces of bright, warm-looking furniture, which were taken into the shack.

Also, on the next following day, he had seen Holly leave the shack about three in the afternoon. Fifteen minutes later, Babs Melchior had come out of the woods in front of the shack and hurried across the clearing and into the house.

He had thought about that. What was most puzzling of all was the active, mysterious commotion coming from within the shack. It seemed to him, from a distance, that Holly had left barely in time to get out of sight. He also thought that Babs Melchior seemed fearful, looking as if she were afraid she might be seen.

She had not stayed long. On Sunday, the only person to visit the shack, except for Larry Carter, was Holly.

On Sunday Martin had arrived early. The farmers were just beginning to come into the village on their way to Sunday School. In the pocket of his windbreaker, Martin carried a little lunch. He sat under the maple tree and watched the shack between scribbles from his pencil, as he wrote verses suitable to the early entrance of autumn, the colorful panorama of nature slowly enveloping the hills in bright shades of dark and golden red, and oranges and browns of all shades.

Holly had come to the shack that Sunday and had stayed most of the day, not leaving until about six in the evening when Martin had to hurry to get home in time to help with the chores. On the following days he noted that Holly remained at the shack until after he had to leave. He therefore had no way of knowing how late she stayed alone with the young man.

His active mind began to form ugly pictures of what she was doing with the handsome stranger, and he became angry, bitter and impatient with her for it.

On one such afternoon when his thoughts became especially and unbearably crude, he could endure them no longer. Carefully he worked his way down the hill, threading a path between the fallen twigs from the trees, and walking softly on the leaves that carpeted the floor of the earth.

At the living room window, he moved forward slowly and then, the hot sun beating down on him, carefully looked through it. What he saw was both a disappointment and a relief.

Holly was carefully dusting off the furniture when he first looked through the window. Occasionally she glanced toward the far corner, where the handsome stranger stood preoccupied with brush and canvas.

The young man wore a loose-fitting pair of pleated blue denims which were turned up about the calves of his legs. His bright plaid socks showed above his shined brown shoes.

He also wore a white cotton T-shirt. His bare arms came up sleek and strong as he used his brush gently on the canvas. The set of his head was thrust watchfully forward. Every so often, he would move back, cock his head to one side, half smile, nod, and return to the canvas as if satisfied.

Watching him, Martin recalled the gray marble statue he had seen in the city park the one time Herb had taken him to Cincinnati: A huge, gray and cold thing that stood upright and naked in the summer sun. Its figure, molded in round, pulsing muscles, sloped gracefully into the curves of his lean figure. Martin had thought that the gray, beautifully built figure was waiting to receive something from the sun, something to come and admire the strength and softness of him. And thinking this, Martin had felt a kinship as if he himself were the one for whom the man waited. And then, for the first time, he had known the strange ache.

Watching the young artist, he felt the ache come alive again. And so he moved away from the window with both disappointment and relief. And although he was unable to stay long enough to see Holly leave the shack, he did not have any more of those awful suspicions that afternoon.

On Wednesday, Holly left the shack early. She seemed reluctant as she paused outside the shack to look back. Then, lowering her head, she walked away dejectedly.

For a second, he thought about again going down the hill, looking in the window at the handsome young man. He could see the stranger in his mind's eye, watch him moving about the shack. Perhaps he was shaving with his bare, round shoulders glistening, and his waist small and firm above his slacks. He was about to head down the hillside when he saw the figure come out of the woods, and skit across the clearing and into the house. Babs Melchior again! God, he thought, what if Jim found out!

Sitting on the knoll, waiting, his mind began that awful train of thoughts, and after a while he moved down the hillside and peered through the living room window.

This time the window was raised a bit, and he could hear the voices long before he saw the two of them on the couch in front of the fireplace.

It was Babs' voice saying, "I tell you, he'll kill you if he finds out, Larry." Then, softly: "Oh, why did you have to come?"

"For you," came the young man's voice, barely above a whisper so that Martin had to strain to hear.

"I'm making good money now, Babs. We can be together again. You won't have to do those things for me again, supporting me like that.

Don't you know I hated that, Babs? I hated knowing someone else was holding you, taking what belonged to me."

The room was quiet, and then: "I had to have you back, baby. Don't you understand that?"

And then their heads moved up over the couch, and Larry Carter lifted her and held her in his arms as they stood up. His head was buried against her throat, under her long blonde hair. There was a strained, painful expression on Babs' pretty face.

Martin lowered himself. He swore softly, and then moved up again, pressing his ear against the hard wood of the shack. His lips were drawn tight and felt dry. He felt a sickening heaviness in his groin.

"You do like me, baby," came Larry's voice through the window. "Say you do, baby. Say you feel it."

Martin looked again. Larry was on the sofa with Babs, his lips mumbling, and his face moving over her. Suddenly her hands caught at him and pulled him against her. A painful, ugly expression was twisted on her face.

It was then that Martin stepped back. He felt paralyzed by what he had seen through the window of the shack. Numb with a sickness that made his stomach uneasy, he could not have moved in that instant even if they had seen him. But they did not. Larry Carter was too busy to see anyone, and Babs' eyes were closed.

Martin moved only after the two glowing bodies disappeared on the other side of the couch. Laughter echoed upward—cheap, vulgar and tantalizingly emotional. Martin turned away, barely aware that he moved. He walked down the path toward the overhanging bridge and headed down the narrow ledge that led to the side of the mountain and the big, wide creek.

Slowly, as in a trance, he threaded his way down the side of the hill, through the sassafras bushes and small pines, going beneath the big overhanging limbs of the golden-leafed maples and tall, splendid oaks. He saw the walnut trees, big and loose-limbed, and the mistletoe growing at its jointed limbs. The parasite—the thing that had no life, the ugly, sucking thing that lived on the bigger, stronger tree. The delicate, useless mistletoe was a parasite.

He stopped alongside the creek and slumped down in a grassy spot on the edge of the bank. A walnut tree stood across the creek, half its limbs extending out over the water. In the crook of its joints grew the parasite.

Martin thought now of what he had seen through the window. He thought of the times he sat on the creek bank with the thing living in the walnut tree so near him. He thought of the ideas that had come to him while at this site. He thought of the comparisons he had made. He thought of the poems he loved to write, of the bronze statue, of the way he had felt watching Larry Carter and the strange sense that he had not seen Babs Melchior at all—because he, Martin, had been there in Larry Carter's arms!

Sitting by the creek he thought about the uselessness of things. Yet he refused to accept this. But there was so little for him to go on, so little from which to draw conclusions; there were only the few books he had read, a few differences about his personal appearance, his actions. But there was nothing obvious, nothing plain—nothing solid to go on.

The next day he was again on the knoll when he thought he saw Holly coming out of the shack. He rose and stood watching her as she went away, again early. But he did not wonder why she was leaving the shack so early. Babs Melchior would soon be coming.

He watched Holly Reed walk slowly down the path; he watched her go toward the edge of the mountain. When he saw that she was going toward the big swimming hole in the creek, he began to walk after her, moving silently, not letting her know that he was following.

She was wearing a pair of rolled up jeans. Her small bare feet looked like those of a kitten threading its way through the underbrush, clutching at the dirt, rocks and grass on the hillside.

Under the big maple, he saw her stop, then bend forward as she stepped out of the jeans. Her arms came up and went back, and she slipped out of the shirt and laid it on the ground by her jeans. She stood with her back to him and she looked brown and glowing in the filtered sunlight coming through the leaves of the maple tree. Her body was lean, long-legged and hard-looking like a boy's.

He went more softly down the hillside, watched as she dived into the pool of water and swam under the surface. Her back seemed to wave and quiver. She looked slender, and her muscles were rhythmic and strong.

A small, joyful laugh welled into Martin's throat. It was the laughter of a boy without worry—the gurgling, happy laughter of a boy with no inhibitions. He stripped to his shorts, his own thin chest somehow taking on a strong, manly appearance in his own eyes. He dived into the water and came up behind her. He saw her turn her head and look back, her eyes puzzled. He did not understand the bewilderment in her eyes.

After a while, she seemed all right again and he swam after her. He caught up with her and pushed her under the water. Instantly, she dived and came up along the edge of the pool. He laughed and swam quickly to the edge and climbed out. Reaching for her hand, he pulled her up onto the bank, where he pushed her against the trunk of the walnut tree, his body mashing against her.

Her body was warm, tantalizing against his. For a moment, he pulled back and held her forearms against her sides. Like a hungry man, he pressed against her, reaching for her lips. And then his eyes fastened on the small, lifted and rose-tipped breasts. And he became like a chunk of ice in the hot afternoon air, melting, somehow suddenly and irrevocably useless.

He pulled back, his brain whirring inside his skull. He couldn't. He just couldn't do it! He looked at her. He saw her face with that expectant, almost eager expression, the soft laughter in her eyes, her long hair falling over her soft shoulders …

But then she saw him and her eyes became puzzled, and suddenly they went cold, full of accusation and pity. *She knows*, he thought bitterly. And the thought was unbearably painful. *She knows!*

"Well …" she said slowly, as if waiting, as if knowing already that he was a child, helpless.

"I can't!" he pleaded, and then he screamed, "I can't! I just can't! It's ugly and dirty and cheap, and I can't!"

She stared at him silently, and he wished she would talk. He wished she would tell him how awful he was. He wanted her to say that he was the one who was cheap and vulgar, and that he wasn't a man. But she only stared at him with that horrible, odd expression in her eyes. Then she slid away from him.

He threw himself against the earth, his long fingers clawing and pulling at it. And then his face sank into the small soft hole of the earth, and his hands stretched out above his head and dug at the grass. His sobs became muffled in the ground.

It would have been better if he had not been born … much better that he should be part of the earth, dead, useless. Better that than the awful, twisted thing he was. Better dead than the parasite!

He didn't know when she moved away down the creek, but suddenly he knew that she was gone. After a while, he stood up and stared with blind eyes at the mistletoe in the joints of the walnuts. He stared while his soul twisted and cursed his inadequate body, and while his insides screamed in the face of his thoughts:

For now he knew, and the knowledge was unbearable. He had found out, and he could not stand the way he had found out. He had tried to be a man and he had been a miserable failure. And now that he knew the truth, he was afraid to live.

His eyes saw the mistletoe and the huge, great limb that extended over the water. But now his eyes were not blind as they fastened on the limb, and somehow he grew calmer as he looked at life's beginning, and life's sudden, ugly end.

CHAPTER ELEVEN

Earlier that morning Holly had left the house. She was wearing jeans and was barefoot as she walked on the wet, cold grass up the South Valley in the general direction of the shack.

In the few days since Larry Carter arrived in the village, her life had become quite different to her; it became filled with a purpose and a meaning. And although she seemed to get nowhere toward fulfilling that purpose, she was somehow more impatient and more calm at the same time. She was impatient for what she sought, yet calmer too because now she knew what she wanted and could wait a little.

Sometimes the waiting was difficult for her. That was when she went to the shack and he was still sleeping in the small back bedroom and she had to call to him. He would appear in a crimson robe to open the door for her. Then while she made his breakfast, he would wash from the pan in the kitchen, and shave while looking in the small cracked mirror. At those times, she would sometimes see his lean shoulders and the waiting would be very difficult.

While he painted, it was easier … until he looked at her and she would see that odd, wondering expression on his face as he watched her. Then she would know such strange, wild desires that she would wonder about herself, about her sanity, about her abilities, about her own youth.

Sometimes when he looked at her, she would become intense with desire and with anger. She would want to stop in her work and say to him, "Am I so different?" and tear her clothes off and show to him that she was the same as any woman.

But then, seeing her watching him, he would look away and return to his canvas. And the moment of revelation for her would pass. With it passed the instant when she might have given herself to him—with courage and lust and desire.

Mostly, though, the days had been wonderful. Usually, she found it enough to scrub his floors, cook his meals and make his bed. She worked for him until she was exhausted. She worked with the idea that she was doing a wife's job, a woman's job for her man.

However, there had been three days she had not worked hard, for in the middle of each one of these days he told her she could stop her chores. Yesterday had been one of those days. He had gotten cross and impatient and had told her she could go home early.

She wanted to question him but she didn't. Instead, when he looked at her restlessly, as if eager to be rid of her, she left without question.

Leaving the shack, she walked by the edge of the hillside and saw the creek shining down on the valley floor. She saw the many colors around it, of the valley, the creek like a silver wire. Soon the weather would be cold, and the valley would be barren and frozen over, and the creek would be closed to her for another winter.

Walking down the edge of the hillside, she took off her clothes under the big maple tree and dived into the water.

Even now, she remembered how good it felt to have the water washing over her naked flesh, smoothing over her like the soft caress of a man's gentle hands.

She thought she was alone, hidden from Brandy's shack by the walnut and the maple tree. No one ever came this far up the valley floor unless he was going to Brandy's stills. And she knew that no one went up there except Brandy—no one at all—and Brandy always went down the hillside a half mile above his shack.

There was no danger of being seen when she swam; all summer long she had done so without being seen. And yet, suddenly, behind her there came the sharp slap of water against a human body. Turning her head, she saw the intent face of Martin Manley.

At first, she felt panic—the panic coming from a strange situation, something she had not experienced before. And then, she became slowly conscious of a desire to be seen by a man … to be liked, wanted and admired in her nakedness.

She began to feel like the hunted, and he, Martin, was playing the part of the hunter. He swam over to her and touched her back and her hard hips, and she had felt the warmth and the muscles of his youthful, slender body. She thrilled to their closeness and felt a sudden, wild desire to rush this thing that must surely happen to her at last.

She swam to the bank edge and smiled as he came after her and pulled her out of the water. Then she lay still, a delicious feeling of warmth sweeping over her as his body crushed her own against the trunk of the walnut tree. And then she waited, almost smiling, as his hands bit into her arms and his lips came toward her hungrily.

Only then did she feel him hesitate, suddenly freezing and then slouching away.

The look on his face in that moment was one of utter disillusionment and startled horror. He seemed to shrivel and then there began that awful twisting and movement under the tight skin of his cheeks. His eyes looked as if they would pop out and suddenly he started sobbing and screaming like a child in pain.

She did not know what to think when he started screaming at her. She was too shocked. She did not know what to think. But when she realized that he was helpless to appease the passion which he had roused, she felt a sudden, sickening disgust for him.

Afterward, much longer afterward, the reasoning process began: he was young and different, and he had truly wanted to take her there by the walnut tree. She wondered if it was his very youth which had stopped him. She began, then, to accuse herself for the failure. Perhaps if she had helped him. If she had urged him on …

Now as she walked along the creek and neared the water hole, she wanted to see if it had changed since yesterday evening when she had—for a brief while—looked eagerly forward to womanhood.

She came along the edge of the creek as it widened gently into the pool. And then she saw a shadow on the wet, tall grass, where she had lain with him yesterday, with his body over her. It was a huge, dark shadow that stretched out from the slanting morning sun … She looked up and her heart swelled inside her and became like a ball of cotton in her throat. Her scream was shrill, and unending in the still, crisp morning air.

There he was—like a ghost—hanging from the limb of the tree. His small, blond head was thrown over to one side and looked like a broken melon. A deep, ghastly cut was on his throat. Swollen, bubbling flesh was around the edges of the rope.

Suddenly she thought, *I might have helped him! I might have helped him* … It was the sudden pounding in her chest made her turn and run … made her run from the thing she had done, from the past which had hurt her … and failed her … and which she, in turn, had failed.

She thought that now she would always be running—running away and forward at the same time. She would have to go faster and more urgently than ever before. Life, somehow, all at once, was a fleeting thing that had to be fulfilled quickly—in spite of anyone and everything!

CHAPTER TWELVE

Brandy Elliot hesitated as he neared the country store. There would be a big crowd of men in there talking about the suicide of Martin Manley. Because he had been the first on the scene after Holly found him, they would question him. But he didn't feel much like talking.

He wouldn't go in at all except that he was out of potatoes, and a man needed potatoes to fry with the bacon and onions. He had done without them for two days now, putting off coming to the store until after the funeral.

It had been a big funeral—the biggest one that had ever been held in the little white church. The regular preacher had been there, too, and lots of flowers, and people all dressed up and walking by the casket to stare with curiosity at the sleeping young man who lay there with his neck broken.

Brandy guessed he was the only one who had not been surprised by the thing. He was only surprised that it had taken so long to happen.

He had been sitting on his front porch that afternoon with those field glasses the deputy sheriff had given him years ago for some of his moonshine. Frequently, he would get out the glasses and scan the hills. He had no intention of letting anyone sneak up on his little manufacturing venture in the valley without his being forewarned.

Brandy had been watching the hills that afternoon when he saw Martin sitting on a knoll under a tree. He seemed to be watching the shack where the city artist lived. Several afternoons Martin Manley had spent squatting up there under a tree and watching the shack. Martin would watch until Holly Reed left, and then he would follow her through the trees. He would go down the hillside, never gaining on her, but sneaking along and watching, like a cat waiting for the right moment to pounce.

Twice, Martin had walked down to the cabin and looked in the front window. That had seemed strange to Brandy, but then it was no more strange than Martin's other actions. On that particular afternoon Brandy had in mind, Martin walked more quickly after Holly, who had taken the path down the side of the hill that led to the creek.

Lots of times, Brandy had sat on his front porch and watched Holly swim in the big hole in the creek. But the air was getting cold and he was surprised to see her go to the creek on this afternoon. As always, she took off all her clothes, not knowing that she had been followed and, of course, not at all aware of Brandy and his field glasses.

Brandy, respecting Holly's privacy, had never watched her too closely as she swam in the hole. But this day he did watch. He sensed that the cat was nearly ready to pounce and he had shivered with fear and also with anger.

The lad acted like a man might be expected to act: swimming after her, himself naked, wanting to surprise her. He passed over her and then she swam quickly toward the bank, and the lad followed eagerly after her. Brandy watched as the lad took her hand and pulled her up onto the grass. He made himself ready.

But then, not surprising Brandy at all, the lad froze. And Brandy felt an intense pity for Martin Manley in that instant of shame. He sensed the lad's aversion, his inability, and he felt sorry and shamed for him.

Holly dressed as the lad cringed in shame against the earth. And in that moment, Brandy had been afraid for the boy, afraid because of the immensity of his shame. He watched as Holly turned and moved away, walking out of the valley. He did not look again at the lad back there by the creek.

In a way, he had been glad the lad had failed. Brandy, himself, had thought about Holly. He had watched her and wanted her for so long it was difficult to remember when it all began. But since the stranger had come, she didn't come to see him as often as she once had.

She worked for the stranger in his cabin and seemed somehow suspended in the middle of space, as if waiting for the stranger to possess her. Also he had noticed that Holly seemed tense, high strung—like one of his bitches in heat, he thought unhappily. Waiting and expecting, but not getting it.

He could tell that she hadn't gotten it because the tension seemed to mount inside her, the craving showed on her young face. It seemed almost to scream out of her with waiting. And he was glad it was still there. Glad that it built higher and higher inside her, because some day she would see that he was the one for her. And she would be like a pure, screaming virgin when he took her.

That fateful afternoon he watched Holly with Martin passed from his mind, until the next morning when he heard her thin, high scream in the crisp morning air. He had hurried down to her and found the naked body of the youth strung up on the limb of the walnut tree. His neck was broken.

Yes, Holly had been stunned and partly shamed by the sight. And knowing what she was thinking, he had taken her to the village and had Alice make tea for her before putting her to bed.

Holly had also been at the funeral. She sat with her face numb, apparently one half of her mind listening while the other half brooded over the thought of what had caused this tragedy.

Holly had worn a different dress; it was like one Babs Melchior might have worn. Brandy wondered if Babs had given it to Holly. The two women seemed to get along surprisingly well. However, Holly sometimes cleaned for Babs, so it was natural that they should get along. Possibly they both had something very much in common. But Brandy knew that if Holly were aware of the truth, she would not have been friends with Babs Melchior.

Holly didn't know, as did Brandy, that Babs made frequent trips to the shack on the East Hill. She didn't know that those two city people had known each other somewhere before, sometime. That fact was apparent to Brandy. But he couldn't tell her. He knew the fierce, possessive nature which was Holly's, even as that same nature was a part of Jim Melchior.

It was something Jim and Holly both had in common: a wild possessiveness, something that could be fierce. Brandy had wondered which of them would have been the more dangerous had they known of the relationship between Babs and the stranger in the shack.

But he told himself that it was a good thing that people weren't always aware of the undercurrent of things. Sometimes things burst apart with the explosiveness of a bomb if too much were known.

Brandy hesitated on the steps of the store. Then slowly, he walked across it and into the store. There were many men inside. They stood around with their funeral clothes still on. They chewed tobacco and smoked, spitting at the stove, grumbling and pronouncing weird premonitions.

Dick Reed spit on the stove and there was a sharp sizzling sound. He said, "I always knew that one was strange. A queer one if I ever saw one," he said sagely, tugging at his trousers which threatened to drop down over his hips.

"Yeah," one of the farmers said, puffing on a homemade cigar. "I always said Herb had a queer one there, too. Always acting funny, with his woman's ways and that fearful look in his eyes. Reckon he was a coward right up to the last, killin' hisself that way."

Jim Melchior gave the man a dirty look, and the muscles of his face grew firm with anger. "Maybe he wasn't such a coward. Maybe he was brave. It takes a lot of guts to kill yourself. I seen it on the battlefields: lads wishing they could die because they feared the unknown, because they feared the future, not knowing what was going to happen to them next. But when it came their time to die, when a man stepped up behind them with a bayonet ready to poke into their back, they always came to life and fought like hell. They wanted to die, but the will to live was a natural instinct inside them and they fought to live."

"Maybe you're right, Jim," Preacher said softly. "Maybe it does take a lot of courage to die. I guess Martin had more courage than most of us. He knew he was different. He knew he wasn't a man; and rather than bring shame on his father, he killed himself."

"Well," one of the farmers admitted, "it's as good a reason as any, I reckon. But for my part, I ain't believin' it was anything brave to kill hisself. He just saved us a lot a trouble. Him being half a man, and all. I reckon sooner or later, we woulda had to do something about him. Ain't right that a thing like that should be runnin' around among our girls."

Brandy stepped up to the stove and touched the speaker on the shoulder. "Nobody knows why Martin wanted to die. If he had a reason, it was his own. And now that he's dead, I reckon we just better leave that reason with him."

"Look who's talkin'," Jeff Buckley laughed softly. "Ain't a man any stranger in the bunch of us than you, Brandy. Always walking around with that yearnin' on your face for a girl half your age!"

Brandy spun like a top, sudden and dangerous, and his hand grabbed up the front of Jeb's shirt. He lifted the tall, thin man up on his toes.

"You ain't talking, are you, Jeb? I ain't said anything against anybody. But I reckon if you forced me to, I could tell a lot about any man in here." His fist held Jeb's shirt, twisting it so that it pulled at the man's armpits. Then the storm passed and he let Jeb down onto the floor. He smiled gently.

"Ain't no sense in talking about a man who can't be here to take up for himself, is there?"

Jim Melchior said, "That's right Brandy. I figure we ain't got any room to talk about a dead man."

"Well … I can't …" Dick Reed stopped talking as he looked into the clear blue eyes of Brandy Elliot. There was something about the red-headed man that froze him, something about the eyes that showed above that flaming red beard, and something about the set of his thick, smooth lips. Dick tugged at his trousers. He pulled them up so that the hair on his belly no longer showed through his buttonless shirt tail. He walked out of the store softly for a man of his weight.

After a while, the other men began to leave too—all except Jim Melchior and Preacher. They set up the card table, pulled out a deck of rook cards and asked Brandy and Jeb to play with them.

"Reckon I might as well play a while," Brandy said quietly. "Ain't nothing much to do on a Sunday afternoon."

Jeb Buckley slid into his chair opposite Brandy, but his eyes avoided those of the red-headed man. After a while, Milly Buckley came into the store and sat down in the rocker by the window.

And soon, the clickity-click of her needle made small intermittent noises as the men played. She started to hum a hymn and Jeb glanced at her sharply.

"Can't you sing somethin' besides that?" he asked sharply.

"Besides what?" It was Ronny speaking. He shut the door of the store and looked at Jeb with inquiring, rather hard eyes for a youth of fourteen.

And Brandy thought, *When he gets a little older, he'll be the boss around here*. But he didn't say anything and pretended not to notice that Milly went on humming the hymn, and that Jeb Buckley became very, very busy with the cards in his hands.

CHAPTER THIRTEEN

Dora Tincher glanced at the front door as Preacher came in from his card game at the store. She wasn't interested, exactly, in the fact that he had come home. She merely accepted it, as she merely accepted, or sometimes only endured, many things about Preacher.

Thinking about it, she wished the people hadn't begun calling him Preacher instead of Karl. She preferred to call him Karl, and she did so now, watching him for some sign of annoyance, which he now rarely revealed to her.

"Will you be home for dinner, Karl?" she asked, and went on changing her clothes, slipping back into the bedroom out of his sight.

She always changed clothes out of Karl's sight, away from those curious, probing, and sometimes hungry eyes of his. If she so much as took off her dress in front of him, he would immediately get that horrible reaction ... and then the inevitable would happen—an inevitability she dreaded and hated.

She wished she had known about that before she married him. At that time, he had been big and tall and good-looking in a clean sort of way. You could tell his mind was never on women. He was preoccupied with his religion, then, and he had been a good young man.

She remembered the first day she had seen him in the pulpit, and how proud she had been. Right then, she had set her mind on Karl Tincher. He was a good man, better than any man she had ever known, and he would be right for her. With him, she would have security. A woman had to marry to get security. And she would have a certain rather lofty position in the village too, him being a preacher.

It had happened exactly the way she planned it, too. Everything went exactly right: the number of dates, chaperoned; the length of time for their courting. There was planning even to the small kisses ... and the better kisses—her interest seeming to increase with the length of time they knew each other. And then at last he asked her to marry him, and it was precisely the day she had planned for him to ask her.

She managed that last with a hand that slid along his forearm as they sat on the farmhouse porch. A slight leaning toward him had been all that was necessary.

It had taken a while. His not being interested in women had made capturing him a long, difficult battle for her. And although she had insinuated a great deal more than she had intended, she had accomplished her purpose. That was a feather in her cap. That was really something: to get what you wanted and still be chaste.

But afterward, immediately afterward, it had changed. She learned too late, that a woman never knows a man until she has to sleep with him. That part had been the most difficult of all. At first she had succeeded in convincing him that she really did love him, acting as if she were giving herself completely to him. Never letting him know the truth.

But eventually, even the acting became tiring, even monotonous. She came to hate it so intensely that she found herself dreading his presence. She began to loath him at times.

However, it was a consolation to her that she never told him that she hated him—a consolation because he would then know her as a hypocrite. And because, lately, since he had changed even more, he might even do that most dreadful of all things: divorce her!

She had known a divorced woman once. No one had anything to do with her. A divorced woman was worse than a whore, worse than Nellie Byrd. And imagine Dora Tincher like that! Why, she was the finest woman in the village, religious, pure, seeming to love her husband so much, and being so considerate of him all the time he was shaming her with his philandering ways.

Yes, she knew all about Nellie Byrd and Karl. She knew about most of the others, too, and the bastard babies. She knew and felt a little proud of it. Secretly, she was glad that he found other women; he left her alone more often. But outwardly, she would lower her head when he talked to her and she would look benevolent, and just a tiny bit hurt—just a tiny bit, though.

In a way, she had no right to say anything about it, to disapprove, that is. When she failed to satisfy him the way a wife should, she knew she had no call to find fault with him. But she didn't really have the right to be glad—and she was that, truly glad.

Whenever he went up the valley to see Nellie Byrd, she would get down her knees on the bed and pray for him. She would plead with God to forgive her husband, and keep him safe, mostly to keep him from getting some horrid disease. She would die if he carried something home, something miserable, nasty and not clean.

She would pray for him and for herself, and then she would crawl into bed and be sound asleep when he came home from seeing Nellie. And if she wasn't asleep, she would pretend a snore so that he would think she was asleep.

And when for a few days, he wouldn't see other women, wouldn't even go to see Alice Reed who lived up the street—why then she would be very careful, about undressing in front of him or touching against him in bed.

It made her a little angry when he called on Alice Reed. Alice wasn't clean like Nellie, and she might be most likely to give Karl some awful disease. It made her sick when she thought about Karl with that little, sickly-acting woman. She had a strange notion that Alice Reed was the most possessive of all the women Karl knew. She just felt that in Alice all the vulgarity of womankind was wrapped up in one solitary bed sheet that was yellow with Dick Reed's sweat.

Sometimes, but not often, she would even envy Alice Reed. It was not anything she could put her finger on. But it was something like jealousy that Alice could be really naughty. Then she would almost wish she were Alice Reed. When she thought that way and put herself in Alice Reed's place, she could almost like Karl.

It was as if she looked at him through Alice's eyes, and could see the big limbs of him and his wide, heavy shoulders, and his lips curled upward, tauntingly. Then she would like the sight of his damp, hairy body, and the feel of his arms under her.

Still, whenever he did get near her and she wasn't envying Alice Reed, she got that strong aversion to him, that dread and hate and loathing so that she wanted to kick out at him, strike him in the thigh and hurt him savagely.

Now, watching him, she quivered a little. He had that worried expression on his face, the wrinkles around his thick lips. As at other times, though, his eyes had that dumb, blank look of an idiot's. She wondered what he was thinking of when he looked like that.

He wasn't thinking of her. She could see that his mind wasn't on her. When she stood in front of him in her fresh cotton dress and looked at him, she began to hate him again. Why wasn't he thinking of her? She had just changed clothes. He had heard her movements, and yet he stood staring at the floor and did not even notice her.

"I asked you if you would be home for dinner," she repeated impatiently. "Looks like you could answer me, Karl. It ain't as if Martin Manley was anything special to worry about. Besides, he's dead, ain't he? God rest his soul, but there ain't nothing you can do now."

For the first time, Karl looked up. He looked straight at her and his eyes held a strange new look.

"Damn you, Dora," he said softly. "Damn you!"

The shock of his words, quiet in the room, froze her in front of him. She was unable to answer, unable to think. The words, sudden, quick and soft, were like a resounding curse.

He straightened his shoulders and brought his head up. He ran his hand through his hair and seemed surprised at himself. He walked closer to her and put his hand under her chin. He lifted her face so that he could look at it. His eyes took in every line, every movement, every frightened jerking of facial muscles.

He smiled patiently at her. "You're a fool, Dora—a cold, ugly fool. You haven't got so much as a breast to hold a man, nor a mouth to suckle, nor a shoulder to lie on. You haven't anything but a great, big, ugly bottom. If you didn't have that, you'd be a tired old bitch trying to make a living just like Nellie, only not as good as Nellie. You ought to be like that, Dora. You ought to let yourself go and have yourself a damned good time for once. You ought to, Dora," he said softly, and took his hand away from her chin so that it dropped.

She stepped back from him, words leaping out of her mouth. Her hands came upward, slapping his face. She stood still while he grinned at her, and she slapped him again, much harder. How she hated him! Loathed him! Standing there, grinning at her as if she was something to be pitied!

Well, she could stop his awful grinning. She could. She brought up her knee, swung inward toward him with a great release of her long pent-up emotions. But he suddenly moved. He moved near her, grabbed her arms and slid a hand around the back of her. He grabbed the fresh cotton dress from her body. He grinned at her and roughly split her slip and stripped her while she clawed at him.

Then he picked her up and carried her into the bedroom. He threw her onto the bed as if she were something rotten. She tried to get away from him, but he caught her. He pushed her back against the corner of the room, and his hands searched her, roughly, impatiently, and with a slow possessiveness. Somehow to her, in those moments his hands were like something foul and hot violating her body, taking it with sure, angry movements. And in that moment, she knew that he was no different than he was with Alice Reed. She knew that the same hot anger possessed him—the same sure movements of degradation, hate and uninhibited lust were bent over her own flesh even as they had bent and burned themselves out on Alice Reed.

She turned away and he put a hand on her shoulder. "I shouldn't have done that, Dora, but you make me so damned mad. You make me hate you and want you without knowing how to stop myself."

She wanted to tell him that she hated him, but she knew that secretly she was very pleased with herself. She was satisfied with the way it had happened, his taking her like that without her consent. Because it defiled him also, and that made her happy.

But suddenly something small within her became very huge and very important. It was a small, unimportant thing that suddenly pushed at her mind and made her uneasy. A strange, small urge inside her …

Something about him, the way he had treated her like a whore, taking her as if she were a prostitute … something about it bothered her. It was as if now, suddenly, she was becoming a woman, awake to the secret passions within her. And these urges which she never could have admitted had somehow found an outlet. The way was there! He had started it. He had made it possible, opened up the secret of her, and brought out the madness and the hungry, awful lust.

She turned to face him. Without looking at his face, she ripped the buttons from his shirt so that his chest was bare. She buried her face against the hair of his chest, and she began to laugh. He pushed her back and stared at her with frightened eyes. She turned and ran to the bed. She threw herself down on it. She looked at him—straight into his eyes. And she knew when he came toward her that he had guessed how it was to be with her. And he didn't mind. He didn't mind at all that she wanted to be like Alice Reed to him. He just laughed as he came down to her.

She said at last, "You hate me."

He got up and dressed slowly, smiling at her. "No. I hated you before. I hated you because you had it to give and kept it from me. I couldn't hate you now. I guess if a man's got a thing like that, he don't need much else. Nothing else but God, maybe, and a kid to teach things to …" He looked at her. "You ain't changed your mind about a kid, Dora?"

She shook her head. She couldn't ever change her mind about that. It frightened her; the thought of it frightened her. Carrying a kid around and being big for so long, and people knowing you had slept with a man …

"No. I ain't changed my mind about that. Ain't it enough that I'm a whore for you? Ain't it enough that you treat me like this? What else do you want, Karl?"

He looked at her. "You were wrong about the other. I guess you could be wrong about a kid, too."

"I wasn't wrong. I didn't just change now. I been this way all the time, only you wouldn't treat me like that. You wouldn't … I had to let you and make you take me like that. You think it's just you? Maybe you think you're just the best there is. Well, you ain't. It wasn't that at all. I just don't like all that fuss, like a ritual, that turned out dirty and cheap."

He laughed. "I never would've guessed you for a cheap one, Dora. I never would've known you could be so damned cheap."

She sat up angrily, ran toward him and began beating his chest. He grabbed her hands and smiled at her. "Cut it out, you little hypocrite," he laughed. "You might hurt me."

"I'll do more than that. I'll kill you. I'll—" She stopped, speechless, and watched him laugh and go out of the house.

She hadn't heard him laugh since they were first married. She listened to his laughter still ringing in the room long after he had gone. Then, slowly, because she had all the time in the world, she got dressed again.

She thought of herself, of the way she had been. And she thought of Alice Reed, but she had no envy. He would not be going back to see Alice Reed again. She was certain of that much, certain that she had her man now, for keeps. That was another accomplishment for her. One she had never hoped to achieve.

It made her feel good, really good inside. She felt like a young woman who had just said good-by to a five-dollar customer, and it was wonderful. It was wonderful because the customer was her husband, and as far as the world was concerned no one need ever know that Dora Tincher was no different from the others.

For their benefit, she would still go to church, still gossip, still be the pure and the helplessly, pitifully wronged wife. But in her own home, with him, she would be just plain Dora Tincher, without any protective covering. She felt that Dora Tincher was in for a wonderfully exciting and vulgar life!

CHAPTER FOURTEEN

Alice Reed sat on the front porch. She didn't feel well today. The weather had gotten uncomfortably warm after the funeral. The autumn heat did things to her small body; it made her feel tired, sick and alone.

She leaned back in the big chair and scratched one finger across her flat belly. The starch was stiff in her print cotton dress, and it irritated her sensitive skin.

That was one important thing about herself: her sensitivity. She was sensitive to the smallest as well as the biggest things. She was quick to feel the prick of a needle against her finger tip. And she was observant, too. She prided herself on knowing as much as Dora Tincher ever knew. The difference between them was mainly Alice's ability to keep her mouth shut and her ears open.

All her life, she had minded her own business, although she did some pure and fancy listening in on other's business. But she didn't talk about their affairs the way most of the women folk did. Why, even at that poor boy's funeral they had talked. The dirty, digging things they said about him and him dead! They even insinuated that her own little Holly had been bad with that boy, Martin. And they made sure that Alice heard, although they pretended they didn't know she was listening. But she had raised her head higher and turned her nose up at them.

Thinking about Holly, she felt proud. Not a lot, but some. Holly had looked pretty sitting at the end of the front bench with her head bent forward reverently. Somehow Holly had looked almost glad, with her lips pulled tight and tugging at the corners of her mouth. And her eyes had a distant, shimmering look about them as if she didn't realize she was at a funeral. It was as if she was seeing him alive and talking and standing in front of her, with his hand motioning and his eyes searching.

Holly had a certain fullness about her at the funeral that Alice hadn't seen before. She wondered if the girl had taken off her undergarments. That way, with her body full and curved, she was suddenly a woman; desirable and almost pretty in a plain, but warm kind of way.

Thinking about it, Alice thought that the change had begun almost the same morning after that artist fellow came to the village. Holly had been spending a lot of time up there at the cabin and she had been bringing home considerable money, too.

Alice smiled contentedly. They had been eating well: meat every day; green beans, too, and corn. And once Holly had brought in a head of that fancy lettuce that Jeb and Milly got in once a month.

She smacked her lips. She saw the familiar figure of Preacher Tincher swinging down the road toward his house. He turned and went inside, and Alice sighed impatiently.

She had been lucky to make friends with Preacher. For a long time, she had wanted to be nice to that big manly man. But he had been so stand-offish and quiet that it had taken years. She had watched him hungrily, like a hen ready to pounce; but all the time he was so pure, preaching the way he did, and being good to that hypocrite of a wife he had.

Ugly woman, that Dora—mean, vicious and homely as sin. She had no shoulders at all, and no breasts, either—not the way a man liked a woman to have breasts. All she had in the whole world was a big bottom that stretched as wide as the doors on Brandy Elliot's gin barn.

But Alice's time had come; it came just like it did to Nellie Byrd. Only Nellie had come out in the open, raping that school kid. Nellie just set herself up for hire, and she made a good living taking anybody that wanted to play in greener pastures. But not Alice Reed.

Alice was smarter. She sat back, respectable and dirty, and pretended not to care. And when Preacher showed signs of weakening for Nellie, well, Alice just got sickly and had Holly ask if the Preacher would come visit her like he was supposed to visit his congregation.

He came the way she knew he would. He sat by her bed, and talked about God, but his heart was not in it. At first, when she made it plain what she wanted, he was angry. He called her bad names, and swore at her. But after he was finished, she just laughed at him. It was a hollow kind of laugh that rocked her whole body, and made her quiver on the bed. The more she laughed, the madder he became. But that was her way. And it was his way, too, she found. Because in his anger, he was exactly as she had known for years that he could be. He was sure of himself, demanding, possessive. That was what she loved most because it was so different from Dick's way of loving her.

Husbands just kind of took things for granted—easy and for granted. Never domineering ... never the beast in them that was not to be denied.

Alice rocked in the big chair and waited. Preacher would be coming out any time now. A man always needed to go out after a thing like that funeral. She knew him so well now that she could guess his every reaction. She sat back and waited, knowing he would come.

He could stay a long time today because Dick had gone up to the gin barn to steal some more of Brandy's moonshine. Preacher would just walk by, tip his hat to her, and he would wait. If she went inside, Preacher would come up the yard and go into the house, hooking the screen behind him.

She twisted uncomfortably in her chair. He had been home too long. Maybe he thought he could come and go as he pleased, and maybe he expected her to wait as if she never had anything to say about it ...

Then she saw him leave the house. She heard his loud, almost happy laughter, and she knew instinctively that he had somehow been appeased by that broad-bottomed woman. Alice swore softly at him.

She watched, craning her neck, while Preacher climbed into his truck and drove up the road, heading from the village. She wondered where he was going. She rose impatiently, angry with herself and with him, and she went inside and slipped into a coat.

Outside again, she looked about her to see if she was being watched. Then she saw that Holly was entering the house by the rear door. She heard her steps going into her bedroom. Alice smiled. Without another thought, she walked up the valley by the creek and climbed the West Hill, going toward Brandy Elliot's cabin.

Strange how a woman got a thing on her mind and couldn't settle her thinking until she had got satisfaction. It had always been that way with Alice Reed. But most of all, she enjoyed the good men like Preacher.

Now, for several days, she had been thinking about Brandy. He was the one man in the country that no woman could claim. Before he set his head on Holly, he had looked at Alice with a mildly interested gaze. Maybe, now that Holly wasn't interested, he would look again at Alice Reed.

She hurried up the hillside. The wind whipped at her coat, and the sharpness of it was like a knife against her legs. But it was not sharp enough to cut out the heat of autumn.

She saw they were all there. The dogs seemed everywhere. Brandy sat on the porch. He was bundled up in his heavy, checkered jacket and he didn't see her. She stole up quietly and was almost to the side of the porch before one of the dogs sat up and growled.

He looked around and there was an unmistakable look of disappointment when he saw her. He rubbed his red beard and his eyes began to narrow.

"Come on up. Ain't no use you chilling to death down there on the ground. Where's Dick? He ain't gonna like you coming here. I bet he'd kill you if he knew you was here, Alice Reed."

She walked up the steps onto the porch and let the wind whip her coat away from her knees. She felt her dress squeeze between her legs, and she turned about so that he saw her outlined under the cotton dress.

"You got a fire, ain't you? It's cold enough for a fire. A woman could freeze to death from that wind, and no man to care if she died of it, either," she said, twisted around, and she went into the cabin.

He followed her, took off his coat, and turned to look at her. She had removed her own coat and had loosened the snaps at the front of her dress so that the round curves of her breasts began to fill out above the dress.

"I'll get you a drink," he said, and went toward the kitchen. He came back and handed her one by the fireplace. He stood looking at her.

"You can go right back," he said slowly, and drank quickly from his glass. "You can go back and get yourself a little of your husband. I ain't liking the way you come here, Alice. I never liked the way you went with Preacher that way, either. Or the others. I ain't wantin' a woman that ain't honest even with herself. You ain't honest. You're a sneak, Alice. You just sneak up to a man and steal it. You don't even come out in the open and give a man a chance to get wind of it first."

"I reckon you got a better place to get it, eh?" she laughed. "Like maybe my Holly, eh?" she giggled, knowing it hurt him. But she didn't care because the moonshine was warm inside her, and the fire was warm at her back. Just looking at him set the heat blazing in her.

"You know me and Holly ain't done nothing. I wouldn't want to do nothing. Me and Holly will get married, maybe. But we won't be like you,

Alice. We won't sneak about it, pretending to be something we ain't."

"Who's sneaking about it?" she demanded sharply. "I ain't trying to fool you none. I'm just telling you, and you're standing there lying in your teeth trying to make me think you don't want it. Well, I don't believe you. I can see it in you. No man as big as you ever lived without it. No man in the hills lives for anything else but that, and you ain't no different. I don't know what you do about it, but I know you ain't different. Not unless you're like that kid was—"

His hand lashed out and suddenly drew back an inch short of her tight lips. She felt the fright rising in her. For a moment, she stood speechless, watching the anger rise in him, seeing the heave of his chest as he breathed.

"You filthy bitch," he said softly. "I ought to do it just to hurt you," he said, and she felt suddenly exalted. "But I wouldn't dare. I'd get sick at my stomach just thinking about it. Now get out of here," he said throwing her coat to her. "Get out and stay out or I'll tell Dick what you really are!"

"You wouldn't dare ..." she said. But she knew that he would and she took her coat and went slowly out.

CHAPTER FIFTEEN

Belle Barker put her son, Nat, down on the blanket before the open fireplace and left him under the watchful eyes of the two old people. Then she slipped into a worn gray sweater and went outside.

From a high knoll on the hill, she crouched beneath a tree. Leaves fell in the crisp autumn sunshine as she waited for Preacher Tincher to come up the valley road and cut off to the hillside that led to the Barker farm.

In the beginning, she had not cared that this respected man had fathered her child out of wedlock. It had been the result of her own unappeased hunger for a man's companionship; it had been because of her unrestrained response to another's hunger on a night which she would always remember.

But many things, especially one most important thing, had happened in the three years since that ill-fated night. And these made it improbable for her to continue raising a child which was actually Preacher's son as much as her own.

How could she have known on that night that the future would bring to her a strange, serious young man who wanted to start his own family?

This young man, who called himself Perry Layton, had literally come out of the woods one day with a packsack over his shoulders, and a week-old beard on his cheeks and chin. Grandpa Barker had decided that not only was Perry the perfect man to work the small farm for them now that they were getting old, but that he would also make a fine prospective husband for Belle, and an excellent father for the adorable, but bastard son of Preacher.

Perry Layton had worked the farm for near onto two years, turning the soil, raising the tobacco, curing it, stripping it, having Preacher haul it to market in the winter, and turning half of the money from the crops over to the Barker's. He even added a little for his own room and board.

At first, Perry had paid little attention to Belle. She was plain, almost homely except for her large eyes, and she was not very clean. In addition, she seemed almost stupid. Neither of them talked much. But as the months passed, the old man made it clear what he expected of Perry Layton. And eventually things began to work out as the old man wished.

Perry began asking Belle what she liked in the way of wild meats. He would hunt for rabbits especially for her, also squirrels. And sometimes they would gather walnuts together. Only last week, they had thrashed the limbs of a walnut tree to bring down nuts. Together they had taken off their shoes and stumped the green hulls off the nuts until their feet turned black with stain.

Perry had told her then that he was willing to marry her. He even declared that he was anxious to have a wife and raise a family. He wanted to "give the old people some kids they could be proud of," he told her. But he didn't want any young 'un that wasn't his and Belle's! He made it very clear that he didn't want Nat.

Belle knew that a hill woman didn't get many chances like Perry was offering her. If she wanted to marry a man, she had to do it the first chance she got. It wasn't a matter of finding a father for Nat, now. It was more a matter of finding a man to take care of her in her old age, someone to sleep with on cold nights. She wanted a man she could cook and sew for, someone to talk to when he wanted to talk—a man she could help and be with.

For this reason, at the funeral for the strange young Manley boy, she had whispered to Preacher that she would have to talk to him. And she knew that he would come, as she wished.

Down the hillside, she saw his truck rolling up the valley; then it turned to the right and came further up the hillside. She walked slowly under the trees to the road; then she went down to the bend just below the house.

He saw her and stopped the truck in the middle of the dirt road and got out. She sat down on the bank with her cotton dress pulled, carefully down over her knees. She waited until he came and stood before her. He looked down at her and then slowly sat beside her. She wondered what he must be thinking, for his eyes were serious and his hands were awkward in his lap.

She hesitated to tell him her wishes, fearing that he might be angry with her. But then she thought about Perry and her own future, and that was more important than avoiding this man's anger.

She said, "I been thinkin' about gettin' married, Preacher. I ain't so young no more. Near twenty now, and I gotta think about myself some before I get old. Perry—he's willin' 'nough to marry me. He told me he would, but he don't like havin' a ready-made son. He don't like that at all, Preacher."

Preacher was silent for a long while, and Belle's hands started to tremble in her lap. She worked her hands together, trying to still them.

"I reckon no man would like that," he said at last, and she sighed a little because his voice was not angry. Instead, it was quiet and thoughtful, and she thought how nice he could be sometimes, how wise, good and strong he could be when he wanted to. When his old woman wasn't being mean to him, he was good.

"I don't know what I'm to do with Nat," she said nervously. "I been thinkin' 'bout it 'til my head near kills me sometimes. I been thinkin' of a orphanage, or … I even been thinkin' of doin' somethin' awful to him," she breathed heavily.

His eyes came full upon her. His eyes showed his shock. "You couldn't do that, Belle! God, it ain't the boy's fault! And killin' him like that … why … we'd all go to hell sure!"

She frowned. "I reckon I wouldn't do that. But I thought of it lots a times—just thought of it. Ain't no harm in thinkin', is there? Besides, I can't let Perry get away, Preacher. He offered me a future, and I gotta think about myself, ain't I?"

Preacher stood up and stuck his hands into his pockets. His back was bowed like a hoop, and his big shoe went out solidly behind a pebble and sent it sailing down the dirt road.

"What do you want me to do about it?" he asked with a tinge of anger in his heavy voice. "You knew what you were doing that night. You might've been a virgin, but you knew what it was all about just the same. Every farm girl knows that. She knows it instinctively the same as dogs and cows and horses. Maybe I was older and I was supposed to be a trustworthy local preacher, but I'm human same as you."

"But I'm a woman!" Belle said defensively. "I can't marry when I got a kid that ain't got a father. A man won't marry a girl like that and raise it with his own kids! I gotta think about me and him and his kids, Preacher. I gotta marry a man and have somethin' in life besides gossip and women laughing at me and my kid, and pokin' fun at him when he gets older. I gotta have my own life now!"

"All right, all right! Just don't get so hot about it," he commanded. "I've been thinking about it. I've been thinking about it for a long time, even before you met Perry, but I couldn't decide what to do. Now, I reckon you just made it necessary, even if you didn't make it easier."

She looked at him hopefully. "You got a idea? You can fix it so I won't have the kid? So I can marry Perry?"

"I might," he said softly. He walked up and down on the dirt road with his hands like fists in his pockets, and his words poured out, one against the other, as if he was afraid to stop until he had said it all.

"Me and Dora ain't ever going to have any children of our own. And I reckon it would be awful lonesome to grow old without any young 'uns to come visiting in your old age. So I been thinking that maybe I could raise the lad better than you. I could adopt him, Dora and me, and raise him that way. He'd have a father and mother, and he could go to school and grow up same as any other kid, and he would seem like our own—mine and Dora's. Because he is mine, ain't he? Well, ain't he?" he demanded, looking at her mercilessly.

"Yeah, he is. Sure, you know he ain't nobody else's kid, Preacher. Ain't nobody, not even Perry, ever done that but you!"

"Well," he said, slacking off on his walking. "I reckon I can do that, then. Want me to take him back with me now?"

She nodded quickly, eagerly, a smile coming on her face, and her heart leaping up happily to his suggestion. She stood up suddenly and kissed him on the cheek so that he flushed a dark crimson, and then she ran up the hill toward the house. Slowly he began to follow her.

Belle gathered up the few clothes she had for the lad and shoved them into a paper bag, the kind Jeb used for groceries at the store. The old people woke up, sleepy-eyed, and looked at Preacher in the doorway. When Belle put the sleeping child into Preacher's arms, the old man got up on his cane and hobbled over to the door.

"I always said you was a good one. You ain't a bad man. I reckon we owe a lot to you fer takin' it like this."

"You don't owe me nothing," Preacher assured him. "Maybe I owe you something. You give me a kid … a son," he said, and his voice sounded soft and proud.

Footsteps came close to the shack, and Preacher stood aside to allow a tall, skinny, unshaven youth into the living room.

For an instant, the eyes of the two men met in silent hostility. The tall young man with the beard and the messed hair and the rounded shoulders, and this bigger, heavier, ruddier-faced man with the neat hair and clean clothes. They looked at each other, and Belle stood a few feet away and wrung her hands.

After a while, Preacher looked at her. "No need to be scared," he said. Looking at the young man he added, "Is there?"

The young man hesitated, looked at Belle, and back at Preacher. "No. I reckon there ain't."

"I'll be going ahead then," Preacher said. "And don't worry none. I'll do what I told you. He'll grow up to be a fine lad, my son will!" And he went out, looking big and awkward, and a little proud with the child still sleeping in his arms.

Perry Layton shut the door and looked at Belle Barker. "You ain't lovin' him none, are you?"

"No! Oh, no," she said, and ran to him with her face twisted, and tears running down her cheeks.

"Well. I reckon we can get hitched, then. You wanta go to town and get hitched now? Got time before dark, Belle."

She looked at the old people. "Yes. Yes!" she said eagerly. And she thought, *With the night I'll have my man. And there will be a pallet fixed in front of the fire, and I won't have to get up from it before daylight comes.*

"Yes," she repeated anxiously, and they went out together.

Together, they saddled up the two horses and rode into the county clerk's office. They had to go to a doctor and get a certificate. But when they returned to the clerk's office, the papers were filled out in five minutes' time.

Then, taking the papers, they got on the horses again and rode back to the village. It was long since dark when they arrived. Stopping their horses, they dismounted in front of Preacher's house and went in together.

Dora Tincher opened the door for them and she did not speak. Her eyes were swollen and red, and Belle knew there had been a fight over the child. But she knew that Preacher had won, because Nat ran up to her. Belle stood silent, making no sign to her son, although her heart pounded with her eagerness to answer.

Dora Tincher said irritably, "Nat! Nat! Get away from that woman!"

When Preacher came in from the bedroom, he smiled sadly. He got a book from the desk and married them quietly, without any recognition in his eyes.

When they left, Perry grabbed Belle's band. "Ain't gonna be long now," he said, and there was possessiveness in his grip and impatience in his voice.

They rode hard and fast up the hills. Soon the horses were standing in the barn. Inside the house, asleep on the pallet in the living room with the firelight blazing over them, were the new husband and wife. Belle would soon raise her own, and these children would bear the name of Layton. For the father would be tall and skinny, and a jealous man.

CHAPTER SIXTEEN

Brandy Elliot's dogs set up a din of barking that would have wakened the entire countryside from the sleep of death. So fierce was their barking that Brandy rose hurriedly, setting his jug of moonshine under the dining room table. He grabbed his shotgun from the hooks over the fireplace.

Brandy was on the porch with the gun even before the visitor had stepped three feet beyond the rim of the woods into the clearing.

When he saw the lone man, Brandy laughed jovially. He called off the dogs. "Hi ya, Sheriff!" he cried cheerfully. "You lookin' for my stills again, eh?"

The man came up closer. "You know darned well I ain't the sheriff, Brandy. I'm just a deputy. But I came to look all right."

Brandy laughed. "Come in and sit awhile, Sheriff," he invited. "I got a jug of the best spirits you ever set lips to."

Brandy replaced the shotgun in its niche over the fireplace. Bringing out the jug from under the table, he handed it to the Deputy Sheriff.

"Try your lips on that, Sheriff. Ain't a better formula for making it in the state. My own personal brand."

Brandy stood back and watched while the big man drank from the jug. The deputy made a face and then looked serious. He was a big, homely man with a nose that could have been used for a corkscrew. He came to the hills every two or three months, looked around just so he could report a search to the sheriff when he went back to town. As a result of the search he also carried away a couple of gallons of Brandy's best moonshine which the deputy hid under the rear seat of his automobile. He also paid a visit either to Nellie Byrd or Alice Reed. Sometimes he visited both of them, depending on his needs and his particular mood.

Knowing this, and anticipating his needs, Brandy suggested, "Reckon we better go searching. Won't be long before dark, and a man can't see a still in the dark."

They went out, carrying the jug and nipping on it at intervals during their walk through the hills. They were careful not to go down into the valley, at the head of which was the biggest outfit for making moonshine in the state of Kentucky.

They covered the barn, but they didn't go near the stacked hay, under which were hundreds of jugs of moonshine. They went through the woods, the thickets and the fields. Then they came back to warm at the fireplace, to talk, and drink the amber liquid from the jug.

"If you ever tell the Sheriff I ain't doin' my duty, Brandy, you'll never make another batch of this stuff!"

Brandy laughed. "I should tell him and lose my income! You must be getting nuts in your old age, Sheriff!"

"Well, sometimes I get to thinkin' about this. About the way I come here knowin' damned well you make the stuff and don't do nothin' about it. Takin' back a load of it for myself and all. And you knowing about Nellie. The sheriff wouldn't like me seein' Nellie when I'm here. She done a bad thing to that school kid and it ain't set well with the county folks, none."

"Nellie ain't really bad," Brandy said smiling. "She's just a woman that likes her man, that's all. She's just honest. None a that sneakin' business about her. Nellie reminds me a lot a my bitches. She just lays and waits for it, and don't make no pretense about hiding the fact that she's in heat."

The man laughed. "And her a waitin' fer you, and you never coming, eh?"

Brandy frowned. "Waiting for me?" he asked, puzzled.

The man laughed derisively. "Don't be actin' like you don't know it. She's been up there watching this hillside for years: waitin' for you to come off it and come up to her. She's been waitin' all the time she beds with them fellows."

"What makes you say that?" Brandy asked. "Why should she? She gets all he wants, don't she?"

"Sure she does. And more, I'll bet. But it ain't what she wants. She got kinda drunk with me once and she told me. She told me, 'You know, Ben, that man's got somethin' no woman ever tasted, and I'm waitin' to take it from him. He's a damned virgin that's as passionate as a dog. And when he finds it out, I'm gonna be the bitch to give it to him so he won't forget.' And so help me, that's what she told me when she was drunk that time."

Brandy felt his face growing hot, and he lifted the jug and put it between his lips. He thought about what Nellie was supposed to have said about him, and he thought about Holly. He knew damned well

Nellie was right about two things: he was a damned virgin all right, and he was plenty damned passionate too. But it wasn't Nellie who would wake him up. It would have to be Holly Reed.

He thought about Holly till his insides knotted up like a twisted wet rope. And he thought about her till he nearly gave in to his passion, nearly gave in to it and went up to see Nellie—almost, but not quite. He wanted Holly Reed and he felt it in his bones that she would need him just as much, and it would be best if he just waited 'til she was ready.

"You think I'm foolin' you?" the man asked, his yellow teeth gleaming in the firelight.

Brandy shook his head. "It don't matter either way. I got my mind on somethin' else."

"The young un, eh?" he laughed. "You're old enough to know better, man. That one ain't for you! Why, I bet she's as cold as an icicle in the middle of February!"

"Maybe," Brandy admitted, and took another drink from the jug. "Reckon I better open up another one," he said, eyeing the inch of the amber liquid that was left. He got up and went into the kitchen, and came back with three jugs of the stuff.

"Two for you to take with you and one for us to drink," he said, opening a jug of it and drinking thirstily. He licked his lips and set the jug beside him on the floor.

"Next to women, I reckon a jug of whiskey is the best thing a man can have handy."

"Yeah," the deputy grunted, himself emptying the first jug. "I been thinking about both for two months. You know, it's a good thing for a man to get away sometimes. Reckon I'd just shrink up if it wasn't for coming here every two months. A man needs something like he gets here. Whiskey and Nellie. He needs it."

"Maybe, but I'd be satisfied if I had me a woman of my own."

The deputy laughed. "No, you wouldn't neither. I got me a woman, but it ain't the same. A woman—she marries you, and right away she gets different ideas. She wants you to make love, and all that mushy stuff, and then half the time she wants you to stop just when you're warmin' up to her. Nope," he said thoughtfully, "you'd be wantin' the real thing. Like this," he said, shaking the jug in front of him. "Straight and pure and undiluted. You take it, and that's that. Like Nellie," he added, twisting uncomfortably.

"Well, if you're going to keep talking about her, you better go ahead and get up there," Brandy said, observing the way the deputy kept moving impatiently in his chair.

"Yeah. You're right, Brandy. Sure sorry you can't see it my way, man.

Nellie sure would like to see you coming up that valley!"

"Maybe someday I will," Brandy said to him on the porch, helping him place the two jugs under his arms. But he didn't believe it.

Brandy went back into the shack alone, and put wood on the fireplace. The feeling had become stronger lately. He felt that Holly was waking up, getting ready and anxious. A man could see it if he knew her and watched her as Brandy did. A man could see the way she dressed better, and the way her cheeks were rosy, and the way her lips were moist all the time and soft and open like a wet rose in the dew of the evening. He could see it the way she walked, and the way her little breasts had begun to show, pointing upward through her dress.

He had the feeling that she was getting awfully ready, and he knew why. Sometimes when he thought about the man who had brought about all this sudden ripening of Holly Reed, he wanted to go across the valley to that shack and shake the rotten hell out of that pretty man who didn't give a damn whether she got that way or not.

He got so mad at Larry Carter, he could have killed him. Holly wanted him, and yet he just let her keep house for him, always chasing her off in the afternoons so that Babs Melchior could sneak over. He reckoned another man would like to kill Larry Carter, too. And he knew that if Jim Melchior ever found out that Larry Carter fooled with his wife, Jim would shoot him like a pig ready to slaughter for fall.

Everybody in the village knew about Babs' visits to the shack on the East Hill—everybody except Jim Melchior. And he didn't know about it because everybody knew Jim would be furious. Every man and woman knew Jim's wild anger and his strange sense of duty. He would kill Larry Carter without thinking twice about it. So they never let him hear them talking, and they never hinted to him that his wife had a secret lover.

Holly Reed was in the same predicament. She didn't know either, mostly because she was quiet, like Jim. One sensed the animal instinct in her and knew without thinking that her anger would work like Jim's. She would kill to protect the man she loved and wanted. She would kill whoever hurt him. She would do it willingly, even anxiously. Danger lay in her quietness, in her naive, animal lustiness.

Therefore, no one talked about what was happening to Holly Reed or to Jim Melchior. But Brandy sensed that not even people with the finest motives could go on forever keeping a dark, dangerous secret. Sometime it was bound to come into the open. And even while knowing what would happen, one couldn't help wondering just exactly how that end would come about.

Brandy sat down with his jug, and he thought about Jim's anger if he learned the truth … and he wondered how long it would be before the truth did, somehow, get out.

CHAPTER SEVENTEEN

Babs Melchior felt uncomfortably ill all day. She woke up with an upset stomach and came dangerously close to being ill while she made breakfast for Jim. He had barely left for work when she ran out of doors to the out-building and was terribly sick at her stomach.

All day long her head felt light and giddy, and at intervals her stomach would act up mysteriously so that she got nothing done. The house went uncleaned, the bed unmade, and she did not every try to make the walk up to Larry's shack.

By evening, she began to have a horrible premonition that she might be pregnant! She realized this when she began to figure the days and found that she was long past due.

It was shortly before Jim was to return from work when she arrived at the added conviction that it could not possibly be Jim's baby that she was carrying.

She knew that Jim would never trick her. He had always been careful, knowing how she felt about having children. But she remembered Larry and his insistence that he would have her back. She knew instinctively that he was the one who had tricked her!

She became unreasonably angry with him—not only because he had tricked her, but because he had done so without believing her. She had warned him about Jim. She insisted that Jim would kill him. Everyone knew Jim's anger, how it could flare up into a volcano of destruction.

And now, thinking about it, she knew that the secret could no longer be kept. Still … was there any reason why Jim should know? He could have slipped, couldn't he? He could have been mistaken just once. It could be his child she carried, couldn't it?

If she told him she was having a child, he would have to believe her—unless Larry told him otherwise, but why would a man risk his life? Surely, Larry would know better than to be so foolish.

Perhaps if she talked to Larry soon … explained to him again how Jim felt about a wife, about purity and things. Maybe then Larry would leave her alone. Perhaps he would even go away once he realized he could never again have her.

She had intended forcing him to go away weeks ago. She hadn't meant to fall back into the old ways. It had just come about naturally, easily.

She had gone to the shack the first time partly for fun and partly to warn Larry that it was all over. And she had intended it to be all over, but he had been unusually sweet that day. It had been so easy to go along with him for a little way, letting him kiss and touch her. And afterward, it had been impossible for her to turn back. It had been impossible because Larry knew of her passion. He could easily take advantage of it, even without particularly wanting to himself. It was a way he could belittle her, possess her again against her will.

Afterward came his threats to tell despite the danger to himself. That had started it: her going back regularly, with the village knowing about it, too; going back to wait until Holly Reed left, and then sneaking into the shack for a few snatched moments of sin.

Each time, she intended to defy him. Her speeches were prepared long before she entered the shack; and yet, each time, she asked herself what harm existed in a few kisses—his soft, expert kisses. Surely, his hands could not hurt her; his arms about her, the insistent cooing—these couldn't cheapen her.

But once she submitted to these smaller, tender attentions, she was pliable to his wishes; he took advantage of her with a viciousness that shamed her to the core. Then, she could not have stopped for she hadn't either the will nor the wish to do so—she would not stop until it was over and done with and she had been defiled by his own wantonness.

Now if she dared return to the shack, if she chanced going there and warning Larry to leave, then she might succeed in keeping the truth from Jim. There might still be a chance—a chance for their marriage, for Jim to live without blood on his hands.

It was dark when Jim came home from work. He barged in with his usual gaiety and gathered her up in his arms. He squeezed her to him, kissing her before he realized that she did not respond. But when he felt the hot tears against his cheek, he put her down and looked at her with worried eyes.

"Honey!" he exclaimed anxiously. "Honey, what is it?"

She blubbered through the tears, trying to talk. Finally she managed to force a laugh. She said, "It's nothing like that, Jim. It's just that … I found out … we're going to have a baby." She dropped her head and began to bawl loudly. Suddenly he started to laugh, and held her close. He kissed her neck and cheeks, and messed her hair with his chin.

"Why that ain't nothing to cry about, Honey!" he teased gently. "Gosh, I'm so glad I could jump a twenty-foot tree without even touchin' it! Now you just stop crying, and set down here while I get dinner for us, eh?" he said, pushing her down into a chair and looking at her fondly.

While he went into the kitchen, she sat and cried softly into her hands so that he wouldn't hear. She knew suddenly how hard it was to be a decent wife and how good it could be if a woman were decent to a man like her Jim.

He trusted her—and she was a whore from a whorehouse. He loved her—and she let herself be degraded by another man. He wanted his child—but she would bear another's. She wept while he made dinner. For he trusted her and loved her all the more for giving him a child—Larry's child!

After dinner, she sat in his lap while he talked softly and consolingly to her. He told her how glad he was that he was to have a son, how much a son meant to a man. And he told her how much he loved her. He called her his little marigold, his little Mother.

He called her all the wonderful, idiotic things she wanted to hear from his lips; affectionate things—and all because he thought she carried a part of him inside her body.

When she answered him, she was hesitant. Having figured out when the conception had occurred, she was careful to be sure that Jim had possessed her at that time. In answering to his questions as to how she felt about it, she showed just enough concern and fear, and just enough happiness that she had made the step. She even told him she was glad that there had been a slip and she had been made pregnant. But when he seemed ecstatically happy about this, she felt a pain and she cursed Larry Carter. Because of him she would have to live a lie the whole of her life.

Rapidly, she made plans. She had to see Larry soon and tell him the truth; she had to warn him again.

She looked at Jim as he held her close. She thought that if it were necessary to keep that happy look on her man's face, she herself would kill Larry Carter. Yes … she would kill him herself if it became essential to keep her husband with that happy, trusting expression on his face.

CHAPTER EIGHTEEN

Holly Reed slipped up the valley and up the side of the East Hill. There was a glow rising inside her. It was like the early morning autumn sun that rose over the tip of the hill, casting orange light over the countryside. Leaves lay in dazzling colors of gold and brown and green.

She felt the skin on her legs tightening and she felt like an apple polished to a red and green glow, waiting for lips to bite into its solid, silken skin.

Inside the apple was the rich, full-bodied flavor. It had been ripening now for several weeks, growing full and round and mellow. It had begun that night Larry came to the village, wakening her sleeping passion. It had also begun since she had talked to the boy, Martin, and felt him swim over her naked body. It had grown since that morning when she found him hanging naked from the limb of the walnut tree. Even while she had looked into his casket, she had half-wished she had made him take her that day on the bank by the creek.

Her cheeks colored a blushing pink when she saw Brandy Elliot sitting on the front porch of his shack, his hound dogs around him.

She climbed the hillside and went across the swinging bridge. Finally she reached Larry Carter's shack. As always, she entered without knocking on the door. She made Larry's breakfast, and quietly hummed a song as the bacon fried in the pan. The coffee perked on the red-hot cook stove.

When breakfast was ready, she carried it into his bedroom and put it on the stand near his bed. She called him gently, forcing herself not to submit to the wild, impulsive urge to crawl in beside him.

He woke slowly, rubbing his eyes and looking at her as if he hardly saw her. "Ah … hi," he murmured. "Coffee. I always need coffee. A man can't be decent until he's had his first cup of coffee," he said, reaching for the cup.

She stood and watched him, until he looked up at her. "What are you doing standing there?" he demanded. "Haven't you got other things to do?"

She turned and went out, working on straightening the main room. She aired it and built a small fire in the grate. When the room was warm, Larry Carter came in slowly, dragging his slippered feet and tying the robe about him. She knew that under the robe was no more than a silly-looking pair of white shorts.

He sat down on the sofa before the fireplace and stretched his legs out before him. The robe slid over to one side.

"What are you staring at?"

He said it so suddenly, she jerked back and looked away from him defensively.

"Well …" he added even more softly, "that's a new dress, isn't it?"

She smiled, pleased. "Do you like it?" she said, turning about so that he could admire the lines.

"It's not bad. Not half bad," he said slowly. "You might be over sixteen after all," he said, looking closely at her.

"I am!" she assured. "I'm a woman!" she added proudly.

"Not much of a woman," he said thoughtfully. "You're flat. Flat and plain." And he leaned back, dismissing her completely.

But she wanted him to know. She said, "I'm not flat. I'm a woman! If you weren't so blind, you'd know I was! You and your pictures! You think I ain't got as much as your pictures, but I have. I've got more because I'm real—I'm alive!"

He looked at her and smiled gently. "So … I believe you," he said, but he didn't mean it. She knew he didn't mean it, and it hurt her. Of all the people in the world, she wanted him to know she was a woman. She had told him and he hadn't believed her!

"I could show you," she said.

He smiled, again gently, teasing her. "Maybe," he murmured.

"But I could! I'll show you I'm a woman!" she unfastened the dress down the front and slid it back off her arms so that she stood in front of him in a cotton slip. She felt her own plainness.

"A child," he said derisively.

"A woman!" she repeated hoarsely, and bent forward and pulled the slip over her head. She turned her back to him, and slipped hurriedly out of the white band across her chest. She stepped out of the faded pink underpants. Then she felt suddenly clean and grown and beautiful. She turned suddenly and faced him. She knew by his eyes that he was not disappointed.

He muttered something softly, like it hurt him, and then he got up and went toward her. He grabbed her close to him. He kissed her again and again … and she wondered if he'd ever stop. His hands moved over her and she thought they were like a woman's hands. She wished he would be quick and sudden. He was so slow.

The door opened suddenly, and it sounded like a crack of thunder. Larry whirled about even as Holly stood there, angry at the interruption.

Babs Melchior stood in the doorway, a horrible damning look on her pretty face. When Larry saw her, he forgot all about Holly Reed—until Babs looked fiercely at Holly. Then he remembered.

"Get out, Holly," he commanded. "Get out."

She stood there, frozen, unable to believe that he could stop now … unable to believe that it mattered whether someone saw.

She walked up to him and pulled at his arm so that he looked at her. She said, "I won't leave. Not now. Not ever, now."

He brought his hand up suddenly, slapped her across the face. "You stinkin' slut," he said angrily. "You ain't any better than that whore of a mother you've got. Now get your filthy butt out of here before I wring it off of you!"

Then, without a word, she gathered up her clothes, and walked into the crisp autumn air. She went to the edge of the hill where the swinging bridge crossed the valley to Brandy's house. There she stopped to wait and put on her clothes. She sat, too stunned by rejection to wonder why Babs Melchior should be in Larry Carter's shack early on a Tuesday morning.

She waited ... wanting only that Babs should hurry with whatever business she had with Larry Carter. She had to return to that big, handsome man with the soft, cuddling hands.

When she looked to see where the noise was coming from, she saw the dogs on the swinging bridge. She saw that one of them was a bitch in heat. Suddenly Holly reached down and gathered twigs and stones, which she threw at the dogs. The stones missed, dropping into the valley and splashing into the creek. As she spent herself angrily upon the dogs she was reminded of her own personal, unanswered need.

CHAPTER NINETEEN

Brandy was sitting on the porch that morning early, a jacket around his shoulders as he enjoyed the morning sun. Soon, now, the weather would be too cold for him to be sitting out-of-doors. So he sat and watched the dogs and listened to the last birds of summer, those that had not yet flown south. He listened to the bright sound of the breeze in the trees, and he heard the whistle of the wind against the corner of the house. Winter would be coming fast.

The sun rose and shone onto the porch. Feeling warm he took off his jacket, and sat rolling his tobacco and smoking, blowing rings into the sunlight.

He saw Holly Reed making her way up the opposite hill, and he smiled as he watched her. He felt good when he saw Holly. He admired her youth, the vigor and energy that was in her, ready to burst out under a man's coaxing.

Later, he saw Babs Melchior go up the same hill toward the same shack. He waited for Holly to come out as always. But this morning, something was wrong. Holly was still in the shack when Babs Melchior went inside.

A few minutes later, Holly Reed came out. She was naked, her clothes clutched to her. Brandy knew what had happened. He knew that something had been going on in the shack, something not completed because Babs Melchior had walked in. And he thought, *Now it's out of the bag. Now Holly knows. And Jim will know, and the trouble will begin.*

He watched Holly go down to the bridge which he had swung across the valley himself. She put on her clothes and sat by the bridge until she saw the dogs. Then he saw her get up, and he knew what she was feeling. He knew of her anger as he saw her throw rocks at the dogs. It wasn't something Holly would ordinarily do.

And then, Brandy, from his own porch, saw Babs Melchior come out of the shack and hurry rapidly down the side of the hill. When she came close to the bridge, he saw Holly turn. Babs seemed to hesitate and then she came on to the edge of the hill.

The two of them seemed to talk for a while. The voices came to him from the distance, and he thought he could bear the high pitch of anger. He saw a sudden movement, as if Babs had lost her footing near the bridge. He watched as instinctively Holly reached out her hand. But she was too late. The rising, terrified scream of a woman falling to her death filled the air.

Brandy lurched up from his seat. He heard the splash that her body made in the creek. Then the world because suddenly very, very still. Not even the wind seemed to blow. The sun went under a cloud, and he saw Holly break into a run. He heard her sobs in the still air and they sounded like deafening claps of thunder … rolling, rising, bouncing against the hillsides.

He thought about rushing down to the creek. But he knew that would be hopeless. Babs had died when she hit that water as surely as a man died when a bullet pierced his heart. The drop was too long. The water would be like a sheet of cold steel. It would have smashed her lungs … her ribs …

Holly was the only one to think about now. He waited until she came running into the clearing, and then he ran down to meet her. He threw the jacket over her shoulders. He helped her up the steps and pushed open the door.

She was mumbling through her sobs, "It was an accident. She slipped. I tried to stop her, but she slipped. And she was sleeping with him. She was his woman— It was an accident."

"I know," Brandy said monotonously, over and over to soothe her. "I know it was an accident. I saw it from the porch. Now rest here. I've got to get her out of the creek. Somebody's got to tell them down at the village. You just stay here until I get back, Holly."

"It was an accident … but she was bad. She slept with him. She told me she slept with him …"

"I know," Brandy repeated. "Now you just stay here and—" he sighted the jug under the dining table and he went after it.

He gave her a big swallow of the whiskey and took a drink himself.

He wiped his mouth and smoothed down his beard. "You just stay here now, till I get back. Take more of this stuff if you want."

Then he went out and went down to the creek. It was a dirty mess getting her out and laying her on the bank. He covered her up with a sheet he had brought along with him. Then he went down to the village. He didn't stay to hear what anyone said; he didn't wait to find out who told Jim Melchior. He just told Jeb Buckley at the store to take care of the matter, and he headed back to Holly Reed.

When he got to his shack, he found her sound asleep. She had passed out in a drunken stupor; the jug beside her was half empty. She sat in a chair in front of the fireplace with her head dropped onto her chest. Picking her up, he carried her into the bedroom and stretched her out on the bed.

For a long time, he stood over her, looking at her and wishing things had been different so that she was on his bed as his wife. He wiped his red beard and went slowly into the living room and got the jug.

The people from the village would be coming soon. They would come to question him, to get the body, and to make plans for the funeral. And Jim would find out that his wife had been with Larry Carter and murder would follow.

Brandy thought about it. He almost felt that the man deserved to die. But then, Larry Carter couldn't have known that he'd have to meet up with a dangerous man when he picked on Jim's wife. Thinking this, he told himself that someone ought to warn Larry Carter.

Brandy kept drinking. When he finished the jug, he brought out another. He had taken the first drink from the new jug when they came. He went with them down to the creek and he didn't even look at Jim Melchior. Jim went ahead of them, the four or five men. He went ahead and stood over her body, and he sounded as if he were choking, as if he were going to cry. He kept talking about how he was to have had a son soon; he said she died with his son. But Brandy didn't look at him. He didn't want to be the one to tell Jim Melchior that maybe the son wouldn't have been his.

They took her body down to the village. Afterward, the deputy sheriff came and asked questions just for his report. Finally, when they had all gone, Brandy Elliot started across the bridge.

The October sun was halfway across the sky when he knocked on the door of the shack where Larry Carter lived. Brandy hadn't set eyes on the young man since he had rented the shack, and Brandy was surprised when Carter opened the door. He was wearing a bright wine-colored robe; his hair was messed and hung over his forehead, looking like a woman's bangs.

"Oh …" Larry Carter murmured, surprised. "The landlord! What have I done, Elliot?"

"Nothing much. Can I come in? Wanta talk to you, Carter."

Larry Carter stepped back, bowed mockingly, and ushered Brandy into the living room. It was a neat, large room—homey looking. The couch in front of the fireplace had pillows that looked recently used.

"Sit down, Elliot. Anything I can get for you? I don't have any of that moonshine of yours, but I've some real stuff. Bourbon. Want to try it?"

Brandy shook his head, fingered his beard. "Reckon you don't know about Babs, then?"

Larry glanced up suspiciously. "Know what?" he asked sharply.

"That she just died," Brandy said shortly. Larry Carter's face turned a funny shade of green, then white, and then red.

"She fell off the cliff into the valley. Died right away, I guess. Or drowned anyway if she wasn't dead when she hit it. They came and took her away a while ago. The men from the village. And her husband, Jim Melchior," Brandy added softly.

Larry Carter got up nervously, poured himself a drink and downed it in one gulp. He looked at Brandy, turned away and poured another stiff drink for himself.

"Why didn't you come tell me sooner? I would have helped carry her to the village."

Brandy frowned. "I didn't think you'd want to meet Jim Melchior so soon. He won't like it when he learns why she was in the hills. She was going to have a baby, you know."

"How the hell would I know?" Larry demanded angrily, twisting the belt to his robe.

"Maybe because it would have been yours."

"Now listen here, Elliot …" Carter began, and stopped because Brandy Elliot had fastened his cold blue eyes on the young man's face. He saw the nerves jumping around Carter's mouth; the young fellow's fingers moved spasmodically, and his head jerked too fast.

"I live over there on the hillside opposite you. I got some glasses I can use when I have to. But most of the time, clear days like this, I can see over here without any trouble. I know the women and men around here by their walk, most. The way they carry themselves, and the size of 'em. I have to know things like that, have to see 'em too, in my business. And I saw Babs come in here today while Holly was here. First time she ever came in before Holly cleared out. But she did today. Figure you hadn't expected her. Maybe she came to tell you about the baby, eh? And afterward, I saw Holly come out, naked. And later I seen Babs come out. She didn't act satisfied. Like maybe you hadn't been very receptive to her talk, eh?"

Larry Carter had sat down. He had listened carefully. And now he looked up at the older, red-headed and bearded man.

"Why are you telling me this?"

"Because, no matter how rotten a man is, he deserves a chance to save his own neck."

Larry paled under his dark skin. He clasped his hands together in his lap. "You mean that silly goof really would kill me?"

"He ain't so silly. Not Jim Melchior. He's a smart man. But he's got a temper, and a strange kind of belief about things that are his, I reckon. Anyway, he'll sure as hell kill you. Mind you, I don't care one bit if he does. Might even consider doing it myself, all taken into consideration. But I thought a man had a right to be warned one last time."

Brandy stood up, pulled his trousers up a niche, and ambled toward the door. Then, as an afterthought, he turned to Larry Carter, who still sat on the couch with his head bowed down.

"Just one more thing I wanta know. You didn't get her, did you?"

Larry looked puzzled. "Who?" he murmured.

"Holly Reed."

He looked back down at the floor, uninterested. "No. I didn't. Babs come in too soon."

Brandy grunted. He smiled softly under his beard, and went out into the sunlight. Maybe it wasn't the way a man should be; maybe he shouldn't be thinking such thoughts when he knew hell was going to pop anytime now. But all the same, he was mighty damned glad nobody had claimed Holly Reed. And maybe nobody else would …

He walked down the hillside to the bridge. But just as he was crossing it, he saw Holly going down the other hill. He sighed. Well, there was still time. And he had lots of time.

CHAPTER TWENTY

Jim Melchior raised the hood of the big car and gazed thoughtfully at the engine of the Buick. The squat, little, fat man behind the steering wheel poked a fat red neck through the window.

"Well?" he demanded. "Can you fix it or can't you?"

Jim smiled casually. "I think so. Just an air bubble in the gas line, I expect. Let me blow it out with the air hose, and I think it will be fine again. Nothing serious from what you tell me. Just ain't getting the gas like it should."

"Well. Get it done then. I ain't got all day. I got things to do."

"Yeah," Jim murmured, and hoped the smile on his face didn't show how hard he was trying to be polite. "Reckon you must be a busy man."

"Fellow's got to hustle if he's going to make out," Bhram muttered, getting out of the car and slamming the door shut. He bent over the fender and also peered at the engine.

"You taking something out of there?"

Jim nodded. "Have to take the valve out so I can blow the line out," he said. Nothing anyone did or said today would make him lose his patience. Not today. Today he was a different man, going from boyhood, kind of, into manhood. Fatherhood, you might say. Why, he was more than just a man. He was kind of a god, and a god had no reason to get angry at the slightest provocation. He was the maker of human beings: Jim Melchior. He had made love with a blonde woman, and now he was to get a … son!

Why, he'd call him something great. Maybe name him after a President of the United States even. A son of his could easily get to be an important man. That was sure when a son came from such happiness, and pure, righteous love.

Jim put the air hose back, closed the hood and looked at Bhram. "There now," Jim said, "I reckon it will run all right." He walked away from the automobile, confident that it would start.

When he was in the garage, he heard the car door slam. A man that slammed a car door like that didn't deserve to drive one. The engine turned over, purred softly. The motor worked all right. His thoughts turned elsewhere.

His life had really begun when he met Babs. His interest in women began then. Although it had always confined itself to just one woman. But Babs had always been enough for Jim Melchior. And now that he was to have a son, well—his thoughts spun on and on.

At noon, he stopped to eat the lunch which Babs had fixed for him. Drinking from his thermos of coffee, drawing in smoke from his rolled cigarette, he thought about Babs and about the baby.

He thought about the way Babs had acted last night: kind of upset. She'd been sick all day. Maybe she would be sick today too. Maybe he should have been more considerate and stayed home with her. They could have stretched the budget to allow him to miss one day of work. He might even make it up at night. Why, if she was sick right now and no one there with her, he'd never forgive himself. It wasn't as if a woman was expected to take all that by herself. He didn't believe that. He thought a man and a woman should share things, everything—even sickness. But a man should take the biggest part of it. He should look after his woman, not just take money home and let her wait on him hand and foot, and be a slave, and sleep with him.

Right from the beginning, he had tried to show Babs that she was part of him, not just a tool for him to use. He tried to show her that he loved her, that he wanted her to be happy and enjoy him just as much as he enjoyed her. Otherwise, he'd feel like she was just another prostitute instead of his own wife, and he had no use for prostitutes.

He remembered that time in Japan. A bunch of the boys had gone up to this little shack and knocked on the back door. A big fat American woman had peeped out, smiled real big and let them in.

They stood around a small dark room and waited. There were three doors that went out of the room into little cubbyholes; and one by one, the men came out and others went in.

He wanted to leave. He felt somehow dirty and unclean, standing there with his hands in his pockets and his chin pulled down into the jacket as if he were ashamed to show his face. But he had been to a movie, an American movie, and watching it had made him suddenly very lonely and warm and impatient. So he stood there waiting in line until it was his time to go in.

He'd never forget that moment as long as he lived. He could still see that olive skin glistening in the lamplight. He remembered those large-tipped breasts sloping down over her chest, the fat thighs.

He'd taken it—with his eyes shut, and his lips pressed so tight against his teeth he could feel the salt from his blood. But he hadn't liked it. He'd hated it—hated the way it made him feel cheap, the way it left him empty and with nothing but a filthy memory.

To cleanse himself he remembered the girl he had met at the USO dance. When finally he got back to the States, he saw her again. It was the beginning of everything as it should be. She was clean and fine—not at all like the prostitutes. She was warm and responsive. So he had spent all their loving moments trying to show her that she was his equal when it came to love. And he felt good about her afterward. He felt as if making love was holy and fine, something good.

"Jim! Jim Melchior!"

Jim sat upright. "Yeah?" he called back through the garage.

The man came up beside him. "Got a phone call from the village about your wife. She's been hurt. Want you to come home right away."

Babs? Hurt? His heart leaped upward, pounded impatiently against his ribs. What of the baby? What of Babs?

It was silly to worry—plain silly and womanish to get upset and nervous. Quickly he left the garage and drove toward the village in his pickup truck.

He closed his mind, blocked it off as if with a valve. He refused to think until he could get home and see how she was for himself. His foot was pressed down on the accelerator.

Later, much much later, he stood in his own living room and thought back carefully over all that had happened since he had raced into the village. So much of it was blurred in his mind, frozen there, numb and unthinking inside his brain. Had all this actually happened? All of it!

As soon as he got out of the truck they told him that Babs was dead. Like a blind man, he'd walked with them up the hills to Brandy's. Then they'd gone down to the creek and found her under the sheet that Brandy had spread over her.

The men talked about Holly being with Babs when she fell from the edge of the cliff. They talked about the stranger in the shack, about Babs having been there, knowing the stranger, seeing him often. They talked as if Babs had been a bad woman, as if she had slept with the stranger, as if the baby she was having might have been the stranger's baby …

It could have been, he thought wearily. He had always been so careful with Babs, knowing that she wasn't ready for children. It could have been— He thought about the stranger. What was he like? Where was he from? Why had Babs gone to see him, and how often? But why? Why? Why?

Suppose it was the stranger's baby? Not Jim's at all? Suppose she went there today to tell him, and he got mad. What if she fell into the creek on purpose, ashamed to face her husband, ashamed to tell him her secret? Suppose the man had tricked her somehow! Sleeping with Babs … with Jim's wife!

Jim Melchior thought until his head hurt painfully. He brought his heavy closed fist down upon the kitchen table and looked suddenly toward the bedroom.

No, he didn't want to do that. It had been so long since he had killed a man, and he didn't want to do it again. Somehow, killing a man did things to the man who killed. It took part of him away, mashed him.

He had seen so many men killed. But for what? He had killed then just to be killing, just because someone said: 'Kill— They've done us wrong, kill them?' And he had killed.

This was different. This was a matter of personal harm. This was one man's sin against a woman and against her husband. And by God, the sin had been against her baby too! Against the whole world! The man was a stain on the face of the earth. One man who could— This was surely different. This killing was necessary.

He walked slowly into the bedroom and lifted his shotgun down from the pegs over the chest of drawers. The wallpaper was bright, new and fresh smelling, and he thought about Babs papering that room for him—

for the two of them to smell and look at, to make love while enclosed in its newness and its freshness.

He broke the gun open. Taking a single shell from the top drawer of the chest, he inserted it slowly. Then he closed the gun. He held it under the curve of his right arm and walked slowly, deliberately through the house and out the front door.

Outside, he walked down the road, not seeing the people on the front porch of the store, not hearing the deafening silence as he passed. He walked to the culvert and cut off and headed up the valley. A little further, he started up the hillside toward the stranger's shack.

CHAPTER TWENTY-ONE

After Brandy Elliot left, Larry Carter stood in the middle of the room. He still could not believe that one man would kill another simply because a wife was willing to do a little playing around with an old husband. After all, Babs had been as much his, as she was ever Jim Melchior's.

But Brandy Elliot had left very little doubt in Larry Carter's mind. The slow voice—calm and deep—had been convincing enough. He remembered the soft chuckle, and then the anger with which Brandy Elliot had told him he was glad Jim was going to kill him. If Jim Melchior didn't kill him, he, Brandy Elliot, might.

People in the hills surely took their women folk strangely. He'd seen life at its rawest since he came to the hills: the dirty little Reed girl who cleaned his house for him and practically begged him to take her—yet that red-bearded old gent wanted her. It was hard to tell just how old the man was behind that beard, but he was considerably older than that immature brat girl.

And that one up the North Valley who had been a teacher once—she with her fine house and her store-bought things. She was not as pretty as Babs had been, but she was the same kind: selling it like that, dressing for it, and letting you either take it slow or fast. It never mattered to her.

Hell, he suddenly decided, he'd tell Jim Melchior he hadn't given a darn for his woman. She just kept coming to see him, and he made love to her. That was all: just made love to her, got her pregnant. But that wasn't his fault any more than it was her own. She should have been more careful. She knew enough about it to look after herself. He had no pity for a woman who didn't take care of herself. It wasn't a man's business to look after that part of it.

Still the more he thought about the matter, standing in the middle of the living room, the more doubtful he became. Suppose this fellow Jim was hot-tempered like they all said he was. He might not stop to think that a man could hang for murder!

But suppose men who committed murder in these hills were not hanged? Suppose it was called justifiable homicide, or something like that? Protecting a man's home, or—hell, Melchior could kill him and not blink an eye if that's the way things stood.

Larry Carter moved to a table and poured a stiff drink. His hands shook and he almost dropped the bottle. He swore softly, drank half a glass of bourbon, and licked his dry lips.

Maybe he ought to get out? He could pack and be gone before that fool of a man got here. After all, Melchior worked in town somewhere. They'd have to call him, get the body and stuff.

He poured another drink, but his hand still shook. His whole body seemed to shake. He wished to hell he had never come to these damn hills anyhow. He hadn't really wanted Babs. Why, she hadn't been any different than a thousand other women he could get. Just more responsive than most, maybe. He'd just wanted to hurt her. He'd wanted her to want him again, want him terribly so he could just walk off with a laugh and leave her.

He had just about been ready to do it, too. When she told him she was going to have a baby, he just laughed at her. He taunted her, called her all sorts of a fool. He told her they were just about even—just about. He even thought about staying around to see what the kid looked like.

Why, now he could come back any time he wanted to and she'd have to come running to him. She would have to! She would be afraid he would tell her precious Jim that it wasn't his baby at all.

But now—why had the silly fool fallen off that cliff? Had she done it purposely? Or accidentally? He wished he knew. Somehow, he thought it would make a difference if he knew why she had fallen off that cliff.

He poured another drink; he looked out the window. It was way past noon and he knew he was wasting precious time standing around and thinking.

He began hurriedly to pack his suitcases. When he had everything, he walked back to the living room with them and set them down. The furniture was his, but that didn't matter—at any rate not as much as his life.

He picked up the suitcases—and stopped abruptly. The door of the shack opened, and a tall skinny man stood unmoving in the doorway.

There was a gun in the curve of the man's arm, and his eyes were two dark, hot pools that burned into Larry Carter like hot sparks of coal.

The man didn't seem to move at all. Yet his arms raised till the gun pointed at Larry Carter's head. And there was a sickeningly loud explosion as the gun spat powder and bullets across the living room. Then there was a soft thud, and the tall man went out and closed the door softly behind him.

CHAPTER TWENTY-TWO

Brandy slowly went up the steps to his porch. He turned once and looked long at the swinging bridge. Beyond it was the shack. There was a bitterness in his mouth that he knew he couldn't spit out. He brought up a hand and put it to his face. He tugged at the rough tangle of his beard. Maybe if he'd followed his first impulse and turned that good-looking stranger away none of this would have happened.

He thought of Jim Melchior sitting in his empty home, sitting there and waiting for what would come next. Everyone had seen him heading up to the shack where Larry Carter was. They'd seen the shotgun and they knew what was to happen. No man or woman thought of stopping Jim. Each knew what had to be done. And then it was—the hollow blasts rolling into the village from the echoing hills.

And Brandy had left the store. The talking would start now, and the deputy would have to get into action. He didn't want to see any of it. Suddenly he turned and headed into the house, a hound dog leaping out of his way. His mind was made up. Some men were mules and needed an explosion to set them to moving. And maybe that's why mules missed some important fun out of life.

Grabbing up a pair of shears, Brandy took them to the mirror over the wash basin. He struck a light and for a long time looked at his full red beard. He'd been sitting on that porch long enough. And if he wasn't going to wind up sitting all his life he'd better get to acting. And then he was remembering young Larry Carter with that smooth face of his. He glared at the rough beard. How could a young gal ever get a romantic thought toward a thorn bush like he had? He started snipping at the beard with quick, decisive strokes.

His face was smarting when he stepped away from the mirror. He felt strangely naked without the beard. He threw the old razor near the wash basin and touched fingers to his face. He'd forgotten that he had a face under that red beard. He turned and headed into the living room, wondering what Holly would say when she saw him. Then he suddenly froze. His shotgun wasn't in its regular niche. He looked quickly around. He saw it nowhere in the room.

He remembered thinking he saw someone move away from the house when he had reached the foot of the hillside. Holly! She knew about his gun. She'd seen it many times. A weakness seemed to pull at his legs. He swung around and lurched for the door.

He stood on the porch a moment, his eyes searching aimlessly over the countryside. Holly was made the same as Jim. She would have to strike for what she lost. She would kill even as Jim had. Any moment he expected to hear the far-off blast from a gun. Then his heart leaped—in the near darkness, he thought he could detect movement on the swinging bridge. He leaped down the steps and started running.

He knew it was Holly even before he could clearly see her. He saw the shotgun held awkwardly at her side. She'd just been at the shack where Carter was probably stretched out. Now she was heading to the village to draw blood. She swung around as she heard his footsteps rush down upon her.

But she didn't try to use the gun on him. In her face was a numbness. She stared unrecognizingly at him, her mouth slightly open.

"Give it to me, Holly."

Then she knew him. It was his voice she recognized. "He's dead," she said. "Jim—he killed him." Her voice held her shock, told of her purpose.

"You give it to me. You don't want to go gunning after Jim."

"He killed my—" and then she stopped and her head fell.

"That Carter wasn't your man. You got no call to take up for him." Brandy reached out and grabbed the gun from her. At first she tried to hold on to it, but then her eyes lifted to his face and she looked wonderingly at it. Her fingers released the gun stock.

"That's better."

"Brandy," she said, in a small voice. "You look so—"

"Like a baby's butt, huh?"

Her face dropped and she fell silent. Brandy reached out and put a hand on her shoulder. It felt warm and full. He drew her to him. "Now, you come to my place."

She raised her head. Her eyes held tears. "Brandy, I loved that Larry feller …"

"Honey," he said gently, "you think about it awhile. He was a skunk. He got what he deserved. Ain't that a fact?"

She didn't answer, and then slowly they began to walk together toward Brandy's shack, Holly's sobs beginning to fall gently from her mouth.

When they got into the house Brandy started a fire going. Then he turned to her. He saw her small, hard body and his desire for her grew.

Something new had entered Holly's eyes. She looked at him as if she had never guessed what he looked like without the red beard: his skin ruddy and his face firm and hard and clean-looking.

"You're not old," she finally said, and her voice had lost its numbness.

"You really think that, Holly?" he said as he drew closer to her.

Her face was lifted to him and she didn't try to move away. She nodded and there was something like a smile on her lips.

He reached out his arms and drew her to him. He felt her quiver against him, as if at long last she was beginning to taste the release for which she had hungered. Slowly he worked his fingers over the buttons of her dress. And then he saw her as he always wanted to see her. And she was more lovely than he had ever dreamed: her body was rich and full-breasted; it was round of stomach and her thighs tapered gently into fine legs.

A moment followed and then she uttered a gasp and ran to him. He met her full, holding her to him, kissing her mouth, her cheeks, her neck. And then he picked her up and carried her into his room.

It was for Holly as she dreamed it would be: gentle and fierce, soft and bold. And in the fullness of its final rising surge she knew at last that she had found her completion …

She lay in the crook of Brandy's arm, a sweet deliciousness filling her. She was smiling, nodding and brushing her cheeks against her lover's chest. Yes, they would be married. Yes, and even as she agreed to Brandy's warm words, she felt a warmth go through her. Because maybe deep within her she had always known that it would be Brandy.

Lying in the darkened room, hearing Brandy's soft breathing, she looked at the dark sky through the narrow window. She felt no anger toward Jim now—only something like pity. He was alone as she had been alone. And she felt a pity for everyone else—for Nellie who continued to live in her cabin waiting for the man who would never arrive, for her own mother who would never come to the point of gentle rest. And she wondered about Preacher. Maybe in getting, finally, a son, he would find what he wanted.

A wind blew against a tree outside the shack. It whistled through the branches. Winter was on the verge of arriving. She pressed closer to the warmth of Brandy's body. Let it come. She didn't care.

THE END

Peter Twist

"Peter Twist" was born Chester Peter Hewitt on November 7, 1922, in New York City. After a single year of college he enlisted in the U.S. Air Corps in 1943. After WWII, he became a civil engineer and worked in construction. After he retired, Hewitt and his wife moved to Mexico City, where he became involved in humanitarian efforts to bring aid to American and Canadian prisoners locked up in Mexican jails. *The Gilded Getaway* is his only novel, utilizing a pseudonym that combined Hewitt's middle name with his wife's maiden name. Hewitt died in the U.S. Virgin Islands on December 15, 1980.

Emmett McDowell

Robert Emmett McDowell was born April 5, 1914, in Sentinel, Oklahoma. The family soon moved to Louisville, Kentucky, where he remained for the rest of his life. McDowell served in the Merchant Marines during WWII where he began his writing career in the pulp magazines as Emmett McDowell. He wrote stories for *Amazing Stories, Astounding Science Fiction, Planet Stories, Jungle Stories* and other genre magazines. In 1949 he began to shift over to detective magazines, switching to novels for Ace Books in the 1950s. In the 1950s McDowell became increasing interested in Kentucky history, and turned to writing historical fiction. He wrote one more mystery in 1965, *The Hound's Tooth,* as Robert McDowell. He died in Louisville on March 29, 1975.

Wilene Shaw

Wilene Shaw was born Virginia M. Harrison in Kentucky before moving to Southern California to become a writer. She wrote seven crime novels for Ace Books in the 1950s and early 60s as Shaw, including *The Fear and the Guilt,* an early lesbian novel.

THREE ACES BIBLIOGRAPHY

Peter Twist

(1922-1980)

The Gilded Hideaway (Ace, 1955)

Robert Emmett McDowell

(1914-1975)

As by Emmett McDowell

Mysteries

Switcheroo (Ace, 1954)
Stamped for Death (Ace, 1958)
Three for the Gallows (Ace, 1958; 3 novelettes)
Bloodline to Murder (Ace, 1960)
In at the Kill (Ace, 1960)

Science Fiction

Citadel of the Green Death (Armchair Fiction, 2019)
The Blue Venus, Sword of Fire, Black Silence & Moon of Treason (Planet Stories, 2021)

As by Robert Emmett McDowell

Fiction

Tidewater Sprig (Crown, 1961; historical/Kentucky)
Portrait of a Victim (Avalon, 1964; historical/Daniel Boone)
The Hound's Tooth (Morrow, 1965; mystery as by Robert McDowell)
The Sour Mash (unpublished mystery)

Non-Fiction

City of Conflict (1962)
Re-discovering Kentucky: A Guide for Modern-Day Explorers (1971)

Plays

Home is the Hunter (1964)

Wilene Shaw

The Mating Call (Ace, 1954)
Heat Lightning (Ace, 1954)
The Fear and The Guilt (Ace, 1954)
See How They Run (Ace, 1957)
Out For Kicks (Ace, 1959)
Tame the Wild Flesh (Ace, 1960)
One Foot in Hell (Ace, 1961)

A TRIO OF LIONS

From the early 1950s—the golden age of the paperback!
Three noir crime novels in each volume!

Lion Books began in 1949 as Red Circle Books, part of the Martin Goodman publishing empire that also included such magazines as *For Men Only, Stag* and *Movie World*, as well as various pulps and the early version of Marvel Comics. Lion Books only lasted for nine years, but during that time at least a third of their books were noir reprints and originals, and featured authors like Jim Thompson, David Goodis, Robert Bloch, Richard Matheson and Day Keene.

Kermit Jaediker: Hero's Lust
Shel Walker: The Man I Killed
Clayre & Michel Lipman: House of Evil
978-1-944520-02-1 $19.95
"A real ten-knuckle page-turner."—Kristofer Upjohn, *Noir Journal*.
"Reading these books are like watching late night film noir on late night TV with the lights out."—Rick Ollerman.
Introductions by Gary Lovisi and Dan Roberts.

Kermit Jaedeker: Tall, Dark & Dead
Frederick Lorenz: The Savage Chase
D. L. Champion: Run the Wild River
978-1-944520-75-5 $19.95
"As hard-boiled as they come."—Paul Burke, *NB*.
"...really races along."—James Reasoner.
"...unequivocally recommended."—*Paperback Parade*.
Includes an interview with editor Arnold Hano.

"Lots of tough-guy, wisecracking fun... reads like a 65-70 minute RKO private-eye movie."—*GoodReads*

Stark House Press
1315 H Street, Eureka, CA 95501, 707-498-3135, www.StarkHousePress.com

Printed in Great Britain
by Amazon

33405826R00175